# WINTER BREAK

A Selection of Recent Titles by Merry Jones

The Harper Jennings Series

SUMMER SESSION *
BEHIND THE WALLS *
WINTER BREAK *

THE NANNY MURDERS
THE RIVER KILLINGS
THE DEADLY NEIGHBORS
THE BORROWED AND BLUE MURDERS

* available from Severn House

# WINTER BREAK

*A Harper Jennings Mystery*

## Merry Jones

Severn House

This first world edition published 2012
in Great Britain and 2013 in the USA by
SEVERN HOUSE PUBLISHERS LTD of
19 Cedar Road, Sutton, Surrey, England, SM2 5DA.

British Library Cataloguing in Publication Data

Jones, Merry Bloch.
  Winter break.
  1. Jennings, Harper (Fictitious character)–Fiction.
  2. Women veterans–Fiction. 3. Iraq War, 2003-2011–
  Veterans–Fiction. 4. Post-traumatic stress disorder–
  Patients–Fiction. 5. Pregnant women–Fiction.
  6. Suspense fiction.
  I. Title
  813.6-dc23

ISBN-13:  978-0-7278-8220-2 (cased)

*All Severn House titles are printed on acid-free paper.*

Severn House Publishers support The Forest Stewardship Council [FSC], the
leading international forest certification organisation. All our titles that are printed
on Greenpeace-approved FSC-certified paper carry the FSC logo.

MIX
Paper from
responsible sources
FSC
www.fsc.org     FSC® C018575

Typeset by Palimpsest Book Production Ltd.,
Falkirk, Stirlingshire, Scotland.
Printed and bound in Great Britain by
MPG Books Ltd., Bodmin, Cornwall.

*To Robin, Baille and Neely*

# ACKNOWLEDGMENTS

Heartfelt thanks to:

My agent, Rebecca Strauss at McIntosh and Otis;

My editor, Rachel Simpson Hutchens, and the team at Severn House;

My fellow Liars at the Philadelphia Liars Club, including Jonathan Maberry, Greg Frost, Solomon Jones, Jon McGoran, Kelly Simmons, Marie Lamba, Dennis Tafoya, Don Lafferty, Keith Strunk, Keith DeCandido, Ed Pettit, Steve Susco and Chuck Wendig;

My family and friends, especially my husband, Robin.

E ven when the second guy walked in, Sebastian Levering didn't realize he was in trouble. He was deep inside the glowing haze of too many appletinis, and in the middle of a deep, passionate candlelit kiss. In fact, he was fully naked, in bed with a gorgeous, popular, sexy, witty, glib trust-fund baby, someone he'd never imagined would notice, let alone be interested in him. Someone he'd assumed was – and even now couldn't believe wasn't – straight. But Evan Lourd had approached him at the bar. Had singled him out and moved in on him suddenly, with disarming directness and irresistible charm.

'I'm here on a bet,' he'd said.

'Sorry?' Sebastian had glanced around, not believing Evan could be talking to him. But no one else had been nearby. The bar had been almost empty due to intersession. Finals were over, and most students had left Cornell for the holidays, would be gone until the middle of January. Sebastian had stuck around, partly to hang out with Brad, but mostly to put off going home for as long as possible. He couldn't delay much longer – Christmas was just five days away. And in four, his family expected him back in Elmira. But they didn't expect what he had to tell them.

He'd decided on his own, not because of Brad. He was simply done pretending. Done hiding. Done enduring the slew of blind dates his mother kept setting him up with: Nieces of friends or cousins and daughters of friends of friends. No. He just couldn't live the lie any more. Finally, in two days, he'd planned to face them with the truth. He was ready.

But then fucking Brad had come up with his ultimatum. Just because they were renting an apartment together, he'd insisted on meeting Sebastian's family. As if they were married or something. 'Take me home with you,' he'd demanded. 'Or else.'

Or else? Seriously? What the fuck did that mean? What gave Brad the idea he could insist on anything, let alone meeting the family? No way Sebastian was going to allow that. None.

After the fight, Sebastian had stormed out of the apartment, gone for a drink. He'd been sitting at the bar, remembering the sting of his fist as it had made contact with Brad's jaw. Christ, what had Brad expected? Damn Brad, picking up the phone to call Sebastian's mother, swearing that he was going to tell her everything. Had he thought Sebastian would just sit there and let him make the call? No, the bitch had asked for it. Brad had definitely crossed a line, had deserved to be knocked out and locked in his big walk-in closet where he couldn't get to a phone to call his own mommy, let alone Sebastian's. He'd stay in there until he cooled off and came to his senses.

Meantime, Sebastian would have a few appletinis, trying to face his trip home and what he'd say to his parents. How to word it. Should he come right out and announce it? Or guide them slowly along, revealing bits of the truth until it finally became apparent? He'd rehearsed both, but couldn't decide.

Option one was to be blunt: 'I have something to tell you.' He'd pictured their faces, waiting to hear his news, expecting him to announce that he was changing majors. Or getting married. Christ. His hands had been clammy just imagining it. Maybe he'd be better off telling his brothers first. He'd been considering that possibility when, from nowhere, Evan Lourd had appeared, talking to him. Saying he was there on a bet.

'I just went through a particularly bad break-up,' Evan's voice had been resonant, deeper than he'd have imagined it. 'My merciless room-mate bet me that I'd spend intersession all alone, feeling sorry for myself.'

Sebastian had been speechless, partly because Evan's Adonis-like good looks had struck him dumb, and partly because he couldn't figure out why Evan Lourd, a member of Delta Phi Omega, one of the most exclusive, wealthy and notoriously hard partying fraternities on campus, was talking to him, an anonymous engineering student struggling to survive on loans and scholarships. And why was he telling him about his break-up? In fact, what was Evan even doing there? Didn't he realize this was mostly a gay bar?

But Evan had moved closer. Actually, too close. Right into Sebastian's personal space. Sebastian had gulped his drink, stared at the pretzels on the bar. Missed the next thing Evan said. Because it couldn't have been what he'd thought it was – that he'd asked him to help him win the bet.

'Am I making you nervous?'

Evan's breath tickled his cheek.

'Okay. Sorry. I was just . . .' Suddenly Evan had backed off, shoulders slumped. 'My mistake. I just thought, since you were here alone – never mind.'

Sebastian had looked up, seen Evan's embarrassment. His vulnerability. 'No worries, man.' He'd said something stupid like that. 'It's okay. I get it. What are you drinking? It's on me.'

But Evan hadn't let him buy their drinks. And he'd made moves, brushing his leg as they'd talked, touching his arm. Leaning close. Teasing with his steady blue eyes, his easy grin, his white straight teeth. His wad of cash on the bar.

At first, Sebastian had been both surprised and flattered that Evan had noticed him, chosen him, approached him when he could have had anybody. Not that there were many guys around. But still. Evan had picked him. After a few drinks, though, Sebastian understood that Evan was truly into him. His confidence had grown, and he'd begun to think more clearly. If things went well, Evan might let him run with his circle of rich frat boys.

Sebastian drank up, and the more he drank, the better his future looked. Maybe he should dump Brad, who was too possessive. Besides, he barely had the money for his share of the rent. Sebastian's name wasn't on the new lease; his furniture wasn't even moved in there yet. He could still get out of it. If things with Evan worked out, who knew what might be ahead. Life was all about who you knew, wasn't it?

So Sebastian hadn't hesitated to go with Evan to the deserted fraternity house; he'd been encouraged that Evan had wanted more than a simple men's room encounter. Maybe, after his tough break-up (had it been with a girl?) he was coming out, ready for an honest relationship. Sebastian tried to read Evan's reactions, to make sure he was having a good time. And, from his breathing and soft moans, he seemed to be.

Until the second guy came into the room.

Instantly, Evan pulled away. 'Shit, Sty,' he barked. He was on his feet, grabbing his pants.

'What?' the second guy raised his eyebrows.

Sebastian froze. Who was this guy? Evan's old boyfriend? Oh, damn. Would there be a scene? He pulled the sheet up around his neck, looking for his clothes.

'What the hell took you so long?' Evan hopped into his pants. 'We've been here for like twenty minutes—'

'I know.' Sty's eyes twinkled, grin widened.

'Shit. You were watching.'

'Truly, Lourd. I never noticed how cute your pink ass is—'

'Sick fuck.' Evan zipped his fly. Didn't seem angry.

Sebastian didn't know what was going on, but he didn't like it. Quietly, quickly, he got up and was gathering his clothes when, in the candlelight, he noticed something glitter in the second guy's hand. Something thin. And metallic. And long.

Oh shit.

As he fled naked out of the room, down the stairs and out the door into the snow, Sebastian had three distinct thoughts, none of which involved Brad or his confinement in the closet.

The first thought was that he should have known a guy like Evan Lourd would never have gone for him.

The second was that it was intersession; no one was around to help him.

The third was that, unless a miracle happened, he wouldn't have to worry about coming out to his family.


Harper Jennings tightened her jaw, picked up her plate. 'Thanks, Lou. Dinner was great.'

'How would you know? You didn't eat anything.' Her mother took hold of Harper's arm, examined her plate. 'You left half the liver.'

Actually, more than half. She'd left all but the two bites she'd deposited in her crumpled napkin.

'You need to eat, Harper. The baby needs the food—'

'I'm fine, Ma. I just don't want to eat right now.'

'Are you okay?' Vivian's voice was ragged and deep from years of smoke and drink. It grated. Wouldn't let up. 'Lou – make her some tea.'

'Ma—'

'Let her be, Viv. She's pregnant. Try to remember how it was.'

Harper bit her lip. Even if he was taking her side, Lou had no business entering a conversation between her and her mother. Then again, Lou had no business being there at all, making himself comfortable in her home, cooking, taking over her kitchen. She hadn't invited him, didn't know him, didn't want to know him.

'So when are you getting your tree?' Vivian sipped white wine. 'It's just a few days till—'

'Ma. We've already talked about this.' Harper stood to take her plate to the sink, took a deep breath. They'd discussed the tree that very morning. She'd explained that, with Hank gone for Christmas, she didn't feel like bothering with the pine needles and the decorations, the tinsel and the effort.

'But it's Christmas. I'd like to have a tree.' Vivian pouted, emphasizing the loosening skin around her mouth. Pouting didn't flatter her.

Harper started for the sink, hoping to end the discussion.

'Leave the dishes, Doll.' Lou changed the subject. 'We'll get them later.'

Doll?

'It's not Christmas without a tree.' Vivian followed her. 'Harper? Why are you being so negative? You wouldn't even eat.'

'I'm not being negative, Ma. I feel fine. I'm just not hungry.' Well, actually, she was. Very. But liver? The thought of it made her gag. She wanted a meatball sandwich. Or hot Italian sausage. Or a greasy cheeseburger. Yes, with onions and pickles. With a black and white milkshake.

But now, Lou was on his feet, following Vivian as she followed Harper, making it a parade.

'So, we'll save it for you for later. Here – give me your plate.' Vivian tried to take it. 'I'll put it in the—'

Harper pulled the plate away. 'No!' Oh dear. Her voice was too loud, too harsh.

Her mother froze, wounded, pouting again, her hands still on the dish. Harper sighed, closed her eyes, regaining her composure. She knew the drill. It was the same as it had always been. Her mother, oblivious, was invading her space, hovering, needing Harper to need her. Needing Harper. Needing.

'Let her be, Honey.' Lou put his arms around Vivian, intervening, giving Harper a half-nod, half-wink. Who the hell was he to intervene? To wink?

Harper let go, giving in, just at the moment Vivian conceded. The plate fell to the floor, shattering. The liver bounced, landed with a grayish-brown splat.

Damn. Harper knelt to pick up the mess.

'Oh my God, oh my God,' Vivian yelped, grabbing Harper's shoulder. 'Look what you've done.'

'Ma, it's just a plate—'

'No.' Lou stooped, grabbing her hand as she reached for a shard. 'We'll take care of it. Go. You're supposed to rest, aren't you?'

Harper met his eyes and saw a spark. It was familiar; she recognized it, had seen the same spark before, in Iraq. In the eyes of a woman, Sameh – just before she'd set off an explosive device. So what was that spark doing in Lou's eyes? Did it mean danger? Was it a warning? Oh God. Harper smelled fire, heard screams, saw a flash of white heat, felt herself flying – NO. She pressed a piece of broken stoneware into her palm, grounding herself with pain. Sent the flashback away. Reminded herself: she wasn't in Iraq any more. She was home. The spark in Lou's eyes was just that: a spark. Not a warning. Not defiance. She was safe in her own kitchen. Staring too long and too hard at her mother's boyfriend.

In fact, both her mother and Lou were crouched beside her; her mother yammering about how difficult and stubborn Harper was being, lamenting the waste of food, the mess Harper had made, the broken plate. But Lou was silent, still watching her. The glimmering spark was gone. But she'd seen it, for sure. Who was this man?

He reached out to help her to her feet. 'Come on, Doll.'

Doll again. What was that about? Couldn't he remember her name?

'Go lie down a while. Your mother and I will clean up.'

Really? Her mother would clean? He must not know her very well. But Harper didn't argue. She didn't take his hand, either; she simply stood. 'Thanks,' she breathed. 'I think I will.'

And Harper dashed away, overhearing them as she fled.

'No Christmas tree? Why is she so miserable? Can't she see how it upsets me – she makes me want to start smoking again.'

'Babe. She's pregnant. She's gonna be haywire. Cut her some slack.'

Harper flew up the stairs, down the hall to her room. Closing the door, finally alone, she let out a breath. Hank had been gone less than a week; would be away at least three more. No way she could survive all that time with those two. Just the sound of her mother's gravelly tobacco-cured voice grated her nerves. Scraped them raw.

Harper ran a hand through her close-cropped hair. She walked across the bedroom to the window, then back to the door, then to the bathroom, then to the window again. Why was she so jumpy?

She needed to calm down, ached for a Scotch, but couldn't even think about it. Not for another five months. Five whole months? God. If only she could get on her Ninja and ride, but it was too cold out, too icy. She turned away from the window, surveyed the bedroom. Stared at Hank's pillow. Felt a pang. Looked away, back outside. Damn, she was turning into a first-class wimp, needed to buck up. After all, she was Army. She'd survived the Iraq war. Not to mention Hank's accident, a drug conspiracy, a psychotic student, a rogue soldier, a gang of artifact smugglers – if she'd gotten through all that, she should be able to survive a visit from her mother. Maybe.

Harper checked her watch. Almost eight. Another three hours until Hank would call to say goodnight. She stared at the phone on the nightstand, willing it to ring. Lord. Why had she let Hank persuade her to let her mother stay with her? She would have been perfectly fine on her own.

'Rest.' She could hear him insist. 'Docta said for. Next. Whole trimesta.' He'd manage to articulate trimester; his speech was improving.

'I'll be fine on my own,' she'd insisted. 'I can take care of myself.' After all, she was a trained, experienced combat officer. And, despite her war-damaged left leg, she was in good shape.

'Hoppa. I won't go. If you're alone.' He'd been adamant. Had crossed his arms and steeled his jaw.

And he'd won. She couldn't have allowed Hank to stay home and pass up his opportunity. For the first time since the accident that had damaged his brain and caused his aphasia, he'd had a chance to work in his profession. His friend Trent Manning had offered him a position assisting on a month-long geologic survey in South Texas. For a thousand reasons, it had been essential that he take it.

Still, Harper had tried to think of alternatives. 'But Hank. You know how things are between my mother and me—'

'Vivian loves. You.' Maybe. But did he think that made up for all the rest?

'Look, what if I promise that I won't be alone?' Harper had tried to negotiate. 'I'll have friends come by. Every day.'

'Who?' He'd frowned, his arms still crossed. 'Friends are away. And whole month. You'll need help to shop. Cook. Clean.'

As if her mother would help with any of that. Harper couldn't even imagine Vivian cooking or cleaning. After her father had gone away, Harper as a young teen had done all the chores, taking care of her mother more than her mother had of her. But Hank had a point. It was winter break at Cornell, and every single one of her friends was traveling. Janet and Dan were skiing in Jackson Hole. Ruth was in Costa Rica. Even Vicki, Trent's wife and Harper's best friend, was going on a cruise. Harper, it seemed, would be the only living soul staying in Ithaca for the holidays. Still, there had to be some other choice – anybody but her mother.

Hank had scowled, waiting.

'Look. I'm pregnant, not helpless. I'll be fine.' Harper had actually stamped her foot.

'Hoppa.' Hank had stepped over, placed his hands on her shoulders. 'Docta said rest. No strain. Listen to her. For baby.'

He'd been right; Dr Parsons had told her to not to exert herself. She'd been having early contractions, and Parsons had threatened bed rest if they worsened. So, Harper had relented. Her mother would stay for a month; Harper wouldn't be alone and Hank would feel comfortable about leaving.

Neither of them, though, had expected her mother to bring a date. Not that Harper was surprised. In the fifteen years since her father had left, Vivian had been through dozens of relationships. Men were essential to her; without one, she shriveled, couldn't survive. Harper had stopped getting to know them long ago; to her, the men blended into a long line of receding hairlines and too much aftershave. This latest one, Lou, was different; he had thick gray hair and no after-shave at all. But what was he doing in her home?

Never mind. Lou kept Vivian distracted; at dinner, he'd even been a buffer between them. Harper stopped fuming, began to let the tension out of her shoulders. And gasped at a sudden flutter in her belly. It wasn't a contraction; this was gentler, deeper. More like a tickle – the baby? Was it moving? Kicking? Harper's hands went to her tummy; her mouth opened, amazed. She wished she could call and tell Hank, but he had no cell reception in the field. Lord, she missed him. Harper held her belly, hoping for another flutter, picturing a tiny person swimming in her body, doing flip-turns. She concentrated, waited, but felt no more movement. Still, she stood at the window, gazing out, not giving up.

Outside, the street was deserted except for a sole black car, driving slowly by the house. The sky was starless, full of thick clouds that promised more snow. The ground was blanketed in white from the street back to the woods, and the fraternity next door stood dark, abandoned for intersession. The night seemed frozen; nothing moved, not Harper. Not the baby.

Harper was about to give up; the baby wasn't cooperating. She moved away from the window, and noticed a flicker of light, coming from the woods. What? She stepped back to the pane, looked into the trees. No light. Nothing but the frigid stillness. Chilled, she stepped away from the window, and – flash – another flicker.

Harper pressed her face against the cold glass and peered outside, her breath steaming the pane. Through the darkness, she saw a flash among the trees, and then a rustle of foliage near the edge of the woods. Was it an animal? A deer? And the flashes – had they been from a hunter's gun? Suddenly, a dim figure burst out of the woods, sprinting away, on two legs. Not a deer – a man. And he headed across the fraternity's back yard to her driveway where the motion sensors Hank had installed in the fall picked him up and, suddenly, the whole area was bathed in light.

Oh God. Harper blinked. The guy was naked? She gaped, confused, as another figure dashed out of the woods, tackling the first, pinning him in the snow, punching him. The naked guy flailed and struggled, rolled onto his back, apparently dazed. But looking up, he seemed to see Harper in the window. His eyes widened, locking onto hers, and his lips moved, mouthing something. Was it 'Help me'?

Before she'd even processed the words, Harper's training kicked in. She grabbed a flashlight from the nightstand and rushed to the door, glancing back out the window to see the assailant flipping the naked guy over his shoulder and carrying him back toward the woods.

Harper's weak left leg nearly buckled as she flew down the stairs, but she kept running. Through the hallway. Into the kitchen, toward the deck door.

'Harper?' Her mother looked up from her brandy.

Harper didn't answer. She pulled the door open and headed out into the night. Vaguely, Harper heard chairs scraping, voices asking: 'Where's she going? What the hell?' But she didn't stop; she hurried out, off the deck, past the end of the driveway across the snowy back yard to the woods.

'Harper!' Vivian's cigarette and whiskey baritone blared. 'What are you doing? It's freezing out—'

'At least get a jacket,' Lou called.

She heard them, breathlessly discussing how bizarre she was as they chased her, but she didn't stop. Her socks got cold and damp as she crunched through ankle-deep snow, but she kept on going, heading for the spot where she'd seen the naked guy emerge.

'What the hell, Harper?' her mother croaked. 'Are you crazy? You don't have boots or a jacket or—'

Harper spun around, lifted her finger to her lips. 'Shhh! Quiet,' she commanded.

'No, I will not—' Vivian began, but Lou grabbed her arm, shaking his head while stepping slowly forward, indicating that they should humor Harper until they caught up to her.

But, despite her lingering war injuries, Harper was in far better shape than they, and by the time they got to the edge of the woods, she had already moved out of sight. All they could see was the intermittent beam of her flashlight.

Harper stepped over twigs and into ice-coated puddles, aiming the light forward, to one side, then the other. Her feet were soaked and freezing; her toes were numb. She stopped and held still, listening for sounds of struggling. Hearing only the persistent carping of her mother and Lou as they plodded after her.

'She'll catch her death – what can I do? She's supposed to be resting, not running around barefoot in the snow. That girl will kill me, I swear.'

Harper moved deeper among the trees, looking for footprints. But here the snow was thin; the branches had caught most of it before it hit the frozen ground. And there was no clear path – just narrow spaces between trunks and stumps.

She paused several yards deep, thinking. Obviously, anyone out here would know she was coming. Would have seen her light. Would have heard Lou and her mother talking. She stopped, not knowing which way to go, how to proceed.

'Hello?' she called. 'Who's out there?'

She didn't expect, and didn't get, an answer from the men. But Vivian shouted, 'Harper, come out of there right now. I'm freezing. Lou's coming in after you – if he falls in the dark and breaks a leg, it'll be your fault.'

Harper pictured Lou in a body cast, plastered to her sofa for months. 'Don't come after me. Go home.' She rotated slowly, shining the light into the stillness, looking for movement or skin tones, or the steam of someone else's breathing. In Iraq, she'd been able to sense the presence of an enemy, a tingle of alert. But now, the only tingle she felt was in her frozen toes. What was she supposed to do? What had those guys been doing out there?

'Harper, I'm warning you. I'm calling Hank—'

'No – don't.' Oh God. She would, too. Her mother would call Hank and leave him some frantic message and get him all upset. 'I'm coming.'

Harper made her way back, stepping over stumps and sticks, frozen wadded leaves and icy puddles, favoring her weak left leg. As she approached her back yard, her mother barked, 'L-Lou – g-grab her.'

Lou obeyed, wrapping an arm around her and holding on the whole way back to the house. 'What the hell, Harper? You got more sense than this. This is nuts.'

Lou was shivering; her mother's teeth were chattering. 'Y-you p-probably gave us all pn-pneumonia. What's wrong with y-you, running outside l-like that?'

Shaking with cold, Harper clenched her jaw, and kept walking. Maybe she shouldn't have run out like that, without a jacket and boots. Or a weapon. What had she been thinking, going after a target unprepared? She looked over her shoulder at the dark hunkering woods. Nothing moved there, and no light flared.

When they got back to the house, Lou put on the kettle to make cocoa and pulled out jackets to warm them. Harper curled into a parka, shivering.

'Feel my hands, Lou, how cold they are.' Vivian put his fingers under his sweater. 'What were you thinking, Harper? Lou or I could have had heart attacks out there. And what about my grandbaby? It's not just you any more . . .'

Harper closed her eyes, trying to shut out the yammering so she could think. But her mind seemed stuck; her only thought was the face of a naked man, mouthing, 'Help me.'

'Got any marshmallows?' Lou searched a cabinet.

'Trust me, Harper wouldn't buy marshmallows. Don't even bother looking.' Her mother's voice was deeper than Lou's, more weathered. As usual, she assumed she knew everything there was to know about

Harper. Harper wished she'd had marshmallows just to prove her wrong.

Lou passed around mugs of hot cocoa and a plate of ginger snaps. Vivian asked for whiskey to spike her cocoa. Suddenly, it was a party.

Harper huddled inside the parka, trying to remember where she'd left her phone. Her brain felt frozen, unable to think. But she remembered plugging it into the charger. So the phone had to be upstairs. She stood, started for the door.

'Now, where is she going?' Vivian talked about her as if she weren't there.

'To get my phone.'

Vivian was behind her, following. 'Why? Who are you calling? Hank? Don't call Hank. He'll only worry—'

'Hold on.' Lou came up around front, standing in her way. 'Why don't we sit down, warm up and talk about things before anybody does anything else.' It wasn't a question.

Harper eyed him. Who the hell did he think he was, blocking her in her own home? Reflexively, instantly, she sized him up – Lou was taller by eight inches, bulkier by some seventy pounds. But he was also at least twenty-five years older. Fit but untrained. She could take him down in a heartbeat. In fact, she'd already taken a stance, balanced, knees slightly bent, ready to strike. But Lou wasn't hostile; he was smiling. Lord, his teeth were so white – were they real? Probably dentures or caps. His arms moved out for her; she blocked them, her hands tightened into fists before she realized that he'd only wanted to hug her. Oh God. What was she doing, preparing to flatten her mother's boyfriend? But wait. She was surrounded, closed in from the rear and the front. Flight or fight responses kicked in, and flight wasn't possible. An annoying buzzing droned on, grating Harper's brain, and she smelled gunfire. Saw smoke, heard the rattle of gunfire. No. She was home, not in Iraq. She needed to startle her senses, prevent a flashback. Harper spun, shoved her mother away to get to the refrigerator, opened it, grabbed a lemon. And bit.

Acidic sour juice rattled her, interrupted her brain. Grounded her with its intensity. Images of Iraq flitted away, leaving her facing a startled mother and gaping Lou. Again, Harper saw that dangerous spark flare in Lou's eyes. She looked directly at it, undaunted, ready to take him on.

'You're eating a lemon?' he asked.

Harper looked at the lemon in her hand. Set it on the counter. Shrugged and smiled, didn't want to explain.

Her mother was finally silent. She and Lou watched her, baffled.

'I need to go get my phone.' She didn't bother pointing out that they had no right to stop her. 'Not to call Hank. I'm calling the police.'

'The police.' Lou repeated. Had his voice faltered? Had his gaze done a quick shimmy?

Harper studied him as she continued, hurrying. Time mattered. 'There was a man out in the cold. Naked, and someone carried him into the woods.'

Silence. Blank stares.

'He saw me at my window, asked me for help.'

More silence. Continued stares.

Vivian plopped into a seat at the kitchen table, poured more whiskey into her cooled cocoa. Took a long drink. Stared at the wall.

Harper went on, aware that a man's life could depend on her. 'Look – the police will have search lights. I need to call them before he freezes to death.'

Lou shook his head. 'Harper. Your mother and I were down here. We would have heard something. Yelling. Or a scuffle.'

'Jesus, Harper. It's just goddam kids. What the hell's wrong with you? Thinking of the worst possible scenario—'

'They're probably doing drugs out there, that's all. Or a party. A bunch of kids, you know, getting it on—'

'You're making a big deal out of something you don't know anything about—'

Harper started for the stairs, stopped as her midriff tightened. A contraction suddenly gripped her. She came back to the table and sat.

'Harper, that's right. Sit.' Lou sat opposite. 'You might not realize it, but you're under a lot of stress.'

What? She inhaled deeply, exhaled slowly.

'Your mother's told me about your husband's accident. How he almost died. How he got brain damage. And now, he's gone away for the first time since he got hurt.'

Vivian sat beside Lou, nodding.

The contraction tightened.

'Besides which, you're pregnant.'

Vivian put a hand on Lou's.

'I don't want to sound sexist; I've had some experience with pregnant women. And that experience tells me that they get pretty off the wall. Hormones fluctate, see.'

Fluctate? Did he mean fluctuate?

'And their emotions take over—'

'He's right, Harper. I was that way with you.'

'So, my point is, things might not in actuality be exactly as you perceive them.'

'Bullshit.' Harper breathed, waiting for the contraction to pass.

'Christ, Harper, you're making me nuts—'

Lou cut her mother off. 'Hear me out. Your own doctor said you're in a fragile state, didn't she? So your body chemistry is changing, influencing your perceptions. You might be interpreting things different than they are. Thinking something's sinister when it isn't. You don't want to embarrass yourself by calling the police. That's all I'm saying.'

'Lou's right.' Vivian clutched her cocoa mug. 'But it's not just her hormones. She has that STPD thing – or no—' She looked at the wall, concentrating. 'It's PTSD. From the war. It makes her have those flashbacks and she loses touch with reality. She sees things that aren't even there—'

'Ma!' Harper sputtered, holding her belly. 'I know what I saw.' Didn't her mother believe her? Did she think she'd invented the guy?

'It's not your fault, Harper.' Vivian turned to Lou. 'But I'm thinking it's her hormones combined with her post-trauma shock disability, combined with Hank taking off—'

'That's enough!' Harper shouted. Her temples pulsed, even as the contraction eased. She wanted to correct – no, to throttle both of them, but she couldn't take the time. A man's life was in danger. She stood, too incensed to speak. Breathing evenly, her belly still recovering, she headed out of the kitchen to the stairs, grateful that, this time, no one followed her. Time was precious, had already been wasted. How long had it been since she'd seen him? Eight minutes? More? How long could a naked man survive in the snowy cold woods?

Shaken, more from the conversation than the contraction, Harper moved carefully up the stairs. Breathing evenly, she hurried to her room, found her phone and made the call.

*   *   *

Detective Charlene Rivers was no stranger to the Jennings home. She'd been there on numerous occasions. First, when Hank had his accident. Later, when some of Harper's archeology students had become involved with stolen drugs and homicide. Most recently, when Harper had been caught in a web of stolen archeological relics and murder. In the last two years, in fact, she'd had to visit the Jennings home more often than any other in Ithaca or Tompkins County, and each visit had connected to the grisliest crimes of her career. So it was with some trepidation that she walked up the path to the front door, and with some hesitation that she rang the bell.

The woman who answered wasn't Harper Jennings. She was older, her skin weathered, as if she'd been around the block and then some. The kind Rivers would see in a bar at three in the afternoon. Too much eye shadow, skinny jeans that struggled to contain her hips, and a painfully tight red sweater. Her long hair sprayed and bouffant, dyed an unnatural shade of auburn/blue.

'It really was nothing . . .' she began when she saw Rivers' badge. Her voice was scraped, gravelly and deep. Too many cigarettes, too much booze. 'My daughter overreacted. She shouldn't have bothered you.'

Her daughter? Rivers blinked, filing away the information. Noting the contrast between this woman and Harper Jennings, with her trim athletic figure, neutral, functional wardrobe, cropped hair, and shiny-scrubbed make-up-free face.

But Harper was at the door now, scowling at her mother – almost pulling Rivers inside. Rivers stepped over the threshold, noting the changes. The foyer had a new floor, new paint. And in an open parka, Mrs Jennings looked to be about halfway through a pregnancy.

'Detective. We don't have much time,' Jennings zipped up her jacket, led the way through to the kitchen, the back door.

Rivers followed, saw a man standing in the kitchen, putting cups away, his back to them. She noted his full head of gelled salt-and-pepper hair, height just shy of six feet. Flannel shirt and jeans. Solid frame, a little thick around the middle. Harper's father?

'You said you saw a naked man out here?' Rivers gazed at the snow.

'Running. Another guy was chasing him. They fought.' Harper hurried to the spot where they'd re-entered the woods. 'I went after them, but didn't find them. Couldn't even find footprints – too much debris on the ground. I'm afraid he'll freeze to death.'

Rivers looked around, saw some disturbed snow near the driveway. Walked to the woods, listened, heard nothing. The story was implausible; even so, Harper Jennings had been reliable in the past. So, somewhat reluctantly, Rivers made a call. Minutes later, floodlights probed the wooded patch behind the fraternity, and three uniformed cops searched the area with high-intensity flashlights.

After half an hour, they'd found nothing. They gave it another fifteen minutes. Still nothing.

Harper had wanted to help, but Rivers ordered her inside. As the search was winding up, they met on the back deck.

'They didn't find him? But, Detective, I saw him – he was back there.'

'The area isn't that big,' Rivers reminded her. 'We saw no sign of anyone, naked or otherwise.'

'But where could he be? He didn't come out this way – and there's a high fence on the other side.'

Rivers watched her. Harper looked strained, shaken. But steadfast. She believed she'd seen this man. 'I don't know.'

Vivian came out the sliding door. 'Nothing?' It wasn't really a question. 'No surprise. Detective, I'm sorry. I told her it was just her post-war condition again. She sees things—'

'I do not see things—'

'Yes, you do – you told me yourself – or it could be her hormones.'

'Ma. What are you saying? This was not PTSD or hormones . . .'

'All right.' Detective Rivers raised her voice. 'I don't know what you saw, Mrs Jennings. But at the moment, nobody is out there. Maybe it was just kids, horsing around, playing polar bear. Streaking in the cold. Acting on some dare. Doing drugs – we get all kinds of crazy calls in the winter.'

Harper looked pale. The police crew was packing up the lights, loading their truck.

'Can we go inside?' Rivers suggested.

The man wasn't in the kitchen any more. Harper wandered to the table, took a seat, seemed distracted.

'I apologize for my daughter. She shouldn't have bothered you,' Vivian droned.

Rivers glanced at Harper, saw no reaction. Harper was apparently deep in thought. 'Nothing to apologize for, Ma'am. Your daughter was right to call. Even if it was a prank or just kids being kids, she had no way to know that. And, given what's gone on around here the last few years, it's best to rule out the worst scenario. Trust me, it's better to call than to be sorry you didn't.'

'Would you like some cocoa, Detective? I can ask Lou to make—'

'No, no thanks, Ma'am. I'll be on my way. You all right, Mrs Jennings?'

Harper didn't answer.

'Harper,' Vivian scolded.

Harper looked up. 'You're leaving?'

'I am. Anything else happens, you let me know. Give your husband my regards when you talk to him. And have a merry Christmas, okay?'

Harper nodded, returned the wishes, thanked her for coming out. Vivian walked Rivers to the door, whispering, repeating that Harper was under stress, having a difficult pregnancy, upset that Hank was gone. Rivers found her apologies disloyal and cloying, her perfume irritatingly sweet. Again, she wondered at the contrast between Harper and her mother. Mused about how odd families could be.

Just to be thorough, before she left, she walked around the property again, looking under the deck, up the driveway, among the shrubs. As she walked to her car, she looked back at the house. A man stood upstairs, watching her from the window, silhouetted by the light.

In a dark bedroom on the third floor of the fraternity house next door, two figures hunkered by the window, peering out. Nearby, on a bed, an unconscious young man lay under a blanket, his hands and feet tied, his body bludgeoned.

'You think they'll look here?' Evan whispered.

'No. Why would they?'

Really? Wasn't it obvious? 'Because it's here.'

'But it's closed up tight. Nobody's here. Remember?'

Evan considered that. Still, he was concerned. 'Maybe we should move him.'

Sty didn't answer. He picked up his flask and drank. Passed it to Evan.

'I mean, just for argument's sake. What if they come looking for him?'

'We won't answer the fucking door, that's what.'

Evan took a drink. Dim light spilled in from the neighbor's

driveway, just enough to create shadows. Just enough that he could see Sty's eyes darting side to side. A sign that he was thinking.

'What?'

'They won't come here.' Sty sounded certain. 'But if they did, they'd need a warrant to come in. And they have no cause to get a warrant. We left no footprints. No evidence leads here. So no warrant, no cops.'

Evan wasn't convinced. He took another swig, mentally replaying what had happened. Making sure that they'd left no sign of themselves in the woods, in the yard of the fraternity, in the driveway of the house next door. Obviously, someone there had seen something and called the cops. But what? How much had the neighbor seen? Enough to identify him? He peeked between the curtains at the police and their searchlights, at the windows of the neighbor's house. He'd seen the couple who lived there, had often said hi. The woman was short and blonde. Perky, sexy except for her limp. She rode a damned Ninja motorcycle. And the guy – he was solid like a linebacker, but he had some sort of disability. Walked crooked. But they couldn't have recognized him – they didn't know him from any of the forty other guys living in the house. And it was dark out. No, if they'd recognized him, the cops would be ringing the doorbell. Which they weren't. Besides, he wasn't even officially there, was supposedly staying at Sty's apartment until the Christmas performances were done. If the police asked, he had answers. They both did.

Sty was silent, drinking. Watching out the window.

Damn. Fucking kid running outside. What had the neighbors seen?

The kid stirred, making an awful high-pitched wail. Like a siren. Sty got up, held the kid's head up and poured some more stuff from the red Solo cup into his mouth. Came back and crouched by the window again.

'I don't think he was really conscious. But if he was, he won't be now. That stuff's strong. It'll keep him out a while.'

Evan shrugged. 'Sty. We really ought to just do it.' Actually, he'd wanted to drop their plan and kill the kid as soon as things began to go wrong. But Sty had stopped him, lecturing him about their higher purpose. Going on again about his heroes, those guys Leopold and Loeb. Christ, Sty was obsessed by those two, even though it had been a century since they'd killed anyone. Evan knew it was useless to interrupt once Sty got started; Sty had to run through his entire speech. That was part of his obsessive personality. So Evan watched out the window, only half listening as Sty recounted the strengths and flaws of the two Chicago killers.

'Those two had everything. Wealth. Education. Sophistication. Genius IQs. And their challenge was simple: commit a perfect crime. Leave no clues. Never even be suspected. Get away with one simple murder.'

Evan watched searchlights bathe the woods, saw police scurry among the trees.

'Picture it. 1924. No such thing as DNA evidence. None of that high-tech CSI shit. All they had to do was leave no overt clues. Yet, despite their superior intellect, they failed miserably, got caught and convicted. Loeb died in jail.'

Evan shook his head, sick of hearing about these two guys. But Sty was fixated on them, reading everything he could find about them, seeing movies based on them, analyzing their philosophies, and he'd become convinced that the two would have succeeded, would never have been caught after killing that Chicago boy, had they not had their eyes on the wrong prize. Instead of focusing on getting away with their crime, he believed they should have concentrated on perfecting the act itself.

For Sty, the critical factor was the experience of murder; he insisted that it be done in a precise and studied manner, not in a haphazard hurry. For that reason, he'd refused to let Evan simply kill their victim.

'We have the benefit of learning from their mistakes, Evan. We take pains at every step. We do nothing swiftly or impulsively. We stick to our plan, adapting it slightly, but we stay grounded, moving with caution, precision and discipline.'

Evan wondered what the cops would find outside. Footprints? Blood? He replayed chasing the kid, how angry he'd been. The feeling of his knuckles slamming into an eye socket. Of landing on the kid's leg, feeling something snap. Of his own blood bubbling and rushing, the sense of floating and looking down at the scene from somewhere up high.

Sty was still talking, insisting that all was not lost, that despite unforeseen obstacles, their plan was still intact. They were smarter than his heroes, would learn from them.

His voice was annoying, but Evan let him ramble on. And they

stayed there, peeking through the curtains until the searchlights went
out and the last of the cops drove away.

Harper lay in bed, staring at the window. Waiting for Hank to call.
Seeing the naked guy running out of the woods, over and over. Stop
it, she told herself. Think of something else. So she thought about
the baby, which brought to mind the contraction she'd had earlier,
when Detective Rivers had been there. Which reminded her of the
police and the searchlights. Which reminded her of her own search
of the woods—

When the phone rang, she grabbed it. Paused a moment, to control
her voice.

'I felt the baby move today,' she struggled to sound cheery.

She heard Hank's grin. 'Kick you? Tough guy?'

'Guy?'

'Girl?'

Either way. 'It wasn't a kick, more like a somersault.'

He chuckled. 'Baby gymnast?'

Harper smiled, but hearing his voice, she ached to have Hank
home. To snuggle against his big bear-like body. To fall asleep
wrapped safe in his arms. Of course, she didn't dare let him know
how much she missed him. Nor did she dare tell him about Rivers'
visit or the naked man she'd gone looking for in the woods.

Instead, Harper put a hand over her belly, determined not to say
anything that might upset either of them.

Hank asked. 'How's Mom?'

'The same as always.' She put a deliberate lilt in her voice.

'That bad?'

Bad? Would 'bad' cover it? 'Only sometimes.' At all other times,
worse.

She felt like a whiner, saying even that. She was Army, had made
it through a war and survived wounds; had no business griping about
small stuff. So she added, 'Her boyfriend cooks.' She didn't mention
that what he cooked had been inedible. 'He made dinner tonight.'

Hank talked about his work and sounded elated. Energized. In
short clear phrases, he told her he didn't mind performing routine
mechanical tasks instead of managing the whole field study, as he
would have before his accident. 'Feels good just working. Again.'

After the call, Harper set the phone on Hank's pillow and lay
beside it, replaying his baritone, 'I love you.' Savoring it, she closed

her eyes. And saw not Hank, but a naked stranger bursting out of the woods.

Damn. She couldn't escape him; his frantic image wouldn't go away. Harper turned over, but kept seeing him hightailing it across the yard, his pursuer at his heels. She saw him hit the ground struggling, and lying pinned down in the snow. And she saw his frightened eyes lock onto hers, pleading, 'Help me.'

She tossed some more, determined to break the endless loop of images. Change channels, she told herself. Think about something else. Not about her mother or Lou, or how they'd discounted everything she'd said. And not about Detective Rivers or the way she'd seemed to doubt her. No. About the nursery – yes, she could think about fixing it up. Buying stuff for the baby. Sheets. Onesies. Diapers. A mobile for over the crib. But, as she pictured the room, a face with desperate eyes kept appearing, replacing woolly lambs on a musical mobile or a box of wipes on the changing table. He was everywhere, and he wouldn't go away. Harper closed her eyes and saw him. She opened them and saw him again. His face desperate and frozen with fear, mouthing: 'Help me.'

*Help me.*

How could she just lie there, doing nothing, when a man had asked her to help him? It was against her nature. Against her training. And yet, there she was. Lying in soft flannel PJs and a warm bed while some poor dude might be freezing his bare butt off, beaten up in the snow behind her house.

But he wasn't there. The police had found nothing.

She turned over yet again, forced her eyes to close. Began the relaxation exercises Leslie had taught her. Breathing deeply. Letting the tension out of her toes, her feet, her ankles. She moved up her body slowly, breathing from her belly, giving in to gravity, letting the bed hold her up. She was concentrating on her shoulders, releasing the stress, when she heard a creak downstairs. And another.

The sounds of old floorboards being walked on.

Someone was downstairs, moving around.

Her mother and Lou had gone to bed around midnight. Harper looked at the clock. Ten after two. So who was downstairs? A prowler? The naked guy? His attacker? Harper sat up, perfectly still, listening. Waiting. Hearing nothing for a minute. Then a creak. And hushed padded steps.

In an eye blink, Harper was out of bed, hurrying through the dark hallway to the staircase. Avoiding the noisy spots on the steps, she glided down silently, descending into the foyer just in time to see Lou going out the front door.

Lou was leaving? In the middle of the night? Sneaking out on her mother?

No, that was crazy, she told herself. Two hours ago, she'd heard their headboard slamming the wall in the throes of their passion. Maybe he was just going out for a smoke.

Harper went to the living room, parted the curtains and peeked out. Lou was not smoking. He was walking off the porch, across the snowy front yard all the way to the street where he disappeared behind the hedges. He reappeared beyond them, walking under the streetlight, past the fraternity and out of sight. Harper stood watching, confused. In a few seconds, Lou reappeared, looking up and down the street. Was he waiting for someone? At this hour? He walked back to the hedges. Passed them. Looked over his shoulder. Stopped to gaze left and right. Kept walking. Kept looking.

Harper kept watching until, finally, he started back towards the house. From the living room, she watched the door open slowly, saw him tiptoe inside.

'What's up, Lou?' Harper crossed her arms.

He actually jumped, yelping. 'Christ, Harper. Shit. You fuckin' gave me a heart attack. What the hell are you doing here?'

What was she doing there? Wasn't this her house? Wasn't it her right to be anywhere in it she wanted? Harper stood to her full five-feet-just-over-three-inches. 'I'm wondering the same about you.'

Lou pushed his hair back. 'What? Me? Nothing. No reason.' His eyes stopped hopping around, settled on hers, widening. 'I, uh, I just couldn't, you know, sleep. So I went out for a smoke, but then, wow. The strangest thing – I could swear I saw something move out there.' His eyes grew wider. 'And I thought it might, you know, be your guy. From before? So I walked around, looking. But I must have been wrong. Nobody was there. Must of been a raccoon or something. Anyhow, I got cold so I came back in. Whereupon you scared the living crap outta me.'

He grinned, walked over, stood too close. His eyes were bulging, forcing themselves not to waver. To look directly into hers. But his bulging straining eyes were unnatural, gave him away. But why? Why would he lie about not being able to sleep?

'Don't know about you, Doll. I got the munchies.' He smiled, baring perfectly even, too-white teeth. His arm snaked around Harper's waist, and she pushed it away but went with him to the kitchen, not because she trusted him, but because, suddenly, she craved cornflakes.

Even as she dug into a big bowl of cereal drowning in two percent, Harper kept her eyes on Lou, trying to figure out what he'd been doing outside, and what he was trying to hide.

But Lou wasn't revealing a thing. 'What's the deal with you and your mother, Harper?' He shoved a forkful of leftover peach pie into his mouth. 'I gotta tell you. You're all the woman talks about. How proud she is of you.'

Not possible. 'Yeah?' Harper picked up her milk, wished it were whiskey. 'How sweet.'

'But then the two of you go at it like a pair of bat shes.'

Bat shes? What, female bats? Unless he meant banshees. Either way, the relationship was none of Lou's business. Harper swallowed cereal.

'She's not as tough as she looks.' He spoke with his mouth full. 'She's been through a lot, you know. Between you and I, I don't think she ever got over that deal with your father—'

'Excuse me?' Harper put her hands on the table. That was it. Lou was completely out of line. Her family's history was not his to discuss.

'He had her completely bamboozled. She had no idea he was doing one of those Fonzi schemes.'

'Ponzi.' Why was she bothering to correct him?

'Bottom line, she was traumatized. She hasn't been able to trust anyone ever since. Especially men.'

As if Harper didn't know this? Did Lou think her mother had been the only one traumatized by her father's deceit? Or that it was her responsibility to deal with her mother's issues? Harper scooped up cereal, letting Lou talk on with a wad of pie in his cheek, his fork pointing at her.

'I get Vivian,' he continued. 'I get why she's picked losers all these years. You know why? Because if they're losers, she doesn't get disappointed. She can't get hurt if she doesn't expect anything from a guy. That's why.'

And what, he was different? Harper looked at the fork waving in her face. The hand that held it was solid, fingers thick, almost rough. But the fingernails were manicured. Polished. A contradiction. She saw the intensity of Lou's eyes. Remembered their dangerous flash. But she held his gaze, thinking that, if he didn't shut up soon, she might just cold cock him. And finish eating in peace.

'So explain it to me,' he went on. 'What is it that gets you two going? She says you're the only good thing she ever did in her life.'

Wait. Harper put her spoon down. Vivian had said Harper was something she'd 'done'? The way a person might 'do' their nails or a kitchen?

'All she wants is to make you happy.'

'Right.'

'I'm serious.'

Really? 'You're wrong.' All Vivian wanted was for others to make Vivian happy.

'Think about it.' Lou licked the last of his pie off his fork. 'You ought to give her a break. Start fresh. She's your mother, after all. And you only got one.'

'Right.' Thank God, she had only one. Harper finished her corn flakes, drank the last of the milk out of the bowl. 'I'm going up. Night.' She stood and carried her dish to the sink.

'It's good we talked, Harper.' Lou stood, too. 'Maybe you gained some insides.'

Harper figured he meant to say 'insights'. But, as she climbed the steps, feeling the weight of her expanding belly and the cereal she'd wolfed down, she figured that Lou was right. The conversation had taught her nothing, but she'd definitely gained some insides.

For a while, Sebastian drifted between blankness and fog. When he finally became conscious, he could only open one eye; the other was swollen closed. It took a few seconds to remember snapshots of what had happened. Then, instinctively, he tried to get up and run, but his hands and feet wouldn't – no, couldn't – move. He gave up and lay still, straining to figure things out. Things like where he was. And how he'd gotten there. He fought the urge to look around, sensing that he shouldn't let on that he was awake. Gradually, he became aware of the pain. It expanded, balloon-like, until it was overpowering, hot and alive, possessing his whole body – his chest screamed with each breath, his face throbbed. Bones must be broken – ribs. And his leg? His hand? Christ. He couldn't separate the pain into pieces. It owned him, head to toe, and now his nerves were spazzing, making him tremble and quake. Or maybe it was the cold. Damn. He remembered now. Evan. Being caught in bed with him. Were they here? If they saw him shivering, would they know he was awake? He listened for their voices. For movement. Remembered their faces, their intense concentration as they held the melon scoop in front of his face, promising to take his eyes out. Oh God. Was that why he couldn't open his left eye? Was it gone?

He almost choked, swallowing a bloody scream. Thrashed, despite himself, remembering. Panicking, trying to sit up. Feeling the restraints on his ankles and wrists. Fighting them, wriggling and twisting, even though he knew he had to be still. Sebastian couldn't close his mouth all the way, tasted blood. Moved his tongue to an empty pulpy space where some lower teeth had been. Tried to remember what had happened. Where he was. Tried to think. Tried to cry. Couldn't do anything. Even breathe. God, his nose was stuffed, probably smashed.

Okay. Okay, he had to think. Had to ignore the pain long enough to figure things out. He closed his eye, focusing, and what came to mind were their faces, watching him. Wearing twin expressions of fascination. And then another memory: the drink they'd given him. Insisting that he drink it. Their curiosity as they studied him while, slowly, his vision blurred, his eyelids sunk. Someone had held an eyelid open, watching his eye. Talking about the iris?

Sebastian's body contorted involuntarily, trying to get free. Recalling how he'd escaped into the woods, how they'd come after him, slamming onto his legs, kicking his face, his chest. Why? Why were they doing this? What did they have against him? He'd only spoken to Evan that one time, at the bar. And the other one? Sebastian was sure he'd never even seen him before. So what could it be? Because he was gay? There were tons of gays. Why him? Oh God, why him? He lay there, wracked by pain, wiggling the wrist of the hand that wasn't broken, trying to get loose, until he heard footsteps.

Above him. Upstairs? So he was someplace with an upstairs. Maybe back in Evan's room? Or in a basement? And were the footsteps Evan's and the other dude's or were they somebody else's? Somebody who might help him? Oh God. Maybe he should call out, shout for help. He opened his eye again and looked up, down, left and right, saw only darkness. He dared, slowly, to turn his head. Saw a sliver of light flat against the floor. Coming in under a door.

The footsteps were coming down the stairs. Leather shoes on wood or tiles. Coming closer, approaching the door. Sebastian's mouth went dry; his stomach churned. He turned his head back where it had been and closed his eye, aware that he'd lost control, had soiled himself. But still he lay motionless, pretending to be unconscious. He heard the door open and, recognizing Evan's voice, he was careful not to move his lips while he prayed.

Vivian slammed her coffee mug onto the table and glared. 'Dammit, Harper. Why are you always trying to ruin things for me?'

'I'm not—'

'Can't you just let me be happy? Is that too much to ask?'

Harper clenched her jaw, wondering why she'd begun the conversation. What delusion had led her to think it would be possible to be open with her mother?

'What is wrong with you, Harper? Always finding fault. Looking for something evil and twisted in everybody – especially everybody who cares about me.'

'All I said, Ma, was that Lou went out—'

'Lou is a decent guy. For once, I found a decent—'

'—in the middle of the night. I didn't say there was anything evil and twisted—'

'—guy who cares about me. And now you have to go trying to—'

'—about that.'

'—ruin it.'

They stopped talking at the same moment, fuming at each other in silence. Finally, Harper stood, took her cereal bowl to the sink, rinsed it, and put it on the dish rack, replaying the last few moments in her mind. All she'd done was ask her mother if Lou had seemed all right this morning, since she'd seen him go out in the middle of the night. How had her mother turned that into finding fault or looking for something evil and twisted?

'You blame me, don't you?' Vivian's voice was even lower and more ragged than usual.

Blame her? For what?

'I did my best, Harper. It wasn't my fault what your father did. I had no—'

'Oh please, Ma.' Not this again.

'Well, I didn't. I had nothing to do with his shenanigans. First I knew about it was when they came to the house to arrest him.'

Harper's hand ran through her hair. She didn't want to rehash everything. 'I know, Ma.'

'But you act like it was my fault. You always have.'

Ridiculous. 'I was just a kid.'

'A judgmental kid. Anyone I brought home, you hated.'

'Sorry,' she lied.

'Seriously. Name one guy you got along with.'

Oh Lord. Faces of her mother's men raced through Harper's mind. What was his name – the hairy one with the stinking cigars? Carl? Or Sydney, the shoe salesman who'd made a pass at her when Vivian was in the shower? Or the so-called personal trainer. Enough. Harper closed her eyes, pushing the memories away.

'You're right.' She came back to the table, sat down. 'I didn't like them.'

'You didn't give them a chance because you wanted your daddy back. But really, Harper. Was I supposed to sit and wait for him for fifteen to twenty? A guy who lied to me and stole from his clients, even his family? Your daddy was a smooth operator, Harper. Handsome and charming, but he wasn't who we – or anybody else – thought he was. So get over it.'

'Fine, Ma.' There was no point saying anything else; her mother wouldn't listen, never had. Harper wrapped her hands around her cup of chai, stared at the rim.

'You've always blamed me, though. Don't deny it. You resented me for trying to move on.'

'Ma, please.' She resented her, but not for that.

'God knows, I tried to be on my own. How many jobs did I take? A dozen?'

More, probably. Harper tried to remember them: waitressing, babysitting, washing hair, answering phones, telemarketing – whatever. Her mother hadn't kept any of them very long.

'But, face it, I'm not educated like you. I couldn't get a good job that would support us even close to the way your dad did. And – honestly? I'm no good on my own. I need to be with someone.' She leaned forward, lowering her voice. 'Look. Lou's not sophisticated or classy like your dad. But he's good to me. I'm happy with him. Don't begrudge me—'

'Ma, stop. I'm glad you're happy. Really.' Lord, how did her mother always manage to turn things around, making her feel that she'd done something wrong? 'All I said was that Lou—'

'All you said was something that would make me suspicious of him. You want me to doubt him.'

Harper shook her head. 'That's ridiculous.'

'He's a good guy, Harper. With a good heart. No fancy PhD like your guy has, but then, he didn't get advantages like you.'

Advantages?

'If Lou'd had the benefits you had – like that GI bill – maybe he'd have a college degree, too. Just because you got somebody to pay for your education doesn't mean you're better than him. Or me.'

Harper's mouth dropped. She was done listening. 'You right, Ma. As always.' She picked up her mug and took it to the sink, biting her lip so she wouldn't say what she was really thinking, that she'd earned whatever advantages she'd received by serving in the Army and nearly getting her head blown off. And that Vivian was completely self-centered and totally off her rocker.

'That's right, walk away. That's exactly the superior attitude I'm talking about,' Vivian sputtered.

Harper said nothing. She hurried out of the kitchen and, trying to ignore the pangs in her left leg, climbed the stairs to her room.

Upstairs, Harper tried to forget the exchange with her mother and work on her dissertation. She sat at her desk and opened her laptop, stared at the screen, unable to concentrate on symbolism in pre-Columbian relics, still smarting from Vivian's words. How dare Vivian imply that Harper had had an easy life – had she missed the part where Harper's father had gone to jail? Or maybe where her friends had dropped her as if she was a criminal, too? 'Don't let Harper get close to your lunch money,' her pal Jenna had taunted. She could still feel her cheeks burn.

Jenna Bradley. Wow. Harper hadn't thought of her in years. Hadn't thought about high school, or how they'd had to move from their suburban Colonial home to that tiny roach-infested one-bedroom, or how, after her father left and all his assets had been seized, her mother had imploded, drinking all day, unable to perform even the simplest domestic chores, let alone to hold a job – no. Enough. Harper would not get stuck revisiting all that. She had a dissertation

to write. Even so, her head throbbed because of Vivian, her oblivious-
ness. As if, at fifteen, Harper hadn't had to nurse her mother through
the night when she'd come home puking and plastered? As if Harper
hadn't had to work after school at the A&P until she'd been old
enough to enlist? As if she'd simply been given the benefits of the
GI bill and hadn't almost died in the war and didn't even now suffer
from her injuries? As if the war in Iraq had been a debutante's ball?
God, how had she let Hank talk her into letting her mother visit?
With Vivian there, Harper was far more stressed than she would
have been alone. In fact, her room was the only place she could
find any peace; she was a prisoner in her own home.

Rubbing her temples, Harper closed the computer and went to
the window. Snow was falling lightly, the sky and ground blended,
grayish and white. Hazy memories drifted by, images of her handsome father. Of their big house, her room with the canopied bed.
Damn. Why was she thinking about all this? It had happened decades
ago. She'd buried it long ago. Except that her mother was here,
raising the dead. Harper's fists tightened, angry that she was still
angry. That she wasn't immune.

Well, she might not be immune, but she wasn't helpless, either.
She had resources, would use them. Her phone was still on Hank's
pillow when she picked it up to call her shrink. Leslie would let
her vent, would help her gain perspective. Would probably help her
find ways to avoid bludgeoning – or even engaging in discussions
with her mother. Would help her survive.

Leslie's voice mail picked up; Harper left a message about an
appointment and reopened her computer. This time, she managed
to open her document file and read half a page before her mother's
voice began carping in her head. 'You've always blamed me. You're
always trying to start trouble . . .'

Okay. Enough. Harper snapped on the television, trying to drown
out the nagging, and turned back to her work. The last section she'd
written had been on parallels among symbols in pre-Columbian and
Greco-Roman relics. 'In discussing the recurring symbols among
these artifacts,' she read, 'it's essential to consider their significance
in the mindsets of the times, especially with respect to the role of
cosmology and the characteristics of the various deities.'

Harper read and reread the sentence, trying to remember what she'd
planned to say next. Where had she been headed with that? She looked
at her outline, searching for the section, so she was only vaguely aware

of the voices on the television. But when a woman sobbed, 'We were expecting him home for Christmas and he never showed up. It's not like Sebastian,' the tears interrupted her concentration, and Harper glanced at the television screen.

'He always comes home right after finals are over. He's never been into drugs or any kind of trouble. He's as straight a kid as they come . . .'

The woman's nineteen-year-old son was missing. Sebastian Levering, from Elmira. Harper looked back at her outline, found the section. Right. She needed to separate the three sub-topics. Talk first about the cultural mindsets . . .

'Authorities are hoping for help from the public . . .'

Harper looked again at the screen, saw the image of the missing college kid. Looked at her computer. Then at the television, at the kid's photo.

Harper was no longer seated at her desk. No longer thinking about the role of artifacts in revealing ancient man and his relationship with nature or religion. Harper stood at the television screen, riveted by the photo of the missing college kid from Elmira, certain that she'd seen him the night before, out in the snow, begging for help.

Except that, no. Maybe not. It had been dark. She'd seen the guy for maybe twenty seconds, and he'd been moving, facing away most of that time. She'd actually seen his face for – what? Three, four seconds? Not long.

The photo was long gone; the anchor had moved on, talking about holiday shopping in downtown Ithaca. But Harper stood, riveted on the screen as if still seeing the man's face. Sebastian was his name? He'd been wearing a suit in the TV shot, probably a high-school graduation picture. His hair had been neater, shorter than the naked guy's. And he'd been huskier.

But this kid was supposed to be in Elmira. Why would he be in Ithaca? Or naked behind her house? Really, there was almost no chance that the guy she'd seen was this missing kid from Elmira. She was forcing herself to see a resemblance because she was upset about what she'd seen. Probably, they were two completely different people.

But maybe they weren't.

Either way, one of them had asked for her help. Damn. Had he just been goofing around with friends, as Rivers suggested? Drinking too much, getting naked on a dare?

Okay. She wasn't going to get any work done. Harper closed her computer, went to her closet, took out her snow boots, pulled them on. She needed to get out of the house. To clear her mind. To move. Quietly, hoping to avoid her mother, she crept down the stairs to the coat closet. She was taking out a down parka when Vivian appeared.

'He's all upset, Harper.' Her whisper was like tires on gravel.

What? Harper put on the jacket.

'He's not himself. He's fidgeting and pacing, and he won't eat anything. I think it's because of you and last night. What the hell did you say to him?'

Harper exhaled, pulled up the zipper. 'Why do you assume I said—?'

'Because you must have. What else could it be?' Her mother worried her hands, following Harper as she went to the door. 'He was fine when we went to bed, and you saw him last night – so you must have—'

'I didn't say anything, Ma. He had a piece of pie.'

Vivian stopped harping, as if this information confounded her.

'If Lou's upset, why don't you ask him what's wrong?' Harper pulled on her gloves, moved to the door, opening it. 'I mean, you say you have this wonderful relationship.'

'We do.'

'Then talk to him.'

Harper stepped onto the porch. Pulled her hood up against the cold. And began walking.

She was halfway down the driveway when Vivian yelled, 'Harper? Where are you going? You need to rest. It's snowing!'

Harper waved a hand in the air and kept walking, didn't even look back.


The suspension bridge was her favorite spot on campus. She stopped halfway across to watch the large snowflakes floating down, the icicles dangling on the rocky walls of the gorge, the trickling frozen stream at the bottom. A frigid wind had kicked up, biting her exposed face, making the bridge sway. Even in the middle of the morning, the light was muted, the sky the typical winter-in-Ithaca gray. Harper stood alone, back to the wind, her thoughts wandering, settling on

nothing. She recalled the hot, sandy winds of Iraq. Wondered if it
was hot or windy where Hank was. Wondered whether the baby
would be a boy or a girl. Realized that walking had aggravated
her injured leg, but that the rest of her muscles were grateful for
the exercise. Enjoyed being away from Vivian. Braced for another
three weeks with her.

By the time she headed home, Harper's fingers and nose were
numb, but she was refreshed. Ready for a mug of hot chai. But as
she walked up the driveway, she stopped, looking into the trees
behind the house, remembering the naked guy being carried there.
Disappearing into the shadows. The police hadn't seen any sign of
him, but they'd been searching in the dark of night; even with their
floodlights, they might have missed something.

And so, instead of going inside, Harper set foot into the patch
of woods behind her house and the fraternity. She stepped carefully
between bushes, over fallen branches and icy rocks, around frozen
puddles. She wandered up the hill to the fence and back down,
edging through dense foliage, examining low branches and the
ground, looking for a sign of what had happened there. A piece of
clothing, maybe. A doused campfire, or evidence of drugs. But,
except for an occasional empty beer bottle, she found nothing.

Snow kept falling, and wind howled through the trees, whipping
her face. How bitter would it have felt without a parka? Without
even a shirt? Harper couldn't imagine. The guy, whoever he was,
would have had to be crazy to go bare-assed outside in this cold.

Wait, maybe that was it. Maybe he had been crazy. Maybe he'd
eaten some bad mushrooms or some other drug; maybe he'd been
hallucinating. Had torn off his clothes and run outside in a frenzy. And
maybe the guy chasing him had just been trying to help him, taking
him back home quietly, without anybody noticing so they wouldn't get
in trouble for messing with illegal substances. It was college, after all.
Kids – even smart Ivy League kids – did stupid things.

Good. Harper felt better. Her theory was plausible. She headed
out of the woods, relieved. Ready to get back to work on her dissertation. Ready even to see her mom. She was focusing on the house
up ahead, not studying the ground any more, so she didn't see the
key at first. It was lying beside a tree trunk, attached to a broken
string. But if she hadn't noticed the flecks of red beside it, dark
against fresh snow, she would have passed it by.

*        *        *

The thing was about nine feet tall and smelled of pinesap, and it stood between the sofa and the fireplace in full glory, greeting her from her living room.

Harper stood in the foyer, motionless, gaping. They'd bought a tree? While she'd been out trying to regain her composure and so she could be more patient with Vivian, she and Lou had run out and gotten it, behind her back? How had they dared? Had she not said, clearly, without ambiguity: No Tree This Year? Was it not her home, her right to decide? Had her mother once again completely dismissed her, openly disregarding and showing complete disdain for her authority?

Obviously. Harper marched into the living room ready for combat, but Lou stepped forward, his hands raised defensively. 'I swear, really, you won't have to do a thing—' he began, trying to appease her. 'And your mother is so excited. She picked out all new decorations—'

'I said I didn't want—'

'Is she back?' Vivian burst out of the kitchen, holding a pitcher of rum-spiked egg-nog and two glasses. 'Harper, I knew you didn't mean it. It isn't Christmas without a tree. Where would we put the presents? Besides, we've always had a tree.'

A childhood memory, a wobbly aluminum lopsided thing from the five and dime flashed to Harper's mind. Yes, they'd always had a tree.

'What, Harper? Don't you like it?' Vivian whined. 'I thought it would add some cheerfulness to this big old place.'

Harper closed her eyes, took a deep breath, opened them. 'Fine, Ma.'

'You're angry? Lou, is she angry?'

'Never mind. It's done.' Harper's jaws were tight. All her muscles were.

'Wait until it's decorated. You'll see—'

'I said it's fine.' Harper unzipped her parka, remembered the key. Damn. She had to call Rivers, couldn't be distracted by her mother's damned pine or spruce or whatever kind of tree. Which she had expressly, in plain English, clearly and more than once said she didn't want, and which had no business being in her living room.

'Lou went all out – he got colored lights, the kind that blink. And spray-on snow. Oh – and wait till you see the angel. She sings "Silent Night" and glows in the dark.'

Lord. She tossed the parka onto a chair, careful to keep the key wrapped in her glove, not to get fingerprints on it.

'You're welcome to help us decorate, if you want.'

Really? She was welcome in her own living room? How fucking unbelievably thoughtful. Harper bit her lip as she went upstairs with the key, deliberately counting her footsteps to prevent herself from letting loose with a reply. Not that Vivian was waiting for a reply; as Lou poured the egg-nog, her gravelly voice rattled on about the magical effect of blinking lights reflecting on tinsel.

Forty-nine. There were forty-nine steps from the bottom stair to her bedroom door. Which she shut, fuming. Grinding her teeth. Focus, she told herself. Focus on what you found in the woods. The key. The blood spatter. She picked up her phone, found a text: Leslie could see her at ten the next morning.

Harper placed her call to Rivers, wondering, as the call went through, how odd it was that she had a homicide detective on speed dial.

'Rivers.'

Harper told her about what she'd found.

'You're sure it was blood?' Rivers sounded skeptical. 'Because the fraternity kids could have spilled wine, or ketchup—'

No. She'd seen enough of it to be able to tell the difference between blood and wine or condiments. She'd seen it wet, dried, pooled, splattered. It was blood.

Rivers sighed. 'Well, the snow's getting heavy. They're saying ten to twelve inches. Whatever you found is going to get covered very quickly, if it isn't already.'

Harper went to the window, saw the thick heavy flakes; a layer of white was already concealing the undercoat.

'I could go get it.'

'The blood spatter?'

'I have the key. But I could gather the bloody snow in a plastic bag.'

'You took the key?'

'I didn't touch it. I had gloves on when I picked it up.'

Another sigh. 'Mrs Jennings. That key could be anything. Somebody could have dropped it months or even years ago. We don't even have proof that a crime has taken place—'

'What about that missing kid? The one from Elmira? I saw it on the news.'

'Are you saying that's the boy you saw?'

Harper hesitated. No, she wasn't. Not for sure. 'Maybe. It could have been. It was dark, but I think it was. Maybe.' She looked out the window. Tried to remember his face. And to locate the spot where she'd seen the spatter.

'Okay, Mrs Jennings. I'll stop by. I have to wrap up something here first. Give me half an hour.'

Harper stood at the window, her hand cradling the key in a tissue, careful not to smudge any fingerprints. Rivers was right: It was just a key, could be for a house, apartment, garage. Maybe a pantry or bedroom. Might have nothing to do with the naked guy, the missing kid or the blood spatter. But the snow was thickening; she had to hurry if she wanted to bag the evidence before it got completely buried.

Pocketing the key and her phone, Harper went back downstairs, grabbed a sandwich bag from the kitchen and threw on her still-cold parka and snow boots. She avoided the living room, but Vivian heard her.

'Now where are you going?' Her mother held a half-empty glass of egg-nog. 'It's a blizzard—'

Harper didn't hear the rest. She'd already slammed the door.

Snowflakes clung to her eyelashes. Tickled her nose. Stuck to her coat and gloves. Dimmed her view as she walked back toward the edge of the woods. The air was raw and indifferent. And, except for the wind, very silent.

The silence suddenly seemed dense, almost tangible; Harper moved through it, gazing through a white speckled haze. The house, the fraternity, the street, the trees – everything was soft, edgeless. Colorless. Suddenly, Harper felt isolated, disoriented. Her senses obscured. She braced herself, heard something in the distance. A motor? Was someone else out there? Maybe on a snow mobile? She looked behind her, saw nothing. Gazed at the street. A single dark SUV drove slowly past the house, the sound of its engine muffled by the snow. Lord. It was just a damned car. She was too jittery. Needed to go find her blood.

Slick layers of ice lay beneath new snow, and Harper slid a few times, nearly falling, but she righted herself and walked on cautiously, finally getting to the spot where she'd found the key. She stooped and scraped away the fresh layer of snow with her glove, but found no dots of spatter. She cursed, looking around, rechecking her location. This had to be the spot – a straight line from the corner of the garage. She'd memorized the tree, the tangled roots at its base, its position. So where was the spatter? She stooped, scraped the snow again. No blood. Damn.

Harper stood, squinting into the wind and snow. Was it possible that this wasn't the right tree? She looked around for a similar trunk and root. Didn't see one. No, this was the tree. Had to be. She pictured exactly where she'd found the spatter, took a few steps to the left. Scraped the snow again and stooped, looking closely for small drops of red or pink or brown or anything but white. Found nothing, all the way down to the dirt. She tried again, a little further from the tree. And then again, closer to it. And again, to the right. And again, even more to the right. Nothing. How could this happen? Had she lost her bearings due to the snow? Had the spatter marks been so tiny that they'd washed away or been blown away in the storm?

The wind was fierce, hurling snow into the woods; places she'd already dug were buried again. Harper couldn't tell where she'd been from where she still had to look.

When her phone rang, her gloves were caked with icy clumps, so she had to pull them off. She reached into her pocket, pulling out her phone with red stinging fingers.

'Harper, what's going on? Get in here,' Vivian whispered. 'That police woman's here again.'

Harper looked around one more time. The snow had camouflaged everything, concealed all the ground cover. No way she would find what she was looking for. Half blinded in white wind, careful of her footing, she started back for the house, holding an empty plastic bag.

Detective Rivers sat on the living-room sofa, holding a mug of hot tea. Lou must have brewed it, but he wasn't around. The monster tree was still bare, except for a cluster of six glittering red Styrofoam balls, hung at chest level. Plastic bags, wires, lights, miscellaneous decorations scattered the floor, chairs, coffee table.

'Shame you won't have any egg-nog,' Vivian slurred. 'It's truly delicious. I wonder why nobody drinks it except at Christmas—'

'I looked, but I couldn't find the spot,' Harper interrupted, trying to divert attention from her mother. Feeling old, familiar shame.

'What spot?' Vivian blinked. 'Where did you go?' She turned to Rivers. 'I told her not to—'

'Where's Lou?' Harper cut her off. Why wasn't he controlling her?

'Dunno.' Vivian shrugged, looking around. 'He was here a minute ago. LOU?' she bellowed, giving Lou three-syllables. 'LOU-OU-OU! LOU—OU-OU!'

'Never mind, Ma.' Harper yanked her coat off, stepped out of her boots.

'But if you want him—'

'It's all right.' She turned to Rivers. 'Let's talk in the kitchen.'

'I don't mind if you stay . . .'

''Scuse us, Ma'am.' Rivers stood.

'Okay. Go ahead. I've got work to do, hanging balls.' She put a hand over her mouth and burst out laughing. 'Sorry.' She slapped her thigh. 'It's just – hahaha – that – haha – sounded so bad – haha. Hanging balls—'

Harper's face got hot. She didn't look at Rivers or Vivian. She just grabbed her phone and the glove with the key and kept walking until she got to the kitchen, where she found a hot kettle simmering on the stove, poured a cup of water, tossed in a tea bag.

'Sorry to subject you to my mother.' Her voice was stiff, and she still couldn't meet Rivers' eyes. She was almost thirty years old, still embarrassed, still apologizing for her mother.

'No need to apologize. She's who she is, not who you are. Besides, I'm not here to judge.'

Harper nodded, poured honey, stirred.

'Nobody gets to pick their relatives,' Rivers added.

'I guess that's obvious,' Harper said as she sat opposite her.

'You should see my family.' Rivers shook her head, grinning. 'Asylums are filled with saner people.'

They snickered. Harper sipped tea, told herself to relax.

'Here's the key.' She unfolded the glove, pushed it across the table.

Rivers glanced at it. 'Yeah.' She didn't reach over or examine it. 'It's a key all right.'

'Don't you want to see what it opens? Or check it for fingerprints? It could be—'

'Tell me about the kid you saw. What makes you think he might be Sebastian Levering?'

Harper finally looked at Rivers. 'I saw his picture on the news, and it looked like the guy I saw being dragged into the woods.'

Rivers took a long sip of tea. 'How long, all told, would you say that you actually saw him?'

Harper frowned. She could tell where the conversation was going. 'Okay. It wasn't long.'

'Mrs Jennings.' Rivers leaned forward, elbows on the table. 'We've gotten to know each other pretty well over these last few years. I've come to trust you, and I respect your powers of observation. But by your own estimation, you saw this man's face for what? A couple of seconds? In the dark? In a highly emotional situation?'

Okay. She knew what the detective was implying: the recollections of eyewitnesses weren't reliable. 'But the blood spatter . . .'

Rivers watched her silently. Didn't have to point out that there was no way to test the alleged spatter.

'He asked me to help him.'

Rivers still said nothing. For a few seconds, they watched each other, not moving. Then Rivers leaned forward, letting out a sigh.

'The thing is, Mrs Jennings. We're in the same place we were last night. Despite what you say you saw and my desire to believe you, we have no evidence to back up your claim. Your spatter is unobtainable and not necessarily blood. This key – frankly, it has no link to any crime. It could have been dropped in the woods by anyone at any time. Beyond that, we have no idea if the guy you saw is Sebastian Levering. Since that news clip aired, literally dozens of people have called, saying they've seen him – he's in Rochester. Miami. Aruba. Cincinnati. Cancun. And now, according to you, he's in Ithaca. But we don't really know what you saw; we still have no proof that it wasn't a prank or bad behavior between drunk friends.' She paused, folded her hands. 'Honestly? Because it's you, I'm inclined to check it out – but how? Where? The dorms and fraternities are all closed for the holidays. The college kids are mostly gone. Nobody's reported any break-ins and no young men have been admitted to the hospital. Frankly, I wouldn't know where to look or who to interview.'

'You could test the key for prints—'

Rivers shook her head. 'I know you're trying to be helpful. But where would there be prints? The manufacturer's name is embossed on the top, so readable prints wouldn't have been left there. Plus, the key was out in the snow, and snow dilutes latent print residue. In addition to which, you wrapped it in your glove, which you carried in your pocket. So whatever prints might have been on it would have been rubbed off or smeared.'

Harper's face got hot. She should have protected it better. 'You mean I destroyed evidence?'

'No. Well, not intentionally. Besides, there was probably nothing to destroy. Bottom line: that key is just a key.'

In the living room, Vivian burst into song. ''Tis the season to be jolly . . .'

Harper swallowed tea, trying to ignore the raspy caroling and absorb what Rivers was saying.

Rivers leaned back in her chair, crossing her arms.

Harper was about to speak when abruptly, the muscles in her midriff tightened. Harper slammed her cup down, splashing tea all over the table. Damn. She closed her eyes, grabbed her belly.

'Mrs Jennings?'

Vivian's voice drifted in. 'Falalalala lalalala . . .'

'Mrs Jennings? You all right?'

Harper sat perfectly still, eyes shut tight, holding her middle, waiting for the stranglehold to ease. 'Fine,' she managed. 'I'm fine.' She even opened her eyes.

Rivers waited, ready to call an ambulance.

'. . . Deck the halls with boughs of holly . . .'

'I hate to say it: your mother's right. You shouldn't have gone out in this weather. You sure you're okay?'

Harper nodded. It was subsiding. Slowly. 'I'm fine. Just a random contraction.'

Rivers watched her for a while longer, then finally stood and took her tea mug to the sink. 'It's not my place to tell you this, but, hell, I will anyway. Take it easy, Mrs Jennings. Don't stress about anything. Especially about that guy you saw; let me worry about him, okay?'

Harper bristled. 'I can't just forget about him, Detective.'

'Mrs Jennings, let me do my job? And you do yours: Be pregnant.'

Harper nodded, even smiled. 'Fair enough.'

'Convey my best wishes to your husband, will you? And, assuming I won't see you in the next few days, have a merry Christmas.'

Harper thanked her, wished her the same. She stood to see her out, but her legs felt weak, and the detective told her to sit and take it easy. Harper didn't argue. She sat, breathing deeply, hearing her mother's dreadful singing. Staring at the key.

Evan was getting nervous. 'I think you killed him, Sty.'

'You think *I* killed him? You beat the fucking shit out of him.'

'But you're the one who drugged him. You must have overdosed him. He hasn't moved all day. And he shit himself. That happens when you die.'

One of them stepped closer; Sebastian could actually feel the heat radiating from the guy's body. He held his breath, willed his heart to slow.

'He's not dead.'

'You're sure?'

Sty put a hand on Sebastian's chest. 'There's a heartbeat. But we have to get Rory a new mattress. This one's totaled.'

Silence. Sebastian waited, bracing himself for the unexpected, barely breathing. Feigning unconsciousness.

Sty put his face up against Sebastian's, lifted the eyelid that wasn't swollen closed. Watched his eye for a sign of awareness. 'Hello? Anybody home?' Finally, he gave up. 'He's out,' Sty said, releasing the eyelid.

Sebastian almost wept with relief. Almost let out a breath. But he didn't dare. Suddenly Sty pressed down on his swollen, probably broken knee, but despite some woozy pain and a dull realization that his leg was exploding, he didn't move. Didn't let out a sound. Gave silent thanks for the drugs.

'You're right. I probably overdosed him.'

'So what do you suggest we do?' That was Evan.

'I guess we wait for him to wake up.'

'And then?'

'And then we proceed as planned.'

More footsteps, moving away this time. Sebastian allowed himself a shallow shudder. Another.

'But I think we should make revisions.'

'Why?'

'Seriously? Why? Look at him, Evan. He's messed up. You went kind of berserk—'

'What did you expect? The fucker stuck his tongue in my mouth—'

Sty was laughing. 'So? He liked you. Who could blame him? I mean, now that I think about it, you're kind of cute.'

'Fuck off.'

'Point is suicide won't cut it any more. As in, he couldn't have beaten himself to a pulp. The authorities would investigate to find out who did.'

Silence.

'Okay. How about this? We conceal the injuries behind bigger ones . . .'

'Like how? Oh, the gorge? No, too risky. We might be seen.'

'Not if we do it at night. Late.'

'And if someone and his sweetie just happen to wander by?'

'It's intersession. Nobody will—'

'I said it's too risky.' Sty's tone was final.

Sebastian let out a breath of relief. He had no desire to be thrown into the gorge.

'Fine. Then what do you suggest?' Evan sounded miffed.

'We could dump him somewhere in town. He'd be just another drug overdose. They happen all the time.'

'Sty. If it's drugs, they do an autopsy. People don't take rufies on their own. They'd find them and look into it.'

More silence.

'I still think he can hang himself. They won't do an autopsy if they find him hanging, will they? We can write a suicide note mentioning . . . I'll copy his signature off his ID.'

'But where? Not here. They'd wonder how he got in. Not to mention why he'd killed himself someplace he doesn't even belong.'

'Right.'

'So we'd have to move him.'

Involuntarily, Sebastian shivered but they didn't notice. Which meant they weren't looking at him. Which meant he could dare to open his openable eye. He did, just a crack, and peered across the room. Evan and Sty sat deep in thought, one on a mattress, the other on a chair.

'The woods?' Evan suggested. 'It's right here. No one would see us—'

'But it's too close to the house. A body found there casts suspicion our way. Nobody else has access to it.'

So he was in a house near some woods. Which didn't mean much; could be almost anywhere around Ithaca. Unless . . . maybe they were still in Evan's fraternity. Of course – Sebastian remembered the woods out back, running into them bare-assed.

'Or we can drive him out to the country. Out near the Falls. It'll be months before anyone finds him.'

Damn. Sty stood. Sebastian closed his eye, heard Evan's chair scrape the floor. They were getting up. Oh God, were they going to take him now?

'Fact is,' Evan said, 'he looks pretty banged up.'

'I doubt his own mama would recognize him.'

'I told you. He pissed me off.'

'Okay, okay. So we put it in the note. He writes that he's been mugged by some violent homophobe, and he can't take it any more. So he hangs himself. What do you think?'

'I'm not a homophobe.'

'Christ, Evan. This isn't about you—'

'Even so.'

'It's a fucking suicide note.'

'Okay. Fine. I get it.'

'And, along that line of thought, we need to untie him. A suicide wouldn't have restraint marks.'

'Brilliant, Sty. What if he wakes up?'

'Seriously? Look at him. His leg – he's not going anywhere.'

Someone came close; Sebastian lay limp. Hands messed with his ankles, then his wrists. His stomach twisted, lungs ached with fear. Oh God. He didn't dare exhale.

'So what time's your date?'

'I'm expected to pick up the lovely Ms. Alicia Lawrence at . . . Oh shit, in twenty minutes.'

'Can't believe you're with a fuckin' townie.'

'A townie with velvet lips, Evan. Don't underestimate the skills of the locals. You're staying here tonight?'

'After that Christmas gig.'

'Good. Because, frankly, I don't want this to get fucked up worse than it is already. The whole idea – our whole reason for doing this was to conduct a study—'

'No worries.' Evan sounded downright cheery. 'I'll be here. And whatever happens, it's all good, part of the process. We're learning as we go, honing our skills. We'll do better next time.'

'Bullshit. You almost fucking let him get away . . .'

The conversation faded as footsteps moved away. A door closed.

As soon as Sebastian heard the click of the lock, he lifted his arms, wiggled the seven fingers that could move, and tried to sit up. His damaged ribs slowed him down, but when he tried to move his legs, the pain was excruciating. Paralysing. The drugs were wearing off. His right knee was the size of a melon. In fact, the whole leg looked purple, inflated and balloon-like: the ankle, foot, even his toes. Never mind. He was alone and untied. He had to get out somehow. Fast. And without making noise.

The door was locked, but there was a window. Slowly, grimacing with pain, he used his left hand to shove his right leg off the bed he'd been lying on. Slid his other leg over the side and tried to stand on it. Wobbled. Flopped back onto the bed. Caught his breath. Tried again and managed to stand on his left leg, but, reeling from pain ripping through his right one, almost fell, barely catching himself by grabbing the desk at the foot of the bed with his left hand. He stood there for a while, panting, steadying himself, and then, carefully, he hopped a step toward the window. Oh God. Sebastian bit down on his lip, stifling wails of pain as he leaned against the desk, preparing for another agonizing hop. Which brought him within arm's-length of the wall. One more hop, and he was close enough to use the wall as support while he continued, slowly and painfully, to edge his way to the window, where he clutched the curtains, parted them to look outside, lost his balance. And fell, howling, to the floor.

Vivian was snoring on the sofa as Harper passed the living room to climb the stairs. The tree was untouched, decorated with the same clump of glittery Styrofoam as before, but the pitcher of egg-nog was empty. Harper thought about the collection of decorations she and Hank had up in the attic, collected together, each representing a special memory. A crystal prism from their first Christmas together. A tiny handmade wreath from a trip to the mountains. A small stuffed bear from a camping trip. A toy soldier for her military stint. A delicate glass snowflake – but why was she itemizing her decorations? Hank wasn't there. She wasn't going to unpack them without him, certainly not for her mother and Lou.

And speaking of Lou, where was he? Harper hadn't seen him since she'd gone out looking for the spatter. Vivian had told Rivers that he was somewhere in the house. Maybe, like her mother, he'd had too much egg-nog and passed out. Except that he'd been too hyper to pass out. Too edgy. Maybe her mother was getting to him.

Finally back in her room, Harper lay down, shaken by the strength and suddenness of her contraction. What if her contractions got worse? What if the baby came too early? Oh God. What if something went wrong? She couldn't bear that thought and held her belly tenderly, trying to sense the person inside, wishing it would flip around again so she could feel it move. Who was in there? Would it be a boy who looked like Hank? Softly, she began to sing to it. 'Hush little baby, don't say a word. Papa's gonna buy you a mocking bird . . .'

Oh God, what had she been doing, running around outside in the ice and snow, risking harm to her child? From now on, she'd focus on the baby and nothing else. Well, except for her dissertation. And her mother. But that was it. Nothing else. Period. Chilled, she climbed under the comforter and, still softly singing, stared out the window at the falling snow. When she opened her eyes again, it was dark.

Something smelled. Incendiary devices? Harper jumped up, reached for her weapon. But wait – there was no weapon. No gear. She looked around, remembered she was home, in her bedroom. Not in Iraq. So the odor wasn't from explosives or the burning flesh of soldiers. She closed her eyes again, reassuring herself. The smell wasn't men; it was meat.

Harper turned, looked at the clock. Lord, it was after five. She'd slept all day? How? Suddenly, she was starving. Ravenous. Even so, she didn't want to move. Her left leg ached, and she felt sluggish and confused, still in the fog of sleep. But this was unacceptable; she'd wasted a whole day.

Harper ran a hand through her hair, missing Hank, feeling utterly alone. No, even worse than alone – alone with her mother and Lou. And the monster tree downstairs. Lord, how would she make it through the month?

Stop whining, she scolded herself. Don't be a wimp. You've gotten through longer months in far worse conditions.

Still groggy, reminding herself that she would see Leslie the next morning, she got out of bed, checked the snowfall out the window. It looked like about ten inches had fallen, and, now that it had stopped, the ground glowed bluish white, reflecting the moonlight, emphasizing the shadowy angles and gables of the empty fraternity next door. The street hadn't yet been plowed, but a dark SUV pushed its way through the snowy street – hadn't she seen it before? Why would anyone be out in this weather? Where could they possibly need to go?

'Harper?' Vivian knocked as she opened the door. 'Good. You're up.' She came inside, arranging her hair, hesitating before she spoke. 'Look. I hope you're not going to make a fuss about the tree. Lou bought it with the best of intentions, so you could make the place more festive—'

'I told you before. It's fine.' She tried to sound sincere.

'Don't be like that.'

'Like what? I said it's fine.'

'Your tone. I can tell you resent it. Why can't you ever be appreciative when people try to show their concern for you?'

Their concern for *her*? Harper bit down on the inside of her cheek, stifling her response. 'I am appreciative, Ma. Thanks.'

Her mother folded her arms, cocked her head. A lock of bluish auburn hair flopped over her forehead. 'Tsk.'

Tsk? Really? 'Ma. The tree makes you happy. It's fine.'

'Good. I knew you'd change your mind.' Vivian stepped over to Harper, pecked her on the cheek. 'What did that policewoman want?'

'Nothing. She was just getting back to me about last night.'

Vivian nodded, turned to leave. 'Dinner's ready. Lou's been cooking all afternoon. Pot roast.'

Pot roast? So that was the seared-flesh smell. Harper looked out the window at the snow. If there was one dish Harper disliked more than cow liver, it was pot roast. How was it possible that Lou had chosen to prepare those two meals on consecutive nights?

'Come and eat.'

Harper couldn't eat anything that smelled like that – she almost gagged at the thought. But she didn't want to start another argument. 'Damn, Ma. I didn't realize.' She grasped for an excuse. Lied. 'I ordered pizza.'

'You what? When? Why would you—?'

'Just now. When I got up. I didn't think Lou should cook every night.'

'Well, you might have asked first, before going ahead. You shouldn't just assume things. How did you know we'd even want pizza?'

Harper didn't respond. Didn't want to start the discussion about asking people what they wanted before deciding on a meal. Or a tree.

Vivian sputtered out of the room. 'Lou – wait'll you hear this . . .'

Harper waited until she was on the steps, reporting the news of the pizza. Then, staring into the snow, she picked up her cell and called Napoli's.

She was thinking about artichokes and shrimp, not paying attention to the view. But she was positive, or almost, that as she repeated her address, in an upstairs window of the empty fraternity next door, a curtain moved.

Showered and dressed, Evan was practicing his harmony while trying to straighten his tie without reopening the wounds on his knuckles when he heard the thunk from upstairs. He froze. Heard nothing more. Tried to convince himself it was nothing. Maybe the kid had come to, rolled over and fallen out of bed.

It was nothing.

Evan began singing again, checking himself in the mirror. Thick wavy hair, strong jaw. Classic, patrician looks. Frankly, he couldn't blame the gay kid for being attracted to him. Singing, he stepped forward and back, turned to the side, spinning through moves from his a cappella group. Rehearsing. It was a tradition for The Quadtones to do Christmas shows at old people's homes. The old codgers loved it, sang along, clapped their hands like little kids.

Evan checked his watch. Time to go. He grabbed his striped blazer and headed for the door.

Thump.

It was faint this time. Muted.

The kid was conscious. Damn. Must be banging on the wall.

Another thump. Another.

Christ, what was he doing?

Evan took his cell phone, called Sty. Got voice mail. Fuckin' Sty, too busy getting laid to answer his damned phone? So what was he supposed to do? Just leave and hope nothing happened? He had to meet the other guys in front of Balch in fifteen minutes. Had to leave. The kid was locked up tight, had no place to go. No phone. No way out. And he'd be back in a few hours. What could happen in a few hours?

Evan took his overcoat from his closet and headed out of his room toward the steps. He was in the foyer when, from upstairs, he heard a crash. And then an ear-bending howl.

Hank called early, right after dinner. He sounded glum, but denied that anything was wrong. 'Nothing,' he said when she asked.

Harper knew, though, that something was. She could tell by his voice. Maybe the work was too much for him. Maybe he was pushing too hard. Getting frustrated or depressed. Or sick? But Hank needed to succeed at this project. Needed to feel competent again – they both needed that. She decided to be positive and encouraging, not to say anything that might upset him. No complaints about Vivian or Lou or the tree. No mention of the missing kid, the key or the blood spatter. Instead, she talked about shopping for baby furniture. About her dissertation. And, as she gazed out the bedroom window, about the weather.

'We got another foot of snow.'

Hank muttered a disinterested reply.

In a lilting voice, Harper tried yet again to cheer him up, reporting that she'd devoured almost an entire shrimp and artichoke pizza, and that she was already hungry again. That the baby had a fierce appetite.

Even then, Hank's response was flat.

Finally, Harper gave up pretending. She sat on the bed in silence, stroking his pillow, pouting, thinking of his chest.

'So.' She bolstered her voice, stared at the window. 'Tell me what's going on.'

'Long day.'

Oh – he was tired. Of course, that was it. Hank hadn't worked full days since before his accident, wasn't used to hours of continuous exertion.

'Sleeping okay?'

'Not. Without Hoppa.'

An aching wave rolled through her. Hank missed her. Maybe that was why he sounded so down.

'You? Resting, Hoppa?'

She thought of her forays into the icy woods, the sharp contraction she'd had earlier. 'Plenty. I slept all afternoon.'

'Good. Baby needs. Naps.'

When they finally said goodnight and hung up, Harper stayed on the bed, holding Hank's pillow, replaying his husky whisper when he'd said goodnight. Feeling the whisper like a caress. An embrace. Oh God. She had to stop. Hank would be home in just a few weeks. She shouldn't whimper and whine as if he'd been ripped permanently from her arms; she was lucky. They both were. In fact, she should go downstairs and celebrate their luck with some ice cream. Yes. Butter almond? Rocky Road? What did they have? She couldn't remember.

And she didn't want to go look. She missed Hank and refused to cheer herself up. Instead, she curled up on the bed, held onto his pillow and sulked, staring out the window at the night, noticing that the curtains in the fraternity window hung motionless and undisturbed.

Evan raced back up the stairs. Across the landing, up to the third floor. When he got to Rory's room, he took the key off the frame, but didn't unlock the door. He stood outside, listening. But heard nothing.

Obviously, though, something had happened in there. Maybe the kid's leg wasn't as bad as it looked. Maybe he was just inside the door, waiting to jump anyone who opened it.

Evan pictured the leg, purple and swollen. He'd felt something smash when he'd pounced on it. No way the kid could walk on that thing, let alone fight. Still, he should be careful. Not rush in without protection.

Again, Evan went downstairs, this time into the kitchen, hoping to find a knife. Drawers, cabinets – everything was locked. Even the refrigerator had a padlock on it. Damn. Okay. He'd have to use his own stuff. He hurried back to his room, grabbed his flashlight and his baseball bat, then reconsidered. Put the bat down, opened a desk drawer and shuffled through pens and jump drives. Found his Swiss army knife and rushed back to the third floor, where he listened again outside Rory's door.

Hearing nothing, slowly, cautiously, he unlocked the door. Held the flashlight in one hand, the open knife in his other. Pushed the door open with his foot.

The room stunk like a damned latrine. Evan flashed the light onto the bed. Saw no kid, just his stinking mess. Panned the light across the floor, finally found the kid lying in a heap, all the way across the room. How the fuck had he gotten all the way over there?

Evan was breathing fast. Damn. He had to go, couldn't be late. They needed his tenor, couldn't do the show without him. He flashed the light onto his watch. Shit. Ten minutes. Okay. He needed to calm down, think. He could just leave the kid where he was. Could re-lock the door, pretend he hadn't heard anything and deal with it later, when he got back. Or better yet, let Sty deal with it in the morning.

Good plan. But he didn't leave. He stood there, doing a best-case/worst-case assessment. Best case, nothing would happen and he could wait for Sty. Worst case . . . Jesus. What would the worst case be? The kid could move. Could get to the window and, maybe, yell for help.

And then Evan had a disturbing thought: What if the kid had already gotten to the window? What if he'd managed to open the curtains and contact someone outside – waving and banging? Had that been what he'd heard?

Damn. Evan flashed the light on the curtains, walked across the room, peered through the gap between the drapes. Flashing his light outside, he relaxed; the window wasn't visible to anyone on the street, just to the house next door and its garage. There was a glow from an upstairs window next door, but not much chance that anyone there would have been watching Rory's window.

Cool. Turning to leave, Evan stepped over to the kid, flashed the light on his face to see if he was awake. And let out a yelp of surprise as his knees buckled beneath him and he hit the floor, sending his knife and the flashlight flying.

Leaning on Hank's pillow, Harper got tired of feeling sorry for herself. She turned on the television, found a marathon of *Psych* reruns and, preparing to settle in, finally went downstairs for ice cream. She took out a giant soup bowl and scooped in a mixture of mint chocolate chip, strawberry and butter almond, which she covered with maple syrup, black olives, whipped cream and wads of super crunchy peanut butter. Decided to wash it down with a tall glass of tomato juice. Took it all upstairs and climbed back into bed to watch the next episode.

An hour later, she turned off the television and lay in the dark, reassuring herself that Hank, the naked kid and her baby were all fine, reciting her list of worries as a rhythmic mantra. She was dozing, her eyes drifting closed when a beam of light flashed into her room.

Harper opened her eyes, watched the light move across her wall and disappear. She got up, looked out the window, couldn't find the source. Nobody was in the driveway or the yard. The street was empty. She looked across at the fraternity, saw it hulking dark and still. Nothing moved. Nobody was there. But the light had come from somewhere. Weird.

Puzzled, Harper stood at the window until she got cold. Then she got back in bed and lay facing the window, watching for lights, listening for movement. Letting her eyelids drop.

He landed on his back, head slamming the floor, showing him pulsing red light. Before he could even wonder what happened, a heavy weight landed on him, grunting and stinking – something on his throat – an elbow? Evan tried to roll, but he was pinned, couldn't move. Couldn't breathe. What . . . the kid? Yes, the kid. Poking at his face with a filthy hand. Evan slapped and shoved at it, but it kept coming back. Scratching him. Pressing on his cheek. Aiming for his eyes. What the fuck? Evan kicked, tried to hit the kid's wounded leg. But his leg hit nothing, swung through empty air. Meantime, his arms were useless, one pushing the elbow off his throat, the other fending spidery fingers off his face.

No way this could be happening. Evan was strong and in good shape; the kid was damaged from head to toe and had been repeatedly drugged. Still, incredibly, he wouldn't give up. Evan moved quickly, using both arms to dislodge the elbow and knock it off his neck. And using the momentum to knock the kid off him.

The kid's scream actually hurt Evan's ears, but he kept moving. His eyes had become accustomed to the darkness, and he could see the kid's swollen eye, his mangled hand, his grotesquely broken leg. A growl rose from his belly as he readied himself to strike, raising a fist to pound the kid's wounds, preparing to kill. Remembering the knife only when he saw it coming toward his stomach, the blade glinting dimly in the kid's hand.

Twisting, Evan grabbed the kid's wrist. The kid howled but hung onto the knife, his body trembling and sweating. Evan squeezed and twisted harder and, finally, the knife fell, clattering on the floor.

The kid wailed, his wrist hung limp, but amazingly, he still wouldn't give up. He reached with his other hand, even though its fingers were broken. Evan watched, catching his breath, simultaneously amused and fascinated at the persistent pathetic effort. The kid kept trying to pick the knife up with a thumb and pinkie. As though he'd be able to wield it, even if he somehow managed to lift it. He glanced at Evan repeatedly with his one open eye, as if he still thought he had a chance.

But Evan had had enough. Annoyed, he punched the kid in his good eye. When he fell backwards, Evan picked up the knife and, without further ado, thrust it deep into the kid's throat. Then, remembering the time, he cursed, ran out of the room and down the stairs. In a minute, he'd changed his shirt, washed his face, smoothed his hair, donned a different blazer, grabbed his overcoat and hurried out the door, manufacturing a story that would explain his lateness and the bruises and scratches on his face.

Harper's eyes popped open. Something had awakened her again. Not a light this time – the room was completely dark. Then what? Faintly, the floor creaked. Footsteps padded softly down the stairs. Harper sat up, listening. Moments later, the motion detectors turned on the driveway lights, beaming white light through her window. Harper climbed out of bed, hearing her mother's car start up. When she got to the window, she saw Lou at the wheel, backing out of the driveway.

Again? Where the hell was he going? She glanced at the clock. It was almost one. What could he have to do at this hour?

She remembered what he'd said when she'd asked him: he had trouble sleeping. Maybe he needed a break from Vivian; she could certainly understand that. Or maybe he just wanted to move, get out of the house, go for a drive. That, too, would be understandable. The snow had closed them in; Lord knew, Harper felt claustrophobic. Maybe Lou had just headed to a bar before closing time to see new faces and connect with life outside her house.

Harper stood at the window, watching the stillness of the empty street. Wishing she could go somewhere, too. Missing her Ninja, the highway. Hank. Mostly Hank. As if to console her, the baby did a shimmy; it felt like a feather dancing in her body. Harper put her hand on her belly, wondering again who was in there. Who it would look like.

'You're awake, too?' She smiled. 'Missing your daddy like me?' She pictured the baby doing flip-turns until the movement settled. Then, wide awake and restless, disturbed by something she couldn't name, Harper walked the floors.

\*     \*     \*

When Evan got back from the old codgers' home, he let himself into the house through the back door, like always, careful to cover his footprints with snow. He'd called Sty again and again, but of course, hadn't been able to reach him. He'd left a text, telling him to call. With exclamation marks. But he knew Sty. Sty wouldn't even look at his phone while he was with that girl. Townie or not, she had him completely whipped. So here he was, alone with the dead kid until morning. But he was not going to think about him.

He moved through the dark kitchen to the foyer, taking off his coat, loosening his tie. Thinking about how fucking cold it was outside, and how fucking cold it was inside because the heat was turned down to like fifty degrees while everyone was gone.

He moved through the foyer, seeing by the night light on the staircase, thinking how absurd it was that the place was closed. His father paid his fees; he ought to be able to stay there year-round without having to sneak in and out.

He moved up the stairs, reviewing his evening. The festive tree and lame egg-nog and sugar cookies. The old folks singing along, even getting up and dancing. That one old guy – he'd been spry, dancing with that old girl even though she had a walker. They'd seemed delighted with the performance, the old familiar songs. And no one had been mad about him being late – they figured it had been the snow. Before they could even ask about his face, he'd said he'd gone tray sliding down the hill behind the Straight, had fallen and landed on his face. Avery had laughed and that had been the end of it. Fucking Avery had a falsetto like nobody. Could hit those high notes like fucking Beverly Sills.

Evan walked down the hall to his room, unlocked the door. He hung his coat and blazer up in his closet, thinking he could just about see his breath it was so cold. Maybe he'd just get undressed and go to bed. Pretend nothing had happened.

He stripped down, pulled on a sweat suit. He hated sleeping in clothes, but it was cold. He went to the john, brushed his teeth, got in bed. And lay there.

Thinking about the kid.

How it had felt to sink the knife into his neck – the rush. Kind of like an orgasm, but on a different scale. Nothing he'd ever felt before. He closed his eyes, reliving the moment.

But what was that? A footstep? No. Just a creak. A noise. The fraternity house was old, made noises. Something howled loudly, rattling the window. It was just the wind, Evan told himself, nothing from upstairs. Stop being so jumpy, he told himself. You stuck your fucking knife in his neck. He was dead when you left, was still dead now.

But what if he weren't?

What if he'd crawled back to the window? What if he'd written 'help me' or 'save me' in blood?

Christ. Evan rubbed his eyes. Cut it out. This wasn't summer camp, wasn't a ghost story. He'd killed the kid. It hadn't gone the way they'd planned, hadn't been done methodically as Sty had wanted. But he'd done it. Dead was dead.

Evan lay staring at the ceiling. Picturing the body above it. The bloody mess up in Rory's room.

Okay, shit. He wasn't going to sleep anyhow; he might as well get a start on cleaning up. He got out of bed, pulled on some sweat socks, stopped at the maid's closet to get a bucket, a mop, some rags, some cleaner, and climbed up to the third floor.

'Knock knock,' he announced as he opened the door. In case the corpse might hear him. But, no, even in the dark, he could tell that the kid was right where he'd left him.

'You know, it was nothing personal. It was an experiment of a sort.' He kept talking as he went to the window. If he pulled down the shade behind the curtains, he could turn on a light without it being seen from outside. That way, he could actually see what he was cleaning.

'We were searching for a specimen, and you happened to be available. Unfortunately, you mucked up our research.' He separated the curtains to reach up for the shade. 'You put up an amazing fight, but in the end, your death was basically a waste. It didn't add anything to our intellectual—'

Evan stopped mid-sentence, looking outside. Directly across from him, in full view, he saw the neighbor woman, the little blonde motorcycle lady, standing at her bedroom window, looking out at the night. Had she seen him? He froze, finally realized that, no, she couldn't have; his room was dark. And she was staring past him, toward the street. Wasn't she? He ducked away. Watched her through the slit of the curtain until she moved away.

He quickly pulled the shade down, closed the drapes, turned the light on. As he scrubbed bloodstains, though, he remembered how the kid had crawled to the window before. How he'd found him there. That neighbor – could she have seen him at the window?

Of course not. She couldn't have. Out of the question. Because, if she'd seen him, she'd have done something. Would have called the police again.

He remembered the police showing up after the kid had tried to get away. The searchlights pouring into the woods. Damn, he'd been scared.

But then again, whatever she'd seen or hadn't seen made no difference. He wasn't on the premises – neither was Sty. Nobody was; the fraternity was closed for winter break. So even if the neighbor lady had seen the kid's bare ass, it didn't reflect on them.

Still, as he mopped and washed, he pictured the easy view from her window. Just to be safe, he'd discuss the possibilities with Sty.

Harper checked on Vivian, hoping she was awake, ready to ask her about Lou. But Vivian, her face masked with cream, was snoring blissfully.

So Harper went downstairs and, hungry yet again, fixed herself a glass of two percent and a banana and mayonnaise sandwich. As she brought them back to her room, she decided that Lou hadn't gone out for a nightcap. No, something about him just wasn't right. Harper had recognized that sharp cold glint in his eye – she knew that he had a dangerous side. If Lou was sneaking out while Vivian slept, it was because he was trying to hide something. And because he was involved with her mother – not to mention staying in her home – Harper had a right to know what that something was, didn't she?

Yes, she did.

And even if she didn't, she was going to find out. She was going to wait for him to come home and confront him outright. Not take 'I couldn't sleep' for an answer.

Meantime, she'd have her snack and watch more TV. She set the snack on the nightstand, climbed into bed, clicked on the remote, and surfed channels. Found some late-night talk show. An old *Seinfeld* episode. Cartoons – Sponge Bob? In the middle of the night? The nation's weather. Lord. Harper kept flipping. She had satellite, hundreds of stations. There must be something to watch.

Finally, she settled on a *Law and Order* rerun. Which broke almost immediately for a commercial. Harper bit into soft bread with sweet and creamy filling, gulped some milk. Took another bite, chewing while she waited for insurance, weight loss and car ads to end, but when they finally did, the show didn't come back. Instead, a news anchor appeared with a recap of the latest news. More snow was predicted. The stock market was up over a hundred points. Harper downed another bite of sandwich and reached for the remote, about to change the channel, but the anchor's next story stopped her. She sat still, holding the remote in mid-air, recognizing the face that popped onto the screen. Sebastian Levering, the missing kid from Elmira. The anchor reported that Levering, an Ithaca College student, still had not been found despite dozens of reported sightings that placed him all over the country. His family feared the worst. 'I know if he could, he'd call us,' his father declared. 'But whatever happened to him, somebody knows something. Somebody must have seen something.' His wife stood beside him, weeping.

Harper stopped chewing, didn't hear the rest of the clip. She sat with her mouth full, no longer hungry, staring at the television but seeing a desperate face, pleading for her help. She blinked the image away and saw snow spattered with blood. But then the snow became sand, and Harper smelled burning rubber, heard gunfire and the buzz of flies around her head. She watched a car pull up to the checkpoint, saw a woman crossing the road, smiling at her with a sharp glint in her eyes, and then – a blast of heat carried Harper into the air – she flew, landing on a burned-out car, unable to move. Somewhere far away, she heard voices. *Law and Order* was back on, but Harper didn't see it. She was caught in her own rerun, revisiting a time when she'd sensed danger but hadn't acted. A time when her inaction had caused people to die.

Harper woke with bright sun shining in her window, a plate with half a sandwich on her lap, the TV remote in her hand, and bits of ripened mashed banana, bread and mayonnaise in her mouth.

She got out of bed, sorting her thoughts. Remembering her flashback, and then the news that had set it off. She was in the shower before she thought of Lou and the reason she'd even been watching TV. She was downstairs, pouring a bowl of cereal before she realized that, for the first time since his arrival, he hadn't fixed breakfast.

She looked out the kitchen window into the driveway. Her mother's car wasn't there.

'Ma?' Harper called. Maybe Vivian and Lou had gotten up early and gone somewhere. 'Ma? You here?' she called again.

'In here.'

Her mother's voice came from the living room. The tree was still untouched, the room a mess.

'I don't know what I was thinking, getting all this stuff.' Vivian sat on the floor, lost amid bags of decorations. She was wearing tights and a sweatshirt, her hair tied up in a topknot. From behind, she looked like a teenager.

'Where's Lou?' Harper asked.

'Good morning to you, too.'

'Sorry, Ma. Good morning. How are you? Fine? Great. Me, too. So where's Lou?'

'Why? You need him for something?'

Oh Lord. 'I want to talk to him.'

Vivian eyed her suspiciously. 'About what?'

'Ma. What difference does it make about what? Just tell me where he is.'

'Out somewhere. I didn't ask for his itinerary. He'll be back any time—'

'Was he out all night?'

'Of course not. Why would you ask that?' Vivian looked away, began emptying a bag: tinsel, spray-on snow. More glittery Styrofoam balls.

Harper came into the room, sat on the sofa close to Vivian. She softened her voice. 'Ma. I heard him go out late last night while you were asleep. He took your car.'

Vivian stiffened. 'So? Maybe I said he could take it.'

'Ma. He hasn't come back. What's going on? Where's he go at night?'

'There you go again—'

'I'm not trying to make trouble. I just want to know. If he's in some kind of trouble—'

'It's business, Harper. That's all it is.' Vivian watched the tinsel.

'Business.'

'Yes.'

'In the middle of the night.'

'He's got a trucking company.'

A trucking company? As if that explained everything.

'His drivers are all over the country. They make deliveries round the clock.'

Harper studied her mother. Did she really think that what she'd said made any sense?

'Ma. You really don't have a clue where he went, do you?'

'No, I don't, and why should I?' Vivian was on her feet, hands on hips. 'I don't keep tabs on him or his business, nor do I want to. I don't give him the third degree. If he tells me he has business to do, I believe him.'

For a few moments, they stared at each other silently. Vivian's nostrils flared. Harper decided not to pursue the conversation any further. She finally stood, said, 'Okay,' and left the room – not because she was satisfied with Vivian's response, and not because she didn't want to cause trouble. The reason Harper dropped the subject of Lou's whereabouts was that she'd left her cereal on the kitchen counter, and she was suddenly monstrously, unbearably hungry. Lou, and whatever he was up to, could wait.

When Sty finally showed up, the sun was high in the sky. He came in through the back, checking to make sure he'd left no footsteps in the hardened snow, and found Evan waiting for him at the foot of the stairs, holding an empty Stoly bottle.

'You don't answer your fuckin' phone?' Evan hadn't gone to bed at all. He'd scrubbed the room upstairs and then wandered through the house, finishing off the last of his Stoly. 'I called you a hundred times—'

'My phone was turned off.' Sty beamed one of his dashing smiles. 'It's rude to take calls in certain circumstances.'

'Well, how about this circumstance? Everything's gone wrong. And you're off getting your cock sucked, leaving all the responsibility to me—'

'Whoa, hold up there, Silver.' Sty stepped over to Evan, stroking his head.

Evan slapped his hand away. 'Fuck you, Sty. I've been up all night, cleaning up this mess. And we still have to get Rory a new mattress—'

'Forget the mattress. It's not a big deal. We've got other issues to deal with first. Let's go check on the kid.' He stepped around Evan, started up the stairs.

Evan let him go. Didn't follow him. Listened to his steps ascend to the third floor, heard him yell, 'You left the fucking door unlocked, you cretin.' And then, seconds later, the door slammed and footsteps descending fast.

Sty sat beside Evan, breathing rapidly. 'So you went ahead and did it without me.'

Evan's mouth dropped. 'That's what your response is? That's your reaction? You're not asking what happened. Or if I'm all right. Look at my fucking face – see any damage? You don't give a crap – you're just annoyed that I went ahead and did something without you and your permission.'

Sty's jaw clenched. 'Damn right I'm annoyed. We were going to do it together, in a controlled manner. Share the experience, study the transition from life to death. That was the point, wasn't it? Like Leopold and Loeb.'

'What? No – they were fags, and, if you recall your own history lesson, they weren't interested in studying anything. They just wanted to do a perfect crime and get away with it—'

'My point is, they did it together—'

'Yes, they did, because one of them wasn't out all night fucking some townie.'

Sty glared, raised a fist, aimed it at Evan's jaw, but Evan stared back, not flinching, not even bothering to defend himself. The moment passed; Sty lowered his fist.

'They got caught, too, by the way.' Evan's voice was flat. He didn't feel like arguing, didn't look at Sty. Wished his vodka weren't gone.

They sat on the steps for a while, not talking. Finally, Sty broke the silence.

'So? How was it?'

How was it? Evan's heartbeat surged. He didn't want to share.

'Tell me everything. What was it like?'

Evan thought back, remembering fingers poking at his eyes, an elbow cutting off his airway. His rage. 'It wasn't like we planned, Sty. It happened fast, in a fight.' He remembered the sense of triumph, his knife ripping through flesh. The pulsing between his legs. 'I just did it; in an eye blink, it was done.'

Sty closed his eyes, covered his face with his hands. 'Fuck.' He sighed. 'So the whole thing from start to finish was a wash.'

'You have no idea,' Evan agreed. 'I've been washing all fucking night.' He told Sty about mopping the floor and the walls, but Sty wasn't listening. He had that look, eyes squinting, lips pursed. He was deep in thought.

And suddenly, Sty hopped to his feet and climbed the stairs. 'Let me get a shower. We'll meet in Rory's room to reassess in, say, fifteen?'

Evan hadn't finished yet, hadn't talked about looking out and seeing the next-door neighbor at her window. But probably, she hadn't seen anything, and Sty was upset enough, would be calmer after a shower. The rest of the story could wait.


At ten o'clock, Leslie showed up at Harper's door and Harper led her to Hank's study. Harper had fixed tea; Leslie took off her coat and took a seat beside her on the leather sofa, poured honey into her mug. Harper closed her eyes, sank into the cushions, felt tension lift from her shoulders just because Leslie was there. When she opened her eyes, Leslie's warm green ones were watching her.

'Thanks for seeing me here.'

'No problem. You're not supposed to exert yourself, so I can come to you.'

Harper picked up a mug, sipped jasmine.

'You're showing.' Leslie smiled, indicating the baby.

'Second trimester started last week.' Harper nodded. 'I've felt it move.'

'Isn't it odd?' Leslie grinned. She had two kids, aged two and four. 'You wonder what the baby's doing in there—'

'Push ups. Calisthenics.' Harper laughed. Noticed that it felt strange to laugh; she hadn't done it much lately.

'Just like mom.' Leslie winked. 'But you're feeling okay? How are the contractions?'

Harper sipped tea, told her she'd had some strong ones. Also told her about her flashback.

'Wait.' Leslie's brows furrowed. 'You're saying the flashback was triggered by a TV show?'

'No.' Again, Harper laughed. That was twice, and in just a few minutes. Actually, what Leslie had said hadn't been that funny; Harper laughed because she felt light. Relieved to see Leslie, to sit with her, drinking tea in a room with the door closed, away from Lou and Vivian.

But her laughter ended abruptly as she began to answer the

question. The flashback had been triggered by a news recap, not an actual show. She described what had led up to it. The naked guy in the snow. The blood spatter and key she'd found in the woods. The resemblance between the guy she'd seen and the face on the news of the missing student from Elmira. When she began to describe his parents and their sense that he was dead, Leslie interrupted.

'Why does all this concern you, Harper?'

Harper cocked her head, not understanding the question. 'What?'

Leslie smiled, rephrasing. 'I mean why are you so personally involved? Why can't you leave all this to the police?'

These questions also stymied Harper. 'You mean why do I care about it?'

'Okay. Start with that.'

Harper crossed her arms. The answer was obvious. 'The guy asked me for help.'

Leslie nodded. Her voice was soft, like fleece. 'And for you, that's a call to action. Harper the soldier, the protector, the fighter. You can't let anyone get hurt on your watch, right?'

Right. Except that she had. She thought back to Iraq. Her watch. Her people getting blown away.

'That's where the flashback came from. I couldn't help them.'

'That makes sense.' Leslie's eyes glowed. 'You still feel as if it's your job to keep everyone safe. But, Harper, you aren't at war now. You're not in charge any more.'

'Of course I'm not in charge. But I can't just stand by and watch someone get hurt – we all have responsibilities to each other . . .'

'Yes. And you faced yours. You called the police. Why isn't that enough for you? Why do you feel that you need to continue your involvement?'

Harper looked away, at a lamp on Hank's desk. Saw the guy's face mouthing, 'Help me.'

'You know, until this happened, you hadn't had a flashback in quite a while.'

No, she hadn't. Not for a few months. 'What are you saying?' Did Leslie think her flashback had to do with Hank being gone? Because it wasn't. No way Harper was going to let Leslie imply that it was Hank's fault. 'This is not about Hank being away.'

'Okay. But something has made you more vulnerable. What else has changed recently?'

Oh. 'You mean the pregnancy?'

Leslie watched her.

'What? You think pregnancy affects my flashbacks?' Was Leslie going to be like Lou, saying everything was because of her hormones?

'I don't know. Do you?'

Harper scowled.

'I think it's interesting that, ever since you found out you were pregnant – until now, your flashbacks practically stopped. And now, with your doctor telling you to rest, you're worrying about the welfare of your baby. Which is something you can't really control, except, hopefully, by resting. But you aren't good at resting, Harper. And you're even less good at not having control – especially about something as important as your pregnancy.'

Leslie paused, letting her words sink in.

'I think that, yes, that streaker in the snow alarmed you. But you were already alarmed about your baby. So almost anything that further stressed you could have pushed you over the top, setting off a flashback.'

Another pause. Unexpectedly, Harper's eyes filled. Leslie blurred, handed her a blurry tissue.

'I'm not saying you don't want to rescue the streaker. I'm just saying you really want to rescue your baby. And that's what I think you should focus on. Your pregnancy. Your health. Resting. Taking care of Harper. Because, trust me, once it's born, it's a separate person. No matter how you try, you will never ever be able to fully protect or control or keep tabs on your child. Your best chance for total control is now, while it's still in your womb.' Leslie smiled, talking from experience. 'Harper, it's important that you enjoy this time. The flutter kicks. The swollen ankles. The ability to eat anything without guilt. All of it. Even the stretch marks. It's all precious.'

Harper nodded and dabbed her eyes. Unsure about the stretch marks.

'This is new territory for you, Harper. A new role for you is emerging, one unlike any you've had before. Being a mom isn't like being a tough high-school kid or army lieutenant or archeology student or wife. It's going to be a challenge because – here's my opinion: I think you're more comfortable with rescuing strangers, protecting artifacts and chasing down enemy combatants than you are with raising a child.'

Harper wiped her eyes. Took a breath. Felt another tear roll down her face. Sniffed. Leslie reached out, put a hand on Harper's.

'You know?' Harper blew her nose. 'You're right. I have no idea what to do. How am I supposed to know how to be a mom? Vivian – I've told you about her – she was never a mom. I never had a role model. Honestly? The closest thing I had to a mom was my drill sergeant – and he was a guy.' The truth of that struck Harper as funny; she chuckled, her face still wet with tears.

'You'll be a great mom, Harper.' Leslie squeezed her arm. 'But first, you have to listen to your doctor. Rest. Avoid stress. Don't go searching the woods for blood spatter and clues – let go of the need to protect the world and focus on protecting yourself and your pregnancy. Let the police do the rest. Can you do that?'

Harper nodded, remembering Detective Rivers asking her to do the same. But, truthfully, she hadn't fully processed what Leslie had said when the hour was up. Walking Leslie to the door, she realized that she hadn't mentioned half the things she'd wanted to. Her cabin fever. Her concerns about Hank. Her friction with Vivian. And, though she wasn't even sure what they were, her questions about Lou.

The waitress brought a stack of buckwheat pancakes for Sty, a feta and spinach omelet for Evan. They remained silent while she refreshed their coffee.

Sty waited until she'd walked away. 'We are still Übermenschen,' he said, pouring maple syrup.

Evan smirked, buttering his toast. When he wasn't invoking Leopold and Loeb, Sty was emulating Nietzsche. 'I doubt that. This disaster is probably not what Nietzsche had in mind when he referred to the work of Supermen—'

'Don't be so self-critical, Evan. The quality of a Superman is that he fully experiences his superior life and power, that his very existence is a form of art. Nietzsche doesn't require that the superior man make no mistakes; rather that he perfect his life as a process, developing until, ultimately, he exerts his will, warrior strength and talent—'

'I see your point,' Evan interrupted with his mouth full. He ached all over, had been up all night. And, frankly, he was tired of Sty's monotonous ramblings about abstract, idealistic principles that had little to do with the situation at hand. Mostly, he was just plain tired. 'What does Nietzsche say about getting rid of a body?'

'Shh!' Sty looked around, scowling. The booths around them were mostly empty; the week before Christmas Eve was slow at State Diner.

'No one's listening.'

'Doesn't matter.' He cut a wad of pancakes. 'We can't afford to be careless. Look what carelessness did to Leopold—'

'For Christ's sake, Sty. Will you stop harping about them? We are NOT like those two—'

'The point I'm making, Evan, is this: Had Leopold not been careless and dropped his glasses at the scene of the body dump, the two would never have been caught. We will make no such error.'

Evan sat back, staring at his half-eaten omelet. Checking to make sure they hadn't been careless. Reviewing everything they'd done so far. Remembering the kid running into the snow. That had been careless of them, for sure; the neighbors had seen him. Still, no one had connected the event to him or Sty or even to Sebastian Levering's disappearance. He'd seen the woman later at her window, but she couldn't have seen anything incriminating; if she had, she'd have called the police again. So, no. So far, no damage had been done. He sat up again, relieved, and took another bite. Added salt.

'According to the news,' Sty swallowed coffee, 'our young Sebastian is traveling all over the country. He's been spotted in Colorado, Ohio, Miami – who knows where. Nobody's looking for him here.'

'So? We've still got to get rid of him.'

Sty nodded, chomping pancakes.

'And the ground's frozen. We can't bury him. We can't get on the water to drop him in the lake—'

'We're going to have to wrap him up and take him on a little trip. There are miles of empty woods and hills around here. In fact, I think I've found a perfect container for him. We dump it; no one finds him until spring, if then.'

Evan bit off a piece of toast. Sty sounded confident. Maybe last night hadn't been as bad an outcome as he'd thought; maybe they were all right after all. He skipped a breath, felt a ripple in his chest, recalling the elation of the kill.

Sty poured more syrup onto his stack. 'Meantime,' he grinned as he cut into his food, 'we start looking for our next project. We're smarter now; we'll do it right this time.'

\* \* \*

Lou was making tuna melts – finally something Harper liked. In fact, they smelled terrific. Harper stood in the foyer gazing out the window, watching that same dark SUV make its way slowly past the house, waiting for the mailman to hike up the walk.

She opened the front door just as he was about to ring the bell.

'Merry Christmas,' he grinned, handing her a package.

'Same to you.' Harper took it and shut the door, excited. The box was probably a Christmas gift from Hank. Thrilled, she rushed to the hall table to open it, but glancing at the address label, she realized that the driver had made a mistake.

Grabbing the package, she ran back to the door and shouted to the driver, but too late; the truck was already pulling away. Damn. She'd have to call the post office and tell them to pick it up. She checked the label again. Odd. The address was actually correct; the post office hadn't made a mistake about where to deliver it. But it had to go back to the sender; the package was meant for someone named Ed Strunk. And there was nobody by that name at her house.

Vivian stuck her head out of the kitchen. 'Come eat.'

Harper set the package on the table in the foyer. Lunch was ready; she'd call the post office later.


'I've been thinking about Louise.' Vivian poured whiskey into her Diet Coke.

Louise?

'Louis, if it's a boy.'

Really? Her mother was thinking of names for her child?

'Well, do you like them?'

Harper took her time, kept her voice calm. 'Actually, Hank and I haven't talked about names yet—'

'Well, that's why I'm suggesting Louise.'

'Why Louise?' Harper dug her knife into her tuna melt.

Vivian looked surprised at the question. 'It was my favorite great-aunt's middle name. I think she should be remembered.'

'And I thought you wanted to name it after me,' Lou swallowed beer, grinning.

Vivian nodded. 'Well, that, too.' She chewed. 'I'm thinking Louise Rosalind. Or Louise Evelyn. Those names are important to me. Rosalind was my cousin—'

'Ma. Thank you, but Hank and I will choose the name by ourselves.'

Vivian looked slapped. 'I'm just trying to help.'

Harper took a breath. 'Fine.'

'Here it goes again.' Lou sat back in his chair. 'You two go at it like an old married couple. We need a damn meditator here.'

A meditator? Harper frowned. He must mean mediator.

'Pass the potato chips?' Lou reached an arm out.

Vivian handed him the basket of chips, then sat up straight, folding her napkin beside her plate, about to leave the table.

'Excuse me, Harper,' she huffed. 'Sorry if I overstepped, but I am the baby's grandmother. And I was just trying—'

'Ma. Please. Let it go. Let's change the subject, can we?'

'Why are you so short with me?' Vivian blinked at Harper. 'I just wanted to help you.'

'Thanks, Ma.' Harper took a bite of her sandwich, determined to avoid an all-out fight.

For a while, nobody spoke. Finally, Harper changed the subject.

'So, Lou. Tell me about yourself.'

'Me?'

'Yeah. Where are you from?'

'Midwest. Ever hear of Cicero? It's outside Chicago.'

'And what's your line of work?'

Lou eyed Harper, then turned back to his food. 'I'm in business. Transportation.' As if that explained it.

'He owns trucks,' Vivian said. 'I told you.'

'No offense, Harper, but I don't discuss business while I'm eating. It's bad for the digestive track.'

'Tract,' Harper corrected him without thinking. 'With a "t".'

He tilted his head and licked his lips. 'So. You found me out: I never went to college.'

'Some of us didn't get the advantages you did,' Vivian chided. 'Some of us have had to make do without—'

'I don't do without, Viv,' Lou cut her off. 'I do just fine. I didn't need a college degree to do okay, did I?' Suddenly, he was jolly again. Wearing a generous, self-satisfied grin. 'I can buy and sell these college kids.'

'That's right, Lou. You've done great.' Vivian smiled cautiously.

Harper drank water and reached for the chips. Lunch was going swimmingly.

When lunch was finally over, Vivian suggested that they decorate the tree.

Harper tried to think of an excuse. Said she had to work on her dissertation.

'Come on, Harper. Just an hour.' Vivian grabbed her hand, began pulling her down the hall.

Harper stopped resisting. What was the point? Her mother would never understand that she didn't want Styrofoam glitter and tinsel all over her living room. And she wanted to reduce the tension between them.

'Okay. But only for half an—' Harper stopped, feeling a tickle. She put a hand on her belly. 'Baby's moving.'

Vivian's eyes lit up, and she placed a hand beside Harper's.

'I don't know if you can feel it from the outside, but it's whirling around in there.'

They were standing at the base of the stairs, their hands on Harper's tummy, when Lou came out of the kitchen.

'What?' His eyes widened. 'You okay?'

Harper grinned. 'Baby's doing cartwheels.'

'I got nothing.' Vivian took her hand away.

Lou, coming down the hall, stopped to look at the package on the table.

'That's not for us, Lou.' Harper and Vivian started for the living room. 'It's to somebody I never heard of. I have to send it back.'

Lou blinked at the package. 'Oh – no, it's okay. Don't bother. I'll take care of it. I'm going out; I'll drop it at the post office.'

Harper thanked him, but as she headed toward the tree, she saw him pick the package up, hold it to his ear, gently shake and turn it.

'Lou?' She turned. 'What are you doing?'

He turned, hesitating. His eyes flashed their spark. 'Just wondering what's inside. You know. Curious.'

'It's for someone else.'

'Yeah. But it's addressed to this house. No harm opening it just to see—'

'That's illegal, Lou, opening someone else's mail,' Vivian piped up. 'I mean I think it is. Isn't it?'

'What? Opening a package addressed to your house and delivered to your address? That's not illegal—'

'But it's not meant for us. So just send it back, Lou. Okay?'

'Whatever. Sure. I'll take it over right now.'

Harper watched Lou get his coat from the hall closet and carry the package out the door. While Vivian unwrapped tinsel, she stood at the window, watching him. Sure enough, Lou didn't get into her mother's car. Instead, exhaling small clouds of steam, he set the package on the hood, looked up and down the driveway, checked over his shoulder. Then quickly, he tore off the brown paper, opened the box and looked inside.

'Son of a bitch,' Harper breathed.

'What?' Vivian scowled. 'Are you spying on him? He said he'll take it; he'll take it.'

Harper picked up a package of sparkly silver stars, began unwrapping it, still watching out the window.

Lou turned and looked up and down the street, then back at the box. Holding it gingerly, he paced in small jumpy circles. Finally, still glancing left and right, he picked up the box and carried it to the side of the garage, opened the trash can and tossed it in.

Harper abandoned the package of stars, filled a plastic bag with ornament wrappings, told Vivian she was going to put them in the recycling can.

By the time she got outside, Lou had gotten into Vivian's car and driven away.

Harper leaned over the trash can, grimacing, studying the contents of the discarded box. The rat was huge, the size of a cat. And its belly had been sliced open, its entrails falling out. Why would someone bother to pull out its insides? Wasn't it bad enough to send a dead rat?

Steeling herself, she stood on tiptoe and reached into the can, rifled around until she found the section of brown wrapping paper with the address label.

The return address was, not surprisingly, bogus: Santa's Village in the North Pole. But the postmark was stamped Ithaca. So the rat had been mailed locally. To her address. To a man unknown to her.

Harper stood beside the trash can, shivering and puzzled.

In her mind, Leslie scolded her: However sick the contents of the package were, the rat had nothing to do with her or her family. It was meant for Ed What's-his-name, whoever he was. If Lou had just left it alone and returned the package, she'd never have even known about it. She should forget about it, go inside and play good daughter and help Vivian decorate the tree.

Harper tossed the paper back in the can, replaced the lid and went back to the house.

Still, she kept thinking about the rat in the trash. Who would send someone a dead animal? Let alone a mutilated one. It was like something from a second-rate Mafia movie. And then she pictured Lou. He must have figured the package was a Christmas gift, something he could quietly claim – a sweater, or fleece-lined slippers. She recalled his surprise – the grayish green color his face had turned when he'd opened it.

Harper couldn't help it; she began to laugh. Was still chuckling when she came into the living room, and Vivian asked her what was so funny.

'Nothing,' she told her.

It was better than explaining how Lou had gotten what he'd deserved, messing with someone else's mail.

Decorating the tree didn't happen. Vivian hung a single glitter ball before falling asleep on the sofa, half soused. Harper went into the kitchen and made some tea, but didn't relax. Her mind was unsettled, trying to make sense out of snippets of information.

Harper held the mug close to her face, feeling the steam. She slid onto a kitchen chair, mentally listing the events that disturbed her, not necessarily in order. There were a lot of them: The dead rat arriving in the mail. Lou secretly opening the package. His unexplained late-night excursions. The naked guy running in the snow, being carried off into the woods. The news reports about a missing student who resembled the naked guy. The blood spatter and key she'd found in the woods. The light flashing in her room, and the curtain she'd seen move in the fraternity next door.

Fine. But the list seemed random. She looked around the kitchen, stood up. Opened a cupboard. Took out Lou's container of Christmas cookies. Told herself that the list wasn't random. Too many odd events were happening in the same place, clustered together in a short span of time. There had to be a connection.

Unless there wasn't. Sometimes unrelated things just happened. Rivers hadn't been convinced that the stains were even blood – and even if they were, who said the blood was human? It might have been from a squirrel or a bird. And the naked kid might have been horsing around with his buddies. And Lou – well, who knew? Maybe Lou went out at night because he had a babe on the side.

But what about the moving curtain?

That made no sense. All fraternities were closed for intersession. Even the housemothers would be gone until the middle of January. So how could a curtain move? Unless . . . Maybe a cat got inside. Or a raccoon.

Or maybe nothing at all. Maybe she'd imagined it.

Oh God. Had she? Was she really off balance because she was pregnant and hormonally fluctuating and stressed out and Hank was away? Was it possible that, as in her flashbacks, she couldn't tell what was real from what was imagined?

No. No way was it possible. She was still herself. Still Army. Still trained to observe, assess and respond. She ran a hand through her hair, shaken by her moment of self-doubt.

Harper took a sip of tea, then put her hand on her belly. Probably, just to be safe, she should pay attention to Leslie and Rivers. She should back off. Stop dwelling on odd packages, her mother's boyfriend and streaking boys, and focus on taking care of herself and her swelling belly.

Speaking of which, those Christmas cookies were dancing to get her attention. A sparkly Santa tempted her – but Harper frowned, ignoring him, opting for a tree.

The cookie was rich and sweet and a little chewy. But two trees later, Harper realized that her selection of a tree over a Santa was no coincidence; her subconscious was still nagging her. She looked out the window at the trees in the woods, remembering the moving curtain, the light shining into her room, her instincts that wouldn't quiet down.

It would only take a minute. And it would involve no risk. Checking to make sure the key was there in her pocket, wrapped in a glove, Harper put on her boots and parka, and headed out across the yard to the fraternity house.

'Put it down a second.' Sty dropped his end of the mattress on the stairs, letting the weight fall to Evan, who nearly toppled backwards. 'It fucking doesn't fit around the corner.'

'So we have to stand it on end—'

'The ceiling's not high enough.'

It was true. The queen-sized mattress they were trying to remove from Rory's room was too wide and too high to fit down the third-floor staircase. Plus it stank from the products of the kid's loose bowels.

'Well, fuck. It has to fit. They got it up the stairs; it must be able to go back down.'

They stood looking at the thing, twisted sideways on the third-floor landing. And then Evan had a genius idea. 'Hold on.' He ran back into the room with the kid's body, retrieved the knife from his neck, returned to the mattress, stabbed the blade into it and started sawing through the fabric. Cotton batting flecked into the air, onto the steps.

'Genius,' Sty smirked.

'Well, it's easier than folding the damned thing in half.' Evan sliced down one side of the mattress, through the binding. It wasn't difficult, but he was sweating. 'You know, you don't have to stand and watch. Look for scissors or something.'

'You're doing fine without me.' Even so, Sty paced from room to room, searching for sharp implements. He was in Alex's room at the front of the house when, through the windows, he noticed movement outside. He stopped poring through Alex's stuff and froze, staring out the window. Not believing what he was seeing. And yet, there she was. The motorcycle lady was coming this way, heading for the front door.

'Evan.' He called softly, as if the woman could hear.

Evan, however, could hear only the sound of a knife ripping through fabric.

Sty backed out of the room, eyes on the window, and scurried to Evan. 'The next-door neighbor,' he whispered.

'What?' Evan's voice was loud. He stopped cutting when he saw Sty's face. And jumped when the doorbell rang.

Neither of them moved. They stared into each other's wide eyes, silent.

The bell rang again.

They waited. Sty held up a finger, mouthed, 'She's alone.'

'Who?' Evan whispered.

Sty pointed to the house next door.

Evan nodded, not surprised. That blonde woman with the spiky hair had been on his mind ever since she'd called the police the other night. He'd seen her staring out her window more than once. What was she looking for? What had she seen? Whatever it was, it was too much because now she was here ringing the bell when no one was supposed to be there. Obviously, she knew something. Or, at the very least, suspected something. He would talk to Sty. Figure out how to handle her. But there was also the matter of her husband. What did he know? In fact, where was he? Evan hadn't seen him for a while. Couldn't remember the last time—

Evan stopped mid-thought, listening. Downstairs, at the front door, there was a faint clicking sound. A metallic scrape or jiggle. Like a key turning in a lock.

'Fuck me,' Sty murmured. He listened for another moment, then motioned to Evan to give him the knife.

Evan pulled it out of the mattress, passed it to Sty who sped silently down the steps. Evan followed him down to the second level, where he stood at the banister, watching Sty position himself beside the heavy carved wood door, knife raised, ready to strike.

The sounds stopped.

A woman's voice penetrated the door. 'Okay. That's that.'

But she didn't leave, and a few seconds later, the key slid into the hole again, jiggled in the lock.

Evan felt his face get hot, his blood pump as he watched Sty ready to pounce. He pictured the surprise on the bitch's face, the spray of her blood. Wondered if she'd have time to scream or fight back. Pictured her gaping slashed flesh.

When the woman took the key out and walked away, Sty exhaled loudly and lowered the knife. Evan shrugged and lowered his head, sorely disappointed.

Harper stood at the curb, preparing to go back inside. Gearing herself up to help Vivian with the damned tree. She needed to be kinder; despite Vivian's self-centered, manipulative, needy narcissistic nature, she was still her mother. Bracing herself, Harper started up the unshoveled walk but, hearing a car approach, she stopped and turned. Saw Lou driving up the street.

He parked in the driveway, got out of the car, smiling cheerily. 'What's up?'

'I saw you, Lou.' Harper hadn't planned to say that; the words just came out of her mouth.

'You saw me?' He walked over to her, as if to accompany her into the house.

'The package. I saw you open it.'

'Oh. That.' He stopped walking, put his hands in the pockets of his down jacket.

'Turned out it was nothing—'

'I saw what it was.'

His eyes flashed, met Harper's. 'Then you know it was nothing.'

'It wasn't exactly "nothing". What's going on? Tell me.'

'What's going on?' His eyes did a nano-shimmy. 'Nothing. I mean, how should I know—'

'Why did you open it?'

'What is this, Harper? The third degree?' His hands went up in the air, defensive. 'Okay. I admit. I shouldn't have opened it. You're right.'

'And?'

'And nothing. I opened it. I thought it might be something good. Like one of those computer tablet things – or leather gloves—'

'But it wasn't.'

'No.' His eyes darted down, then sideways toward the woods, then back at Harper. 'Look, what do you want me to say? I was wrong. I shouldn't have opened it. Sorry. Okay?'

Harper watched him shift his weight. 'We need to call the authorities.'

Lou's eyes narrowed ever so slightly. 'For Christ's sake, why?'

'Sending materials like that through the mail is illegal. It might be considered a terrorist threat—'

'God, Harper,' he interrupted. 'What is it with you? Making everything into some big deal—'

'Are you saying this isn't a big deal? Someone sent a mutilated carcass to my home—'

'Okay, fair enough. It's a big deal, but a small one.' Clouds of breath puffed short and swift from his mouth. 'Look, Harper, if you call your authorities, I get in trouble for opening a package not addressed to me. What's that called – meddling with the mail or something? Do you really want to open that can of worms?'

She said nothing. Pictured her mother's hysteria if yet another of her men got arrested.

'Besides, this wasn't terrorism. There was no public threat. No bomb or amtracks powder.'

Amtracks? Like the trains? 'You mean anthrax?'

'That's what I said. Look, nobody got hurt except an effing rodent. It was probably a sick private joke. In fact – you know what? I bet they meant it for those frat boys next door and they got the address off by a couple numbers. Go ahead – ask those boys if they don't have a guy by that name – Ed Whateveritwas. I bet they do.'

'The place is closed for winter break.'

'Well, so what. It doesn't really matter who was supposed to get it. Whoever it was, he ought to be glad I opened it for him. I mean who wants to get a package like that?' Lou laughed, slapping her on the shoulder.

'Come on,' he grinned. 'Let's go in – too cold to stand out here yapping.'

Harper crossed her arms, reluctant, but she was cold and went along. She wanted to ask Lou more about his late-night wanderings, but her instincts told her to save it. At the moment, his guard was up, worried that she'd turn him in for tampering with the mail. More questions would only make him more defensive.

They were halfway up the front walk when Vivian, bundled in her bright red down jacket, burst out the front door, waving. 'Where were you two? Go lie down, Harper. And Lou, remember we're going shopping. I'm ready.'

Harper headed inside, put the key back into her pocket. And kept her eyes on Lou as he embraced her mother and led her away.

'What the fuck was that?' Sty lowered the knife, letting out a breath as the woman left. 'She thought she had a key? Why was she trying to get in?'

Evan came down the steps, peered through the blinds of the dining room to watch her walk away.

'Shit, Evan. Our neighbor lady knows something. She must have seen you—'

'What she saw was a bare-assed kid running outside in the snow. We already know that.'

'If that's all she saw, why is she here snooping around? She called the cops and they did their thing. So what is she doing? What's with the key?'

'Who cares? It isn't ours. It didn't fit.'

Sty stepped close to Evan, breathing into his face. 'Are you absolutely certain she didn't see anything? Willing to bet your entire future on that conclusion?'

Evan stepped away. 'What if I'm not? What are you suggesting? That we eliminate her?' He had no objection to killing her, was still pumped from the excitement of moments ago when she'd stood a door's width away from death, the anticipation of the attack.

Sty stood still, brows furrowed, arms crossed, the knife still in his hand. 'First things first,' he finally decided. 'We can't allow events to spiral out of control. No tangential moves. Let's finish upstairs; then we'll decide.'

Evan disagreed. 'But who knows what she's up to. We're wasting time—'

'Then let's get this done quickly. One task at a time.'

Evan muttered, 'Who made you fucking king?' But Sty was already on his way up the steps without listening, without looking back.


Harper hung her jacket in the closet and stood for a moment, touching Hank's parka and overcoat, missing him. Thinking about how slowly time was passing. How long it would be until he came home. She listened to the emptiness of the house, chided herself for wallowing. Changed her focus back to Lou, his secretive excursions late at night. His theft of the package, his casual reaction to the gutted rat.

The man was up to something. She was sure. In moments, Harper was upstairs in the guest room, going through his things. She opened a drawer, felt around in his socks and sweaters. Found a wire leading from the drawer to a socket, attached to a cell phone. Odd to have a cell phone in with his socks, but not incriminating. She opened the closet. Checked the pockets of his blazer and suit jackets. Felt the shelf above the clothes.

Nothing.

She sat on the bed, frustrated. Maybe she was wrong. Maybe Lou just wandered around at night, opened other people's mail, indulged her mother and made malapropisms. Maybe he was simply what he appeared to be.

But she remembered the edge to his voice, the quick flash in his eyes. And her instincts insisted that no, Lou was not as he appeared.

Sitting on the bed, she gazed around the room. What had she missed? The nightstand? She reached over, opened the drawer. Found a flashlight, a novel. Things she'd put there. She got up, went to the other side of the bed, looked in the other nightstand. Her mother's spare reading glasses. Earrings. Vials of pills – oh, her mother was taking cholesterol medicine. And Zoloft? Wow. Was Vivian depressed?

Harper pondered that, replaced the pills, closed the drawer. Looked under the bed. Luggage. Stepped into the guest bathroom, rifled through Lou's shaving kit, the medicine cabinet. Found only what belonged there. Soap, toothpaste, razor and shaving cream. She shut the medicine cabinet door, stared at herself in the mirror. What was she doing? What was she looking for? She looked away. Walked out of the bathroom, through the bedroom. Stopped at the linen closet and, just to be thorough, opened the door. Towels and bed sheets.

Enough, she told herself. Go lie down and rest. She looked around, making sure the room looked untouched. As she smoothed out the spot where she'd sat on the bed, her foot bumped the suit-case. Harper hesitated, aware that she had no business looking inside. That there was probably nothing in there anyway. But it was the only place left that Lou could have hidden something, so she pulled it out and opened it.

And gaped at the contents. She'd never seen so much cash before. Thick wads of it. Hundreds, fifties, twenties. Harper couldn't even estimate how much there was – or why Lou would have it with him. She started to count, and sat surrounded by money. She'd gotten to seventy-five thousand and hadn't made a dent when she was interrupted by a soft musical tone.

It came from inside the dresser drawer. Lou's phone had begun to ring.


For the next few hours, Evan and Sty attended to the noxious mattress, cutting it into chunks and neatly depositing them into green plastic trash bags that they lined up at the rear door of the fraternity house. Then they made sure Rory's floor and walls had been scrubbed clean, scuffing them up again to make them look pretty much the way they had at semester's end.

Finally, there was just one more item to dispose of.

Sty sat on Evan's box spring, staring at the body.

Evan squatted, examining it. Poking the stiff and rigid muscles. 'We could do the same with him.'

Sty rubbed his eyes, sighing.

'Seriously,' Evan continued. 'We cut him up, throw him out. The bags are in the junkyard. Nobody finds him. No sign he was ever even here.' He stood, suddenly enthusiastic about his idea.

Sty pursed his lips, took a few breaths before answering. 'And how do you propose we clean up the mess that would make?'

'We do it in the shower. Use some bleach.'

Sty lay back on the box springs. 'It's unnecessary—'

'So what's your idea?'

'As we planned originally. We deposit the body—'

'Where someone might find it within hours. This way, there's no chance of that.'

Sty sighed. 'Do you have any idea how much gore we'd have to deal with? The mess?'

'It's meat, that's all. No different than dressing a deer.'

'As if you've ever hunted a deer. Besides, he's still in rigor. We'd need a damned chain saw.'

Evan thought for a minute. Tried to move one of Sebastian's arms. It was fixed, hard as steel. 'We could go buy one—'

'Great idea. And they could trace the purchase to us.'

'Not if we pay cash. Besides, why would anyone care if we bought a saw? We could be cutting firewood or a Christmas tree—'

'Dammit, Evan. We can't keep improvising. Haven't you listened to a single word I've said? We need to stick to the plan. We follow it step by step, meticulously. That way, we won't make careless mistakes like Leopold—'

'Fine,' Evan snapped. 'Whatever you say.' Sty was being irrationally inflexible, but Evan couldn't bear another Leopold and Loeb lecture. 'But we better dump him soon, or we'll never get the stink out of here.'

Sty got off the bed. 'Right. We should get him out of here. You take the shoulders.' He reached for Sebastian's feet.

Together, they carried the body down the steps. As they reached the second-floor landing, Evan grunted, 'Dammit.'

'What?' Sly stopped.

'We're giving my mattress to Rory. So where am I supposed to sleep?'

'I'll lend you my inflatable.' Sty flared his nostrils. Sometimes, for a smart guy, Evan was shockingly, annoyingly oblique.

Harper opened the dresser drawer and pulled out the phone, held it and saw the name on the screen: Rita.

Rita?

Slowly, she raised the phone to her ear and pressed the button, answering the call but saying nothing.

'Ed?' The woman was breathless, urgent. 'Ed? Why the hell haven't you answered my calls? What's going on?'

Harper waited while saying nothing.

'Okay, don't even answer. Don't talk to me. I guess I don't blame you after what happened. Still, I wish you'd understand the position I was in. I had no choice. It didn't mean—' She stopped, lowered her voice. 'Anyway, I owe you. So I'm letting you know: I'm pretty sure Wally knows where you are. For the last few weeks, all he's talked about is: "Where the fuck is Ed?" Now nothing. Now, he's restless, not sleeping, jumpy as shit, and you know what that means.'

The woman stopped talking. Waiting. Harper waited, too; she had no idea what it meant.

'Ed?'

Harper didn't dare breathe.

'Ed? You still got nothing to say to me? Not even: "Thanks, Rita"? Not a word?'

She paused, giving him a chance.

'Okay, well, fuck you. We're even now, and you can go to hell. But Wally's waiting to hear that you're dead, so take my advice and watch your fucking back.'

Rita hung up, and Harper repeated her final words. Wally, whoever he was, was waiting to find out that Ed, who was obviously really Lou, was dead. Had he arranged for someone to kill Lou? Harper recalled the package, addressed to Ed. Had the dead rat been a warning? A message saying that Wally knew where he was, had his address, could get to him? Could make him as dead as the rat?

Harper replaced the phone where she'd found it, thinking about what she would do. Whoever this Lou or Ed guy was, he was staying in her home. And, if people were trying to kill him, then her mother and she and the baby were also in danger. And that, she would not allow.

The gun was hidden under the mattress. A Colt .45 with a box of ammunition. And a bunch of papers, a handful of passports, drivers' licenses with Lou's picture and different names: Frederick Lowry, Peter Flemming. Oliver Hines. Damn. Who was this guy? A spy? A con artist? And how dare he bring a gun into her house? Harper sputtered, lifting the mattress to see if other weapons had been stashed there, remembering too late that she wasn't supposed to exert herself. A startling stab shot through her abdomen, and she dropped the mattress, cursing. Flopping onto the bed in a fetal position, waiting for the pain to pass. Wondering what it was – it hadn't been a contraction. Maybe a pulled muscle? Whatever it was, she had to take it easy. Couldn't lift things. Lying on the guest bed, she looked around the room, identifying hiding places. Was anything behind the vent? Taped under the dresser? Inside the toilet tank? When she got her breath back, she took her time, moving from spot to spot, feeling and reaching and looking, but finding nothing more. She was examining Lou's pockets, when she heard her mother's car pull into the driveway. Quickly, she closed the closet door, surveyed the room to make sure it looked the way she'd found it. Stepped into the hallway just as Vivian called from the foyer.

'Harper? Are you awake?'

Harper leaned over the railing.

'Come downstairs and see what we got!'

Oh Lord, Harper thought. They'd already brought in a monster tree. What now? An inflatable Santa? But she had bigger issues than awful Christmas decorations on her mind. For example, the identity of the man standing beside her mother. And the possibility that someone named Wally had put a hit out on him and was, at this minute, waiting to hear it had been carried out.


Vivian was sitting beside the still undecorated tree while Lou hauled packages in from the car, beaming at Harper.

'You won't have to buy a thing for the baby – by the way, have you thought more about Louise? Such a beautiful name.'

Harper didn't answer.

'Anyway, we got everything – diapers, onesies, teething rings – look at this.' She held up a tiny T-shirt with the slogan MY GRANDMA SPOILS ME.

Harper sat on the sofa, stunned. 'Ma, I told you not to buy stuff—'

'Listen to this, Lou,' Vivian interrupted as Lou walked in, arms loaded with more shopping bags. 'She's complaining that we shopped. She thinks it's bad luck to buy anything until the baby comes.'

'Ma, I didn't say it was bad luck—'

'Isn't that ridiculous? How's she going to shop *after* the baby comes?'

'—I just said that, with my complications, I wanted to wait—'

'Don't be superstitious, Harper.'

'She's right.' Lou set the bags beside the tree. 'Besides, your mother got great pleasure shopping for her grand-baby.'

And her mother's pleasure clearly superseded her own.

'Somebody's got to get supplies for poor little Louise, or Louis. And, obviously, you can't.' Vivian made it sound like she was doing charity. As if Harper were a dire failure for having to rest.

'You know, you should be grateful you have a mother willing to do all this,' Lou chided. 'Not everybody's so lucky.'

Harper wanted to smack him. How dare he tell her how she should feel? He who'd brought a gun into her home, who wasn't even really named 'Lou'? She glared at the packages; some were huge. Good God, what had Vivian bought? Or rather, what had she gotten Lou to buy? Harper had wanted to shop with Hank for the baby. Pick out a high chair, a stroller, a mobile for over the crib. But, from the look of the boxes, Vivian had taken over, made all the choices for her.

Assert yourself, she thought. Explain that this is your child, your home. That your decisions need to be honored. Go on. Tell them to take the stuff back to the store.

But, as usual with her mother, Harper swallowed her anger and said nothing. She sat watching Vivian arrange boxes around the hideous imbalanced tree. What's the matter with you, she scolded herself. You fought insurgents, you commanded armed soldiers in combat, but you can't tell a spindly-legged middle-aged woman to back off? Speak up.

'Ma,' she began, her voice too soft.

'I got you a few things, too.' Vivian placed a package under the tree. 'But, Harper. Don't worry about shopping for us. I don't want you to go to the trouble, not when you're supposed to be resting. Don't bother. I mean it; I'm serious.'

Harper felt a stab of guilt. Just when she was about to stand up to her, Vivian had to say something to make her feel inadequate and indebted. Obviously, Harper hadn't shopped – hadn't even gone to the grocery store. But now, by bringing it up, Vivian made it clear that Harper should have managed somehow to get her mother something for Christmas. After all, she'd sent something to Hank by shopping online. Lord. Why hadn't she done the same for Vivian? She hadn't even thought of it. The truth was she hadn't wanted to have Christmas this year. With Hank away, she didn't feel like celebrating. But Vivian would expect a gift. And Christmas was just days away. Harper's mind raced through the house, the closets, the attic, making an inventory of items that could pass for presents – and

she thought of the cozy slippers her friend Vicki had given her
before she'd left on her cruise. Damn. She liked them. But never
mind. She'd re-gift them. Her mother would never know.

Meantime, the living room was a hodgepodge of decorations and
wrappings and boxes and a big, tall lopsided tree. Lou, having
brought in the last of the packages, began hanging more glittery
Styrofoam balls as Vivian sorted gifts and hummed carols. Out of
place in her own living room, Harper stood to go, stopping in the
foyer to watch them. Focusing on Lou. Thinking about the gun he
had upstairs. Watching him flick specks of glitter off of his shirt.

On impulse, she called out, 'Hey, Ed!'

Reflexively, Lou's shoulders tensed and his head jerked up. His
eyes met Harper's with a flash of danger. He recovered quickly.
'You say something, Harper?'

Vivian looked from Lou-who-was-really-Ed to Harper, a question
on her face.

Harper didn't reply. She headed to the kitchen to cool her temper
with a tall glass of two percent.


Sure enough, by the time she'd closed the refrigerator, Lou had
joined her.

'Who the hell are you?' She set the carton down, facing him.

'What's that supposed to mean?' Lou lowered his voice and
looked over his shoulder, making sure Vivian hadn't followed him.

'You tell me, Ed,' she poked him in the chest. 'And while you're
at it, explain why you have a gun and a ton of money upstairs—'

'What – you went through my stuff?'

'Damn right.'

'Where'd you get the nerve . . .?'

'Seriously? Where'd *you* get the nerve to bring that stuff here?'

Lou sputtered, opened a cabinet. Took out a bottle of Scotch.

'That package with the rat,' Harper kept after him. 'It was
addressed to Ed Strunk.'

'So?' Lou turned, facing her. 'Oh wait – you think I'm Ed Strunk?'
He smiled, almost convincingly. 'No – Ed's just a guy I know. Not
me—'

'So why'd you open his package? Why'd someone send a dead
rat to him here, where you're staying?' Her voice was hushed so
Vivian wouldn't hear, but it rumbled like a threat, and she stepped
closer to him, her head tilted up to hold his gaze.

Lou blinked. 'He's a business associate, that's all – a guy I'm helping out.'

'And the money is his, too? And the gun?'

Lou took out a glass.

'First, the guy gets a package here. Then a phone call.'

Subtly, Lou's eyes bulged. 'A phone call? Here?' He poured Scotch. 'When was that?'

'While you were out shopping.'

'Really? Who was it?' He lifted the glass to his mouth.

'She said her name was Rita.'

Lou swallowed too fast. Coughed. 'Rita? She called your phone?'

'No. Yours. I heard it ringing upstairs and I answered it. Ed.'

Lou put up a hand. 'Look, Ed's a friend. I'm holding his stuff for him, that's all. The phone, the gun, the money – that's all his . . .'

'Don't bullshit me.'

He poured another a finger of Scotch. 'Okay. Here's the honest truth. Ed was doing stuff he shouldn't have done for a client he shouldn't have taken on.' He finished the drink. Poured another.

'What the hell does that mean?'

Lou's eyes darted left, then right. He lowered his voice. 'He was hauling illegal substances. And cash. And I guess he . . . borrowed some of the cash.'

Christ. Harper ran a hand through her hair. 'You stole from a drug dealer?'

'No, not me. Ed—'

'And you put my mother and me in the middle of it?'

'You're not in the middle—'

'Lou?' Vivian called from the living room. 'Where's my drinkie?'

'On its way,' he shouted, watching Harper. 'Look. It's Ed's business. Nothing to do with you or your mother—'

'A gun in my house? The mob coming after money hidden in my house?'

'You're right.' Lou stared at the ceiling. 'I agree, Harper. I was careless, and I apologize. I'll take care of it. Okay?' Lou took out another glass for Vivian, poured Scotch.

'Lou!' Vivian yelled. 'I can't reach the top of the tree. I need help.'

'We done here?' He picked up the drinks, eager to go.

'Take care of it fast.' Harper watched him carry the glasses out

of the kitchen. 'By the way, Rita said something else.' She put her
glass in the sink. 'But I guess it doesn't matter; the message was
for Ed.'

Lou spun around. 'What'd she say?'

'Like I said . . .'

'Tell me. I'll let him know.'

Harper made herself sound casual. 'She said that Wally knows
where Ed is, and Ed should watch his back.'

Lou said nothing. He nodded slightly, and Harper thought his
skin drained of color before he turned and walked away.


Harper said she was tired, and ate spaghetti in her room, watching
television. According to the news, that boy from Elmira still had
not been found. She dozed off during *Jeopardy*, was awakened by
the gong of her phone.

Hank called early. His voice was dejected again. 'Nothing wrong.
I'm fine.'

'Don't even say that. I can hear it—'

'Ankle twisted,' he blurted.

Damn. 'How? What happened?' Harper clutched the phone.
Hank's right side had been weakened by his accident; maybe he
wasn't strong enough for fieldwork.

'Not bad. Slipped. On rock.'

'Is it swollen? Make sure to elevate it. And ice – do you have
an ice pack?'

'Hoppa, stop,' Hank snapped. 'Care can take of it fine know what
to do.'

Okay. Apparently, Hank was frustrated. Probably in pain and
not wanting to admit it. Harper was concerned, but kept quiet,
didn't want to question Hank's abilities. After all, he was an experienced outdoorsman, a PhD geologist and strong athlete, didn't need
her advice about first aid. So she said nothing, just lay on their
bed, worrying silently, staring out the window at the silhouette of
the fraternity house against the night sky. Waiting for Hank to
continue the conversation. Missing him.

'Tell me.' Hank broke the silence. 'You? Baby?'

She thought of the gun upstairs. 'We're fine.'

'Tell me. What's wrong? Something.'

Hank knew. Of course he did. He could hear the tension in her
voice. 'Nothing. Just I miss you.'

'I miss. You, too.'

Silence again.

'Vivian?' he asked.

Harper took a breath and let her answer spill out. How Vivian had bought everything for the baby – high chair, car seat, stroller, toys, layette. How the whole living room was full of who-knew-what.

'Trying to be nice.' Hank made excuses. 'She wants to give—'

'No, Hank. She's not being nice. She's trying to tell me what to name the baby. And she knew – I told her not to shop, I said we wanted to pick things out ourselves. I made it clear that we were waiting until later—'

'Hoppa. Breathe.' His voice was firm, commanding. 'Don't upset. Rest. Calm. Name we'll pick. Return gifts later, shop later.'

He was right. She had to stop getting upset with Vivian; it wasn't good for her or the baby. But the problem was bigger than just Vivian.

'It's not just Vivian,' she blurted. 'It's her boyfriend. He has—' She barely stopped herself before she said 'a gun'. No point making Hank worry when he was hundreds of miles away and could do nothing.

'Boyfriend has what?'

'I don't know. Insomnia?' Whew. Good thinking, she told herself. 'He creeps out in the middle of the night. He spends wads of cash and won't say how he's earned it. He's . . . I don't know. Sneaky?'

Hank chuckled.

'What?'

'Sorry. Not funny really. Just you're surprised. At sneaky? What kind of man. Vivian with ever? Expect what? Saint? Scholar?'

Hank was right. Her mother had neither great taste in nor much luck with men. The best of them, after all, had been Harper's father, a professional liar, embezzler, swindler, cheat. A distant memory flashed: strong arms scooping her high and holding her up in the air. The sense of being safe. And of something else – pride? She closed her eyes, crushing the image, replacing it with another one: those same arms locked in handcuffs as police led him away.

'Nice to her?'

What? Nice? Oh, wait. He meant Lou. 'Too nice. And affectionate.' She thought of their bedpost bumping the walls the other night. 'He seems nuts about her.'

'So?'

'You're right. He's probably okay.' Even though he has a gun. And a suitcase full of cash. And fake IDs and an alias. And a hit out on him by a guy named Wally.

They talked some more. About Harper's expanding belly. Her upcoming doctor's appointment. Life in Texas. Their first Christmas apart. When they hung up, even though she hadn't told Hank everything, Harper felt reassured. The sound of his voice, even though he was far away and in pain, grounded her. And at least for a little while, she felt calm.

The body was too stiff, wouldn't cooperate. They got it down the steps, laid it on the floor.

Sty shook his head. 'Obviously, this is not going to fit in the back of my car.'

Evan crossed his arms. 'No shit.' He was out of breath. Tired of cleaning and carrying. Tired of listening to Sty.

'He'd fit after rigor passes, but that could take up to three days.'

'Which we don't have. I've got to get home Christmas Eve.'

'So do I.'

'So what do we do? We have to leave, and he can't just lie here—'

'I didn't say he would, did I? I believe all I said was that he wouldn't fit into my car—'

'Don't go semantic on me, Sty. What you said or didn't say isn't the fucking issue. The only fucking issue is what the fuck are we going to do with him?'

Sty's lips curled into a snaky smile. 'Getting testy, are we?' His eyes were cold and lizard-like. 'This kind of reaction is beneath you, Evan. Don't give in to childish fits of pique. They make you careless and panicky. We can't afford them.'

Evan felt his face heat up; he fought the urge to strangle Sty. His fingers ached to close around Sty's throat. Evan imagined his tongue protruding, his eyes bulging. But he held back; even though Sty was turning out to be a pompous arrogant asshole, he still needed him. Looking away, Evan deliberately slowed his breath, waiting a few beats before speaking. 'So. What do you suggest?'

'I mentioned before that I'd given the problem some thought and come up with a viable solution.' Sty pointed into the sitting room. Against the far wall, beyond the sofas, in a corner wedged between a grandfather's clock and a bookshelf, stood a hideous oversized armoire.

'That?' Evan's eyebrows rose.

'No one would miss it. If they did, they'd just assume it finally got junked. I've measured it. The interior space is ample: seven feet four inches tall by forty-two inches wide. We load it up, strap it to the top of my car, and dump it as planned.'

Sty led the way across the sitting room, Evan followed and, even grunting and straining, the two were unable to lift the bulky armoire. Finally, they tilted it and, after moving sofas and tables out of the way, inched it into the hall. There, they opened it, lifted Sebastian and managed to stuff him into one side, leaning him against a bar that divided the thing into two parts, pressing against the doors until they clicked securely shut, closing Sebastian into what was now his casket.

For a moment, they stood, winded and recovering. Evan eyed the armoire cautiously, as if expecting it might hurl out its occupant.

'Should we load it onto your car?' He wiped sweat off his forehead.

Sty stretched his back. 'Not yet. Let's finish up here.'

Evan cocked his head.

'Put the furniture back where it was. And move your mattress into Rory's room.'

Really? 'My mattress? Now?' Evan didn't relish the idea of sacrificing it.

'Of course, now. We need to be thorough. Everything has to be completed, calmly, neatly and efficiently before we leave campus. Let's get this done.' Sty started up the stairs.

Eyes narrowed, lips pursed, Evan watched him. 'Then that includes you giving me your inflatable.'

'Tsk tsk. Fear not, little Evan. You will have it by bedtime. I'll even read you a story.'

Evan's jaw tightened. He had to take a moment at the base of the stairs to quell the urge mounting in him. By the time Evan quieted down and got to his room, Sty had pulled the sheets off the bed and lugged the queen-sized mattress to the door.

Together, under the dim hall security lights, they managed to push, twist and drag it up one flight of steps, over the railing and across the hall to Rory's room. Once inside, though, Sty caught his foot on the bed frame and stumbled into his end of the mattress, shoving it into Evan, who was knocked off his feet against the window.

'Christ,' Evan struggled with the mattress, shoving it aside, standing again and righting the curtain.

For a few seconds, Sty held his shin, wincing in pain. Then, wordlessly, they lifted the mattress, shoved it onto the box springs, in place of the one they'd disposed of. When it was done, Evan stormed out and headed down the stairs. But Sty took a moment at the door, checking the room one more time, making sure that they'd thought of everything, that the place looked untouched.

Harper didn't want to work on her dissertation, didn't want to read or watch television or sleep. Her body ached from lack of use; it wanted to work out, to move and stretch and jog and lift. Longed to get on her Ninja and roar through town, along the highway, around the lake. Anywhere out of the house.

But she couldn't. Instead, she put her hands on her baby bump, gently patting it, remembering why the doctor had ordered her to rest. Picturing the baby – a chubby miniature Hank. Imagining holding it, smelling its hair. Feeling its little toes and velvet skin.

'You comfy in there?' She pictured the baby curled up tight inside her belly. 'Or are you claustrophobic like your mom?'

Of course it wasn't. The baby felt secure and warm, not trapped; her womb wasn't a prison, confining like her house. She gazed at her bedroom walls. Four more months, she thought. Four more months of sitting down, lying down, staring at walls. Lord. Her muscles whined, longing to work. Begging to.

Stop it, she told herself. She would see the doctor, talk about her restrictions. Maybe they'd be eased; she hadn't had many contractions lately. Just a few. Maybe she could at least take walks.

Harper sat up, fluffed her pillows. Turned onto her left side too fast; pain shot from her left hip down her leg. Damn. She flipped onto her back, letting the pain subside. She needed exercise; her left leg was weakening from too little use. The war injury was flaring up again. Never mind. She couldn't complain. At least she was alive, unlike the rest of her patrol. Again, she saw them at the checkpoint; the flash of light, the sense of flying through hot white air—

No. She would not revisit those memories; they sucked her into a useless endless vortex of sorrow. She lay back, resisting the spiral. Reminding herself that she had more pressing issues to deal with. Like Lou, his case of money. His gun.

Carefully, she rolled onto her right side. Maybe she should call Detective Rivers and tell her about Rita's phone call. About Wally and the hit that he'd supposedly taken out on Ed. Then again, she had no proof of what Rita had said. No proof that Lou was actually Ed. Didn't even know who Wally was. And wasn't eager to raise havoc with Vivian by calling police on her boyfriend.

Still, she had to do something. Didn't trust Lou. The package with the rat, his late-night wanderings, Rita's phone call, his fake IDs, the gun and money – Lou was trouble. Might be endangering her mother and her – and the baby, and that was inexcusable. She'd give him the night to think about their talk. But in the morning, she'd tell him to get his affairs in order or she'd call Detective Rivers and let him explain himself to her.

Her decision wasn't satisfying, but it was the best she could do for the moment. Harper reached over and turned out the lamp on the nightstand, lay in the dark, staring out the window. Her eyelids were growing heavy, and she was about to shut them when, in a window of the fraternity house, the curtains slid to the side, and something – a man's head? A mattress? Something fell against the windowpane. Arms reached out, yanking the thing away, quickly straightening the curtains again.

For a moment, she stayed there, trying to deny what she'd just seen. This was the second time she'd seen the curtains move. Which meant that someone was definitely in the fraternity house, which was supposed to be closed and empty. Oh God. Was it the hit man watching for Ed? Or maybe it was the naked guy? The missing kid from Elmira – could he be in the house? Hiding there? Or being held prisoner?

Ridiculous. She was overreacting, putting things together that didn't fit. Maybe the curtain hadn't moved. Maybe she'd invented that scenario out of boredom. The same thing often happened to prisoners of war – when they were held in seclusion many began hallucinating because of sensory deprivation. Harper wasn't that far gone, wasn't hallucinating, but the same principle could apply. Her mind might be compensating for the unbearable monotony of her doctor's ordered bed rest – might be creating its own stimulation. Imagining movement. Connecting unconnected events. Exaggerating the significance of details. Distorting.

She was still considering those possibilities when, careful not to alert Vivian and Lou, she snuck outside into the darkness. And she

was still contemplating them when she stood on her front porch,
shivering, toying with the key in her coat pocket, waiting for
Detective Rivers to arrive.

'Tell me again what you saw?' Detective Rivers was tired. She'd
pulled a double shift twice that week because Boschi was out with
the flu. She was beginning to wonder about Harper Jennings – was
she off balance? Her pregnancy affecting her? Her husband was away,
and her mother visiting. Still, she'd been a reliable – if too
independent and daring – source in the past. Rivers owed it to her
to come out personally to follow up on her call.

Harper described what she'd seen. A man falling against the
window. And maybe a mattress. 'It's not the first time I've seen that
curtain move. I think someone might be in there who shouldn't be.'
She held off voicing her suspicions about the missing boy. Stuck
to the facts.

'So you think someone's trespassing?'

'Maybe. Someone was in there.'

Rivers sighed, eyeing the fraternity. It hunkered dark and silent,
slumbering in the snow. 'Okay. I'll go check it out.' She stepped
off Harper's porch, into the snow.

Harper hustled, going with her.

'Mrs Jennings, I can handle this—'

'Please, Detective. I won't get in your way – promise.'

'It's not protocol for a civilian to come along—'

'Okay – I won't actually come along.' Harper waited and let Rivers
move ahead through the snowy yard. 'I'll stay way behind you.'

Rivers didn't bother to argue. The call, after all, was trivial, the
danger level nil. No doubt the disturbance would turn out to be
nothing. Some fraternity boys sacking out in the house when they
shouldn't be. Maybe with some girls. Small stuff. She climbed the
front steps, rang the doorbell, heard it chime inside. Waited. Got
no answer.

'You wait here,' she told Harper. She stepped off the porch, took
a hike around the perimeter of the building, flashing her light left,
right, up, down. Behind the house, by the back door, she saw some
disturbance in the snow, as if someone had tried to brush over footprints. Large green trash bags were lined up beside the kitchen door
with the trash cans, waiting for pickup. Something bothered Rivers
about that; the house had been empty for almost a week. Shouldn't

the garbage have been picked up? She'd have to check the sanitation schedule – possibly it was different during the holidays. She kept walking; saw no tire tracks in the driveway. Went to a window and flashed her light through, saw a dining-room table lined with chairs. A dim glow coming from the hall – probably a security light. But no sign of life inside. She moved on. Looked into the kitchen, games room, sitting room. Came back around to the front of the house, saw Harper waiting for her at the front door. Which was now wide open.

Evan and Sty sprawled on a plush leather sofa in the shadows of the sitting room.

'What did you tell Phil about why we needed his truck?'

'To move a senior's furniture out. But he didn't seem to care, just said go ahead and take it.'

Evan eyed the armoire. 'But we can't lift that thing,' Evan reasoned. 'So how are we supposed to get it into the bed?'

'Are you serious? It's obvious. We drag it out the kitchen door. I pull the pickup over to the porch, and we tilt it onto—'

Chimes suddenly rang out, interrupting him. Evan and Sty froze, mouths open, mirroring each other. Who was at the door?

'Who is that?' Evan whispered.

Sty put a finger to his lips. 'Shhh.'

The chimes peeled again.

'Who the fuck . . .?' Evan's blood had stopped pumping; he slipped off the sofa and scuttled backwards into the corner.

'Stop, you imbecile,' Sty growled. 'Hold still.'

For a moment, they sat motionless, waiting. Then a light flashed from the porch into the dining room.

'Shit,' Evan breathed. 'The cops?'

Sty said nothing.

'We're screwed.' Evan hugged his knees.

The flashlight moved away, shining in again through the next window.

'Christ,' Evan got to his feet, hugging himself. 'They're going around the house? The garbage bags. They'll find the mattress—'

'Shut up,' Sty's voice deepened, rumbled a threat. 'Just for once stop yammering and use your brain.'

'Use my brain? Why? You're the genius. You're the one with all the plans. What are we supposed to do—?'

'I will tell you again, Evan.' Sty stood slowly. 'Your panic is counterproductive. Panic is the enemy, the opposite of thought. We will have to improvise, yes. But if we think carefully and follow a rational plan, we will not fail. Just calm down and go along with whatever I say.' He moved through the shadows to the foyer, noticing a shape – a face pressing against the glass, steaming up a sitting-room window. Sty ignored it, proceeding directly past the armoire and across the old Oriental rug.

'What are you doing?' Evan's voice was an octave too high.

Sty didn't reply; he simply pasted a smile onto his face and unlatched the heavy carved wood double door.

As Detective Rivers walked away, Harper rang the bell again. For a moment, she stood waiting. Then she set out in the opposite direction, moving from window to window, pressing her face against the glass, trying to see inside. Dim light from the foyer spilled into what looked like a living room, filled with leather sofas and easy chairs, portraits on the walls. Nothing moved. She went to the next window. From there, she could see into the foyer where there was some light. At the bottom of the staircase, she saw a lumbering oversized cabinet standing awkwardly out of place. And movement – a silhouette skirting the cabinet, heading for the door.

Harper straightened up, cleared her throat, hurried back to the front door, just as it swung open, wide.

A young man smiled a greeting. 'Are you here to sing carols?' His hair was perfectly gelled; he wore a red Polo sweater and khakis.

Another guy stood behind the first. Paler, skinnier. Dark pants, white shirt, untucked. Harper checked over her shoulder for Detective Rivers.

'I live next door.' She said it as if it explained her presence.

The guy's smile broadened. 'Yes. Of course. You're the Ninja lady – you recognize her, don't you, Evan?' He turned to the second guy. Evan. Even in the dimness, Harper could see that Evan had bruises on his face. Had he been in a fight? An image flashed to mind: a naked guy getting beaten up in the snow. Could the assailant have been Evan?

'Harper.' She extended a hand. 'Harper Jennings.'

'I'm Sty, and this is Evan. Come in?' He shook her hand.

Harper didn't move.

'Okay, look. I bet I know why you're here. We aren't supposed to be in the house. It's officially closed. And you noticed someone was here, am I right?'

Harper nodded. 'I was concerned—'

'As you rightly should have been, Ma'am. It's reassuring to know that people in the neighborhood are looking out for our property, keeping an eye on what's going on in the area.'

Harper's gaze moved to the armoire.

Sty followed her gaze. 'Oh, that?' Sty laughed, gesturing to Evan. 'She likes our armoire, Evan.'

Evan didn't move, didn't speak.

'You want it? If you outbid our customer, it's yours. We sold this online and – actually, that's why we're here. We're delivering it to our customer.'

Harper nodded. 'I saw someone upstairs. In the window . . .'

'Really?' Again, Sty laughed, turned to Evan. 'She saw you!' He turned back to Harper. 'As long as we're here, we moved a bed for a fraternity brother. For next semester. But Evan slipped – smacked right into the window.'

'A bed.' Harper repeated. That explained why she'd seen a mattress in the window. They'd been moving furniture. Perfectly plausible. Still, there was something odd about them. A tension. Excitement? 'Well, that explains it. I was concerned that someone might have broken in—'

'Understandably. Thank you for checking. We're lucky to have a neighbor like you.'

Finally, the beam of Rivers' flashlight came around the corner, moved toward them. Rivers climbed the front steps and adopted a cop's stance, legs firmly planted, arms at her side. 'Want to explain what you boys are doing in here?'

Sty began again, from the start.

'You have permission to be here?'

Sty looked sheepish. 'Well, unofficially. This is our fraternity. And we aren't staying long; our parents expect us for Christmas.'

Rivers didn't smile. 'How long have you been here?'

'Oh, just a day.'

'So you weren't here when that guy was running around naked.'

Sty chuckled, glanced at Evan. 'What? Are you serious?'

Evan stood with his hands in his pockets, elbows straight, a frozen smirk.

'You're saying you didn't see him?' Rivers asked.

'I think we'd remember – wouldn't we, Evan?'

Evan shrugged. Nodded. Still smirking.

'So what was he doing, some kind of Polar Bear club initiation?' Sty suggested. 'Or maybe it was a case of husband-walks-in-and-catches-naked-guy-with-his-wife?' He laughed. 'Guy exits quickly, not bothering to grab his pants.'

Evan snickered, amused. Took his hands out of his pockets, crossing his arms.

'Must have been quite a show. Sorry we missed it.' Sty smirked, and his gaze rested on Harper's belly. 'Oh, dear. We're not being very hospitable. Please. Come inside. We don't have much in the way of snacks, but I'm sure we can fix some tea—'

'No, no.' Rivers stepped back. 'Look. In honor of the season, I'm going to take you at your word that you're here with permission. But I do not want to get called back here and regret letting you slide.' She peered past Sty, eyeing Evan's bruises. 'Been in a fight?'

Evan opened his mouth to answer, but Sty cut him off. He was telling Rivers about Evan's collision with the window when, suddenly, a contraction sucked away Harper's breath.

'Can I—?' She took Rivers' arm. 'Can I sit down?'

Before anyone could answer, she started into the house, but the contraction was fierce; she wobbled and might have actually collapsed if Evan and Sty hadn't grabbed her and carried her to a cushiony leather chair.


Detective Rivers walked Harper out the door, down the fraternity's front steps. 'Are you sure you're all right? You should see a doctor and be checked out.'

Harper felt shaken; the contraction had been strong. But, while Evan and Sty had walked Rivers through the house, just to make sure no one had broken in and was lurking there, she'd recovered. 'I'm fine now. My doctor's watching the contractions. That's why I'm on house arrest.'

They walked several steps through the snow in silence. Then, 'Mrs Jennings—'

'Detective—'

They both spoke at once.

'Sorry,' Rivers said, as Harper said, 'Go ahead.'

'No, you first,' Rivers insisted.

Harper glanced over her shoulder, checking to see that they were alone. 'So? What do you think? Because those boys send red alerts through my bones. Their smarmy smiles. They're way too – I don't know. Confident? Smooth? Like they think they're smarter than everyone? And their story, that they were moving furniture. Well, it explains what I saw in the window today, but it doesn't explain why I saw the curtain move last time. Or the light beams that someone flashed through my window the other night.'

'Light beams?' Rivers scowled.

'Oh – didn't I mention them? I must have forgotten, with everything that's been going on . . .' Harper stopped, realizing that Rivers had no idea what she was referring to. 'It's not just the naked kid in the woods and odd goings-on in the fraternity house,' she explained. 'It's also that a package came to my house with a dead rat in it.'

'A what?'

'It was addressed to someone who doesn't live here. But it shook me up.'

A black SUV turned onto the street, cruised slowly down the snowy road. Harper turned to watch it. 'Detective, I swear. That same car has been driving past my house every night, as if someone's watching us. As if they're casing the area.' She watched the car move away, then realized that they'd stopped walking, that the detective was studying her, eyebrows knit.

'What?' Harper asked.

'Let's go inside.' Rivers gripped Harper's arm. 'We'll talk there.'

Harper went along, hearing snow crackle under their boots, and beyond it, the silence of frigid night.


'What the fuck was that?' Evan sank onto the stairs, covering his face with his hands. 'What the hell were you thinking? Offering her the armoire. "If you outbid our customer, you can have it." Why didn't you just open the thing up and let her look inside? What would you have done if she'd tried—?'

'Damn it, Evan.' Sty put a hand on the newel post, facing him. 'Can you please get hold of yourself? You're clucking like a perturbed hen.'

A hen? Evan stood. The steps made him higher than Sty, gave him an advantage. He pictured pouncing, twisting Sty's neck, hearing it crack.

Sty didn't look up at him; his eyes peered into the distance, thinking. 'There was absolutely no chance she would inspect the armoire once I'd invited her to do so. If I hadn't offered her a look, she might well have taken one.'

'How could you possibly know that?'

Sty raised an eyebrow. 'It was a matter of probability. Human behavior is fairly predictable. You'd know that if you'd study it.'

Evan opened and closed his sore fist. He hadn't eaten, and his muscles ached from all the cleaning and moving.

'Don't get ornery, Evan.'

'Who said I was ornery?'

'I know you, my friend. You are a man of passion; that passion is what first attracted me to you as a superior individual. But remember, passion needs to be balanced by rationality and self-control.'

Evan leaned against the wall, exhaled, saying nothing. He wished Sty would drop his affected intellectual posturing. But Sty was a genius, couldn't help it. And they needed his genius if they were going to get out of this mess.

'So, what now? Should we get your car and load this thing?'

Sty frowned. His eyes moved toward the door. 'Not yet. Obviously, we have to alter our plan.'

'Again?' Evan snorted. 'I am not moving that guy again. I refuse—'

'Calm down, Evan. I mean it. We're both tired, but we need to remain steady and clear-headed. There's no need to move him again.' Sty took a step up and sat below Evan. 'Think about it. We've already informed the police that the armoire has been purchased by a third party. That's why we're here, right? To deliver it?'

Evan nodded. 'That's what we said.'

'So, when and if they find it abandoned and discover the body, they'll also assume that that same third party is responsible. After all, we're just college boys; what possible motive would we have for killing anyone? And, more pertinently, why would we have offered it for our visitors' inspection if we'd had a corpse hidden inside?'

A slow, relieved grin stretched across Evan's face. How was Sty so talented at planning ahead, anticipating snafus, dodging bullets, making contingencies?

'Think about it. In the worst case, down the road, all we'll have to do is invent a false identity for the buyer of the piece, and profess our absolute ignorance of what they did with it after purchase.' Sty reached up, put a hand on Evan's shoulder, and squeezed. 'You all right, compadre?'

Evan looked at the armoire. 'What do we do with that?'

Sty removed his hand, stood. 'Nobody's here but us. We can leave it for now.'

Thank God, Evan thought. He rubbed his shoulder, doubted he could move the thing another inch.

Sty went for his coat. 'Come on. Let's go get some dinner. I'm so hungry, you're starting to look like rare steak.'

As they locked the door on the way out, Evan was still uneasy. The police car was still in the neighbor's driveway. And even though he knew she wasn't, he felt as if Harper was watching him from the upstairs window.

Back in her bedroom, lying down again, Harper turned on the television but ignored it, glaring out the window at the fraternity house. Rivers had advised the boys to leave and lock up, but she hadn't questioned them sufficiently. Hadn't seemed to notice the coincidence of their presence just yards from the site of the assault she'd witnessed. Or the possibility that the victim of that assault might be the missing boy from Elmira. Or that the key she'd found could belong to that boy – might even open the door to his apartment.

In fact, Rivers had flatly dismissed every single one of Harper's concerns, even the dead rat. Even the SUV that kept cruising the neighborhood.

'You need to rest more and take better care of yourself.' Rivers had made Harper sit down in the living room beside the tree, among the decorations and baby gifts, and she'd proceeded to scold her. 'Your body is under more stress than you realize. That contraction next door – it was alarming. You need to talk to your doctor, Mrs Jennings. You don't want to put your health or your baby's at risk.'

Harper had been indignant. She didn't need a lecture, was quite aware of her condition and her responsibilities. Resented the detective's tone. 'Thank you. I assure you I'm following my doctor's instructions and trying to rest. But how can I rest with all that's going on around here? Disappearance, assault, threatening packages, trespassers – the baby and I might be at risk from more than contractions—'

'Please, Mrs Jennings. Listen to yourself.' Rivers had looked down at her boots, studied them, then looked back up. 'I don't know how else to say this, so I'll just be blunt. You're imagining problems where there aren't any. You're taking random events and inventing connections between them, inferring the worst possibilities. Honestly, things aren't as sinister as you seem to think they are. Simply put: you're overreacting.'

Harper had felt slapped. Stunned. Was she overreacting to a dead rat in the mail? A fist fight out her window? Young men prowling around in a house that was supposed to be empty? Why was everyone so determined to dismiss her? Her mother, Lou, Detective Rivers. Why were they all so doubtful? Had they sent out a memo? Had a meeting and decided to explain away whatever worried her as being the result of hormone fluctuations or stress?

An hour later, when the phone rang, she was still seething. She ran a hand through her hair, shut off the television and answered, not taking her eyes off the building next door. Asking herself what was wrong with everyone. Confident, now, that the errors in reasoning or perception were not her own.


Hank had news. 'Hospital. Today. Went.'

Oh God. 'What? Why?' Harper could only make short syllables. The walls around her suddenly slipped away and, as if from above, she saw herself in the garden before his accident, planting tulips, looking up to the roof where Hank was making repairs. Seeing him slip, falling, hitting the ledge below. No—

'Hoppa?' How long had he been talking? Harper had missed it. 'You there?'

Harper grunted, biting hard on her lip, causing pain that she hoped would ground her and fend off the flashback. Hank. What had happened to him?

'. . . Trent took me. For X-ray.'

X-ray? Harper was still floating, looked down at Hank lying on the hedges, unconscious. Saw a rush of gurneys, hospital beds. She bit down harder, felt a rip of pain, tasted blood.

'Not worry. Hoppa. Okay?'

Not worry? Hank had gone to the hospital again, and she wasn't supposed to worry? 'What happened? Why didn't anyone call to tell me you'd been hurt?'

'Did tell you. Hurt my ankle.'

Wait. Harper thought back; Hank had mentioned that he'd twisted his ankle. 'But you didn't say it was that bad – bad enough to go to the hospital. You made it sound like no big deal. Like everything was fine—' She stopped short, aware that she'd also been omitting things from their conversations, making things sound fine. Apparently, each had been trying to spare the other.

'Not broken,' he assured her. 'Just tendon.'

Just? 'Damn. Can you walk?'

'Crutches. Okay. Will be.'

Again, Harper saw him falling, his head slamming the ledge. She dug a fingernail into her palm, focused on the pain.

'Hoppa?' Hank penetrated the flashback. 'I'm fine. Don't worry. No. Big deal.'

Harper looked out the window. Evan and Sty were leaving the fraternity. Harper ran a hand through her hair, watching them.

'You okay?' His voice was gentle, distracting.

Harper closed her eyes, not able to bear how much she missed him. 'Fine.' Her voice was lumpy and raw. She swallowed, regaining control. Repeated herself. 'I'm fine. Why?'

'Know you.' Two words wrapped around her like a hug.

Harper's eyes flooded. Damn. Cut it out, she told herself. She was stronger, more resilient than this.

'Tell. Me. What?'

She reached for a tissue, blew her nose. 'Nothing.' Nothing except that everyone around her discounted everything she said and implied she was losing her mind. 'Nobody takes me seriously, Hank. I feel like I'm the only one who sees what's going on—'

'Like what?'

Harper opened her mouth and words flooded out. But she didn't tell him about the naked boy in the snow, the missing kid from Elmira, the key she'd found out back, the odd behavior in the fraternity house, Rivers' implication that she was imagining things because of her frustrating isolation at being in the house all the time. She didn't mention anything about the dead rat or Lou's gun, fake IDs and suitcase full of money. Those things would make Hank worry. Instead, she railed about the ugly unwanted Christmas tree, prematurely purchased baby presents, the garish God-awful lights Lou was going to hang all over the property . . .

'Leslie,' Hank interrupted.

Leslie?

'Will you? Call Leslie. See Leslie.'

Wait. Hank was telling her to call her shrink? 'Why? You think I'm overreacting because I'm pregnant—'

'Not saying that—'

'Seriously, I'm pregnant, but that doesn't mean I can't be taken seriously—'

'HOPPA.' Hank stopped her. 'Listen. I'm. Not there. Vivian no help. Nobody. With you. That's why Leslie. Trust Leslie. See her.'

What?

'So you. Aren't all alone.'

Oh. Tension began to ease from Harper's muscles. Hank wasn't doubting her; he was trying to find her an ally.

'I'm okay, really.'

'Being careful?'

Damn, he knew her too well. 'Of course.' Unless she counted sneaking around the woods and the fraternity house, or snooping through Lou's things. Or answering a strange phone to find that hit men might be stopping by.

'Baby?'

'The baby's busy. Moving.' She remembered her last contraction twisting the air out of her, wondered if the baby had felt it, too.

'How about dissertation?'

Harper rolled her eyes. How was she supposed to write about Pre-Columbian symbolism with the upheaval going on around her?

'Work good for you. And ask doctor. Maybe you can exercise. Some.'

Really? How could she exercise when she couldn't lift anything and could take the stairs only a couple of times a day? She knew that Hank was only trying to help, offering suggestions to help her feel less trapped and closed in. But Harper was bothered by far more than just her close quarters. Maybe she should open up, tell Hank everything that had happened.

But that wouldn't be fair, dumping all those worries on him.

Harper held onto the comforter, missing him.

'Promise, Hoppa. See Leslie.'

Harper promised. And she agreed to ask the doctor about exercises. After they hung up, she pulled the comforter up around her neck, refusing to cry. Yes, she would see Leslie. But keeping secrets from Hank made her feel as if she was doing something wrong. As if she couldn't really open up to anybody. As if she were utterly alone.

\*     \*     \*

When a cloud of buttery sweetness drifted into her room, Harper looked at the clock. Almost eleven. She'd been lying there, staring at shadows, feeling glum for over an hour. And oddly, at this late hour, her room was filling with the aroma of baking goodies. Obviously, Lou was in her kitchen again. Taking it over, without as much as asking.

So what, she told herself. So he's making cookies. Get over it.

Except that it wasn't just that Lou was making cookies in her kitchen without even asking. It was also that he had a gun and a wad of cash in the guest room.

But she wouldn't have known that if she hadn't snooped. And he'd explained that he was holding that for his friend.

But Lou might have lied about the friend. He might really be that guy Ed Strunk, who might have hit men after him.

Maybe she should go downstairs and ask him.

As if he'd tell her the truth. As if anyone would believe her story about him if he did. Oh Lord. Harper didn't want to confront Ed, didn't want to think any more. She rolled over, grabbed the clicker, switched on the television. The news came on and her phone rang simultaneously. Probably Hank again, calling to make sure she was all right. She grabbed the phone, anticipating his voice. But the caller wasn't Hank.

'I just got a call from your husband.' Leslie didn't bother with 'hello.'

'Hank called you?' Harper sat up and bent her legs, winced as her left knee protested the bending.

'He's worried. He thinks you're too alone.'

'I know.'

'So, what's going on?' Leslie's concern felt like a hug.

Again, Harper's eyes filled. What the hell was wrong with her, crying so much over nothing? She'd never been a sap, never a whining wimp. She tried to answer but choked on a sob.

'Harper?'

'Uh huh.' She reached for another tissue. Blew her nose.

'What's going on? Talk to me.' Leslie's voice was like silk. Or flannel. Or fleece.

Harper took a breath. 'I'm fine.'

'Don't lie. I'm your shrink.'

Harper sniffed, dabbed her eyes. 'Okay, maybe not entirely fine.'

'Flashbacks?'

'Not really.' Not if she didn't count the ones about Hank's fall.

'Let's make an appointment. Tomorrow at ten?'

Tomorrow at ten seemed a long way off.

'Fine, yes.'

'Good. I'll come by then.'

Harper agreed, but sat fuming. Lord. She couldn't even drive ten minutes to Leslie's office. She was a pathetic shut-in. Felt like a prisoner. She looked at the walls of her room, ached for a hatchet. Then again, swinging it would be too much exertion. She couldn't even trash her own house. Damn. Harper's fist clenched, she picked up a pillow and punched it once, then again.

Finally, needing to move, she swung her legs over the side of the bed to stand. She stopped, though, when she heard the news anchor mention Sebastian Levering. According to the report, there was still no sign of him. A reporter interviewed his mother, who cried, pleading for him to be home before Christmas.

Outside a car door slammed. Harper stood and went to the window. In the glare of Lou's Christmas lights, she saw a pickup truck in the fraternity's driveway, and Sty coming around it, removing a large box from the back. Evan got out the passenger's side, walked through the snow to the front door. He had something in his hands, too. What was it – a gun? She leaned closer, squinting to see it better. No, not a gun. A blow dryer? What were those two doing? Why would a couple of guys need a hair dryer?

Sty followed Evan into the house, carrying the carton. And the heavy wood carved door closed behind him.

Harper stood at the window for a while, thinking until she couldn't stand it any more. Besides, the aroma had grown too tantalizing, and it tugged at her, nagging until she gave in and let the scent of warm sugar pull her down the stairs.

The cookies were cooling and Lou was gone. Harper fixed a tray of milk and sugar cookies. Comfort food. Brought it back upstairs and crawled into bed. Fell asleep with the television blaring and crumbs sprinkled over the mattress.

She woke up early, hearing voices. Realized they came from the television, one of those cheerily annoying early-morning shows, people smiling and blabbing just to fill airtime. Snapping off the television, she showered and dressed, preparing for her appointment with Leslie, and just after nine a.m., she went downstairs, carrying her empty glass and tray. Halfway down, she heard Vivian's deep voice braying in the kitchen. Her gravelly laughter. And then male laughter, joining in. More than one man's laughter. Not just Lou's.

Harper stopped on the stairs, listening, trying to identify the voices. But the only voice was Vivian's, and it was talking about her.

'Ahh. The Ninja Lady? Really? That's what all you boys call her? Very funny. Harper will love that—'

'Ma?' Harper came into the kitchen. Her mother was perched on her chair, across the table from Evan and Sty.

'Good morning,' Vivian beamed. 'We were just talking about you. Harper, these are members of the fraternity next door. This is Evan, and that's Sty—'

'What are you two doing here?' It sounded more unfriendly than she'd intended.

'Harper?' Vivian's jaw dropped. 'These are our guests—'

'Good morning, Mrs Jennings. The truth is we came over because you gave us a scare last night.' Sty leaned back and crossed his legs. 'We came by to look in on you, make sure you were okay. And your lovely mother was kind enough to invite us in for some coffee.'

Vivian looked at Harper, confused. 'What's he saying?'

'That's right. You seemed pretty wobbly when you left.' Evan leaned forward on his elbows, eyes twinkling.

'When you left where? Harper?' Vivian frowned, looked from face to face. 'Will someone explain?'

'It's nothing, Ma.' Harper brought her tray to the sink, rinsed her glass.

'Actually, she's being modest.' Sty spoke to Vivian but watched Harper. 'Your daughter is an active and concerned citizen. That's why she came over to the house last night—'

'What? She did what?'

'Ma. It was nothing.'

'No.' Sty's smile was crooked. 'It certainly was not "nothing". It was, in fact, a prime example of civic responsibility. So many people these days witness wrongdoings and do nothing. They don't get involved. But not your daughter. She had an indication that something in the house was amiss – so she summoned the authorities and followed through, investigating personally.'

Vivian's mouth was a gaping hole.

'But while she was there,' Evan added, 'she almost passed out. We thought she was having a seizure or something.'

The hole aimed at Harper.

'I had a contraction, Ma. That's all. It was—'

'So you really went out? You went over there? Why? Without even telling us?' Vivian stood, gestured with her coffee mug. 'What the hell is wrong with you?' She turned to Sty. 'She's having a difficult pregnancy and that's why I'm here, to help her while she's supposed to be resting. But she never listens to me. She keeps over-exerting herself. Going out in the ice and snow, looking for God-knows-what in the woods or, now, trekking over to your house. You know what? It's no surprise she had a contraction. She's lucky she didn't go into labor.' She turned to Harper again. 'What were you thinking?'

Harper glared at Sty, then Evan. Sty shrugged, smirking. Evan glanced away, at the door to the deck, which was swinging open. Lou came in, shaking snow from his boots, looking around the room.

'What is this, a party?' He unbuttoned his coat, stepped over to give Vivian a kiss hello.

'No, it's not a party.' Harper still hadn't accepted that she had no control of what went on in her house.

'Of course it is – these nice young men dropped by to look in on Harper,' Vivian was practically singing. 'They live next door—'

'Yes. I'm Sty, and this is Evan.'

Sty held up a platter. 'Care for a poppy-seed muffin?'

They were still there, in the kitchen, having coffee and munching pastries when Leslie arrived. Harper excused herself to answer the front door, but the guests wouldn't let her make the effort, and Sty was on his way before she'd gotten to her feet. Harper protested, but he scampered ahead, welcoming Leslie and offering to take her coat as if he lived there. As if he were hosting a gala.

'I'm here to see Harper.' Leslie kept her coat, looking past Sty at Harper who was standing in the hall, holding her belly, looking pale.

Leslie rushed to her. 'Contraction?'

Harper nodded, breathing through it.

Sty approached, crowding them. 'Oh God, another one?' He spoke too loudly.

'Another what?' Vivian called. Her chair scraped the floor as she pushed back from the table. 'What's wrong?' She rushed to the hall, saw Leslie holding Harper's hand, Harper leaning against the wall, Sty hovering over her.

'You should get off your feet.' Leslie's eyes held Harper's.

Vivian crowded them, blocking their way. 'Should I call the doctor?'

Harper shook her head. 'No, Ma. It's okay.' She moved slowly away from the kitchen, hanging onto Leslie's arm, whispering. 'Hank's study.'

Vivian followed. 'It's a contraction? Lou – she's having another contraction—'

'Should we go to the hospital?' Now Lou was in the hall with them; it was a parade headed at a snail's pace toward the study at the end of the hall.

'Harper? Should we call an ambulance?'

'She'll be fine.' Leslie's voice was strong, commanding.

'How would you know?' Vivian's hands were on her hips.

'Ma!' Harper bellowed, squeezing Leslie's arm. 'Back off.'

Vivian covered her mouth, and Lou put an arm around her, shaking his head. 'You shouldn't talk to your mother that way – you've hurt her feelings.' He turned to Sty. 'I'm sorry you had to see this.'

'No,' Sty insisted. 'I have a family, too.'

Evan wandered over, taking up the rear.

'Please. Everyone.' Leslie turned to face them. She raised a hand. 'There's no need to follow us. Just go back to whatever you were doing – Harper's going to be fine. She and I are going to sit a while and relax and talk. By ourselves.'

Vivian stood still, eyes wide, her hand now at her throat; Lou whispered something to her and guided her back to the kitchen. Sty, though, wouldn't back off. 'So you're certain that she's fine? Are you a doctor?'

That was enough for Harper. The contraction had peaked; she had breath enough to talk. She pivoted, using her officer's bark. 'Sty. Go.' She pointed to the kitchen.

For a nanosecond, their eyes met, exchanging sparks. Then Sty grinned. 'Just a concerned neighbor, trying to help.' And he turned away, joining Lou, Evan and Vivian.

As she and Leslie went into the study, Harper heard Lou telling them not to run off. 'Wait, boys. I just baked these sugar cookies. I'll wrap some up; take some home with you.'

And her mother apologizing for her daughter's behavior. 'She's not herself. The pregnancy and all.'

\*    \*    \*

The study smelled like Hank. Well, not like him physically. But like his stuff. Old leather and books. A hint of whiskey. And something spicy, almost but not quite like cloves. The room hadn't been changed since he'd left, but without Hank, his possessions had shifted; the room felt altered and abandoned. His big leather easy chair and ottoman reached out, offering – maybe needing – comfort, and Harper responded, planting herself on them, letting the big leather arms and oversized cushions embrace her. Briefly, she scanned his desk, his mementos. His sofa and overflowing shelves. His absence. But even without him, she was safe here, on Hank's private turf, guarded by his photos and papers and periodicals and books.

'You all right?'

Harper clutched the fat arms of the chair, nodding.

'So who are those guys?'

Harper leaned back, pulled an afghan off the arm of the chair, snuggled under it and began, 'Just guys from the fraternity—' But she stopped, started over.

'You know what, Leslie? I'm really not sure,' she began, and then she went through all of it. The fight she'd witnessed, the late-night police search of the woods, the key she'd later found and tried in the fraternity house lock, the incidents involving strange flashes of light and moving curtains in the supposedly empty fraternity. Last night's visit there with Detective Rivers, during which they'd encountered Sty and Evan, who shouldn't have been in the building, much less in her house this morning when she'd come downstairs.

'I don't know what they're into,' she concluded. 'But I doubt they're there moving furniture.' Then she talked more about the SUV that had been cruising the neighborhood, the money, IDs and the gun she'd found in Lou's room, his lame explanations about why he had them, the dead rat in the package, the telephone call warning of a hit against Ed Strunk, Lou's odd late-night wanderings. When she stopped talking, her head ached.

Leslie watched her from the sofa, her expression soft, her green eyes glowing warm. She hadn't made a single comment, just sat still, letting silence blanket them.

'What?' Harper was confused. After everything she'd told her, didn't Leslie have anything to say?

'How have your flashbacks been?'

Flashbacks? Why was Leslie changing the subject? Had she not even listened to what Harper had just said? Didn't she believe her? 'Okay. Not bad. Why?'

More silence.

Wait. 'What are you saying? That everything I just told you – that my impressions of what's happening around me are like flashbacks? You think I'm losing touch with reality—'

'Whoa. Slow down. I didn't say any of that, did I?'

'No. But then, you didn't actually say anything at all, did you?' Harper crossed her arms, shifting in her seat. 'Lately, nobody takes a thing I say seriously, so you have plenty of company. Detective Rivers thinks I'm imagining things because I'm suffering from too much rest, cabin fever and sensory deprivation. My mother and Lou say I'm too hormonal and stressed by Hank's absence to know what I'm talking about. Hank thinks – hell, I don't know what Hank thinks – he's so far away, it feels like he's been gone forever. And as soon as I gave a single hint that I was upset, he dodged and called you. Referred me to my shrink. So bottom line, everybody I talk to finds some reason to avoid what I'm saying. What the hell, Leslie?' She stopped talking because her voice was thick again, but she refused to give in, swallowing away the urge to cry.

Leslie waited a few beats, then got up off the sofa and walked over to the easy chair, sat on the ottoman beside Harper's legs, leaned over and took her hands. The tenderness at first infuriated Harper, but Leslie's warm eyes steadied her. And gradually, the tension and anger began to fade.

Finally, Leslie spoke. 'I don't think you'd confuse reality with flashbacks, Harper. Besides, none of your typical triggers have been involved in the events you've described. And you've said that lately your flashbacks have been minimal.'

Their eyes locked. Harper waited. After a moment, Leslie continued. 'To be honest, I don't know what's going on, Harper. I trust your observations and your instincts, but I can't explain what those two frat boys are up to or what kind of dude your wacky mother is dating. And frankly, I don't care all that much, except that they affect you. Because you are the person I'm concerned about. And you are clearly miserable. So, for a minute, let's put aside all the reasons you're upset – the fight, the boys, the dead rat, even the gun – wrap them all in a mental package and set it aside for now. We'll deal with that package later.

'The more pressing issue is that you're emotionally stressed and tense. And being emotionally stressed and tense can take a toll on you, your health and your pregnancy. Agreed?'

Harper hesitated. What was Leslie doing? Finding a psychobabble way to explain and wipe away all of her concerns? Was she no different than the others, convinced that Harper was losing it? Harper studied the familiar green eyes; they never wavered. She heard Hank saying, 'Trust. Leslie.' And her gut echoed his words. Hell, if she couldn't trust Leslie, she could trust no one.

Harper shrugged. 'Agreed. So?'

'So. There's something I want you to do – before you even begin to deal with any of the weird events you told me about. And that is: take care of Harper. Step One: get rid of the crippling damaging tension. So we're going to work on relaxation techniques. We've done this before, but not in a while—'

'Seriously? That self-hypnosis crap?' There was a gun upstairs and strangers all over her house, and she was supposed to hypnotize herself?

'Yes, Harper.' Leslie smirked, squeezing Harper's hands. 'That self-hypnosis crap. Now focus. Let's start with breathing. Inhale through your nose, out through your mouth. Slowly, from the belly. That's right. And close your eyes, envision a place where you are perfectly at ease. Where you are safe and secure and there's no need to be on guard. And breathing deeply from the belly, let the tension out of your toes. And breathe. And let the muscles of your heels and ankles relax until they're light enough to float. And breathe. Now your calves . . .'

Leslie moved Harper up her body, releasing tension muscle by muscle, and, even though she wondered if Leslie believed her, by the time they reached her shoulders, Harper felt lighter. Easier. By the time they passed her neck, she felt more optimistic, half convinced that she wasn't engulfed in skulduggery and danger. And when they were finished, for the first time in days, she felt refreshed and calm.

'Damn,' she smiled, stretching as if from a nap. 'I meant to offer you tea before – would you like some? We have fresh cookies.'

'You're feeling better,' Leslie grinned. 'I'd love tea, but I don't want you to get it. Tell me where everything is and I'll fix it.'

'No, we'll both go.' Harper got up slowly, started for the door.

In the hallway, Leslie checked her watch. 'I can only stay a few more minutes. I have more appointments—'

An explosive crash interrupted her. Instantly, Harper ducked, pulled Leslie to the floor. Saw a car pull up to the checkpoint, and – bam. Her patrol vanishing in a flash of white heat. She smelled burning rubber, burning flesh. Felt herself flying . . .

'Harper?'

Leslie crouched beside her, repeating her name. Harper. Harper? Harper blinked, and Iraq slowly faded, replaced by the hall outside her kitchen. She took a breath, recovering, and got to her feet.

'Sorry I pulled you down. Conditioned response – you all right?'

Leslie nodded, standing, breathing shallowly. 'Are you?'

Harper had already headed toward the sound. 'What the hell happened?' It had come from the front of the house. The dining room? 'Ma? Lou?' she called, but got no response.

The air mattress took forever to inflate, and Evan was sick of the sound of the blow dryer. In fact, he was sick of this whole week. Even though Sty wouldn't admit it, everything had gone wrong, from the very first night when the kid had run outside into the snow. The motorcycle lady had seen him and, even though she hadn't recognized them, she was suspicious. She kept calling the goddam cops. Had even brought them to the house. And if he hadn't moved fast enough to stand in front of it, with Sty saying they were selling furniture, that nosy bitch might just have tried to examine the armoire. He could see her, opening a door, looking inside. The idea sent adrenalin through his veins. Because they'd have had no choice; they'd have had to kill them both.

He thought about it, how close they'd come to actually doing those two babes. And killing a cop? Wow. Way beyond what they'd talked about. Finally, Sty would have to shut up with his lectures and let go of his tedious self-important plans; they would have propelled themselves far beyond the limp and tiresome crime of his role models, Loeb and Leopold. Instead, they'd have had to live in the moment, improvising. Acting on pure impulse, relying on their most basic and primitive instincts. He pictured what might have happened. Strangling would have been good. He'd have liked watching hope fade from their eyes, feeling the shift of vertebrae as life yielded to the force of his hands. Drowning one of them would also have been interesting. Filling the tub – maybe with icy water – no, that would freeze his hands. So nice warm bathwater. He imagined holding one of them under – maybe the cop. Feeling her body resist, then ease. Watching the release of bubbles. The fixed stare of her eyes.

Evan pressed the blow dryer against the valve of the mattress, watching the material expand, amused that the mattress was not the only item on his lap that was expanding. And the beauty part was – or would have been – that if they'd killed those two, no one ever would have caught them. They'd have disposed of the bodies far away from here and from each other, and there would have been no evidence linking the deaths to each other, let alone to them. He and Sty would have been long gone by the time the corpses were discovered. Home for Christmas. Not even close.

'You almost done?' Sty stuck his head into the room. Deflating the fantasy. 'We ought to move the armoire.'

Damn Sty, constantly pestering, interrupting, pushing, antici- pating, speechifying, intellectualizing, philosophizing, talking, talking, talking. And worse, cozying up to the Ninja Lady and her family. Becoming too visible, even though he was the one who insisted on meticulously sticking to, never deviating from his all- important, immutable, carefully devised, ultimately perfect and utterly fucking infallible Plan. 'Yep. Just have to make a pit stop. Go on downstairs; I'll be right there.'

Evan turned off the dryer, listened to Sty's footsteps descending the stairway. Plugging up the air valve on the mattress, he considered that maybe, if the constant prating became too intolerable, he might eliminate Sty, too.

The two of them stood silent, wrapped in each other's arms, staring at the metal pipe that had shattered a dining-room window.

'Ma? You okay?' Harper hurried in, looked them over, saw no wounds. 'What the hell happened?'

Vivian watched the pipe and shook her head.

'Lou?' Harper demanded.

Lou's eyes darted to the window. 'We were in the living room, working on the tree, when: bam. We came in and saw this.' He kissed Vivian's forehead. 'It's all right, Viv. No harm done.'

Really? No harm? Harper eyed what was left of her window. 'Did you see anyone?'

'No.' Lou's answer came fast.

'A black car,' Vivian sniffled, crying now.

'That was nobody,' Lou growled. 'Just a passing car.' His hand covered Vivian's head, stroked her hair.

Leslie stepped in, looked at the window, the pipe. It was about eight inches long. 'Oh dear.'

Harper moved behind her mother, circled around the pipe. Saw a cell phone duct-taped to the thing. Damn.

'Everybody – OUT!' she yelled. As she started for the door, Harper saw writing on the tape. Just one word: BOOM.

'Let's go – now!' Harper commanded in her lieutenant's voice. She shooed them, shoving them like a snowplow.

'What? Out of the house? Why – is it a bomb?' Vivian stopped crying.

'Out.' Harper grabbed coats from the closet and kept herding, meeting Leslie's eyes, letting her know that, indeed, the place might blow up.

'Who would toss a bomb into the house – I'm calling the police.' Vivian stopped, looking into the living room. 'Where's my phone?'

'Nobody said it was a bomb, Vivian,' Lou guided her forward, ignoring the coat Harper held out to him. 'Don't get all hypersterical.'

Vivian tilted her head. 'Don't get what?'

'Ma. Move. Out.' Harper gave Leslie her coat and put on a parka. 'Hurry.'

But nobody obeyed. Lou blocked Vivian, who was trying to go to the kitchen. 'I've got to get my phone,' Vivian insisted.

'Calm down, Viv.' Lou put his hands on her shoulders. 'Think about your blood pressure—'

'Ma! Forget your phone. Just get out!' Harper held the door open, waiting.

'You don't need to call the cops, Viv. It's just a broken window—'

Suddenly, the walls trembled and the air cracked; Harper gave an ear-shattering whistle.

Everyone froze, gaping.

'Listen up, will you? That thing could go off any time. Get out of the damned house.'

She ushered them outside just as in the dining room, a cell phone began to ring.

Reflexively, Harper followed her training and threw herself at the others, knocking them down the stairs, as far as possible from the bomb. She braced herself for the oncoming explosion, aware that the cell phone was the detonator, that its ring might be the last sound any of them heard. In nanoseconds, the house would blow, and they might, too.

Flying down the steps, Harper had no time to think, only for snapshot impressions. Making impact, body-slamming her mother, shoving Leslie. Seeing Vivian fall and Lou try to grab her. Leslie grabbing the handrail and trying to balance, but tripping, bumping down the steps on her backside.

And the sense of the ground slipping away as she lost traction. Her legs sliding, her body curling to protect the baby as she rolled downward into the snow. And Vivian's hoarse screams. And the shock of cold snow on her skin as she lay flat, waiting for the searing jolt of the explosion. The hot blast, the caustic smell. And the inevitable flashback that would carry her back to Iraq, to another time, a different bomb.

Harper wasn't sure how much time passed before she realized that nothing was exploding, that the bomb wasn't going off. She got to her feet, yanking Leslie's arm to take her along, calling to her mother and Lou to move with them. Gathering everyone together at the street, where they stood clustered.

And waited some more, just to be sure.

Gradually, Harper realized that she was the only one watching the house; everyone else was watching her.

'We were lucky; it was a dud,' she finally said.

'Harper. You pushed me down the stairs. You could have killed me or at least broken my legs.' Vivian rolled up her pant leg. Her knee was pink and scraped. Swelling.

Lou knelt beside her, examining the damage. Blood trickled down his forehead. Damn. How had he hurt his forehead?

'You all right?' she asked Leslie, who hadn't said a word since they'd left the house. And whose skin looked oddly blue.

Leslie didn't open her mouth. She merely nodded.

'Let's go back inside.' Lou took Vivian's arm. 'Your mother needs to get off her feet.'

'Uh uh.' Harper blocked their path. 'Not till the bomb squad says it's okay.'

'The bomb squad?' Vivian seemed surprised. 'Ithaca has a bomb squad?'

'Seriously? You're making your mother stand here and freeze?'

'Has anyone called the police?' Leslie was coming back to life.

'Nobody would let me get my phone, remember?' Vivian shifted her weight from leg to leg, exhibiting her pain.

'I have a phone.' Leslie took it out and dialed.

Lou watched her, looked at the sky, chewed his lip. 'I seriously think we don't need to call any cops.'

'What?'

'Are you crazy?'

'Are you serious?'

All three women responded at once.

'Lou, my knees are killing.'

'Maybe those boys would let us wait in their fraternity—'

'No.' Harper wouldn't consider it. 'I saw them leave earlier. They aren't there.'

Vivian frowned, climbed onto the porch, sat on the bench swing with Lou beside her. Harper sat on the front steps while Leslie called to report a broken window and a bomb. When she hung up, she said, 'Oh my God, Harper. I have an appointment now. I have to go . . .'

'Can't you call and cancel?'

'No. Not for this guy. He needs to see me. But I'll come back. Right afterwards.' She started for her car. Holding her backside and limping.

'Are you hurt?'

Leslie grinned. 'Good thing I have so much padding. I bet I'll have some nice big bruises, but I'll be okay.' Suddenly, she stopped and rushed back to Harper, losing her grin. 'Oh my, Harper. We're so concerned about your mother's knees and my bottom. What about you? Are you all right? The baby?'

Harper hadn't had a chance to assess herself yet. But she nodded. 'We're fine. Both of us.'

'Lord. Someone threw a bomb through your window.' She stepped close, whispered in Harper's ear. 'After what you told me, Harper, I'd keep an eye on Lou. In fact, maybe you should come with me?'

'No, I'd better wait for the cops.'

Promising to be back as soon as she could, Leslie gave Harper a hug, hurried to her little BMW convertible, eased herself in and drove off.

Harper looked up the street, wondering what was taking the police so long. Then she turned toward the fraternity, saw the footprints leading out and back through the snow. The empty front porch. And suddenly, Harper was very cold.

Even with the parka on, Harper couldn't stop shivering. She closed her eyes, picturing what had almost happened. Her house in flames. Her flesh burned away. She'd seen what it looked like when bombs went off. Could hear men screaming, even now.

Vivian was talking to Lou. 'Who would do such a thing? And why? Can you believe it? And as if that wasn't bad enough, Harper decides to tackle me. And I mean tackle. She threw me down the steps—' She stopped, examining her knees. 'Oh, God. Look at this. I'm all scraped up – my knees are going to be purple.'

'You'll be fine, Ma. The police will be here any second.' Harper watched the street. 'I'm sure they'll bring an ambulance—'

'Oh for the love of Pete,' Lou grumbled. 'Nothing happened. A window broke.'

'Lou, someone threw a bomb into my house.' Harper crossed her arms, fuming.

'But it was a dud. Why the hell can't we just forget about it? Leave the police out of it.'

'Why are you trying to avoid the police, Lou?'

'Harper! How can you ask such a thing?' Vivian scolded. 'Good Lord, I could use a Scotch.'

Harper could, too. But unable to have one for several more months, she listened for sirens and thought about Lou. About why a bomb had been tossed into her dining room. About what would have happened if it had gone off.

Gazing at the fraternity, Harper had another idea. 'When did those boys leave, Ma?'

'What?'

'This morning. How long did those two guys stay after Leslie came over?'

'Oh, they left right away. Right after Lou wrapped up their cookies.'

'And did you see where they went?'

'No.' Vivian frowned. 'Why would I? What's your point?'

'Yeah, what are you getting at?' Lou leaned forward, elbows on his knees. 'Are you saying you think that they're the ones who threw the bomb? Why would you think that?'

Harper didn't know why. But suddenly, she suspected it. Wasn't it a big coincidence that they'd come over for the first time that morning and that, as soon as they'd left, a home-made explosive device had come crashing through the window? In fact, maybe they'd come over simply to see the layout of the house to decide where to throw it.

'No way.' Lou's growl was low. 'Why would they? Besides, those guys are too soft. They wouldn't get their hands dirty building a bomb. If they even knew how to go about it. Which they wouldn't. You think that's what they teach at a fancy place like Cornell? How to blow up houses?'

'You can get the recipe on the Internet.' Harper rubbed her hands, trying to warm up.

'They're not the type.'

'No? I think they are. I think those two are hiding some—'

'No,' Lou barked. 'You're getting it all wrong.' He stood up, faced Harper, then Vivian. 'The finger pointing at innocent people stops right now. Listen. I'm going to hurry up and tell you this before the cops get here. But what I say stays between us three.' He stopped. Cleared his throat. 'I'm sorry, Vivian.' He looked at the floor. 'I haven't been completely honest with you. I have a confession to make.'

Lou's eyes darted around as he told them about the unhappy former clients who'd been tracking him, threatening him because of some lost goods.

Harper didn't buy it. Not with the money and gun in Lou's room, his story about Ed Strunk skimming cash, and Rita's phone call warning of a hit. Besides, what kind of unhappy clients employed bombs instead of lawyers?

'My trucks haul all kinds of cargo. We take everything everywhere. Some cartons apparently got lost in transit.'

'Cartons.' Harper echoed. 'Weren't they insured?'

'Well, yes, but . . .' Again, Lou cleared his throat. 'We don't actually check the contents of shipments. They were insured for paper goods. But it turns out these guys were using my trucks to move cash—'

'Oh, Lou!' Vivian covered her mouth, swooning.

Harper watched her and stopped breathing; she'd seen that same swoon before. A memory surfaced: Her father's hands locked in cuffs, the police taking him away.

'Anyway, they blame me for their money going missing. Even though I had nothing to do with—'

'Bull. That's the money you said was Ed's? The money in your room?'

Lou gaped at her.

'What money?' Vivian did, too.

'That money. That money has nothing to do with this.'

Harper just looked at him.

'Harper!' Vivian scolded. 'Wait. Are you saying you snooped in—?'

'It's my house,' Harper said flatly. 'I have a right to know who and what is in it. Is that their money?'

'There are limits,' Vivian huffed. 'You had no right to pry.'

'Yes, I did have a right. And you should be glad I did, because that's how I got the telephone message—'

'Okay. Let's just forget it—'

'—about a hit on Ed Strunk. Coincidentally, just before someone threw a bomb into the house.'

'A hit?' Vivian gasped. 'On Ed Who?'

For a moment, there was silence. Vivian turned away, her eyes vacant and dull.

'It's okay, Vivian.' Lou knelt in front of her. 'I'll explain this later. But don't worry; I'll take care of it.'

Again, Harper pictured her father, his glib explanations.

Lou stood again, put his hands in his pockets. 'These clients are trying to scare me.'

'So, Ed Strunk.' Harper didn't let up. 'That's really you.'

Lou pressed his hands together as if in prayer. 'Okay. God's truth: I had to establish a new persona. It got ugly with these guys. Ed – it's who I used to be. I'm sorry, Vivian. I truly didn't mean for you to get mixed up in this. I thought it was over. I'd put it behind me. But – I don't know how. But they found me, and they've been circling the house, watching me. The bomb – it was just to let me know they know where I am.'

Harper thought of the black SUV cruising the neighborhood, scouting. She hadn't been imagining it after all.

'Anyway, they gave me a deadline of this morning—'

'This morning?' Vivian gasped.

'That's when they said I had to get them their money. But I negotiated with them.'

'You what? How? You've been with me.'

'At night, Viv. When you were sleeping. I had meetings.'

Vivian's eyes closed. She sat perfectly still. Sirens wailed in the distance.

'Anyhow.' Lou glanced out the window, into the hall again. 'I met their guy last night and explained how I couldn't meet their deadline because I don't have and never did have their frickin' money.'

'But you do have money—'

'That's not a half of what they're looking for. Anyhow, I convinced him to give me a few more days, but he said there would be consequences for being late.'

'Consequences? Like a frickin' bomb in my house?' Harper was ready to clock Lou. Her knuckles itched, aching for impact.

'Oh my God.' Vivian still didn't move. 'What have you done, Lou? What are we going to do?'

The sirens grew louder, closer.

'Vivian. Harper. Listen. This isn't your problem, either one of you. I'll take care of it. I swear. Don't worry. Look, I'll call a guy to replace the window. And I'll deal with my clients—'

'Exactly how are you going to take care of it if you don't have their money?' Harper didn't back down. 'What are you into, Lou? Or should I say "Ed"?'

'I told you. They gave me an extension—'

'And what happens when that extension runs out? What will they do next? Set my house on fire? Plant IEDs along the driveway? A minefield on the front lawn? Maybe they'll mail us some anthrax.' Harper's voice was rising. 'I can't allow this. I'm pregnant. I can't have you in my house, endangering my child. You're going to have to leave—'

'Harper?' Vivian began.

'No, Ma. It's final.'

'She's right, Vivian. Until this thing is resolved, I shouldn't be around you. Either of you. I'll go—'

'You're not going anywhere without me,' Vivian insisted. 'If you go, I go, too.'

That was fine with Harper.

'We can't leave Harper alone—'

'Yes, you can,' Harper offered. 'I'll be fine.'

'No. We'll stay until you can find someone else—'

'Seriously? You're a walking, breathing danger to me and my child, and the sooner you leave, the better.'

'Shh!' Lou looked into the hall, put a finger to his lips.

Police cars careened onto the street, sirens blaring.

'Look,' Lou whispered. 'Just don't tell anyone about this, okay?'

Vivian motioned that she was zipping her lips.

'No way.' Harper shook her head. 'We have to tell the cops . . .'

Lights flashing, the cars pulled into the driveway.

Harper stood to go meet them, but Lou grabbed her sleeve, meeting her eyes. 'I'll take care of it. I promise.' He squeezed her arm. 'Please don't tell them. Please.'

The technician wore protective clothing. His thick glove held up the bomb. 'This is why it didn't detonate, Detective.' He pointed to a loose wire. 'My guess is it detached during impact with the window. But it could have just been amateurish work. The device is as simple as they come. Whoever made it might not have attached the wires tight enough.'

Harper stood outside on the porch, straining to hear. Watching the specialists remove the bomb, observing their techniques. The war had taught her more than she wanted to know about improvised explosive devices. She'd known to run the instant she'd seen the phone taped to the pipe; the electric charge resulting from a call would have detonated the bomb. If not for a loose wire, she and her baby – and possibly her mother and Lou – might have been badly hurt, even dead. As the technician walked off with the bomb in a container, she went into the house, wrapped herself in her parka and sat shivering in the living room, remembering another bomb. She touched her damaged left leg, rubbed her scarred flesh. Pictured a boy whose face had been blown away. Realized she wasn't having a flashback, just a memory.

'Quite a tree.' Detective Rivers eyed the gaudy lopsided monstrosity.

Harper no longer noticed it. Now she looked at it anew. The thing was almost invisible beneath all the red and gold, silver and blue glittered balls, silver and gold tinsel, spray-on fake snow, and blocked off by a dozen huge boxes covered with baby wrapping.

'Your mother and her boyfriend are waiting with officers in separate rooms.' Rivers sat on the sofa, facing Harper. 'I want to talk to each of you separately.' She paused. 'First of all, are you okay? Do you need to see a doctor?'

'No. I'm fine. I have my regular appointment next week. I'm good until then.'

'So.' Rivers crossed her legs and sat back. 'What's the deal, Mrs Jennings? Lately, I'm here more than I'm in my own house.'

Harper took a breath. 'All I know is that thing came through the window. I saw the detonator and we ran.'

A pause. 'Let's go over the last few days. You called because you saw a naked man being assaulted. Then you called again because you thought you saw someone trespassing next door. Now this bomb.'

'So?'

'Do you think these events are in any way related?'

'Related?' Wait. Did Rivers suspect Evan and Sty had thrown the bomb? 'All I know is that this morning, Evan and Sty came over with some pastries.'

'Very suspicious behavior,' Rivers smiled. 'Were there any cream-filled?'

'No. But there are some left – would you like one?'

'No, no. Go on.'

'They said they had come over to look in on me after that big contraction. Like concerned neighbors. The bomb came in not long after they left.'

Rivers nodded, pursed her lips. 'Do you have any idea who would want to blow up your family or your house?'

Harper swallowed. She should repeat what Lou had admitted about his client's money. Should at least reveal that his name was really Ed Strunk. Again, she saw the blood rush from her mother's face, her father being led away by police. Heard Lou beg her not to say anything.

The fact was, she could verify none of what he'd said. Had no idea who – or even if – the 'clients' actually were, no independent knowledge of their relationship. And he had promised to leave.

'I don't, no.' It felt like a lie. In fact, it was a lie. Why was she lying for Lou/Ed who had endangered her home, her life and her child? Again, she saw her mother's drained expression. Her hopeless lost eyes.

'Maybe my house guests do.' There. She felt better. At least she'd pointed Rivers in the right direction. 'Oh – and I've seen an SUV driving around. Slowly. As if it's on surveillance.'

'Okay.' Rivers watched her, not moving. 'You look pale, Mrs Jennings. And given what's happened, I'd like to suggest that you and your family leave the house. Stay in a hotel for a few days.'

'You think they'll try again?'

'I don't know.' She paused. 'But just in case.'

Harper sat up straighter. Refused to retreat. No one was going to chase her out of her own home. 'We'll be fine here. Really.'

Rivers sat motionless. 'I think you should reconsider.'

Neither spoke for a while.

Harper didn't budge. 'Is there something else?' she asked.

Rivers tilted her head. 'Actually, I'm not sure. It's a hunch, really. And I'm debating whether to talk to you about it.'

Harper waited.

'Okay. I might as well. It's not about your bomb. It's about that boy who went missing. That kid from Elmira.'

Really?

'Turns out he was still here in Ithaca the night he disappeared. Staying at his girlfriend's. A couple of his buddies say he was in a pretty serious relationship, hardly ever came back to his own place.'

'Did you talk to his girlfriend?'

'Thing is, his friends claim they don't know her name. Neither had ever met her. And his parents say he never even mentioned having a girlfriend. We searched his apartment, but nothing there indicated who he was seeing.'

Harper was confused, not certain why the detective was telling her this.

'So here's the deal, Mrs Jennings. Sebastian was reportedly in Ithaca and disappeared the very same night you saw that assault out your window – that makes me wonder: What if that wasn't a coincidence? What if you were right, and that naked guy you saw fighting in the snow really was Sebastian Levering?'

'Detective, I've spent days wondering the same thing.' Unconsciously, Harper's hand wandered into her jacket pocket, toyed with the key she'd found in the woods.

'If it was Sebastian, then your second call to us might take on new significance. What if someone besides those two boys has been hiding out next door in the fraternity house?'

The questions rattled Harper's skull. 'You think he's in there? But Evan and Sty would have found him—' She stopped, mid-sentence. The house was big, had probably twenty or thirty bedrooms. If he were hiding, they might have no idea.

And if he were badly injured or dead, Sebastian would make no sounds.

Rivers misunderstood the silence. 'Right. It's far-fetched. But, even so, I can't reject the possibility. I spoke to the boys – Sty and Evan? They say they haven't seen or heard anything out of the ordinary there.'

Harper nodded. Fingered the key.

'And I don't know what to think about the girlfriend. Because if Sebastian had somebody here in Ithaca, where is she? Why hasn't she come forward? Is she involved in his disappearance?'

'Maybe she's missing, too,' Harper offered. 'Hell, maybe they eloped.'

Rivers rubbed her eyes, sighing. 'Maybe. But nobody's reported a missing woman. If she went with him, why hasn't anyone noticed her gone?' She started to get up. 'Sorry to trouble you with all of this, Mrs Jennings. You have your own crisis. Plus, you need to take it easy. I just thought you might have some insights.'

'Only this.' Harper pulled out the key. 'Remember? It was in the woods the day after the fight. You said it probably was nothing, but if it fits Sebastian's apartment, then—'

'Then we'll have evidence that he was the guy you saw.' Rivers smiled, taking it. 'It would be another piece of the puzzle. Good thinking. Thanks. I'll let you know.' She stood, getting ready to go. 'What? You look like there's more.'

Yes, there was. Lou, of course. But also, Evan and Sty. They bothered her. She had no evidence that they'd done anything wrong, nothing to indicate that they even knew Sebastian Levering. No reason to think that they'd ever tried blowing up anything but an air mattress. 'No,' she said. 'Nada.' And again, even though it was technically the truth, Harper felt as if she'd lied.

By the time Rivers was finished talking to Vivian and Lou, Leslie had returned. Harper introduced them, when she realized Leslie had been present earlier, Rivers took her into the living room to interview her. Lou, Vivian and Harper sat around the kitchen table.

'So.' Lou took a deep breath, folded his hands.

'So?' Harper's adrenalin rush had passed; suddenly, she was spent.

'So. What did you tell her?'

Oh. 'You can stop worrying. I told her what I knew for sure. Not what I'd been told by you.'

Vivian looked at Lou, who looked at Harper, his face a question. 'You didn't mention—'

'I said nothing about your clients or your fake identity or your stolen stash—'

'Harper. Keep it down.' Vivian looked around. 'She'll hear you.'

'You know what, Ma? If she hears, she hears. You two do what you want, but I'm not going to conspire with you to hide things from the police. You have a couple of days. That's it, and then I want you out, Lou.'

'A couple of days? Be realistic, Harper. That's Christmas.'

Harper rolled her eyes. 'Really? Okay. Then leave the day after.'

Vivian sniffed. 'I can't believe you're behaving this way, Harper. We came here to help you in your time of need, and you're completely ungrateful. Think about how this makes me feel – kicked out by my own daughter?'

'I'm not kicking you out, Ma.' Harper began to explain that the only one getting kicked out was Lou, but she stopped. Her mother would always find a way to feel like a victim.

'Bottom line, Harper. You didn't say anything that leads to me?'

'She already told you, Lou,' Vivian snapped. 'She didn't. She wouldn't do that.'

'And you, Viv? What did you say to her, just so I know?'

'Nothing.'

'You were with her half an hour. That's a long time to say nothing.'

'Okay, let me think.' Vivian thought, rubbed her forehead. 'You know, I really wish I'd never stopped smoking. I'd kill for a cigarette.'

'Vivian.' Lou leaned forward, pressing her. 'Tell me.'

'I told her I had no idea who threw that. Then she asked if I'd seen anything unusual around here lately. I didn't tell her about you going out at night. Or about your business with the money. All I said was that I'd seen a car driving around – you must have seen it. A black SUV?'

'You said that?' Lou sat back. 'But you didn't tell her the make?'

'I don't know the make. What's wrong? You didn't tell me not to tell her about any car—'

'Go on. What did she say?'

'About the car? She asked for details. Like the license, the model. I didn't know any of that.'

'But why did you even mention that car, Vivian?' Lou whined. 'For all you knew, it was a neighbor. Now she's going to have every cop in town out looking for black SUVs and, what with the holiday, there aren't many around.'

'Why would she, Lou? Just because I saw it driving around doesn't mean the bomb came from that car.' She paused, watching him pout. 'Why wasn't I supposed to mention it – is that your client's car?'

Lou drummed his fingers on the table, blinked rapidly at air.

'Oh, cut it out, Lou.' Harper headed for the refrigerator, deciding not to mention that she'd also told Rivers about the car. 'There are a ton of black SUVs. Nobody's going to pick that one out. Besides, you said you're working it out with them. So they can just stay the hell away.'

'I don't understand why you even mentioned it, is all.' He pouted at Vivian. 'I mean why would you even mention it?'

'I didn't know I wasn't supposed to – it just came out. Sorry, Lou. Really. I didn't know.' Vivian reached over, put her arms around Lou's neck, planting kisses all over his face.

Harper tried to ignore them, focusing instead on the leftover pastries from the morning, grabbing a piece of apple strudel, pouring a glass of milk. Chewing, she closed her eyes. They would leave in a few more days. Just a few more days.

Leslie stayed for a while after Detective Rivers left, making sure that Harper was relaxed. She was, in fact, beyond relaxed; her eyelids drooped and she almost dozed off in her chair while Lou and Vivian chattered on. Lou insisted that Leslie stay for cookies and coffee, apologizing for the scare that morning, asking about her bruises and scrapes, complaining about their own, raving about the boys next door and how thoughtful they'd been. Leaving Leslie and Harper no chance to talk privately.

The house, meantime, was freezing; cold air poured through the smashed dining room window, crept into the living room, the kitchen, the hall. As soon as Leslie left, Lou began sweeping up shards of glass and taped sheets of thick plastic to cover the ugly gaping hole. Harper didn't thank him; the damage was his fault. Cleaning up the mess was the least he could do. Still wearing her parka, she went upstairs to nap. Her head ached, her body felt swollen, and she missed Hank. Wanted him to come home. Didn't care, at that moment, about his career or his opportunities. Just wanted him there with her. Climbing under the comforter, she wondered what he'd have done about the bomb. How he'd have reacted to Lou and his shady, no doubt criminal dealings. She tried to picture it, but fell asleep almost immediately, questions still on her mind.

Two hours later, Harper woke up with a start, as if she'd just heard Hank's voice. Of course she hadn't; the voice had been a dream. But, popping out of bed, sitting at her computer wrapped in her parka, she wondered why she hadn't thought of Googling Ed Strunk days ago, when the package had first arrived.

\*   \*   \*

She didn't find Ed Strunk or Edmond Strunk. Or Edward Strunk. But she did find Edgar Louis Strunk. There were a bunch of articles, and photos of Ed, aka Lou. He was originally from Elizabeth, New Jersey, and owned a small trucking company, just as he'd said. But what he hadn't said was that he was wanted by the federal government for questioning regarding conspiracy in connection with mob activity. Harper pored through the stories, some of which mentioned Lou only in passing. And gradually, putting pieces together, she got a clear picture of the man who was dating her mother.

Ed Strunk was a bagman. Lou, the guy staying in her house, had been suspected of collecting gambling debts, loan sharking and drug money for a mob boss named Vincent Parks (aka Wally Parks, aka Vinnie Wallace) and transporting it for him across state lines, using his trucks and legitimate shipments as cover. The Feds had been about to arrest him in 2010, but he'd disappeared suddenly, and foul play was suspected.

Foul play? Harper clenched her jaw, considering it. After all, if authorities thought the man was already dead, what harm would there be in making them right? She stared at the computer, rereading random sentences, muscles braced to fight, until she couldn't hold back any more and stormed out of her room, bellowing, 'Lou!'

She found him in the living room beside the behemoth tree. Cuddling Vivian by the fireplace, sharing rum and egg-nog.

'A word, Lou.' She was panting, hands on her hips.

'Harper?' Vivian drawled. 'Good God. Again? What's the problem now?'

'This doesn't concern you, Ma. I'm talking to him.' She pointed an accusing finger.

Lou stood. 'What's on your—?'

'No, Lou.' Vivian grabbed his wrist. 'Sit back down. She can't just barge in here like that, with that attitude, pointing her finger. It's rude – it's bad enough what she did earlier, telling us to leave. As if we were vagrants.'

'It's all right, Vivian.' Lou patted her hand. 'I'll be right back.' He pecked her cheek, drained the egg-nog in his glass, and followed Harper into the dining room. 'What's up, Kiddo?'

Kiddo? Harper wheeled around and jabbed him in the chest. 'Don't play dumb, Edgar. I know the whole story about who you are and what you've done. I don't know what game you're playing with my mother, but how dare—'

'Hold on. Shh. Keep your voice down—'

'—bring mob money – stolen mob money – into this house. Are you insane?'

'Harper, I swear.' He glanced around, making sure Vivian wasn't there. 'I'm not playing games. That's not who I am any more. That's all behind me.'

'Behind you? Seriously? That's why they threw a bomb—'

'I already told you. It's taken care of – or almost. I got it all worked out . . .'

'You do?'

'I do.' Lou made the sign of the cross on his chest.

'Exactly how?'

'Fine. I'll tell you how,' he whispered. 'I'm giving them what they want. Their money. All of it. With interest.'

'With interest? And how are you going to do that, rob a bank?'

'I was thinking maybe a convenience store.' He tried to smile.

Harper glared until all traces of his grin had disappeared.

Lou drew a deep breath. 'Okay. I'll be honest – I don't have it all. I spent a chunk of it. Look, I had to; I was keeping a low profile and couldn't touch my assets. So I had to use some of it to live off. But—'

'Wait. You're saying you don't have the money?' She was ready to pummel him.

'Listen to me. That's what I'm trying to tell you.' He looked around again. 'I'm getting it – I got a guy who'll cover it.'

'What do you mean, "cover it"?'

'He's an old friend. We go way back; we were kids in Jersey. He's going to spot me the cash.'

'A loan.'

'Fine. A loan. Call it whatever—'

'So how will you pay him back? Or is he going to come after—?'

'Don't worry about that. This is legitimate. I'm signing an IOU.'

'Yeah? With what name this time?'

Lou put a hand on her shoulder; she yanked it off.

'Okay. I get that you don't like me, Harper.'

Like him? What? Harper stepped closer until her belly bumped him. He was almost a foot taller than she, but she looked up, piercing him with her eyes, snarling. 'Listen, asshole. Liking you isn't even on the radar. I don't even want to know you. And if it were up to me, my mother wouldn't either. She wouldn't bother to wipe her shoes with you – you're scum.'

Lou took a step back and looked away, wincing. Harper saw his chin quiver and, for a moment, regretted her words. Lord, was he really going to cry? She bit her lip, dreading it, but told herself that it didn't matter. What if he did? After all, he deserved far worse than tears for all the trouble he'd caused.

But Lou didn't cry. He rubbed his eyes and regrouped, not responding to her insults. 'You don't have to be mean, Harper.'

Mean? He thought she was mean?

He sniffed. 'You have my word. In a few days, it'll be all taken care of. Wally will be happy as pie. No more black SUVs patrolling the street. No more bombs or rats. And best of all, no reason to throw your mama out of the house.'

'I never said anything about my mama. It's you I'm throwing out.'

'Even still. There'll be no need.'

Harper didn't back down. 'Really? What about the government? I believe the Feds are looking for you, too.'

'The Feds?' He scoffed. 'Naw. They think Wally offed me a while ago. And anyway, they got nothing on me. They just wanted me to testify against Wally.'

'I bet they'd be thrilled to find out you're still breathing.' Harper ached to take him down. She pictured cold cocking him, his eyes rolling as he sank to the floor beneath the plastic covered window.

'Look. I get how you feel about me,' Lou whispered. 'But your mother. Honestly, she's the best thing that ever happened in my whole life. We're good together. I swear, Harper. Ed Strunk – he really is dead. She changed me. I'm a new man, living right. All I want is to spend the rest of my life making your mother the happiest woman alive.'

Harper opened her mouth to answer. Closed it. Saw no point.

'Give me a chance. Let me take care of business like I said. Let me make it right. I'm asking you, Harper. What else can I do? Should I get on my knees?' He did. He got down on his knees, folded his hands as if praying and looked at her with wide, sorry, sincere eyes. 'There. Look. I'm begging.'

Harper looked away. Then back at him. Then away. The man was shameless. Manipulative. Dishonest. Slippery.

'Please.' He kept at it. 'Not for me – I'm nobody. But for your mother.' His pleading eyes tugged at her.

Lord. Harper felt a flutter and held her belly; the baby was moving. Twirling?

'Lou?' Vivian called, again giving 'Lou' three-syllables. 'Where are you? You said you'd be right back.'

Lou didn't answer, didn't move. He just watched Harper. The baby distracted her. Was it doing cartwheels?

'I have to consider my baby,' she said flatly. 'You have until Christmas. Take care of your business. But if you can't by then, you need to go.'

He scrambled to his feet, threw his arms around her, pressed his mouth to her cheek. 'You won't be sorry. I swear. I said I'd take care of it and I will.'

'Lou?' Vivian gaped from the doorway. 'The fire's dying.' She furrowed her brows. 'What are you two up to?'

Lou danced over to her, snaked an arm around her waist and kissed her head. 'Spreading peace and good will, Viv. It's the season, after all. Isn't that what it's all about?'


Icy sleet was falling fast, collecting on tree branches, coating the streets. Driving was treacherous.

The armoire was beginning to smell.

'We've got to get that thing out of here. Can't we just stick it on the porch?'

'Absolutely not. If we leave it outside, we have no control over who has contact with it.'

'In this storm? Seriously, Sty. No one's going to come up and look at—'

'What about the Ninja Lady? Or that detective? Wouldn't they wonder why we'd put the armoire, an item we've supposedly just sold, outside where it might be damaged by the precipitation? We have to expect the unexpected. Be patient.'

Evan was itchy, couldn't stay still. Hives were forming on his arms and stomach. Nerves. He went into the living room, sprawled on an easy chair, bouncing his foot.

Sty sprayed air freshener around the foyer, adding artificial lavender to the pine forest scented candles he'd lit all over the first floor of the house. 'It's not that bad,' he scolded. 'Stop whimpering.'

'The plan was to dump the body right away.'

'Yes, Evan. It was.' Sty stopped spraying. 'But as you well know, unforeseen matters led to modifications of that plan. We can't very well go out driving in this weather.'

'So we're stuck here until the roads clear. Wonderful.' Evan pulled a baggie out of his hip pocket, began rolling a joint. 'By the way, isn't that what brought down your friend Loeb – unforeseen matters?'

'Please don't numb yourself with marijuana, Evan. We're going to need all our faculties.'

Evan took out his lighter. 'Not tonight. Nothing's happening tonight.'

Sty walked into the living room. 'You don't know that. You're a liability if you're stoned. And, to be clear, it wasn't careful and timely modification of their plan that brought them down; it was carelessness. Leopold dropped his one-of-a-kind designer glasses near the body at the dumpsite. Plain and simple carelessness.'

Evan lit up, inhaled, held the smoke in his lungs. Held the joint out to Sty.

'Damn it, Evan.' Sty slapped his hand away, sent the joint flying. 'I told you not to smoke.'

'Really?' Evan's eyes narrowed, nostrils flared. He jumped to his feet, shoving Sty, meeting him nose to nose, pushing him, backing him up. 'You really just smacked me?'

'Stop. Calm down.'

'No – no I won't calm down.' He shoved Sty against the wall, leaned into his face. 'I'm sick of hearing about your fucking idols, Leopold and Loeb. I'm sick of you acting like you're some goddamned superior infallible all-inspired Superhuman – and most of all, I'm sick of you telling me what I can and cannot do. Let me ask you: Who made you chairman of the board? Just answer that – who?'

'You're right.' Sty stood perfectly still. 'I have no excuse.'

'And you know what else? I'm sick of your rigid unbendable uncompromising thinking. The almighty Plan. Everything's got to be planned and thought out and predigested and analyzed. Nothing is spontaneous. Can't you just for once let go and enjoy yourself? Do something – anything – without dissecting all the possible ramifications first? Can't you ever take even a small fucking risk?'

'I didn't realize you felt this way, Evan. I suppose you're right. I should occasionally give in to my impulses,' Sty said softly. Looking into Evan's eyes, he raised his arms, set his hands fraternally on Evan's shoulders.

Evan began to settle down. He stepped away, and Sty lunged, knocking him backward, throwing him to the floor, pouncing on top of him, landing a fist in Evan's gut. Evan roared and fought back; the two rolled on the carpet, bumping furniture, punching and grunting, until, finally, Sty pinned both of Evan's arms back and pressed a knee into his throat. Evan writhed and kicked, but Sty's knee jabbed into his neck, cutting off his air, silently threatening to crush his larynx. Evan held still.

'How's that for acting on impulse?' Sty asked.

Evan looked away, lip bleeding, gasping. Nostrils flaring.

'Anything else on your mind?' Sty released him, and Evan lay panting, holding his stomach. 'No? Good.'

Sty sat, rubbed his sore jaw. After a few minutes, he picked up the joint, made sure it had gone out, pocketed it. 'Get cleaned up,' he got to his feet. 'We have some caroling to do.'

Lou had gone out 'to take care of things,' and Vivian sat with a bottle of wine, sulking in the living room beside the tree. Harper was in the kitchen, staring into the refrigerator, considering fixing a mayonnaise and raisin sandwich. Thought about what else to put in. She opened the cold cut drawer, pulled out sliced turkey.

Vivian must have moved to the family room; the television came on in there. Munchkins were singing their welcome song to Dorothy and her friends. That show ran every year around Christmas. Hank hated it, said it had given him nightmares as a child.

Hank. She slapped mayo and turkey onto wheat bread, thinking of him. He should call soon to say goodnight. Should she tell him that her mother and Lou were leaving? No. Better to save that until the last possible moment; he had enough problems with his injured ankle. And how bad was that ankle? Was it serious? Worse than he'd told her? She poured raisins, black olives, sliced bananas. Found some apricot jam. Pictured Hank in traction in a hospital bed; her chest tightened and the kitchen faded away . . . She was out in the backyard, seeing Hank fall, sliding off the roof, hitting his head . . .

'Harper.' Vivian tapped her shoulder, startling her. Gaping. 'What in God's name are you eating?'

Harper looked at her sandwich. She had no idea what was in it, but she took a bite, found it delicious. Waved a hand at her mother. 'I was hungry.'

But Vivian didn't leave. She looked over her shoulder into the hallway, as if expecting someone. Fluttered around, taking out coffee mugs. 'Did you know that one of those boys next door is a singer? He performs with an a cappella group.'

Harper watched her, aware now of voices. Not Munchkins from Oz. Deeper cheery voices, singing in harmony. And approaching the kitchen.

'Fa-la-la-la-la,' Sty beamed, spreading his arms with a final crescendo. 'La la la la.' His cheek was swollen. Or was it?

Evan sang along, looking pale, his lips puffy and scabbed, maybe cold sores?

'Harper – where's your cocoa?' Vivian searched the cabinets. 'Lou normally does this, but he's gone out,' she explained to the boys. 'I have no idea where anything is.'

Harper started to go get it, but Sty gestured that she shouldn't bother. 'No, no. Sit.' His voice was too loud. Booming. 'We came caroling, and your gracious mother invited us in for hot cocoa.'

'It's on the second shelf,' Harper pointed. And she made her way around Sty and Evan, down the hall to Hank's study, where she closed the door. And made a call.


'I'm fine,' Hank answered on the first ring. He sounded groggy, as if she'd awakened him. Why would he be sleeping so early? It wasn't even dinner time. But his voice relaxed her. She wanted to wrap it around her like a shawl.

'You? Okay?'

No. Not even a little bit. 'Of course. Fine.' Her eyes filled; she smeared the tears away, refusing to allow them.

'Called why? Not wait for me later?'

'I don't know. It's just. We're having an ice storm. I'm lonely. And a little claustrophobic.' She didn't mention that she was evicting her mother and Lou. Or that Rivers had talked with her about the missing kid. Or that some fraternity boys were currently raiding the kitchen.

'Tight. Quarters with Vivian.'

If only he knew how tight. 'I miss you.' Damn. She wiped her eyes again. When had she become such a sap?

She could hear the smile in his voice. 'I miss you. Too. Hoppa.' His words were private and throaty. Sexy. She pictured his bear-like shoulders, his solid warm chest. Could almost feel the scratch of his stubbly cheeks on her face. 'Won't be. Much. Away. Longer.'

She didn't say anything. Couldn't trust her voice.

'Baby?'

Her hand rested on her stomach, told him about the baby's somersaults and cartwheels. Hank asked if she was resting enough, having contractions, working on her dissertation. The same questions he asked every night. Harper gave the same answers. And then, when they'd finished with those, there was silence. Two people, breathing into the phone.

'So,' she tried to sound casual. 'How's your ankle?'

'Oh. Will be. Fine.'

Will be? So it wasn't yet?

'Told you. Doctor said. Will be fine.'

'Harper?' Vivian knocked on the study door.

Harper clenched her jaw, closed her eyes. Couldn't her mother let her have three minutes to herself?

'Don't. Worry. Fine, Hoppa.'

The door opened and Vivian announced, 'Your cocoa's getting cold.'

Harper turned away, huddling over the phone, whispering for another few moments. After the call, she stayed in Hank's study, sitting in his easy chair, watching the shadows of his lamp and his desk. Feeling his absence. Oh, tough it up, she scolded herself. Stop being pathetic. Hank's fine, you're fine, the baby's fine. And this separation is only for a few piddling weeks. It's nothing. Get over it.

'Are you coming?'

Harper whirled around; Vivian was still waiting at the door, regarding her icily. Indignantly. Unforgivingly. Harper looked away, rubbing her eyes as if she were sleepy. As if she weren't a sorry weakling, wiping away tears.


Dinner time approached with no sign of Lou. And no sign of Sty or Evan's departure. They sat with Harper and Vivian around the kitchen table, their cocoa mugs and the plate of cookies long since emptied.

'Don't you guys have to be somewhere?' Harper finished off a bag of cheese doodles, wondering if pizza places were delivering with all the ice on the roads.

'Not anywhere to which we can get. Evan's performance got canceled.'

'Aren't you going home for the holidays?' Harper wondered.

'We were both supposed to leave in the morning.' Sty looked at Evan. 'But the weather might make us revise our plans. We still have a few days, but Evan's nervous about getting home in time for Christmas, aren't you, Evan?'

'They're sure to salt the roads.' Vivian wrung her hands. 'I mean, aren't they?'

'Sooner or later. Evan and I are counting on that.' Sty smiled, crossed his legs.

'I hope they do it soon. Lou's out driving in this.'

'He'd call if he had a problem, Ma.' Unless, of course, the mob had snuffed him.

Vivian met her eyes, and Harper saw her mother's alarm. They both knew where Lou was; presumably, he was out meeting the guy who was going to loan him money so he could pay back the mob guy who'd taken a hit out on him. Vivian had reason to worry, and not just about slippery roads. But Harper couldn't think about that right then; the only thing on her mind was food. Hungry yet again, she went to the kitchen counter, opened the drawer with the take-out menus. Rifled through them until she found one for Napoli's pizza.

'Why don't you call him?' Sty suggested.

'He told me not to. He doesn't want interruptions while he's doing business.'

'Business? Today? In this storm?'

Vivian nodded, chewing her lip.

'What kind of business is he in?' Evan ignored Sty's scowl.

Vivian looked at Harper, who was studying the list of optional toppings and hadn't even heard the question.

'Well. He does a few different things.' Vivian stood, began collecting empty cocoa mugs. 'This is a finance deal, I think.'

Sty glared at Evan who sneered back.

Harper picked up her phone, punched in the number. Decided to be cordial. 'Anyone else want pizza?' The call was ringing.

'You're ordering pizza?' Vivian fretted. 'What about Lou?'

'Ma. We don't know when he's coming back. I'm not waiting.'

'But he should be back any time now. He bought food.'

'So? Wait if you want. But I'm not, and Lou's not here to cook his food—'

'No problem. We'll cook it,' Sty stood, rubbing his hands together.

'Napoli's.' The guy had a Brooklyn accent. 'Hold a sec.'

'Seriously. Nobody's delivering pizza on these icy roads.' Sty raised his eyebrows, waiting for approval. 'And Evan and I are quite accomplished in the kitchen. It would be our pleasure.'

'No, really.' Harper shook her head. It was time for the boys to go. 'It's okay.'

'Why that's lovely of you,' Vivian spoke at the same time. 'Lou went to the supermarket yesterday.' She opened the refrigerator, gesturing for them to join her. As Harper waited on hold, her countertops filled with chicken breasts, fresh garlic, baking potatoes, olive oil, lettuce, walnuts, apples, cheese, and she gave up, disconnecting the call. Soon, the kitchen smelled of sautéing garlic. Dishes clattered and commotion reigned, and, despite the tantalizing aromas and her mounting appetite, she once again marveled that she had nothing to say about what happened in her own home.

About halfway into the meal, Harper stopped chewing long enough to tune into the conversation. It took a few more minutes for her to realize that Vivian had begun pointedly to ignore her. Not speak to her unless it was absolutely necessary. Not even look at her except with disdain. When she asked her mother to pass the rolls and Vivian ignored her, even Evan noticed it.

'Here, I'll get them.' He reached across Vivian to get the basket, glancing from mother to daughter with caution.

'So,' Sty tried to stimulate conversation. 'The storm seems to be letting up.' He nodded at the sliding doors to the deck.

'Maybe Lou will make it back soon.' Vivian knitted her eyebrows. Her food was almost untouched, but she'd emptied most of a bottle of wine. 'I thought he'd be back by dinner.'

'He's probably being cautious.' Sty sprinkled pepper on his potato. 'In these conditions, he's probably moving slowly. Did he go far?'

'He's fine, Ma.' Harper's tone was flat and final. She slathered butter on a sourdough roll. 'Stop worrying.'

Vivian turned to Sty as if Harper hadn't spoken. 'What have you boys been doing for fun now that it's winter break?'

Evan cleared his throat.

'Not much. I'm pretty boring, I'm afraid,' Sty said. 'But Evan's been busy with his singing group, doing community performances.'

'Really?' Clearly, Vivian wasn't listening. Her mind was elsewhere, with Lou.

'Retirement homes, hospitals, malls. Places like that.' Evan swallowed wine.

Vivian stared into the air, not touching her food. Not responding.

'How nice.' Harper answered for her.

Evan smiled awkwardly.

'In fact,' Sty served himself salad, 'a few nights ago, when Evan returned from a performance, he found you and the police combing the woods under boom lights. It appeared to be quite a circus, right, Evan?'

Evan looked at his baked potato.

Harper stopped chewing. 'Were you both there?'

'Oh, no.' Sty glanced at Evan. 'I was out, at a social engagement. But Evan told me about all the commotion. What exactly were you looking for? Detective Rivers mentioned an assault?'

'I saw a fight.' Harper watched his reaction. Sty was looking at Evan with a faint smirk. As if he were taunting him.

'A fight? Because we – well, Evan and I – obviously, we've talked about it. And we've come up with a theory. Tell them, Evan. Or should I?'

Evan shrugged sullenly. Licked his sore lip. Refilled his wine glass.

'Our theory was – oh, wait. Have you been following the news? Because our theory involves a recent news story. Coincidentally, a young man went missing – what was his name again, Evan?'

Evan glowered, didn't answer.

'Sebastian Levering,' Harper said.

'Yes. That's it. So you're aware of the story? Well, are you also aware that he was last seen on the very same night that you summoned the police here? So here's our theory: We think that there's a connection between his disappearance and whatever you witnessed in that patch of woods out back.' He put his fork down and leaned over his plate. 'We think that you might even have actually witnessed his abduction.' He looked at Harper, waiting for her to respond.

Harper dabbed her mouth with her napkin, concealing her expression. She had the distinct sense that Sty was playing with her. Or maybe with Evan. Either way, he was clearly amusing himself with this conversation. And with this topic.

'Well?' He grinned. 'What do you think? Is our theory credible?'

Harper swallowed chicken. 'I have no idea. I saw a fight, that's all.'

'But couldn't Sebastian Whatever-his-name-was – couldn't he have been involved in the fight?'

'Good God, Sty. How would she know?' Evan squeezed the stem of his glass. 'If she'd seen that kid, she'd have told the police, wouldn't she?'

'That's precisely what I'm asking.'

'You're asking her what she told the police?' Evan's jaw tensed.

'Like I said, I told them I saw a couple of guys fighting.' Harper tried to sound light. 'But the police didn't find anything, so they assumed it was just some kids messing around, drinking too much.' Well, they assumed that at first, anyway. She thought of the key she'd given Rivers, wondered if it would unlock Sebastian Levering's door.

Evan and Sty were still silently watching each other. Exchanging ugly glares.

'What, Evan? You look upset. You've told me that I should be more spontaneous. So I'm trying; I'm making spontaneous conversation. I thought you'd be pleased, but apparently, I've offended you.'

What was he talking about? Spontaneous conversation? Maybe Evan was tired of Sty constantly dominating the conversation. Or maybe it was something else – something to do with the topic of Sebastian Levering. Again, Harper pictured the fight, the naked guy struggling in the cold, being dragged off into the woods. Maybe it really had been Sebastian. Maybe the key would fit his door.

Maybe Evan or Sty had been involved.

Sty sipped wine. 'Well, it's just a theory. Actually, they'll probably find that young man alive and well very soon. Disappearances like his aren't uncommon. Thousands of people go missing every year; most turn up unharmed on their own. In fact, statistically speaking, he probably simply ran away.'

They sat quietly for a few minutes, eating. Except Vivian. She hadn't eaten a bite, hadn't said a word, wasn't paying attention to the conversation. She drank wine, checked the clock, kept sighing and fidgeting.

'Dinner was delicious,' Harper felt the need to speak, compensating for her mother's silence. 'How did you guys learn to—?'

'Oh – shh! Listen!' Vivian sat straight. 'Is that a car? Is it Lou?' She bolted out of her chair, flew to the window.

Harper followed. Outside, a truck lumbered up the street, plowing and spreading salt. No sign of Lou.

'He's all right, Ma. Relax. He'll be back soon.'

Vivian's only response was the quiver of an eyebrow.

Harper went back to the table and, with the boys, began clearing plates. But, shoulders sagging, Vivian stayed at the window, watching the street.

Evan was on his second shot. The bar of the Pixel Lounge in Collegetown wasn't crowded, only a few lonely losers who had no place to go for Christmas week. It had taken him the better part of an hour to walk there, but he'd refused to go back inside the fraternity. Not just because of the room freshener smell. Mostly because, if he had to spend another minute with Sty, he'd kill him. The thought of Sty, their fight and his smugness afterwards, his arrogance – and that taunting conversation at dinner – as if daring the motorcycle chick to put it together. Evan gulped his whiskey and ordered another. His stomach churned, his chest burned – his fingers tightened, aching to dig into Sty's throat.

Sty. Evan had him figured out: Sty needed to feel that he was in control. It was that simple. He was all about being in charge. And now that Evan was rebelling, he was beginning to come apart. Like that conversation at dinner about the kid and their so-called frickin' theory? Suggesting to the motorcycle chick that she might have witnessed the kid's abduction? What the hell was he doing? What happened to being careful and not deviating from his all holy Plan?

No. Evan was done. Finished. Walking away. Literally. After dinner, he'd kept walking, gone right past the fraternity. And Sty had been frantic.

'I'll spray more air freshener. Besides, you're up on the third floor; you won't smell a thing.'

Evan kept moving down the street.

'Where are you going? It's a skating rink out here; you'll fall on your ass. Come on, Evan. Come back.'

But he hadn't gone back. No way was he going to obey Sty. He'd slipped and slid all the way across campus to Collegetown, deciding that he was done, finished. He would help Sty dump the kid, simply for the sake of self-preservation. But then, to hell with him.

Maybe he'd kill him. He stared at the warm glow of bottles behind the bar. Thinking about sneaking into Sty's bedroom, slitting his throat. Watching his eyes open in surprise.

'It looks like some kind of fairy land out there, doesn't it?' The guy slid onto a stool beside him, even though there were plenty of empty ones. Invading his space. He ordered a beer. Put a twenty on the bar.

'Glad I have my Jeep,' he told Evan. 'It can take the ice. Otherwise, I'd be holed up down by the lake. Man, I had to get out of there. Cabin fever.'

'Trust me. I know what you mean,' Evan nodded. 'This whole week, I've felt like the last guy on earth, all alone in a fraternity house.'

'Yeah?' He shook his head, pulled his jacket off. 'So you know what I'm talking about. It gets weird being alone in the dark and cold – I lost power. Ice must have pulled the wires down. So I can't even watch the tube. Shit, I can't even see where I am.'

'Well, no worries, man. You made it here. Let me buy you a drink.' Evan patted the guy on the back. Looked him over. He wasn't skinny like the first kid, but he wasn't exactly a lumberjack, either. No question: With the element of surprise on his side, he could take him. Besides, he was experienced now. Knew how to avoid mistakes.

Evan smiled, asked the guy why he was still in town. Found out his room-mate was away until next semester; his parents newly divorced and, to avoid choosing between them, he wasn't going to see either of them.

So no one would be looking for him for a while.

Evan told him he'd lost both his parents in a car accident. That going home wasn't an option. They stared at the bottles together. Evan ordered shots.

He pictured Sty, the look on his face when he'd find out what Evan was doing. Evan almost laughed out loud, imagining it. No question, this move would shift the balance of power, would teach Sty a lesson so that, maybe, he wouldn't have to get his throat slit.

The guy's name was Steve. Evan figured he was about 5' 9", weighed about 160. He was kind of scruffy, hadn't shaved lately. Other than that, he'd make a perfect Christmas gift.

Ice coated the sidewalks and street, the snow on the ground. It glazed the trees, making their branches crystalline. It hung from eaves, coated parked cars. Under the streetlights, it made the night glisten.

Harper gazed at the ice from her bedroom, its beauty lost on her. Its only effect on her was to make her feel even more imprisoned. She longed to escape, take off on her Ninja, roar through the streets, feel wind slapping her face. 'Not for a while.' She patted her tummy, reminding herself that she wasn't alone, not the only one imprisoned. In fact, the baby had it worse, had no diversions. No television, no phone.

'It looks like fairyland out there,' she told it. Slumping against the pillows, she turned on the television. Thought of Lou, wondered if he was driving around on slippery streets. He had finally called and talked with Vivian for a long time. Afterwards, Vivian had seemed calmer, but still wouldn't talk to Harper. Wouldn't even say where Lou was or when he'd be back.

'Is he okay, Ma?' Harper had asked.

Vivian had turned her back. 'What's it to you?'

Harper had refused to argue. 'Is he on his way home?'

'All you need to know is that Lou has taken care of business, just as he promised. He has the money to pay back his client, so you won't be inconvenienced any more.' With that, Vivian had retired to the guest room, leaving Harper without as much as a goodnight. Punishing her.

Harper refused to feel guilty. What did her mother expect – that she would welcome a criminal into her home, even with bombs flying and hit men after him? No. The man had lied to her – even about his name. He had hidden a gun in her house. The list of offenses went on and on. She had no reason to feel the slightest bit of guilt.

So why did it bother her that Vivian wouldn't speak to her?

Stop it, she ordered herself. You're taking a stand. Defending your home and unborn child. Setting standards. It's Vivian, not you, who's in the wrong.

She looked at the television, then out the window. Felt rotten. Despite everything, Vivian was her mother, her blood. Right or wrong, they should at least be on speaking terms.

Except that she wasn't the one not speaking to the other. Didn't she have to draw a line? Was it wrong to insist that Vivian respect her – or at least not endanger her?

Right or wrong didn't matter; Vivian would never understand those subtleties. Couldn't see beyond her own needs.

Even so.

Harper's mental argument went on. At one point, she got out of bed, walked down the hall to the guest room, even raised her hand to knock. But she froze, unable to bring her knuckles to the door. She stood there for a moment, then returned to her room, got in bed and stared sleeplessly at the television or the stack of dissertation materials – the papers and books piled up beside her computer.

At some point, she dozed off, television still on. So the sounds of tires cracking ice and a car engine didn't rouse her at first. But when a car door slammed shut, she opened her eyes, sat up and looked outside. Lou was back.

'You're still up?' He closed the front door. 'Where's your mother?'

'In bed.' Harper sat on the stairs. 'She was worried about you, driving in this.'

He nodded, smiling. 'I talked to her. She didn't need to worry. I'm all right.' He set a duffel bag on the floor, unbuttoned his coat. Moved lightly, almost dancing, to the closet. 'Well, you can relax now, Harper. My old pal Ritchie loaned me the money so I can pay Wally back in full, with interest and a margin for error. All I got to do is let Wally know so he'll lay off us. Maybe you and your mother will make up and we can stay the way we planned. Everything's gonna be fine.'

He looked up the steps past Harper, then at the satchel. 'You know what? I think I'll do that right now.'

Now? It was one in the morning. But Lou didn't seem to care. He took out his phone, placed a call. Walked into the living room to talk privately, but his voice got louder, less cheerful. 'Really? Well, you tell him he's not getting a red fucking nickel unless he backs off.' Silence for a moment, as he listened. 'Bullshit, Rita. You tell him this: tell him what goes around comes around.'

Harper eased down the steps, listening.

'He crossed a line with that bomb . . . You don't? Well, you do now. He had a damned bomb thrown in the house . . .' Another pause. 'Warning? I didn't need a warning. I already was getting his money – he had my word. Really. Well, neither is his mother's. Guess what – you tell him this: He messes any more with my girl or her family, he better put his affairs in order. You bet I mean it. He's not the only one with connections. I got his money. So tell him to lay off. Whenever he wants. Fine.'

Lou dropped the phone into his pocket and turned around, cursed when he saw Harper at the door.

'You shouldn't ease drop.'

Ease drop?

Grumbling, Lou walked past her to the plastic-covered window. 'You could get in trouble.' He moved a curtain and peered out of an undamaged pane.

'What just happened, Lou?'

'Nothing. Everything's fine.' He looked up the street and down before stepping away.

'Bullshit. Who were you talking to? Was it Rita, that woman who called?'

Lou licked his lips, avoided Harper's eyes. 'She's an old friend. Wally and her – they're off again on again. She says Wally won't take the hit off me until he's got the money in his hands. After that, he says he'll back off and leave you and Vivian alone. And maybe – get this – *maybe* he'll even let me live. Asshole. As if he's some big-time Al Capone. Needs to get his balls kicked.'

Lou grumbled and paced. Despite her anger, Harper felt sorry for him. No matter how utterly stupid and irresponsible he'd been, he was trying to make things right.

'So how do you get him the money?'

'I just asked Rita to make an appointment. I don't think he'll bother us until then. But with Wally, you never know. Wally messes with people just to show he can.'

Great. Harper's chest tightened and her eyes darted around, half expecting a missile to come flying through another window. What was she supposed to do until Lou paid the guy? Be on permanent guard duty? Play watchdog? She closed her eyes, reminding herself that he and her mother would be gone in four – wait, it was after midnight – in just three more days. Right after Christmas.

Lou stood slouched and dejected, staring at the satchel.

'Did you eat?' Harper didn't know what else to say. 'Want a sandwich or something?'

He shook his head, lifted the bag and headed up the steps. 'It's been a long day. I'm just gonna go to bed.'

Harper started to follow him upstairs, then reconsidered. She was wide awake now, listening for hit men. Hyper alert. And, as long as she was near the kitchen, a sandwich seemed like a good idea.

Sty was snoring on a sofa in the sitting room.

'I thought you said the place was empty.' Steve looked up at the domed ceiling of the foyer, nodded toward Sty.

'Officially.' Evan turned up the light on the chandelier. 'That's just my buddy. So what will it be? Beer? Whiskey?'

'Whoa, what's that smell?' Steve scrunched his nose. Went straight to the armoire.

Damn. Could he smell the kid? Or was it the air freshener?

'What is this thing?' He knocked on it, looked it over, up and down.

'It's nothing. We're selling some old furniture.' Evan stepped over, preventing him from opening the armoire door. The guy was out of line, asking too many questions. 'Come on in here.' He led him into the sitting room, wandered over to the fireplace, as if to start a fire. 'Have a seat.'

Steve didn't sit. He wandered around the room, looking at portraits, bookshelves. Took a volume down. '*O'Henry*.' He opened it, leafed through.

Evan was losing patience. This guy wasn't cooperating, didn't seem interested in drinking. And how could Evan slip him a rufie if he wasn't drinking? 'So what can I get you?'

'You know what? I'm actually kind of wiped. Thanks, but I think I'm just going to take off.' He replaced the book.

He's just going to what? Evan casually picked up a poker, stoked the dying fire. 'No, really? Let me at least show you around the house. It has fascinating architecture.'

Sty snorted, coughed, turned over.

Steve glanced at him. 'Maybe another time.'

Evan's hand tightened around the poker. Damn. He couldn't let him just walk out – he'd pictured the whole thing. What he was going to do, how it would feel. How he would try things, taking his time. 'Well, suit yourself. Thanks again for the ride.'

'No problem. With roads this bad, you'd have had a hard time finding a cab.' He moved toward the foyer.

Evan crossed the sitting room in three long strides. When he was behind the guy, he pulled his arm back, raised the poker and swung.

The impact sounded like the splitting of a coconut shell. The guy's knees folded, his arms didn't even move; he went straight down with a thud. Evan checked his pulse. Couldn't tell, wasn't sure. But he chortled as he pulled up the guy's jacket, covering the wound and containing the blood, and his chest almost burst with laughter as he dragged him back into the sitting room, depositing him at Sty's feet.

Vivian was asleep with the lamp on, sitting up in the bed, her head tilted to the side, a half-empty glass of whiskey on the nightstand. She'd been waiting up for him. Careful not to wake her, Lou put the duffel bag on the top shelf of the closet, got undressed noiselessly. Started for the bathroom, stopped and looked back at the closet, reconsidered the bag's location, went back and moved it to the floor, behind the laundry basket. He stood at the closet a while, looking, considering whether to move it again or not. Finally, he got ready for bed.

But once he was in bed, he didn't sleep. Couldn't settle his mind. Couldn't rid it of Wally, that asshole. How he was going to make him back off and leave them alone. It wouldn't be easy. After all, he'd wounded Wally's ego, getting the better of him, and Wally couldn't stand that. Might want to make an example out of him, show the world how nobody should mess with him. Even when he got the money back, even when he got paid interest, he wouldn't be satisfied. He'd want to get even. Because for Wally, it wasn't just a matter of money; it was a matter of pride.

And that wasn't all. There was also the matter of Ritchie. Ritchie was good people, for a dealer. He'd come up with the loan pronto, no questions asked. But now Lou had a new problem: How was he going to repay Ritchie? He wasn't working for Wally any more, wasn't earning. So, borrowing from Ritchie didn't solve anything. All it did was buy some time. Truth was, he was replacing one problem with another. No, not even replacing – adding. Piling one problem on top of another. Making a skyscraper, a mountain of trouble. And it might all come crashing down.

Beside him, Vivian was snoring, her mouth open a crack. Sleeping like a baby. She looked younger when she slept. Smelled like flowers. Lou lay beside her, eyes closed, the covers pulled over his head, wide awake.

Sty was not amused. 'What the . . .?' He sat up, gaping at the guy on the floor. 'Who the hell's that?'

'That is Steve.' Evan sat on the arm of the sofa, striking a casual pose.

Sty's mouth hung open. Not fully awake.

'Surprise, Sty. He's our next project.'

'What? He's who?' Sty sputtered, got to his feet. 'Good God, Evan. What the hell have you done?'

Evan pouted, feigned hurt feelings. 'I brought you an early Christmas present. I thought you'd like it.'

Sty knelt beside the body, felt for a pulse. Moved the jacket aside to look at Steve's head. 'What did you do? His head is smashed in – he's dead.'

Dead? Really? Damn. 'He can't be – I just smacked him once—'

'Well, you killed him.' Sty checked Steve's throat again. 'No pulse. He's gone.'

'Shit.' It didn't seem possible. It hadn't felt like he'd been killing someone. The guy hadn't even seen it coming. Hadn't registered Evan's power. Just poof, crack – it had been over. Like hitting a damned baseball. No chance to savor it. Zero satisfaction.

'What were you thinking, Evan? This is completely—'

'I was thinking that we should move on. I saw an opportunity—'

'So you just brought someone here and killed him? What's wrong with you? We agreed to think things through. To follow our plan—'

'To hell with your plans, Sty. At the risk of getting into fisticuffs again, let me just say that I'm sick of being limited by you and your constant planning and thinking. The whole point is to act. To do it. To experience the kill—'

'And to fry? Because that's what will happen without careful thinking and planning.'

Evan stood, walked across the room, glared out the window.

'Look, we can't keep bickering. We have to work as a team.'

'A team?' Evan sneered. 'What does that mean? That you decide everything? You decide what to do and when to do it?'

Sty crossed his arms, fuming. 'Of course not.'

'You decide to model your life after your heroes Leopold and Loeb. You decide we live to correct their mistakes. Oh, and you suddenly decide to deviate from your own plan and theorize with neighbors about the fate of our first victim? Well, for once, Sty, I decided something. I selected a specimen on my own, impulsively, without a plan and without Your Grace's permission—'

'Did you also decide to crack his skull open?'

Evan shrugged. 'Accidents happen.'

'That's my point. We can't afford accidents. We can't risk having things "just happen". We need to control our actions.'

'We can't fucking control every aspect—'

'Yes, we can. We have to.' He went to the window, put a hand on Evan's shoulder. 'Okay. The guy's dead. No point arguing over it.' He met Evan's eyes, didn't release his shoulder until he felt the tension ease. Then he turned away, watched the body. 'We now have two bodies to dispose of. Think back, Evan. Did anyone see you two together?'

'Just at the bar. You know, drinking.'

Sty kept asking questions: How had Evan gotten home? Had anyone seen him leaving with the guy? Where was the car now? On and on.

Finally, Sty stopped interrogating. He walked around the room, regarding the body. Then to the front of the house, peering out the window at the Jeep in the drive.

'The roads are awfully bad tonight.' He pulled his coat off the sofa, put it on and stood by the dead guy's feet. 'It would be a terrible tragedy if a car slid off the road and slammed into a tree.'

'Sty.' Evan shook his head. 'You want to go out tonight?'

'It makes sense: the guy's been drinking and his car skids out of control.' He smirked, shaking his head. 'At the risk of offending you by telling you what to do: Get your damned coat on. We're taking your drinking buddy for a ride.'

Icy tree branches sparkled in the moonlight. Harper gazed out the kitchen window, washing her plate, still chewing the last of her peanut butter sandwich. The baby was fluttering.

'What are you doing in there, a spin cycle?' She dried her hands. 'It's time for bed. Settle down.'

But Harper wasn't ready to go to bed either. Her senses were on high alert, the way they'd been in Iraq. She watched the street for a black SUV, listened for sounds of crunching ice. She felt danger as definitely as she felt the baby's movements, as concretely as she felt the dish towel in her hands. It was nearby, closing in, but she couldn't see it yet. She braced for it, just the same.

Harper reached into a cabinet, took out a package of chocolate chips. Opened it, started munching, thought about her conversation with Lou again. He'd tried to convince her that he had his problems under control, but she wasn't at all convinced, kept replaying what he'd said, one sentence in particular: 'Wally messes with people just to show he can.'

Wally had already messed with her once. What if he wasn't satisfied with Lou's offer of cash? What would he do next? Harper sat vigilant, a soldier on guard duty. Wally, whoever he was, had underestimated her. He'd surprised her last time; this time, she'd been forewarned.

Not that she knew what she'd do, exactly, to defend against an unseen cowardly drive-by assault. But if he dared to send an actual person, that person would regret it. She'd been trained, knew how to defend her home—

Harper lost the thought in the middle. Someone was outside. She got up, peered through the window, saw a figure on the porch of the fraternity. Sty? He disappeared inside for a moment, but came out again, backwards this time. Carrying – a person's legs? Yes, with Evan following, carrying the other end, holding him under the arms.

Harper stared, disbelieving. Watching them carry a man to the Jeep parked in their driveway. Loading him into the passenger's side. The guy was limp – had he had too much to drink and passed out?

Or was he dead?

Harper recalled their dinner conversation about Sebastian Levering. Sty's interest in the topic – had it been too avid? Had he been testing to see what she knew, what she'd seen? She thought about the moving curtain, the light flashing from an upstairs bedroom next door. The fight she'd seen in the snow. She should call Rivers.

Then again, they could just be driving a fraternity brother home, and Rivers was already tired of her calls.

Evan climbed into the back seat; Sty started the engine and the Jeep pulled away. And a heartbeat later, figuring she'd just be gone a minute, Harper was into her boots and parka, on her way to the fraternity house.

The door was wide open, the chandelier turned on in the foyer. Harper's left leg throbbed with exertion; she'd dug her heels into the ice with each step as she'd walked over. But, looking over her shoulder, making sure no one was around, she climbed the steps to the fraternity house, dried her boots off on the mat and went inside.

Immediately, the odor triggered a reaction. She saw a faceless boy in the street, flies swarming around a lifeless insurgent. A blown-off foot beside the road. No mistake: death was there, in the house. Or it had been. Evan and Sty might have driven it away in the Jeep.

Then again, they might have been carrying a drunk friend to his car. And the smell could have been from a dead squirrel or raccoon inside the walls, might have nothing to do with the boys.

Except that Harper's instincts told her otherwise. She sensed danger and brutality there, at that moment, as clearly as she could smell the reek of death. Someone had been killed there. Violently. Recently.

She stepped away from the door, her back to the wall, careful to make no sound. The house seemed empty, but she couldn't be sure. The bulky armoire still stood awkwardly in the foyer. Harper gazed past it up the staircase, saw darkness and dim night lights. She peered into the sitting room, noticed embers dying in the fireplace. Stepped inside, found an open Scotch bottle, a glass. And, on the Oriental near the doorway, a poker.

A poker? She stooped, looked at it more closely. Saw something clumped on its tip. Blood? Not just blood. Some hair, still attached to a patch of skin.

Harper stopped breathing. In the distance, guns fired; men shouted. She smelled burning rubber, felt the itch of swirling flies and clinging sand. A car sped up to a checkpoint, and then a flash of light—

No. She strained to resist the flashback, biting hard on her lip. She couldn't afford a flashback now, had to get her phone and call Rivers, had to tell her about the poker. About the body she'd seen Evan and Sty carrying. But the checkpoint kept returning, the car speeding toward it – no. The car wasn't there, wasn't about to explode. The checkpoint had been in Iraq – not Ithaca. Pain pierced her lip and she tasted blood. The sand dropped away from her skin; the gunfire faded.

But the sound of the car didn't. Tires crunched snow. A car door slammed.

Oh God. Evan and Sty were back? Already? Harper looked around the sitting room for a hiding place. Nothing – even if she squatted behind a sofa, she'd be in the open.

'I'll drive the pickup; you take the jeep.'

'Why? Are you afraid of—?'

'No. You killed him; you drive him. I'm driving Phil's truck – I'm the one he lent it to.'

Snow crunched. Footsteps. 'Hey. The door's wide open. Didn't you close it?'

'I thought you did.'

Harper dashed into the foyer; if her weak leg hadn't slowed her down, she might have had time to run upstairs, hide in a dark bedroom. But – no time.

'Sty. Look. Footprints – they go into the house. From . . . next door?'

'Shit.' Another car door opened and slammed.

Oh God. They were right outside. In front. No time to make it to the stairs. She should have taken the poker. Could have used it to fend them off. Maybe she could take them both on anyway. Or make up an excuse for being there . . .

'And look – they only go one way.'

Harper hunkered behind the armoire. In seconds, they'd be inside. Damn. She looked around.

'Yes, they go in but not back out. So. It seems that we have a guest.'

Harper dashed around the armoire. It wasn't an escape, but it was her only choice. Opening the door, she hopped inside, stood beside the vertical wooden bar in the middle of the wardrobe, pulled the latch until it clicked shut.

Instantly, even in the pitch darkness, she knew that she wasn't alone. The stench made that clear. And when she moved, trying to get comfortable in the narrow space, she bumped an arm. Recoiled. Reached her hand up and around the wooden bar, tentatively. Felt an ear. Oh God. A cool, stubbly cheek. A clammy nose. Harper froze, struggling to stifle her gag reflex, her urge to scream, her impulse to bolt out and face Sty and Evan. She tasted bile. Covered her mouth.

'Well, to hell with her. Let's get this hideous thing out of here and she can stay as long as she wants.'

Something banged the back of the armoire.

'You got it?' Sty's voice.

'Yup.' It was a grunt.

The armoire jostled and tilted; Harper slid against the rotting corpse. Couldn't breathe. Needed to get out. She pushed the door, but it wouldn't open. The latch, she thought. Undo the latch. But then the armoire lurched the other way; the body and its dead weight slid onto her, pinning her so that she couldn't move. More bumps. More tilts. Loud grunting and scraping sounds. Then a harsh bouncing collision. Harper landed flat on her side, pressed against the hard wooden wall. The armoire twisted, jostling her until she lay flat on her back, and then she had the sense of rolling, as if the armoire had suddenly grown wheels.

When the bedroom door opened, Lou instinctively threw himself over Vivian, covering her with his body. Protecting her from Wally's thug. Closing his eyes, awaiting bullets.

'Hoppa?'

Lou ventured a gaze over his shoulder, saw huge shoulders, a hulking frame silhouetted in the doorway.

'Hoppa in here?'

Vivian pushed Lou aside, sputtering, eyes wide. Terrified and not yet awake. 'What? What?' It seemed to be all she could say.

The stranger now stood at the foot of the bed and pointed out the door. 'Not here? Where's Hoppa?'

'Hank?' Vivian managed. She rubbed her eyes.

'Hank? This is Hank?' Lou tried to stop shaking. To adjust to the facts. Wally had not sent someone here to torture and kill him. The guy was just Harper's husband. Bigger than he'd imagined. Built like a damned grizzly.

'What happened? Why are you home?' Vivian struggled to sit up, reached for the light on the nightstand. Turned it on. Squinted and blinked. Noticed the crutches.

'Hoppa. Where is she? Late. Not home.'

'Of course she's home.' Vivian fluffed her hair. 'She's in bed.'

'Not. There.' Hank turned, hobbled out of the bedroom.

Vivian grabbed her robe and followed, Lou right behind.

'Hank – what are you doing here? You're not supposed to be back for weeks. And it's the middle of the night. What's going on?'

But Hank didn't answer. Using the crutches, he hurried down the hall, searching every room, then navigated his way down the stairs, calling Harper's name, moving through the house, stopping to search the view from windows. Finally, eyes haunted, he plopped onto the living-room sofa, holding his head. His skin reflected red and green flashes of light from the tree. 'Where is she?' His voice was both anguished and accusing.

Vivian worried her hands, shook her head. 'I don't know. Is the car here? You know Harper. She gets ideas and there's no stopping her—'

'She was here when we went to bed,' Lou cut her off. 'She can't have gone far.' Unless Wally had sent someone to come and take her somewhere far, just to prove that he could. Just to teach Lou a lesson, make an example of him.

Hank repositioned his leg. Winced.

'What's with the crutches?' Leo eyed the leg, came closer; Hank glowered so fiercely that Lou cringed, backed away. 'Hey, relax. Sometimes she can't sleep. Wants a breath of air. She might have gone for a walk. Did you try her cell?'

Hank eyed him. 'Kitchen. On table.'

'She'll be the death of me.' Vivian scowled. 'It's freezing out – and she didn't take her phone?'

Christ. She'd left her cell phone? She'd never have done that willingly; Wally really must have taken her. Lou struggled to stay cool, not to let on what he knew. 'So, with no phone, she wouldn't go far. She'll probably be home any minute. Meantime – I'll make us some coffee.' He backed out of the room. Hank took no notice.

'Lou,' Vivian called after him. 'Do you think she went next door? To see those boys?' She stood as if about to run over to check.

'Why would she do that?'

'Same reason she does anything. To make my blood pressure skyrocket. She's killing me, Hank. She really is – did she tell you she's throwing us out?'

Hank blinked, confused. 'Out?'

'She gave us till the day after Christmas to leave. After all I've done for her – coming here to look after her – dropping my whole life.'

'Vivian, don't get started. Let the man sit.' Lou stopped her before Hank could ask questions. 'Harper's been hormonal, that's all. Nothing to worry about.' With that, he escaped into the hall and up the steps to get his phone. He wasn't sure how, but he was going to convince Wally to bring Harper back immediately, no matter what it cost.

\*      \*      \*

The smell transported her. Locked in the dark, Harper saw lifeless faces, limbs lying abandoned by the road. She felt flies swarming in the relentless desert heat, heard random gunfire and men howling in shock and pain. But suddenly, violently, the world shifted, rolling her onto her side, tossing her sideways. The impact of slamming into slippery dead flesh jolted her back to the present; Harper put her arms over her belly, gagging from the stench.

'Watch it!' Sty's voice, scolding Evan.

'I can't hold it – it's too heavy—'

'Hang on, hang on—'

And then the armoire tilted as if being hoisted unevenly, unsteadily, rising bit by bit, one end at a time, until finally, with an unkind thud, it was planted on its side. Harper lay on top of her companion, thinking about maggots. Crawling, sucking, burrowing, writhing. Harper scratched, slapping her skin, finally retching and wiping vomit from her chin. Oh God.

Straps or maybe ropes hit the armoire, along with grunts of pulling or pushing. And then, the start of an engine, the crunch of snow under wheels. The ride was rough but the corpse under her absorbed most of the vibration, protecting Harper like a slimy cushion.

Lou dashed upstairs into the bathroom, phone in hand, spun in circles while the call went through. When Rita answered, her voice was low and dreamy, half asleep.

'What the hell has he done?' He tried to sound strong rather than frantic, but his voice scraped raw. 'I told you I got him his money – with interest. But I swear if he wants it back, he has to let her go. I'm serious.'

'Lou?' As if she weren't sure who was calling.

'He has no business with her. He shouldn't mess with people he doesn't even know.'

'What are you talking about?' Covers rumpling. She was stirring, waking up.

'She's pregnant, for Christ sakes – and guess what? She has nothing to do with me. She's just the kid of some woman I was seeing . . .'

'I don't understand – what woman? Who's pregnant?'

He stopped spinning, ran a hand through his hair. Could it be Rita didn't know? 'Look. Wally's doing what Wally does. Playing games. Taking collateral. But this time, he's gone too far.'

He heard a match strike, her draw on a cigarette.

'Wally thinks he's sending me a message. But I'll tell you what: I have a message for Wally. I got his money, but he's not getting it – not a fucking penny – until she's home safe. Unharmed. You hear me?'

'Lou. Be honest. Are you drunk?' She sounded baffled.

'Don't play dumb—'

'Whatever you think Wally did, you're mistaken.'

'Yeah? Well, maybe your boyfriend isn't telling you everything. A pregnant woman? He's that low? Endangering two lives—'

'Trust me. The only life Wally wants to endanger is yours. He wants his money. In fact, he intends to come get it personally.'

'What aren't you hearing? I said he's not getting it – not until she's back.' Lou stood at the bathroom mirror, caught a look at himself. Saw red lines pulsing through his eyes. Pasty flesh. Took a breath. 'You tell him what I said. And get back to me. I mean it, Rita. Fast.'

When the call ended, he shoved the phone into his pants pocket, splashed his face with cold water. Stared at his reflection. Damn. Time to get packing again. Now, while he still could. He didn't want to. Closed his eyes, already missing Vivian. For once, he'd thought he had the real thing. A relationship he hadn't messed up, one that would last. But never mind. No choice. Being with her, he was bringing her trouble. Her kid was gone. Her grandkid. No. He had to go. Had to come up with something, an excuse to take off. Vivian would cry for a while, but she was tough, had been down a few rocky roads; she'd survive. And taking off would make Wally realize he shouldn't have messed with Harper, that Lou wasn't going to grovel and twist just because she was missing.

Drying his face, he thought of Harper. Wondered if she were still alive.

And, if not, how Vivian would handle it.

Felt a pang.

Damn. He had to get out of there before the shit hit. When his breathing was even, he went downstairs to make coffee.

When he got downstairs, the front door was open. Hank stood on the front porch with Vivian, staring out at the snow.

'She has to be over there,' Vivian told Lou. 'Look – footprints.' She rushed down the steps into the snow.

Footprints? Lou hurried over, stepped outside, checked out the ground. The porch light was dim, but, yes, for sure. There were tracks in the snow, leading next door. And they seemed fresh.

A wave of relief rolled through Lou. Maybe he'd been wrong; maybe Wally hadn't taken her. Maybe Harper simply hadn't been able to sleep and had gone next door to hang out with the college boys. Maybe he'd jumped the gun, worrying for nothing. He rushed over to Vivian, put an arm on her shoulder. Kissing her head. Maybe he wouldn't have to skip after all.

'Come on.' Vivian tugged at him, plowing ahead. 'She's over there – I'm sure of it.'

Hank was having difficulty negotiating the steps on his crutches, but he wobbled down and along the path. Halfway down, he slipped and fell, landing with a thud. Letting out an angry grunt.

'Here. You all right?' Lou stopped, grabbed Hank's crutch and held it up for him. The man was solid muscle but off balance, struggling to right himself. Lou was freezing; they were outside without jackets. The wind whipped up suddenly, and he shivered, waiting for a man twice his size to climb, stumbling and tottering, to his feet. Vivian had rushed ahead, calling Harper's name. By the time Lou and Hank got to the fraternity, she was already at the door, peeking through windows.

The light was on in the foyer.

'Hoppa!' Hank pounded the door. Thrust his shoulder against it, threw his body at it until the wood around the lock finally broke and he shoved his way inside. 'Hoppa?' His voice circled the rotunda of the entrance way, crashed into the sitting room, bounced against the walls. He followed it, charging on his crutches through the shadows of the first floor, finding no one.

Vivian stood at the door, hugging herself, coughing, yelling for Evan and Sty, her voice scratchy and deep. Lou wrapped himself around her like a stole, trying not to collapse under the weight of what he now was certain that he knew. As Hank and Vivian had raced inside, he'd lingered out front. In the snow, he'd seen multiple footprints leading to the tracks of a vehicle. And tracks of something else – a sled, maybe. Or a cart.

Damn Wally. He hadn't messed with just Harper. His people must also have taken the boys. Those two boys must have seen Harper in trouble, must have stepped in to help her. And now, all of them, all of them were gone, being held God knew where. All because of him.

Vivian left his embrace, began running around, up and down stairs, hollering names, looking like a trapped bird.

'Nobody's here, Viv. The place is empty.'

The facts were obvious, but she didn't seem to accept them, fluttering around until the big guy lumbered back to the door and slowly
started home. Vivian suddenly regained her focus. 'Hank? Wait –
where are you going?'

He didn't turn around or stop moving. As he swung his body forward
on his crutches, his voice slapped the air like wind. 'Calling. Police.'

The thin wooden post in the middle of the armoire had broken under
her weight, and gravity kept Harper right on top of the body. She
pushed at it, trying to rearrange it, but the armoire kept bumping,
tossing them, and the thing kept sliding around. Beneath her, she
felt a cold arm. A hand. A puddle of puke. Shivering in frigid total
darkness, she resisted the stench, the images it conjured – the explosion, the white heat, the motion of flying and the screams – no. She
kept fighting the flashbacks. Had to think, had to figure out how to
get out of the armoire, away from the body. From Sebastian Levering.
It had to be him. Evan and Sty – they'd killed him. Harper cradled
her belly, protecting the baby from banging the hard wood encasing
them as they rolled along. A contraction snaked around her, and
she breathed, assuring the baby or herself. 'Don't worry. It's okay.'

Of course, it wasn't okay. The contraction intensified, strangling
her mid-section. 'It's okay,' she repeated. Her baby wasn't even
born, and already she was lying to it. Gradually, slowly, the contraction eased, leaving Harper breathless, cold and damp. Suddenly, the
armoire lurched to an angle, propelling Harper against the wall. She
leaned on it, pressed her arm and a leg against Sebastian, pushing
up and away. How long had he been dead? Three days? Four? Rigor
mortis had passed; he was limp, clammy. God. Harper had to get
out, had to. She leaned an elbow, lifting herself away from him,
used her other hand to grope the wood, searching for the latch. If
she could find it, maybe she could undo it, open the armoire door,
climb out, escape without Evan or Sty seeing. Her hand moved
along the wood, desperate and inefficient. Where was the damned
latch? It had to be there, in the middle somewhere. Sebastian
bounced; his arm flapped against her. She kicked it away, finally
locating the latch.

'I have it,' she told the baby, trying to calm herself. 'I found it.'
And she fingered the metal, feeling for the release, pushing and
twisting it slightly, catching a finger on a sharp edge, feeling a prick
of pain. Damn. She kept working the latch, pressing on it, hoping

to hear a snap, feel the door give. But she felt no give, heard no sound above the noisy engine and the crunch of a snowy road.

Finally, she understood. She couldn't get the door open because it was fastened from outside. The doors were tied shut. And the armoire had to be tied onto the vehicle. So, even if she'd unfastened the latch, no matter how long or hard she pushed, she wouldn't be able to open the armoire. She was trapped.

And she was losing perspective. Had no idea how long she'd been in there, how far they might have gone. She let go, slumping against Sebastian, questions darting through her mind. How much longer would they drive? What did they plan to do with Sebastian? And what about the other body she'd seen them carrying? Who was he? Was he dead, too? How would she get away? Harper leaned on Sebastian, her left leg starting to cramp. Think, she ordered herself. Design a maneuver. But, digging her elbow into Sebastian's ribs, the best she could do was to tolerate the fetid air and minimize the bouncing, protecting her belly with one arm.

By the time Detective Rivers arrived, Hank had already called Leslie as well as Harper's obstetrician to see if either knew where Harper might be. Neither did. Both were concerned; Leslie offered to come over but Hank said there was no need. He met Rivers at the door and, on crutches, ushered her into the living room where they found Vivian, chain-smoking Camels and draining a bottle of Scotch.

'Back off,' Vivian growled, hugging the cigarette pack. 'It's not my fault. Don't blame me for starting again. I was doing fine, but your wife finally pushed me over the edge.'

Hank glared; she snuffed the cigarette and downed her drink.

Rivers made them review everything that happened: Hank's sudden return, Harper's absence, the trek next door following footprints. 'I thought you were supposed to be away for a few weeks.'

'Surprise Hoppa.' Hank's voice was thick. 'Christmas. Came home.'

Rivers eyed him. 'So Harper didn't know you were coming?'

He shook his head, flopped onto a wing-backed chair, clung to the crutch.

'What's with the leg?'

'Hurt.' He scowled. 'Ligament. Not rele. Vant—'

'Mr Jennings, please bear with me. Everything is relevant at this point. I'm gathering information to get a sense of what's going on.'

Vivian raised a glass. 'I'll tell you what's going on.' She gulped

Scotch. 'My daughter is out of control. She's completely self-absorbed and oblivious to the feelings of the people around her. Trust me, you're getting upset over nothing. She probably got bored again and went next door to see the boys. Probably they all went out for a ride around town. That's all. She'll turn up. You don't need to worry about Harper.'

'Has this happened before?'

'What, that she's gone over there? You bet. Look, you saw the footprints. I'm telling you, that's what happened.'

'Do you know their names?'

'You have them – they're the same kids from the other night.'

'Other night?' Hank's gaze moved from Vivian to Detective Rivers.

'Yeah. When Harper made all the fuss about that missing boy.'

'What. Missing boy?'

'Hank, you have no idea how impossible she's been. Thank God you've come home. Harper's been over the top on one thing, then another until, like I said before, she's decided to throw us out.'

Hank seemed doubtful. 'Never told me that.'

'Of course she didn't. She knew you wouldn't put up with it. But she gave us a firm deadline to vacate the premises. Her own mother. Don't look so surprised. I'm not kidding. It's been crazy here with her. She imagines things – it started with the naked guy in the snow . . .'

Hank's brows furrowed. 'Naked. Guy?'

'Everybody stop.' Rivers put her hands up, sighing. Clearly, not everyone was on the same page. She settled onto the sofa, looking around for Lou. 'Any chance we can get some coffee?'

Lou was already in the kitchen, waiting for his phone to ring, concocting more than coffee. As hot water dripped through ground beans, he practiced his lines, the excuse he'd give to Vivian.

'My brother-in-law called.' He would try to make his eyes water, his voice break. 'It's serious. My sister. She's been in a car accident.' He would pause there, waiting for the expected, 'Oh no!' or, 'Is she all right?' He pictured Vivian's face, the alarm and disappointment in her eyes. Would she sense his deceit?

Maybe he should forget the accident story, go with a cancer diagnosis instead. Although cancer might be less pressing; there would be treatments or surgeries that lasted weeks or months. But a car accident, well – that could suddenly put his sister, if he'd had one, on the verge of death. Could be a reason he'd have to drop everything and come.

'I know it's bad timing, what with first my client being angry and now Harper missing,' he would say. 'But she asked for me. And she doesn't have long.'

Damn. It sounded phoney even to him. Never mind; if he presented it sincerely, she'd buy it. He couldn't risk telling Vivian the truth. Poor kid. Well, there was no choice. The lie, his departure – they were for Vivian's own good. As long as he was with her, she and those close to her were in danger. At least until he squared things with Wally. But after that, he'd still have to deal with Ritchie. Damn. Lou stopped, rubbed his eyes and took a breath, steeling himself. What a mess he'd made of his life. What a goddamned mess.

But there was no going back. He'd brought this onto Vivian's family, and he'd have to make it right. He'd get Wally to bring Harper home, then move on before anything else could catch up to him. He stopped for a moment, wiped his eyes with the back of his hand; apparently, he wouldn't have to fake tears. Taking a deep breath, getting control of himself, he opened a cupboard, pulled out a box of shortbread. Arranged some cookies on a tray, poured steaming coffee into the mugs. Headed into the living room, eager to tell Vivian about his sister, to get it over with.

When he set the tray down, his hand slipped; he almost dropped the thing and spilled coffee all over the table, interrupting their conversation. He apologized and tried to steady his hands as he wiped up the spill and passed out mugs of coffee. The detective was talking to Hank and Vivian; no way he could announce his news right now. He'd have to wait until the detective was gone. Interrupting would draw too much attention, and the last thing he needed was too much attention from the cops. Especially not while he had almost half a million dollars upstairs. Speaking of which, he needed to pack.

The red and green Christmas lights kept blinking, taunting Hank with their happiness. Surrounded by unopened gifts, leftover wrapping paper, spare decorations and the hulking oversized tree, Hank tried to sort out the stories Vivian and Rivers had just told him. One about a missing student from Elmira. Another about a snowy brawl in their own back yard involving the assault of a naked guy. Most upsetting was the news that Harper had been consumed – and according to Vivian, obsessed – by these events. And that, despite their importance, she had deliberately neglected to mention anything about them during their nightly phone calls.

And now she was missing.

Hank didn't know what to do. Even while the detective was talking, he pulled himself to his feet, limped to the window. Stared out at the night. Harper was out there somewhere. Where? Was she hurt? Frightened? Was she even alive?

Dishes clattered behind him. Vivian gasped.

'Sorry—' Lou fumbled with a tray, dropping it onto the coffee table. Reached for napkins, kneeling, dabbing spilled coffee off the hard wood floor. Rivers hopped to her feet, helping him. 'I'm sorry, I—' Lou broke off, sank to his knees. Covered his eyes.

Vivian ran to him, knelt beside him, caressing his shoulders, his head.

Lou took a moment, meeting Vivian's eyes. Embracing her. 'It's just—'

'I know,' Vivian croaked, burying her head under his chin. 'I don't know what I'd do without you, Lou. You're my world.'

'I'm so sorry this is happening to you, Baby.'

They stayed there, fiercely locked together in the middle of the living room. As if Harper were irrelevant. As if Vivian were the victim.

Hank tightened his jaw, couldn't be distracted by Vivian and her need for drama. He made his way to the table, took a mug of coffee and hobbled back to the window. He needed the caffeine. Needed to process what was going on, to clear his head so he could sharpen his instincts, clear his senses. Problem was, at the moment, he couldn't quiet himself enough to sense anything other than panic. Even Rivers seemed at a dead end, passively waiting for some new development. God. Where was Harper?

Hank gulped coffee, blinked at Vivian and Lou who were still fawning over each other. Thought about how bizarre and inappropriate they were, stroking each other, staring into each other's eyes while Harper was missing and in trouble. Obviously, Vivian was caving in, imploding, grabbing onto her boyfriend in desperation. But Lou – what was his excuse? The guy was off somehow. Just wrong. Trembling like jelly; Vivian just about had to hold him up. Hank glanced at Rivers to see if she was catching this, but Rivers was pointedly ignoring the display of affection. She munched shortbread, studying the red and green Christmas lights bouncing off her shoes.

\*     \*     \*

By the time the jostling stopped, Harper's feet and hands had long since gone numb from the cold, and, though she'd found a way to breathe by pressing her face against a crack in the wood, she'd become convinced that she would never rid herself of the stench. Closed in this casket-like closet with Sebastian, she had absorbed the smell of death through her pores; it penetrated her bloodstream. Her mind seemed frozen and useless.

Even so, when the armoire finally jolted to a stop, Harper grabbed her belly and bolted to attention, alert again. The ride was over; whatever Sty and Evan were planning to do with Sebastian would happen now. She had to be ready; surprise was one of her best weapons. Maybe her only weapon.

Harper's eyes strained in darkness, and she felt around, hoping to find a nail, a splinter – anything that could slice or puncture. She found nothing, reached into her pockets. Maybe there would be a pen or pencil – nothing.

Car doors slammed.

'Come on, Sty. Get over it.'

Footsteps. Silence.

'What difference does it make, really? We were going to do another one anyhow. So we did it earlier than you wanted.'

The armoire shook. There was shaking, then whip-like sounds, as if ropes were being unfastened, slapping the wood.

'Are you just going to ignore me forever? Look. I'm sorry. I acted impulsively – but I've got that out of my system. I'm ready to take more time and do more planning.'

Suddenly, something slammed against the armoire. Flesh pounded flesh. Somebody grunted. Somebody moaned.

'Imbecile,' Sty breathed heavily. 'You'll bring us both down. I should kill you and leave you here to rot with them—'

'Stop, Sty. Cool it.'

'Have you learned nothing? Has nothing I've told you penetrated your thick pathetic skull? You don't even know who your victim was. You don't know who or how many will be looking for him. You aren't sure that he can't be linked to you . . .'

'No. I told you a hundred times.' Evan's words slurred. He spit, probably blood. 'Nobody saw me with him.'

Silence. Then more shaking of the armoire, more slapping of ropes. Harper clutched the key with one hand, stroked her belly with the other. Wiggled her feet to get the blood circulating. Prepared to leap, swinging.

'Sty, look at it this way. It's experience. The more we have, the better we get. I needed to do one on my own. To feel the transition for myself—'

'Don't say anything more, Evan. Don't speak. The more you say, the more I realize how little I can rely on you, how faulty your judgment is.'

'Really? Like you're perfect? Who let the dude get out in the snow?'

Something – maybe a fist – slammed the armoire. 'Seriously? You're reinventing the facts so you can shift the blame? You were a mistake, my friend. I should never have taken up with you.'

Coughing. Then: 'But you did. You did and there's no going back. We're a team, Sty.'

Silence. Stillness.

'Come on, Sty.' More coughing. 'The next one will be better – I swear.'

More silence. Then a thump. 'Take your end. Pull it down.'

The armoire leveled out. Harper slid across the wood, away from Sebastian, drawing a breath and forming fists, bracing her cramped legs, ready to spring. The armoire slammed down hard; in the impact, she slapped the wall, emitting an involuntary whelp. But then, Harper heard nothing. No engine. No voices. Just the closeness of reeking cold air and the rapid bursts of her own breath.

She waited. She counted. She shivered, ignoring occasional screams of wounded, rattles of gunfire, buzzes of flies. Finally, convinced that Sty and Evan were not close by, Harper felt for the latch, worked it, pressed down and undid the lock. Slowly, cautiously, soundlessly, she lifted the armoire door an inch, felt cold fresh air, took in a delicious breath. Paused and listened, heard no reaction. Not a sound. Lifted the door higher, just a finger's width. Inhaled more frosty clean air. Heard a loud bang, like a crash – and then nothing. No voices. No car engine. No footsteps in the snow.

Harper counted seconds, being cautious. Her ears strained, listening as trained for insurgents, or hostile forces, or Evan and Sty – her instincts searched for the tingle of danger, the pulse of the enemy. But she heard and sensed only an empty howl of night wind. Her legs were stiff and numb; her body ached, but she waited until she was sure it was safe. Then, giving her belly a reassuring pat and leaving Sebastian pooled in a heap beside her, she eased the armoire door open all the way, slowly stood, cautiously looked around.

Ducked down, and scampered away.

\*      \*      \*

Detective Rivers kept trying to put pieces together, couldn't make them fit. She replayed the events of the last few days. Harper Jennings' report of seeing a naked man beaten outside, her insistence that someone was being held in the fraternity house. Rivers knew that Mrs Jennings wasn't given to baseless hysterical claims, but her pregnancy might be a factor; it had caused hormonal fluctuations and premature contractions. Plus, Mrs Jennings was bored and lonely, trapped in a house with her half-drunk narcissist mother. It was possible that Mrs Jennings might have overreacted, misinterpreted.

It was also possible that Harper's disappearance had nothing to do with the other missing persons. She might simply have gotten fed up with her mother and the boyfriend and gone out for a little bit.

Except Rivers didn't believe it. Her instincts told her that Harper's disappearance meant serious trouble. Meantime, Harper's husband was simmering, about to erupt into probably highly emotional and counterproductive actions; she wouldn't be able to contain him much longer. And Vivian was drunk and useless, passed out in the arms of her numbskull boyfriend.

Whom she should probably check out, just for the sake of being thorough.

'Need to follow. Car tracks.' Hank stood, clutching his crutches. His jaw rippled, determined. 'Drive. Road.'

'I already put a car on that. The tracks from the frat house disappeared on Thurston. It was plowed.'

Hank took a few steps, glared at the broken dining-room window. Pivoted. 'Can't just sit here.'

'Mr Jennings, there's nothing you can do right now. Police are looking for the fraternity boys, are checking pickups and ATVs. But the fact is, we aren't even certain that your wife is in trouble—'

'Find. Hoppa.' Hank bent forward, nostrils flaring, eyes searing.

Reflexively, Rivers leaned away. She wasn't doing any good at the house. Probably ought to take off. Still, something told her to stick around.

Lou cradled Vivian on the floor near the wing-back, stroking her forehead. Rivers rubbed her temples. There was no reason for her to stay. In fact, she might do better driving around looking for a pickup truck. She crossed her arms, trying to regain a sense of authority, then nodded out the window at the patrol car. The truth was that she'd lost control of the situation. In fact, she wasn't even sure what the situation was.

Lou put a pillow under Vivian's head and got up, trying not to draw attention to himself. His cell was vibrating, so he hurried away from the others and ducked into the kitchen, huddling over the phone, keeping his voice low.

'Wally wants to see you. One on one. Face to face.'

To see him? 'What the fuck for?'

'How do I know? Maybe he wants to get things straight.'

'You told him what I said? I'm not paying until he lets the woman go?'

'I told him what you said.'

'And?'

'And nothing. He wants you to bring him the money personally – two hundred twenty with one-eighty interest—'

'What one-eighty? Hell – the interest was one-fifty—'

'I'm telling you what he said, Lou. You want to argue, argue when you see him. He'll come to you.'

'He can't come here. No way—'

'He'll pick you up and take you somewhere. Have his money ready.' She gave him a time. Christmas Eve, twelve noon.

'Christmas Eve?'

'It won't be a long meeting. His mother-in-law is expecting the family back in the City for dinner.'

It was crazy. Lou had just a day and a half. But that meant that in a day and a half, Wally would have to let Harper go. Which would be good news for Vivian. Meantime, he had to get ready to split. He got off the phone, peeked into the living room, saw Hank pacing, heard Vivian's soft snore. And went upstairs.

Closing the guest-room door, Lou took out what was left of Wally's money, just over a hundred and sixty grand. He tossed it into his duffel bag with the two-fifty he'd borrowed from Ritchie. Damn. If Wally wanted one-eighty in interest, he was short. And he'd have nothing left, not a penny.

Lou hefted the bag; it was heavy with cash. At the moment, Lou was a wealthy guy.

He sat on the bed, thinking that, with all this money, he and Vivian could live the life. Happily ever after. He pictured it, a small – what did they call it – a hot sienda in Mexico. Drinking tequila by the beach.

But what was he doing? Wally would never let that happen. For one thing, if Lou skipped with the money, Wally wouldn't let Harper go – he'd kill her and the baby. And then he'd track Lou down and kill him and Vivian, too. Would make an example of him, showing the world what would happen to someone who cheated him.

If he could find him.

It was too big a risk. There would be almost no chance for him and Vivian. They'd have to watch their backs forever, even with the best of new identities. No, if he wanted her to be safe, he'd have to leave her behind, act as if he didn't even care about her. Hope that Wally would believe it and let Harper go and leave Vivian and all of them alone because there would be no point messing them up if they meant nothing to the guy he was trying to get back at.

Meantime, he had to pack. He took his shirts out of the closet, socks out of the drawer. Rolled all his clothes into a bundle. Stuck them in his suitcase. Wiped his eyes with the back of his hand, smearing tears. Damn. What a mess. Who'd have imagined how wrong things could go? Harper going missing right at Christmas. Her husband suddenly home. And him suddenly having to take off in an eye blink, not even able to see Vivian's face when she opened her gift.

Well, at least she'd have that. He'd spent a chunk of Wally's money – twenty grand on it.

He had to sit, was out of breath. Couldn't stop his damned crying. Pictured the next morning, telling her that he had to go. The hurt on her face.

He heard her respond, clear as a bell. 'You never said you had a sister.'

Damn. She might see through his lies. She was sharp, Vivian.

But he'd stick with his story. 'No? I guess I didn't think it mattered.'

He could see her chin quivering, her eyes registering the news. 'You're leaving me, aren't you, Lou? Just say it.'

He would meet her eyes, hold her chin in his hand. 'Just for a few days, Viv.'

Even the thought of lying to her hurt his heart. He closed his eyes. Considered again the impossibility of taking her along. Running. It was out of the question, a death sentence. So he kept moving. Packing. Throwing things into his bag. Preparing to pay Wally before Wally did something permanent to Harper. And he had other business to

take care of. A new identity to get used to. A new name to choose
– he had papers for Jake Mateo. Or was it Jake Martino? Something
like that. And some for Oliver Hayes. No, Hines.

He had to check and make sure to pick a name Wally and Ritchie
wouldn't know about. That the papers hadn't come from anybody
they knew. Meantime, he kept moving, getting stuff done. But he
wept, envisioning the morning. Dreading the talk with Vivian.

'Don't lie, Lou,' she'd demand of him. 'Just tell me why – aren't
you happy? What happened?' Shit. Would she suspect the truth?
Would she think he was leaving because of his business problems?
Would she connect them to Harper's disappearance?

He had to prepare himself, be ready to swear that he was telling
the truth. That his sister was really sick. That he had nothing else
to tell. That Vivian was still his girl. She would search his eyes, hers
full of pain. He wouldn't be able to bear it, so he would kiss her
quickly, as if he was just heading to the grocery store, and carry the
bag of money and the suitcase out the door.

Meantime, he was packed and ready. He shoved the bags against
the wall, felt the solid weight of the money. When he went downstairs, he found that Rivers had gone. A police car sat watch in the
driveway. Hank paced through the house on his crutches. Vivian lay
snoring, passed out right where he'd left her. Lou poured what was
left of her Scotch into a glass, downed it and felt the burn, still
looking for a way out. Still considering his options.

As she headed away from the truck, the headlights came on, bathing
her in white blinding light.

Harper blinked, unable to see into or beyond them. Exposed.

And then she took off, diving blindly into the snow. Running on
legs numb as stumps. Ducking down in brush. Freezing. Hunkering
behind a fallen tree, shivering, gathering her wits. Listening.

Neither Evan nor Sty had said a word, not a syllable. The only
sounds she heard were those of her ragged breath and boots plowing
through snow. Now, crouched low, she could make out slow and
steady steps, small crunches of powder moving closer through
darkness. And breathing that wasn't hers.

Her eyes adjusted to the glow of snow at night; the ground
reflected light, filtered it through clouds, exposing spots even
where trees blocked headlights' glare. Harper saw a frozen slope
leading to an ice-covered lake. A cluster of pines with a jeep

smashed into one – the jeep she'd seen them put a body into? Was the crash what she'd heard before? Oh God. And not far from the trees, an abandoned wood-slat house. Beside it, a collapsing barn.

'Harper?' Evan called out. She estimated ten yards away. 'You'll freeze your ass off out here. Come get warm.'

Harper didn't dare breathe. She rested a hand on her belly, waiting. Thinking.

'Shut up, Evan,' Sty growled. 'Why don't you just send up flares showing her where we are?'

'What's the difference? She's not going anywhere.'

'I swear. If you make another sound, I'll shove your larynx up your ass.'

She could see them, just three or four yards away. Could almost touch them. If they looked down and to the right, they'd see her huddled behind the tree trunk. If they climbed over it, they'd step on her.

Sty was panting, stopped to catch his breath. 'Jesus. What the hell happened?'

'You all right?'

'Fine. Peachy.'

Evan stood beside him, put a hand on Sty's shoulder. 'I guess you didn't plan on this.'

'So?'

'So, all your planning didn't prevent this unexpected event.'

Sty stiffened. 'You think this is funny?'

Harper heard Evan's smirk. 'Actually, yes. I do. All your great genius and painstaking preparations are thwarted by the unpredictable pranks of a woman.'

'Nothing has been thwarted. This is just another obstacle. We'll deal with it.'

Silence. Harper shivered, wondered if they could hear the rattle of her bones.

'I can't wait to hear how she got in there. Oh, and how she got along with her travel companion.' Evan laughed out loud, almost a cough. 'Christ. Imagine being locked in with that thing.'

Sty wasn't amused. 'Just find her.' He took a breath and pressed ahead toward the lake. After they'd passed, Harper waited a few seconds and darted out of the trees, across the open field to the barn. It didn't look sturdy or warm, and undoubtedly, they'd see her footprints leading there. Still, she might be able to climb up a level and get the advantage of elevation. And who knew? There might be something inside – an old pitchfork or rake. Something she could use as a weapon.

When she neared the barn door, a contraction began, and she leaned into the shadows, breathing evenly, holding her middle until it eased. 'Okay, baby,' she whispered. 'Calm down. We're okay.' Then slowly, silently, she slid the door open and stepped into total darkness, reaching her arms out, groping air, hoping that the floor had not rotted through, that the ground ahead wouldn't swallow her. That she and the baby would survive until another dawn.

Back at her desk, Rivers tried to absorb the news. She blinked at Sgt. Lavoy, who had just told her that yet another young man had gone missing. The third disappearance in a week.

She took a swig of watery coffee and eyed her notebook.

'Brad Sterling.'

'I took the call myself. Parents say they haven't talked to him in weeks. They don't even have a current address, said he was about to move into a new place with a friend.'

Rivers stared at him. Lavoy must have been dieting; his uniform didn't seem as tight.

'I know what you're thinking,' Lavoy went on. 'If they never talk to him, what makes them think he's missing? I asked them that very question.'

'And they said?'

'It's Christmas. They expected him.'

Rivers sighed. 'Yeah. Well, not showing up at Christmas doesn't mean he's missing. He might be in the Bahamas.'

'That's what I told them. Only I said Cancun.' Lavoy wandered away.

Rivers looked back at her notebook, reviewing Harper Jennings' disappearance. Going over events of the past week, trying to see a pattern. She reread her notes about Mrs Jennings' various calls, making sure she'd been thorough enough. Of course, she had. She'd investigated the brawl, even searched the woods for signs of an assault. She'd gone next door to the fraternity to follow up on Mrs Jennings' reports of a shining light and moving curtain. She'd tried out the key Mrs Jennings had found in the woods and interviewed the only two fraternity members who were present, observing their demeanors, checking the interior of the house. She had followed protocol to the letter. And she'd found nothing – no evidence of wrongdoing. No evidence of anything except a stressed-out pregnant woman.

Still, Mrs Jennings was missing. Clearly, she had stumbled into something that Rivers had missed. But what? Rivers was furious that she hadn't spotted it, hadn't prevented the disappearance. She strained to figure out what she wasn't seeing. The pieces were all there; Rivers just had to fit them together. Three people were missing, two of them young men. And those frat boys – Evan and Sty. They bothered her; their smarmy attitude set her off. Could they be behind all this?

Just for the sake of it, she followed that possibility. What if the naked guy Mrs Jennings had seen was Sebastian? What if Sty and Evan had kidnapped him, and he'd tried to escape – that would explain the fight. And, if Harper had been onto them, they'd have taken her, too.

So far, it all made sense. It was a good theory.

But Rivers had not a shred of evidence to back it up.

She picked up a pencil, doodled. Wrote the word: Why?

Why, indeed? Why would two rich college boys suddenly go around kidnapping people? They had no motive. Rivers felt physic-ally ill, angry with herself. She got up and went to the coffee pot, poured another cup, set it down. Couldn't swallow it. Damn. Where was Harper Jennings? How could she have just disappeared? She was tough – a veteran. She'd survived combat and serious injuries. Was not likely to be duped or taken by force. How could two puny college kids get the best of her?

She thought of Mr Jennings, the husband, his frantic rage. And the mother's drunken stupor. The mother's boyfriend, holding her head in his lap . . . Speaking of the boyfriend, he'd been acting strange, hadn't he? Jittery. Tiptoeing around. Peeking from the hallway. Rivers frowned. Had he had something to do with Harper's disappearance? Her instincts said no, but she needed to be thorough, couldn't make assumptions. Should have him checked out.

'Hey, Lavoy.' She wrote down Lou's name, handed it to him. 'Check this guy out, okay?'

Lavoy ambled over to her desk, took the paper, didn't leave. Stood there, watching her.

'What?'

'You okay, Detective?'

She shook her head. 'Peachy.'

Lavoy rested a hip on the edge of her desk. 'Hell of a way to spend Christmas week.'

She shook her head. 'I keep thinking I'm missing something.'

'Sometimes it helps to talk things over. Saying it to someone else can shake things loose.'

Rivers pulled a chair over, offered him a seat. Started over, from the top, reviewing her notes about Sebastian and Harper again. Looking for leads she knew she didn't have. When she finished, Lavoy summarized the facts about the newest missing person, Brad Sterling. He was twenty-two, a former Ithaca College student. He was from Florida but was staying in the area, moving to a new place with his room-mate.

'That's the connection, of course.'

'What's the key?' Rivers frowned. 'One pregnant woman and two young men who don't seem to have common friends or live in the same neighborhoods. Other than all of them being in Ithaca, I don't see any connections. I just don't.'

'Well, you got to admit. If the thing about Brad's not a connection, it's a pretty damn big coincidence.'

Coincidence? 'What is?'

Lavoy reached over, picked up a paper from the pile on her desk. 'Charlene, have you even looked at this?'

'What is it? I haven't had a chance.' Lord, why didn't he just tell her what it was? 'I've been focusing on the Jennings—'

'The room-mate? The guy Brad Sterling was moving in with – it was the first missing kid. Sebastian Levering.'

Rivers sat back, rubbed her temples. Her head hurt. She didn't know what else to do, so she reached for her notes, and started reading again.

Lou sat in the dark in the guest room, trying to keep up with his mind. Why would Wally want to meet him face to face? Why was he coming to pick him up and drive off someplace? Lou was pretty sure he knew why: Wally was planning to do more than just accept his money and Lou's sincere appreciation for loaning it to him.

Wally was going to kill him.

Lou had already called Rita to try to wangle out of the meeting. 'I mean as long as he gets the money,' he'd said, 'I don't see why I can't just drop it off—'

'He wants to see you, man to man.'

'But why?' Lou had persisted. 'Does he want to talk? Because we can talk on the phone—'

'It's his terms. You know him. His terms aren't negotiable.'

Finally, Lou had given in. He'd agreed to hand over the money and interest personally, and face whatever fate Wally had in mind.

He'd agreed, but that didn't mean he'd accepted it. Maybe he'd stand Wally up, simply not show at the meeting. He thought about it. Thought about grabbing Vivian and taking off – but he'd already decided he couldn't risk it.

Poor Vivian. He was going to break her heart. He was going to join the list of men who'd dumped her, literally every man in her life. He pictured her eyelids raw and puffy, her body limp on the bed. If only he could do right by her. But that seemed impossible.

Because as far as he could see, he was cooked. Even if he could convince Wally to let Harper go, Wally would probably kill him. And even if Wally didn't, Ritchie would. Not that Ritchie had a right to complain; in all fairness, Ritchie shouldn't have made him the loan to begin with. He knew that Lou had no collateral, no actual income besides what he earned from Wally, who obviously would no longer employ a man who'd skimmed – rather, borrowed – from him. No. Ritchie should have figured out that Lou wouldn't be able to pay him back. So, Ritchie's loss should be on Ritchie. Not that Ritchie would accept that fact.

Either way, the thing with Ritchie had to wait. First things first. In just a day, Lou had to deal with Wally. He glanced at the duffel bag. Damn, he liked having all that money. Imagined Vivian in a hammock under a palm tree, drinking pina coladas, listening to tin drums. Someplace where it never snowed.

If only he could keep the frickin' money.

He rubbed his forehead, thought again of Vivian, the way she smelled of booze and flowers. The way she laughed, her voice deep as a crater, scarred from staying alive. He thought of how he was going to make her cry.

But all his thinking was getting him nowhere. In a day, he was going to drop a bomb on his life, destroy his happiness, hurt the woman he loved. There was no escape; it had to be done. Lou reached onto the nightstand, picked up the remote, turned on the television. Popped a few aspirin into his mouth. Wished his head would stop throbbing.

He wanted to go downstairs and be with Vivian. Didn't dare

because he'd fall apart. He covered his eyes with his hands, wiped them. Cursed. His mouth tasted bitter from the aspirin. He opened the bottle, took a couple more.

The news was on. Some drunk driver had killed a whole family on their way to a church meeting. A dog had identified a suitcase full of heroin at Newark airport. Lou eyed the duffel bag, wondered how much money a suitcase of heroin was worth. The anchor reported that another young man had been reported missing. Some kid from Florida. And an elderly woman had been found frozen in a state park.

Lou leaned back on the bed, gazed out the window at the night. Listened to the weather report; it was supposed to snow again the next day. Perfect. Wally's car would skid and slide all the way to wherever he was going to kill him.

When he closed his eyes, he imagined the woman's frozen body in the park. Why was he thinking about that? It was just a news story, nothing to him. And then – Eureka – it came to him – a way out.

Lou sat up, whooping out loud. He was giddy, laughing despite his troubles. Finally, he had a plan. A way to keep the cash, get both Wally and Ritchie off his back, and live happily ever after with Vivian. Thanks to that frozen dead woman, he was going to be okay.

All he had to do was die.


Rivers stood, moved around to get her blood circulating. Then sat again, rereading her notes. After talking to Lavoy, she was sure that the disappearances were related. Now she was determined to find a fact, a comment – anything she'd written down that could help her. After a while, she gave up, let out a breath, rubbed her eyes.

Lavoy ambled over to her. 'You're not going to like this.'

Rivers waited.

'Another missing persons call. This one's premature. He's only been missing a few hours, but his mother's frantic. He lives alone on the lake. She hasn't been able to reach him and asked a neighbor to check. His place is empty and his car is gone—'

Rivers ran her hands through her hair. 'He's not even been gone twenty-four hours—'

'I know. It's probably nothing. But under the circumstances, I thought you'd want to know.' He started to walk away.

'Hey, Lavoy? What's the kid's name?'

'Steven. Steven Mills.'

'Let me know if he turns up.'

'Yes, Ma'am.'

Rivers sighed, turning back to her notes. Trying to remember where she'd left off.

She couldn't remember, so she started over. Brad, Sebastian, Harper. And maybe Steven. What linked them? Who knew all of them? Brad and Sebastian were linked; they were planning to live together. But Harper? She had no apparent connection to either. And who knew about Steven?

Rivers drew a map, connecting Brad to Sebastian.

She added Evan and Sty, connected them to Harper. Drew a dotted line from them to Sebastian, in case he'd been the naked kid.

Rivers' desk phone rang. Lavoy had yet more information, wasn't sure it was relevant.

'Shoot.'

'Just got another call from Florida. Mom says that her son and Sebastian weren't just room-mates. They were honeys.'

'Gay?' Rivers was confused; Sebastian's friends had said he'd had a girlfriend.

'Brad was open about it. But according to Brad's mother, Sebastian hadn't come out. Brad said he going to tell his family over Christmas.'

Rivers thought about it. Maybe the girlfriend was really a boyfriend – none of Sebastian's friends had met her. In fact – were Sty and Evan gay, too? Had either of them been involved with any of the missing men? That might be the connection. Except: what would their relationships have to do with Harper Jennings?

Her mind was tangling. She started over. Began with Sty and Evan. Read her notes about meeting them at the fraternity with Mrs Jennings. Going inside, looking up the dim staircase. Walking into the dining room, the sitting room. Moving awkwardly around that ugly oversized wardrobe – they'd called it an 'armoire' – which was smack in the middle of the foyer. They'd claimed that they'd sold it and were about to deliver it to the buyer.

Rivers froze. Suddenly, she had it: the wheel and tire tracks outside the fraternity. The empty space inside the front door. Of course. She knew where Harper Jennings was. Now, all she had to do was find that hideous wardrobe.

Harper moved slowly in the darkness, her arms stretched ahead, searching for obstacles, her toes tentative, testing the floor. Gradually, she became accustomed to the shadows, made out shapes in light that filtered through the barn's shattered roof. Saw lumps of what was probably hay. A ladder leading to a loft.

Behind her, the door swung open. Damn. They'd found her. Harper's left leg buckled and she stumbled, but she righted herself and ran for the ladder, forgetting about testing the strength of the floorboards. Moving fast, before their eyes could get used to the dark, taking advantage of their temporary blindness.

'There!' Evan shouted. 'I see her!'

'Where?' Sty bolted into something, sent it clattering to the floor, howled in pain. 'Shit.'

Harper didn't slow down. Felt Evan's heartbeat, his breath closing in. Wished she had something – a hoe or a shovel. Took a leap, grabbed the ladder, felt for a rung with her left foot. Began to climb.

Sty was back on his feet. 'Where the fuck are you, Evan?'

Evan's voice was alarmingly close. Inches away. 'I've got her.' It was almost a whisper, meant not for Sty but for her.

Harper scrambled upward. Evan got to the ladder and shook it, trying to knock her off. She hung on, was almost to the loft, but she felt Evan's weight beneath her. He'd climbed onto the first rung, was reaching up, trying to grab her ankles. His hand brushed her foot, almost nabbed it.

Harper pushed on, was eye-level with the edge of the loft. She lifted her right leg up two rungs, pushed off and swung her hips, landing sideways in the loft. Winded, she hopped up, put both hands on the ladder and centered her strength so she could shove it away, knocking it over before Evan made it to the top. Harper stepped back, then forward, thrusting the ladder . . .

'Gotcha.' A hand firmly gripped her wrist, promising to take her with it if it fell.

She rolled and twisted her wrist, trying to wrest it away, but Evan wouldn't release it. He was climbing onto the loft when she swung, connecting with his eye, but he pounced on her with savage force, pummeling her head. Harper fell, dizzy, having the sensation that, like her unborn baby, she was doing flip turns.

Okay. Lou knew what he had to do. He had to fake his death. When he was officially dead, no one would bother to look for him. They'd try for a while to find the money, but after a while, they'd give up. Meantime, he'd become someone else. He'd start over like he'd done before. Become a new man with a new name. Use one of the identities in his suitcase. Something he could grow old with, maybe Oliver Hines. He said it out loud: Oliver Hines. Ollie. It was a good name, but was it him? Wasn't it too fussy? Truth was, he was a simple guy, needed a simple, regular sounding name. But he'd already used most of those. Had been a Pete and a Bill. Maybe it was time for something classier. As long as Wally and Ritchie couldn't trace him – shit, he'd be Linda if he could be sure it was safe. Anyway, he'd use a name those guys didn't know about, and when he got himself set up, he'd send for Vivian, and they'd live the dream south of the border, with sombreros and siestas, mambos and margaritas.

Lou laughed out loud, got out of bed, grabbed the satchel of money and started dancing with it, singing out loud. 'Wastin' away again in Margaritaville. Searching for my lost shaker of salt . . . Some people claim that there's a woman to blame, but I know . . .'

Suddenly, his mood took a dive. He slumped on the side of the bed, letting the satchel slide to the floor. What the hell was he doing, living in fantasy land? He had details to work out. Lots of them. For example, he needed an exact location for the accident. Someplace not too far away so that when he died, he'd be identified right away. Well, not him; the car. Vivian's old Camry was going to be mangled and burned in a terrible accident, smashed at the bottom of a gorge. Very sad.

After that, there was only one other problem: how to make it look like he'd died in the crash without an actual body.

Harper opened an eye, saw darkness. Closed it again.

'. . . I think we should take advantage of it. This opportunity fell into our hands, like a gift—'

'No.' It was Sty's voice. And it sounded close.

Harper tried to remember what had happened. Feigning unconsciousness, she lay still, assessing her situation. The smell of death lingered on her skin, reminding her of Sebastian's body, riding with it in the armoire. She remembered getting out, running through snow and trees to escape from Sty and Evan. Heading for a barn. Climbing to a loft.

After that, she remembered nothing. Where was she now? Up in the loft? Or had she fallen? Oh God – the baby. Was the baby okay? Without moving, she focused on her belly, waited. Finally felt a flutter. The baby was moving, must be okay. Harper let out a breath, relieved. But she was still unsure of her situation, didn't even know her own condition. How badly had she been hurt? Silently, she took inventory of her body parts, feet to head. Only her head registered pain. So probably she was okay, just stunned. But where was she? Harper tried to move a hand out, to feel what was around her, but couldn't. Her arms were bound at the wrist. Not with rope – when she tried to move, the bindings didn't cut into her skin. Maybe tape? She was lying on her back, her head turned slightly, rough straw-like scratches against her neck. She inhaled through her nose. Smelled mildew and hay. So she was probably in the loft.

Sty and Evan were still arguing. 'No.' Sty insisted. 'We've deviated too much already. We can't afford to take more chances.'

Chances? What kind of chances? Her head swam, but she strained to remain alert.

'This isn't a chance. It's an opportunity. Besides, we have no choice. We can't exactly let her go.'

Sty grunted.

'So why not make the best of it? Make her a project.'

'Evan, you have no sense of order or discipline. First of all, she doesn't fit the test group. She's the wrong victimology. The wrong size, the wrong age, the wrong gender—'

'So? Wouldn't it be interesting to study age and gender – all kinds of differences? We can record the data and save it, and compare it with our original group later—'

'No.'

'No?'

'That's right. No.' Sty's voice was tight. 'Everything's spinning out of control. We've got two bodies already. And she'd be – Christ, Evan. What are you doing?'

Harper heard the swish of steps approaching through hay. 'You didn't like my suggestion, Sty. So I might as well just get this done.'

'Wait – without thinking it through?'

'Christ almighty, Sty. If we leave it to you, we'll never finish here. Just let me do this.'

'Whatever. I'll get started outside.' Sty descended the ladder, his boots clicking on the rungs.

Harper lifted an eyelid. In the dim light, she saw Evan kneeling beside her. Saw his shoulders lean forward; his fingers reach for her throat. Heard his shrill, spine-shattering howl as, in a heartbeat, she raised her head, opened her mouth and chomped down as hard as she could on his hand.

Even as he yowled, Evan swung with his uninjured fist, slamming her in the side of the head. Harper saw a flash of white light, then nothing.

When she woke up, she was cold. Not sure how long she'd been out. Minutes? Seconds? She expected Evan to be still on top of her, punching, so she tried to roll over to dodge his blows. But the blows didn't come. And she couldn't roll. Couldn't move her arms or legs. Damn. She remembered; they'd bound her.

Shivering, Harper listened, heard soft moaning. Someone was still nearby. Evan? She tried to collect her thoughts. To remember. Why was he moaning? Had she hurt him? And where was Sty? She closed her eyes, opened them again. Tried to slow her breath. To think – oh God – the baby. Was it okay? Harper held her breath, felt dizziness, sharp pain in her head. If the baby was hurt . . . No. She wouldn't allow that thought. Fear was the enemy, would paralyse her. She forced herself to relax her muscles, found her core, focused on it. The baby would be fine. They both would be – had to be. Silently, she began wriggling her hands, trying to get free. Her head throbbed, her hands and feet were freezing and her skin itched from the straw, but she persisted, pressing her palms against each other, pushing her arms apart, trying to stretch her bindings until she was panting and her shoulder muscles cramped. For a moment, she stopped to rest her wrists. Wiggled her fingers for circulation. And felt something sharp scrape her forefinger. Something sharp? Quickly, silently, Harper moved her fingers around in the straw, searching. And found it – a nail. Sticking a few inches up from the floor, but jammed in tight.

Harper tried to stop shivering as she wrapped a cold, stiff hand around it. Tried not to move the rest of her body as she grabbed and jimmied, pulled and turned, pushed and twisted it until, finally, it came free and, letting out a breath, she lay back, oddly exhausted. Probably, it was the cold – she was losing too much body heat. Developing hypothermia. Damn. Her feet were numb, and the pain in her head had faded, become vague. She lay still, waiting, listening for Evan or Sty, the nail with its cold sharp point clutched in her fist.

'Evan?' Below, footsteps crossed the barn, climbed the ladder. 'What are you doing up there? Everything's ready.'

Harper didn't move, pretended to be unconscious even when a foot slammed her shoulder.

'Shit – why's she so close to the ladder? I could have tripped on her and fallen off—'

'Sty. I need help. I'm hurt.'

A heavy weight thudded onto her legs and sat there. 'Look what the bitch did,' Evan groaned, cursing.

'Holy shit!'

A flashlight glared in her eyes. She didn't react.

'What the fuck happened?'

'What does it look like? She bit my fuckin' hand off. When she wakes up, I'm going to knock her teeth out. I'll peel her skin off—'

'Let me see that.' The light moved away. Harper squinted, saw Sty aiming it at Evan's hand, examining it. 'You got to bind that, stop the bleeding. She tore off a chunk—'

'Don't you think I fucking know that? I'm bleeding to death.'

Sty snorted. 'You'll live. We need something to wrap it with.'

'Use your shirt.'

'Why not yours?'

'Mine? Seriously? I'm fucking going into shock as it is—'

'Dammit, Evan. This is hand-tailored.' Sty pulled his jacket off.

Harper lay cold and silent, heard ripping fabric, groans of pain. And slowly, carefully, she moved her hand, repositioning the nail, jamming it up toward the binding on her wrists.

'You're going to have to clean that wound out – the human mouth literally teems with bacteria—'

'And how would you suggest I clean it, Sty? You have running water? Or a bottle of disinfectant on you? Maybe some antibiotic cream?'

'Hold still – I'm trying to tighten this—'

'Don't tell me what the fuck to do. Ouch! Dammit—'

'Too tight? It's got to be tight to stop the bleeding.'

Harper twisted her hand, pushed the nail with her fingers until she felt it puncture something. Then she stopped pushing, used her other hand to ease the nail down maybe half an inch and reposition it. And pressed it up again, felt another puncture.

Suddenly, the weight on her legs lifted; Evan stood up.

'Careful – you've lost some blood. You might be light-headed. Don't fall.'

'Where the hell is my knife?'

She heard Evan stomping around in the hay. The flashlight aimed in her eyes again. She didn't move, not even an eyelash.

'Settle down, Evan.'

'I need my fucking knife. I'm going to cut this bitch to shreds.'

'Not yet.'

'Why the hell not?'

'Let's not argue again, Evan. She's tied up; she'll wait. But think about it: You're impaired; you have limited energy, and we've got that heavy armoire to unload and deposit.'

'Fine. But let's be quick.' Evan's breath was rapid, shallow. The light visited her face again. 'Because when we're done, I'm coming right back.'

Footsteps climbed down the ladder. Alone, shivering, Harper worked the nail, pushing it up, puncturing the binding, repositioning it, pushing again. And again. Wincing when she felt a jab, a warm gush. Damn – she'd aimed wrong, pushed too hard, stabbed her wrist; the blood made her fingers slippery. She was cold, her fingers stiff and almost numb, having trouble gripping the nail. But she had no choice, had to proceed. Envisioned her hands free, her legs running.

'Come on,' she said aloud. 'Get it done.' Steadying herself, she pressed her wrists together to stop the bleeding and began again, working her fingers, placing the nail, pressing it up through her bindings. Cutting her way to freedom, one puncture at a time.

About three in the morning, Vivian woke up and wandered into the guest room. She sat on the bed beside Lou. Noticed the bags.

'Lou?' Her mouth hung open. Her eyes registered new facts.

'Don't get upset.' He reached for her, pulled her close. 'I wasn't going to say anything until morning—'

'Say anything about what?' She pulled away, sat straight, her eyes wide and accusing.

Lou sat up, too, leaned over and tried to take her hands but she wouldn't allow it. 'Something's happened. It's my sister—'

'Your sister.'

'Yes. She's had a stroke—'

'You told me you were an only child.'

Wait. He'd said that?

'Don't fuck with me, Lou.' She was on her feet, hands on her hips.

The air came out of his lungs, wouldn't go back in. He couldn't speak, had no voice.

'You're taking off? Where the hell you going?'

'You're wrong, Vivian. I'm not going anywhere unless—'

'Not going anywhere? Not anywhere?' She repeated the words several times, kicking his suitcase, his duffel. 'You need these bags to not go anywhere?' Breathless and panting, she waited for an answer.

'Harper wanted us out.' He thought it was a good answer. 'So while you were sleeping, I got started packing.'

Vivian's eyes grew, looked like they'd launch out of her head. 'So why'd you lie about a sister if you packed because of Harper?'

'Look, Harper wants us out by—'

A sudden bellow, like a police siren, came out of Vivian's throat. She covered her face with her hands and sunk to the floor. Lou ran to her and held her.

'Vivian, it's okay. We're leaving, starting over,' he covered her head with kisses. 'Both of us. Together. Everything will—'

'Starting over? What are you talking about?' She pulled away.

'We'll go someplace far away, just the two of us—'

'Lou. Stop. What's wrong with you? Don't you get what I'm going through? My daughter is missing. I'm a mess. Until she's found, I'm not going anywhere.' Vivian ran a hand through her hair, simpering.

Lou sat still, trying to figure out what to say. How to explain. How much of the truth to tell her. He had to take her car, total it and set it on fire. Had to make Wally think he was dead, make him see the futility of hanging on to Harper. Had to get far away with the cash. And with Vivian.

But Wally wouldn't release Harper until he thought Lou was dead, and Vivian wouldn't leave until Harper was released. So somehow, he had to fake his death, make sure Harper was home, and then whisk Vivian away before Wally could find out there was no body in the crash and he was actually alive.

Vivian sat on the bed, legs crossed. God, she was gorgeous. Had legs that went all the way to the ground. A face that he could look at forever, not smooth and blank, but lined, character etched into it. Vivian wasn't just a woman; she was his counterpart, the female version of him. Just like him, she'd done what she had to in order to survive. Learned to compromise. To protect herself. And despite that, just like him, she still had a heart.

Vivian took out a pack of Camels, lit one. Lou got up, sat beside her on the bed. She didn't move, didn't acknowledge him.

'I didn't want to do this.' He put an arm around her waist.

She exhaled smoke, didn't look at him. 'Do what?'

He sat for a moment, thinking, making sure. 'Vivian. Fact is I'm not a great catch. But I'm nuts about you.'

Her eyes flickered; she turned to face him.

'Do you love me?'

'Seriously? You're leaving and you ask me that?'

'I need to know, Vivian. Please. Just tell me honestly.'

'Oh, Lou.' She put a hand on his face. 'You know I do. You must know that.'

Lou's eyes filled. He smeared away a tear. 'Believe me, Viv. I didn't want any of this to happen. But you're going to find things out about me – things I wanted to protect you from. Things I was afraid to tell you because I didn't want to lose you. But now . . .'

'What?'

'Things are at a point. I have no choice but to tell you everything. Even if it means you might want nothing to do with me—'

'That would never happen. Not ever.' She leaned over, kissing him.

Lou's chest got warm; his vision blurred with yet more tears. Lord, he loved this woman. His instincts told him to hold back, make up a story. Not reveal the truth. Not risk confiding. But she was too smart; she'd know if he lied. For better or worse, he had to trust her.

Lou picked up her hand, kissed it. 'Two things. First, if after I've finished talking you want me to leave, I will.'

'I won't want that. But okay.' She put out her cigarette.

'Second. No matter what, even if you throw me out and never want to see me again, promise that you'll keep what I'm about to tell you secret. Between us.'

Vivian nodded. Lou took a deep breath, avoiding her eyes, and tried to decide where to begin.


Harper was cold. Beyond cold. Her teeth chattered and her body quaked. She'd been lying still for far too long in frigid air, wearing no coat, just a heavy sweater. Tried to remember facts about hypothermia. How to deal with it. But her mind was muddled and slow. Wasn't that one of the symptoms? Confused thinking? Maybe if she drifted off, took a nap, she'd be clearer when she woke up. But wait – that was part of it, too – yes. Fatigue was a sure sign of hypothermia. She had to remember that, not let herself fall asleep. Probably, she should keep moving, increase her circulation. Get her body temperature up. But moving was tough with her arms and legs bound. No way she could flex them, let alone do jumping jacks. Damn Sty and Evan.

She listened, couldn't hear them. For a while, they'd been banging and clunking, bickering outside, but now, she heard nothing. Were they gone? Evan had threatened to come back, but maybe he'd changed his mind. Maybe he was just going to leave her there to freeze to death. Harper wanted to shut her eyes, take a break. Her hands were frozen and painful, craved stillness, but she kept working the nail into her bindings, pulling and twisting her wrists, trying to rip her bindings apart. Her hands were clumsy, though. And her fingers wouldn't obey, felt dull and swollen. Uncoordinated. She tugged on the bindings but they wouldn't give. Finally, panting and frustrated, she lay back and rested. Maybe she could sleep for just a few minutes. What would be the harm? She closed her eyes, but the door groaned, rousing her. A light flashed up at the loft. Harper watched, willed herself alert.

The old wooden floor creaked under someone's steps. Harper yanked her wrists apart as hard as she could, fighting to separate them. She heard a tiny rip, but her hands wouldn't come free, so she lay still, her eyes open just a crack.

The ladder trembled under someone's footholds.

Evan emerged slowly. His bandaged hand, then his head, his shoulders, finally his legs. Once he was up on the loft, he squatted beside her. 'I know you're awake. Don't bother pretending.'

Harper opened her eyes, met his. Her eyes were well accustomed to the dark; she could see his smirk. 'Why don't we chat?'

'Untie me.' Oddly, her mouth didn't work; her teeth chattered and her words garbled, came out, 'Nd yme.'

He laughed. 'Ymago nngawa.' Mimicking her.

She thought of Hank, how hard he'd worked to speak after his accident. When Evan and Sty knocked her out, maybe she'd suffered a brain injury, too. She was so cold, too cold to think. Maybe her mouth was frozen, her words distorted by the cold. She tried again, more slowly. 'Un. Tie. Me.' Her voice quaked with cold.

'No, see. You don't get to tell me what to do. In fact, you don't get to decide anything. You made a big mistake, biting me, so here's what's going to happen. Later on, in a little while, you're going to die.' He watched her.

Harper shivered but didn't react.

'Nothing sudden. You're going to go little by little.' He aimed his flashlight at her face. 'And I'm going to watch.'

Harper didn't say anything. Didn't want to waste energy. Slowly, with the ice-cold stumps that were her hands, she worked the nail, felt another tiny rip of fabric. But still couldn't free her arms.

Evan set the flashlight down in the hay, took out his knife, held it with the hand she'd bitten. The fabric around the wound was bloody, but he held the weapon steadily. The knife was formidable, much like army issue. Harper blinked, straining to stay alert. Her eyes burned, aching to close; her body begged to give in to the cold, to let go and simply fade. But Evan waved the knife in her face. Wouldn't let her drift. Made her focus on its seven-inch stainless-steel sawback blade.

'Thing is, I can't decide where to start.' He held the blade against Harper's cheek, then her throat. He lowered it slowly to her belly – oh God, the baby? Harper's thoughts were slow; she didn't flinch, didn't show fear, so he kept it moving down to the thigh, the tendons of her strong leg. Then back up to the right side of her face. Slowly, deliberately, he pressed down, slicing a thin line along her lower jaw. Letting blood ooze. 'Any preferences?'

Harper slowed her breathing. Had been trained to resist torture. The cold had dulled her sense of pain, but the sting of the knife revived and infuriated her. She refused to let Evan get sick pleasure from hurting her, and deliberately shifted her thoughts away from him and his knife, concentrated instead on working the nail. 'I want.' She worked her mouth carefully. 'To sit up.'

Evan chortled, repeating. 'You want to sit up?'

'I don't want to die lying down.'

Evan held the knife to her ear. Traced its edge down to her earlobe. Dug a small hole in her forehead. 'Your third eye,' he grinned.

The pain was almost unnoticeable, thin and shrill. Harper focused on resistance, relaxed her muscles. Refused to flinch. Would not let him see fear. Worked the nail.

'All right. I don't see why we can't grant your final request.' He stood behind her head, lifted her by the armpits. Helped her sit up.

Harper bent her knees and straightened her back, slowly finding her balance, she rotated toward the ladder. Blinked a trickle of blood out of her eye. Pushed the nail, jabbing her bindings again.

Evan walked around to her face, examined it. Frowned. 'This won't do. You're asymmetrical. Looks like you've got half a grin.'

He moved the knife to her chin, where his first cut had ended. He knelt in front of her and pressed the knife to her skin, smiling.

But his smile vanished when Harper swung her torso forward with all the force she could muster, butting him in the head with a harsh crack. Evan flew, arms flailing, off the edge of the loft.

Lou couldn't meet Vivian's eyes. Couldn't bear to see the sadness – or maybe the anger – that would undoubtedly erupt there. But he steeled himself, determined to tell her the truth, even the worst parts, even the parts she might never forgive. He would tell her from the start about his past. About coming up the ranks, being a bagman for Wally. Collecting money, delivering it, lots of it. So much that he figured Wally would never miss a little. And he'd begun to take a little off the top. Then a little more.

He'd stop then to explain about Wally's temper. How he'd chopped a guy's hand off because the guy had touched a woman he liked. How he'd thrown a guy off a bridge because he'd left Wally out of a real-estate deal. Blown up a guy's dad's house to get him to do business. He'd tell her how Wally had no conscience. How he wanted people to be afraid of him, so he didn't hesitate to maim, kill, blow things up, smash things – like Harper's window.

Once Vivian understood the kind of maniac Wally was, Lou would explain that Wally had found out he'd borrowed some money from him. And then he'd have to tell her the worst part, that Wally had taken Harper – and probably those two boys next door – as collateral. And it was his fault.

Lou took Vivian's hands. How was he supposed to tell her about Harper? How could he tell her that, even if he paid Wally back, Wally was likely to make an example of him by doing something outrageous – killing him or those he loved? So not just Harper, but Vivian herself was in danger. Because of him.

Probably, she'd throw him out, have nothing to do with him after she found out Harper's disappearance was his fault and her own life was at risk because of him. But he had to tell her. Couldn't lie any more. Couldn't ask her to go away with him on false pretenses.

If he was going to make a fresh start, he needed to come clean. And so, as Vivian waited beside him, he let go of her hands. And began.

'After you hear this, Vivian, you'll probably want me to get lost. And I won't blame you.'

'Ridiculous.' She put her hand on his arm. 'Nothing could be that bad.'

He turned and looked at her. Saw the strain. Looked away. Told himself just to spit it out. Took a breath. 'First of all. My name. It's not Lou. It's Ed. Ed Strunk.'

She didn't say anything.

'I've had a lot of names over the years. In fact, I have a new one I'm about to start using now—'

'Why are you telling me this?'

'Vivian, just hear me out. I've done some stuff – worked with some really bad people—'

'No. I don't want to hear it. I don't. The past is over; I don't care about it. I have a past, too. Do you want to know everything I've ever done?'

'This is different—'

'It's not. I promise you. We all have stuff in our pasts. Why would I want to hear every nasty detail of yours?'

'Because my past – because there are consequences.'

She looked him flat in the eye. 'So? So why now? Why are you choosing to tell me this now? Can't you see how much stress I'm already under?'

He couldn't help it. He needed to look at her. Her face was tired, her skin pale. But even now, with all her anxiety, her eyes were filled with tenderness. Lou reached over, put his hand on her cheek.

'I'm telling you this now because I want you to go away with me. Marry me. Now. Let's leave everything behind and start over fresh – we can go anywhere . . .'

Vivian's mouth opened. Her arms encircled his neck; her body crushed against his. 'Yes.' She kissed him again and again. 'Of course, I'll marry you, Lou. Or Ed. Or whatever your real name is . . .' Suddenly she sat back, the sparkle fading from her eyes.

Obviously, she was thinking about Harper. 'Vivian. That's part of what I have to tell you. Harper might not be able to come back until I'm gone.'

'I don't understand.'

'I think I know who took her. It's because of me.'

And there it was, that look in her eyes. Hurt. Betrayal. Fury. All of it and more.

'But when I'm gone, I think they'll let her go.'

'What? Why?'

'I have a plan. You and I leave. And then, when we're gone—'

'You know who took Harper?' She stood, facing him. 'Why didn't you say something? Why haven't you told the police? What kind of man are you, Lou – or whatever your name is? I'm calling that policewoman. You can tell her what you told me. And you know what? After you're done telling her everything you know about my daughter, I want you to leave.' Her hand went up and came down hard.

Lou felt the slap for a long time after it happened. The sting traveled along his skin like ripples on disturbed water. He sat still, the pain on his face echoing throughout his body and heart, and he stared at the bathroom door behind which Vivian loudly sobbed.

Harper leaned over the edge of the loft, peering through the shadows. Evan's body sprawled on the barn floor, his head twisted in the wrong direction. His neck broken.

Shivering, she shimmied away from the edge, pushing the nail with wooden fingers, twisting her wrists, ignoring the dull pain of misdirected punctures and strained muscles. 'Almost,' she grimaced. 'Just a few more jabs.' She spoke out loud, trying to convince both herself and the baby that they would soon be free.

Wind howled, buzzing through loose beams. But otherwise, the barn was silent. Where was Sty? What was he doing? It would have taken both Evan and Sty to unload the armoire. Probably they'd done that while she'd been left alone. But whatever Sty was doing now, he'd be finished soon. He'd come looking for Evan. And for her.

Hurry, she urged herself. The nail got stuck; she must have jammed it into her numb flesh again. Damn. She pulled it back, felt another small warm dribble on her wrists. And lost her breath as a contraction lurched around her middle, choking, refusing to let go. Alone and freezing in the dark empty barn, she forced steady breaths, counting seconds to remind herself that the contraction would pass. Assuring herself and the baby that somehow they would be okay. Straining her ears for sounds of Sty. Clutching the nail.

Gradually, the stranglehold eased. Harper sat for a moment, mind muddled, teeth clenched with cold. How had she managed to get into this mess, putting her baby in danger? What a rotten mother she was, even before she'd given birth. She pictured Hank, holding a squirming newborn in his big calloused hands. Wondered if he'd forgive her. If she'd see him again. But she was wasting time, needed to get back to ripping the bindings. She steadied the nail with freezing fingers and bent her raw and bloodied wrists, shoved the nail up. Oops, too fast – the nail slipped, fell from her grasp. Landed with a soft whoosh in straw. Damn.

Wailing in anger and desperation, she swung around to search for the nail, straining her back and shoulders, reaching down behind her body into the hay.

Hearing a rip as her hands separated.

Harper pulled her arms forward, stretching in delight. She wiggled her deadened fingers, quickly assessed the oozing punctures on her wrists, touched the crusty bump on her skull. Decided that her injuries weren't life-threatening. Then, hurrying, she bent her legs, peeled duct tape off her ankles with fingers she couldn't feel. Then, unsteadily, she stood, balancing on the heavy stumps that were her feet. And realized how close she was to the edge of the loft.

Harper backed away, steadying herself, wobbled over to the ladder and lowered a numb foot onto a rung, shifted her weight onto it, holding on with numb hands. Watching the door for Sty, she carefully climbed down, stepped around Evan's broken body. And ran out the open door of the barn.

Sty threw the last of the branches over the armoire, climbed halfway up the hill and looked down. Couldn't see the thing at all, even when he flashed his light on it. The snow around it was trampled, but the next storm would come in a day or two. Would cover it completely. Besides, nobody ever came out here. The place was abandoned; when they'd arrived, except for their own tire marks, the snow had been undisturbed.

He took a breath, looking over at the car they'd smashed against a tree. The body in the driver's seat. Damn Evan. He'd been so proud of his solo kill. Defiant, even. He didn't seem to comprehend the consequences of carelessness. Or maybe he didn't care. Maybe he was out of control. Clearly, Sty was going to have to assert himself before Evan inadvertently led the police to them. He recalled the frames of designer glasses that unraveled Leopold and Loeb.

Meantime, they had their neighbor to dispense with. Sty grimaced, displeased at the thought. Evan had insisted they could use her in their studies, but frankly, Evan had zero depth when it came to science. If he had, he would realize that a woman could not be substituted for a man; in research, members of the test group had to share a basic profile, including age and gender. The subjects had to have similar characteristics to Sty himself; they had to be male, in good health, between the ages of eighteen and twenty-five, when they would least expect to face death. Sty had no interest whatever in studying the death of a woman – let alone a pregnant one. That experience was irrelevant; he could extrapolate nothing from it. No, the motorcycle lady's death was merely pragmatic. With all she knew, they simply couldn't let her live. But it was a nuisance, best accomplished quickly. Evan would simply have to control himself.

Speaking of which, he hadn't seen Evan for too long. Where was he? Oh no – had he gone ahead, begun carving up the neighbor? Damn it. Sty turned, heading for the barn. Hurried up the hill, stepping carefully over fallen trees and snow-covered brush, envisioning what he might find. The door was open; he stepped in and flashed the light up at the loft. Saw no Evan. No woman.

'Evan?' His voice sounded hollow. 'Are you up there?'

Nobody answered. He lowered the flashlight, aiming it across the floor toward the ladder. Froze for a moment when he saw what looked like Evan's bandaged hand. Evan's jacket. Evan's face. Sty ran across the barn, screaming Evan's name. Knelt beside the body, holding his head.

Sty scanned the area for Harper, but didn't see her. Cursing, he got to his feet and headed out of the barn, catching sight of the woman as she stumbled down the hill.

The bathroom door finally opened. Vivian stepped out, her eyes red and swollen, her face and neck blotchy. She wore her silk robe, tightened the sash.

'I've been thinking.' She stepped over to the bed where he'd been sitting, waiting for her to emerge.

'Sit down.' He patted the mattress beside him.

Vivian sat. Dabbed her nose. 'Harper is my daughter. My blood.'

Lou nodded. She was going to send him packing. He deserved it, too, after everything he'd done.

'And, from what you've said, she wouldn't be in trouble if not for you. The people who took her were really trying to send you a message, am I right?'

He nodded again. 'Vivian. I'm so sorry. If I could take it back, in a heartbeat, I would. I'd do anything—'

'I know that. Like I said, I've been thinking. You say that paying this guy back won't help. He might not let Harper go anyway?'

'It's fifty-fifty.'

'But if you take off, he might let her go?'

'I'm not going to lie, Vivian. He might. He might not. He'd have no reason to hold her, but that's no guarantee.'

Vivian folded her hands. 'Then, no matter what we do, it sounds like there's a fifty-fifty chance of Harper coming home. Which means you ought to take off. You should split while you can. Lou, I mean it. Do whatever you can, but get away from that sonofabitch and start fresh someplace else.'

Lou's eyes filled. Was she really sending him away? Without her? What was the point of starting a new life if Vivian weren't going to be with him?

'Go, Lou. I mean it.' She faced him, her eyes clear and loving. She touched his chest.

He covered her hand with his, squeezed. 'But, Vivian. I don't – I can't leave without you.' His voice broke. His shoulders slumped.

'Get real, Lou. I can't go anywhere while Harper's missing.'

'I understand.' He understood why they called it a broken heart. His chest hurt; his heart felt as if it had been chopped in half.

'She's my blood, like I said. That's why I'm here for her.' Vivian reached for the Camels, lit one. 'But honestly, Lou, I can't make the guy who took her let her go. I can't make her pregnancy go smoothly. I can't control any goddamned thing for her.' She inhaled. Exhaled smoke.

Lou waited, unable to speak or move. Afraid he'd crumble.

When Vivian continued, her voice was deep and ragged. 'Truth is, I'm getting up in years. I can't base my life on what my daughter needs. At some point, Harper's got to fend for herself – and it's not like she's alone in the world. She's got Hank. She's got her fancy education. It's me I need to worry about. I have needs, too, and I have to do what's right for me; I deserve some happiness, too, don't I?'

Lou didn't understand at first. He gazed at her, uncertain.

'So go, Lou. Set things up. I'll stay here and see what happens with Harper. I'll be here in case she comes home. And when you've got things together, I'll follow as soon as I can. How does—?'

Vivian couldn't say any more. Lou grabbed her so tightly, she could barely breathe.

\*     \*     \*

Harper's weak left leg kept caving in; her head hurt, her body felt sluggish, and she was shuddering from the cold, but she had to keep going. Had to get to the pickup truck. Had to remember where it was. She looked around, thought she saw it parked in a clearing down the hill. But Sty – had he seen her? Was he chasing her? She looked over her shoulder, slipped on an icy patch and went down, breaking the fall with unfeeling hands. Panting, pushing herself back onto her feet, she noticed a dark stain in the snow. Glanced at her hands, saw bloody gouges in her wrist, recalled her accidental thrusts of the nail. She felt no pain. Never mind. Shivering, panting, she looked again for Sty, saw no one, nothing moving, and started again for the truck. With any luck, the keys would still be in it. Otherwise, she'd have to mess with the wires.

Harper's legs dragged. Unable to feel her feet, she had to test each step so she wouldn't slip again. Her lungs burned with the cold as she grabbed onto tree trunks, pushed away low branches with hands that sensed nothing. Maybe she should sit a minute, catch her breath. She stopped and looked for a spot, saw one under a pine. Headed for it, but remembered she couldn't sit; she had to get to the truck. She was almost there – it was only about fifty yards down the hill. But maybe that wasn't right; maybe she wasn't seeing things right. Because the truck had seemed only about fifty yards away when she'd started out, hadn't it? Her body quaked as the wind gusted, passing through her, rattling her ribs. Searing her eyes. Why hadn't she worn a coat? Her sweater was useless. In fact, she might as well take it off, leave it in the snow. And lie down for a minute. The ground looked soft, invited her to stretch out and rest. She knew she shouldn't. But why again? She tried to remember. In fact, why was she outside? Where was she going? She stopped, looked ahead. Saw a truck down the hill. Yes, she was going to the truck. Not real sure why. She was tired, needed to sit.

'No.' Whose voice was that? Was someone there?

'Keep going,' it said. Harper didn't have strength to argue. She pressed on, tottering on frozen stumpy feet toward a truck that seemed unreachable. She wrapped numb arms around her belly to keep the baby warm, vaguely remembering something about extreme temperatures. About freezing to death, how the limbs slowed down, became uncoordinated. How the body pulled all its heat to its core. She thought about that, how she couldn't really feel her arms or most of her legs. But she wouldn't freeze to death; she was Army, had been trained to survive in all kinds of conditions.

She slogged on, trying to recall what she was supposed to do. One step, another. She was so tired, tried to focus – couldn't. Her mind was slow. She had all the symptoms, must be freezing. Actually, it wasn't so bad; didn't hurt. Seemed gentle. Easy. The snowy blanket, the huddled trees, the blank night sky would watch over her while she slept. She stopped, selecting a spot to curl onto.

Hypothermia, she remembered the name. 'Hythemi.' Even though her mouth wouldn't work, she made herself say the word. Her voice sounded thin and fragile as she sank into the snow.

Suddenly, the baby kicked. Delivered a punt, right to her gut.

The baby? Was it strong enough to kick so hard? Why wouldn't it let her rest? Harper stumbled back onto her feet and pressed on. One step. Two. She focused on the truck, counting steps to make sure she was moving.

Finally, limping and hunched, she came to the clearing, had maybe twenty more steps to the truck when her iced-up mind reminded her to look for Sty. Harper hesitated, glanced around, saw Sty running down the hill. Crouching low, she dashed toward the cab. By the time Sty got to the clearing, she was an arm's length from the truck. With a final effort, she flew forward, grabbed the handle with numb fingers, pulled it open. Climbed in and, clumsily, violently, slammed the door. Looked out and saw Sty racing, just seconds away. The keys . . .

The keys were there. With fingers too frozen to hurt, Harper turned them, started the ignition. Put the truck in gear and stepped on the gas.

The truck lurched; the engine burped and stalled. Damn. She tried to think. What was she doing here? Whose truck was this? And why was she running?

'Never mind.' The voice was back. 'Just go.'

Harper followed orders, shifted back to first gear, pushed the clutch and started over, turned the key again. Checking the windows and rear-view mirror, she stepped carefully on the gas, crawled up the hill, shifted into second. Accelerated slowly but steadily, looking around for Sty. Wondering where he'd gone. Finally, when she'd rolled past the abandoned house, she exhaled.

That's when she heard a thump, felt the truck bounce, checked the rear-view mirror. And saw Sty, standing in the truck bed, right behind her.

Damn. Harper pressed her foot down, shifted to third. Steered the truck to the left, veered sharply to the right, trying to shake him off. Watching the mirror, seeing him holding the side of the truck, swaying as she turned.

The ground was steep and snowy. Harper aimed for bumps and rocks. Sped up. Skidded off the property onto an unplowed but single-lane road. Saw Sty in the truck bed, hanging on. She raced ahead, slid into fourth, doing fifty, sixty. Suddenly, jamming on the brakes, hoping to send Sty flying.

The truck screeched and zigzagged, spun around. When it stopped, she checked the rear-view. Didn't see Sty. She looked out at the road behind her, in the side mirrors. No Sty. She grabbed the steering wheel and boosted herself up so she could see into the back of the truck. From what she could see, it was empty. Maybe he'd been thrown off the road, into the woods?

Still shaking, she reached over, restarted the ignition, turned on the heat. Maybe she should climb out of the cab, make sure he wasn't crouching in the blind spot below the window.

But warm air was blowing from the heater. Her hands burned, beginning to thaw out. Her mind was beginning to function, deciding not to go back out into the cold for any reason. She stepped on the gas, shifted into second, steered the truck past wooded areas and vacant lots, empty farmhouses, hoping to find a main road. Nothing outside looked familiar or even occupied. Where the hell was she? Why wasn't there a gas station or a mini-market anywhere? Harper was lost, had no idea what time – even what day it was. Christmas Eve? Or maybe Christmas? She pictured the ugly tree her mother had bought, the flashing lights. And all those gifts. And then she realized that Hank would call – he'd find out she was missing and contact the police. In fact, maybe he'd done that. And the FBI, too. Maybe they were already searching . . .

Something popped, then whooshed. Harper turned and saw Sty reaching through an open space where the rear window had been. He'd taken out the window? She swerved, but Sty grabbed the back of her seat, steadying himself. She veered the other way, pushing the gas. Gaining speed, trying to knock him over. Sty's arm went out, snaked around her throat and squeezed, choking her. Harper steered with one hand, grabbed and scratched his arm with the other. She couldn't breathe, couldn't get leverage to fight him. She floored the pedal, felt the pickup zoom ahead, jammed her foot on the brake, then the gas again. The truck slammed forward, then back. The force made Sty lose his grip, sent him flying backwards into the truck bed, slamming his head against steel.

This time, Harper climbed out and into the back of the pickup. Sty's eyes rolled and he struggled to get up, but she lunged, cold-cocking him, watching to make sure he was going to stay down. Noticed blood pouring from the back of his head. Even so, Harper waited a moment to see if he'd stir. Finally, when she was sure he wasn't going to come after her, she got back in the cab, turned the heat up, and somehow found her way to a main road. As the sun peeked over the horizon, she headed home.

Lou put his suitcase in the trunk. The duffel bag would go up front, beside him in the car. He wasn't going to let it out of sight, brought it with him to the kitchen. Vivian was bleary-eyed, sitting at the table, poking French toast around her plate. Pretending to be fine.

How could he leave her this way?

Well, he had no choice. He sat beside her, picking up his mug. 'All set,' he said as he took a last swig of coffee.

She nodded, her body braced as if for the lash.

'As soon as you're ready, you'll join me.'

She nodded again. Sighed.

'Vivian. Talk to me. What? Are you having second thoughts?'

She didn't look angry, just defeated. 'Look, Lou – I mean, Ed – see? I don't even know what to call you—'

'Try Oliver.' He smiled, took her hand. 'Or Ollie.'

Her eyebrows lifted. 'Ollie?'

Outside, a car door slammed. Damn – Wally? So early? Lou grabbed Vivian and ducked, pulling her under the table. It had to be Wally or his people. Who else would be here at sunrise? Wally must have psyched him out, figured that he'd take off. Showed up early for his money.

'Shh,' he told Vivian. 'Get against the wall. Don't move.'

On hands and knees, he crawled to his duffel, got his gun. The kitchen door swung open; Lou saw a pair of fleecy slip-on boots. Heard Vivian scream. And looked up.

\*    \*    \*

She'd made it. She was home. She wasn't sure how long she'd been driving, not sure how she'd gotten there, but seeing a light on in the kitchen, she'd climbed up to the deck, pulled the kitchen door open and stopped, unable to take another step. Exhausted, her whole body sore, she leaned against the wall and sunk to the floor, gradually taking in the scene. The aroma of fresh coffee – and of something else. Pancakes? Lou on his knees beside her, for some reason, holding a gun. And her mother huddled under the kitchen table, peering out with a ghastly expression, hoarsely barking her name.

And Lou kept repeating her name. Asking questions. 'How did you get away? Did you run or did they let you go? What did they say?' Her mother skittering across the floor, smothering her with hugs. And then thunking noises in the hall. A large dark figure bursting through the door. And Harper stopped breathing.

Hank? Hank was home?

'Hank?' She tried to stand but couldn't convince her legs to support her. And her mother was draped around her neck.

'Hoppa!'

Crutches clattered to the floor. Hank dove down, grabbed her from Vivian's arms, peppered her with kisses. Hank? Why was he home? What had happened?

'Hurt.' He studied the wounds on her forehead and cheek. 'Bad?'

'I'm okay. I'm fine.' Her speech was still slow, even though her words were no longer slurred by the cold. 'How come you came home?'

'Surprise. You.' His eyes welled up, his gaze traveling across her face, down her body. A hand rested on her belly. 'For Christmas. Home.'

His other hand squeezed hers; she winced in pain.

'Hurt?' He frowned, looking at it. It was discolored. Almost purple at the fingertips. He took her other hand to examine it, saw the thick clots of blood on her wrist. 'Vivian,' he ordered. 'Make a bath. Warm not hot.'

The next minutes blurred in a flurry of probing, examining, fussing. Hank dabbed the cuts on her face with a warm cloth, pressed sterile compresses onto the jagged tears on her wrist. Lou gave her hot coffee and circled her, agitated, asking where she'd been. How she'd gotten away. If they were coming after her. What they'd said. She shook her head, not ready to go into all that, not sure why Lou cared so intensely. Why was he so interested in Evan and Sty? Hank asked him to stop, but Lou kept asking questions.

'Did they mention me?' His voice sounded urgent.

She shook her head, no. Winced as Hank pressed harder on her wrist.

'Do you know why they did this? What they want?'

'I don't. No.'

'Was a guy named Wally there?'

Wally? 'No.'

'Let her be,' Hank growled.

'Lou, relax. I'm okay. It's over. Stop worrying.'

Lou nodded, pursing his lips. He blinked rapidly, checked the clock. Ran a hand through his hair. Looked out the kitchen window.

'I have to talk to your mother.' Holding his duffel bag, he dashed out of the room.

The questions didn't stop. Hank asked what had happened to her wrist, her face. Whether she could feel his touch on her fingers, toes, ears, nose. If she knew where Sty and Evan were. She couldn't keep up with all the questions; her mind – her whole body – was still slow. And before she could form an answer to one, another question came at her.

At some point, Lou and Vivian reappeared, holding hands, heads together, whispering. Oblivious to the trouble Hank had with his crutches as he helped Harper to the bathroom where he gently undressed her, helped her into the tub. Harper lay back, eyes fixed on Hank, trying to grasp that he was really home, really there with her, perched on the side of the tub. The wooden numbness of her hands and feet thawed in warm water; as blood began to circulate again, her nerves woke up, too, firing angry piercing shots of pain. Hank gave her pills. Ibuprofen? Aspirin? Something. He stayed with her, reminding her about hypothermia and frostbite. Explaining that rewarming would hurt, that the pain was normal. That she'd be okay.

Harper soaked, rewarming. Hurting. And finally, Hank called out, asking Vivian to bring soft fleece clothing, warm gloves and socks, and, when Harper got out of the bath, he helped her dress in soft layers of warmth. Leaning on crutches, he walked her to the living room, settled her on the sofa. Wrapped her in blankets.

Detective Rivers greeted her from the wingback chair. Rivers? When had they called her? How long had she been there? There

were also EMTs scurrying about, messing with her, insisting on
checking her temperature, her still-open wounds, her pupils, her
tender fingers and toes, her pulse, her baby's heartbeat. They wanted
to take her to the hospital. The tall one, Jerry, said that she had a
concussion, that she needed a thorough exam.

Harper had no energy. Refused to go anywhere. As long as the
baby was okay, she said she'd stay home and see her obstetrician
in a couple of days.

'No. You're going.' Hank's voice held no room for negotiation.
'I'll be with you. Not be there long. But going.'

Jerry took that as a signal to hook her up to an IV.

'What's that for?' she asked.

'Just in case.' He rolled up her sleeve and began tying a ribbon
of thick rubber around her arm, looking for a vein. The band looked
too much like duct tape; Harper yanked her arm away. Her flesh was
still tender, still defrosting. And she didn't want anything tied around
her arm. 'Please. I'll go to the emergency room. Don't do that.'

Instantly, Hank was beside her, holding her, urging her to think
of the baby, saying that they needed to take every precaution. And
before she knew it, Harper had an IV in her arm and Jerry and the
other guy were lifting her onto a gurney. Gunshots and shouts echoed
in the distance; she smelled smoke, recalled another gurney, other
wounds. She kept her eyes on Hank, using his image to root herself.

As they tied her on, she told them to wait. 'Ma?' she called,
sitting up, looking for Vivian.

Vivian was in the hall outside the kitchen, hugging Lou, who
was dressed in his down jacket, carrying a duffel bag. She made
him wait, ran past the EMTs and Harper to the Christmas tree,
retrieved a small gift, ripped the paper off, took a thick gold chain
out of the box. Hung it on Lou's neck. He kissed Vivian, held her
for a moment and, nodding to the group around Harper, headed out
the kitchen door.

Vivian didn't move. She stared after him, as if not hearing Harper's
voice.

'Ma?' Harper called again.

This time, Vivian spun around, startled. Her face was bloated,
wet with tears.

'Where's Lou. Going?' Hank asked.

Vivian looked over her shoulder at the empty spot where Lou

had been. 'Oh, nowhere.' She gathered herself, squaring her shoulders, and came to join them.

'Nowhere?' Harper persisted. 'With a duffel bag?'

Outside, a car started.

'He's taking your car?'

'Of course. He always uses my car. We're a couple.' Vivian's chin wobbled.

'So where's he going?'

Vivian shrugged, smeared away tears. 'He has . . . It's a business trip.' She faked a smile.

Business? What kind of business did he have to do on Christmas Eve? 'Today?'

'On Christmas Eve?' Hank frowned.

'It's no big deal. You're the only big deal here, Harper.'

The EMTs were running out of patience. 'We have to get going, Ma'am.'

'Don't worry, everybody.' Vivian made herself sound cheery. 'Lou will be back in a day or two.' Her mother was lying. Harper saw it on her face.

'What happened, Ma? Did you just break up?'

Hank and Rivers, even the EMTs, turned to look at Vivian.

'Of course not.' Vivian worried the tissue in her hands. 'I told you. It's just business. It came up suddenly.'

Outside, the car engine purred. Probably Lou was warming it up. For a minute, they stood awkwardly, everyone staring at Vivian.

'It's no big deal. The only big deal here is that my daughter has come back.' She stopped, her voice choking. 'Please. Everyone, would you stop minding other people's business?' In tears, Vivian turned away and ran up the stairs.

'Ma – wait.' Harper tried to get up and go after her, but Jerry grabbed her shoulder. 'Hank, go after her – please. She can't take another break-up.'

Hank started but fumbled on the steps, clumsy with his crutches.

'You stay with Mrs Jennings. I'll go,' Rivers volunteered. She ran upstairs, calling Vivian.

'Ma'am, we need to go,' Jerry insisted.

'Just another minute – please. I can't leave my mother alone now. She's fragile. Believe me.'

Jerry crossed his arms; the other EMT rolled his eyes and sat on the floor. A few moments passed and Rivers returned. 'Let's go.'

'But my mother—'

'She insists she's just upset because it's Christmas Eve and he had to work. She swears they didn't break up.'

Harper wasn't convinced. Her mother was pretending to be okay, had done that before. Had also swallowed several bottles of sleeping pills before. But Jerry tightened the straps of the gurney around Harper's blankets, swaddling her like a baby, and Harper gave in, lay back, watched the ceiling and the top of the door frame as they wheeled her out. Heard Vivian's car shift into reverse as Lou pulled out of the driveway. Turned her head to see him, but a black SUV blocked her view. Felt the baby doing flip turns, safe and indifferent to the world.

When they moved the gurney down the front steps, a cold wind rose and slapped her face. That's when she remembered Sty.

'Wait! I forgot . . .' She lifted her head, pointed to the pickup parked by the kitchen door. 'Sty! He's over there.'

Hank furrowed his brows. 'Who?'

Rivers stepped over to the gurney, told the EMTs to wait a minute. 'You're saying Sty's in that truck?'

Harper nodded. 'In the back – unconscious.' How could she have forgotten that? It had to be the hypothermia, she told herself. Her brain was numb. She wondered if Sty had hypothermia, too, lying in the cold all this time. Or if he'd frozen to death. Oh God, had she killed him? How could she have forgotten he was out there? She remembering coming home, driving up to the house, pulling herself up the steps to the deck, not feeling her lower legs or hands. She'd been thinking of Sty then – thinking she'd get Lou to call the police and help take him inside. So why hadn't she? Harper thought back, closed her eyes, saw herself falling into the kitchen. Smelling maple syrup. Letting her legs sink to the floor.

And seeing her mother crouching under the kitchen table. Why? What was wrong? Vivian's face contorted – screaming. And Lou – she saw him again, crawling to her. Holding a gun . . .

'Are you sure he was there?' Rivers was back, exhaling short rapid clouds.

Harper nodded. 'Out cold.'

'There's blood on the—'

'We fought. He fell back and hit his head—'

'Mrs Jennings, there's no sign of him. We checked your garage, too. He might still be around, maybe in the fraternity. Do we have your permission to look in your house?'

When Hank climbed into the ambulance beside her, Harper saw Rivers on her radio, putting out an APB and asking for officer support to conduct a search.

They didn't find Sty in her house or the fraternity. They didn't find him in the woods or anywhere. Somehow, he'd slipped away.

It was early afternoon when Rivers arrived in Harper's hospital room. Harper's wrist was wrapped and her jaw lined with butterfly strips. Half-eaten meatloaf and mashed potatoes sat in a puddle of gelling gravy on her tray. Rivers greeted Hank and Harper, took a seat in one of the two guest chairs, asked how Harper was feeling, waited a beat, and said she had a few questions.

'Baby okay?'

'Baby's fine.' Harper smiled, felt it swimming.

'Hoppa not.'

'It's no big deal. A concussion. They want me to rest.'

'And wrist. And frostbite. And—'

'What do you need to ask, Detective?'

'I want to go over everything again. Tell me what happened. From the start.'

The start? What was the start? Harper sighed. Hadn't she already told Rivers everything? She must have. Why couldn't she remember?

Rivers was waiting. Hank watched her.

She thought back, saw herself in the fraternity, hiding in the armoire. Then suddenly, the memory kicked in and she grimaced, almost gagged. 'I was next door.'

'Next door?' Hank's eyebrows furrowed. 'Why?'

'Mr Jennings, please,' Rivers scolded. 'Let her talk.'

'Sty and Evan came home and I couldn't let them see me, so I hid in that big old armoire.'

Rivers raised her eyebrows.

'But someone was already in it. Dead. I think it was Sebastian.'

'Who?' Hank scowled.

'I told you about him, Mr Jennings. The college kid from Elmira who disappeared.'

Hank looked from Harper to Rivers. 'Hoppa. You found him? Dead?'

'Mr Jennings, we need to focus. I'm trying to find out the facts. You can ask your wife questions later.'

But Harper was distracted by Hank's question, worried that he was upset. 'I didn't tell you about this because I didn't want you to worry—'

'But need to tell. Said no secrets—'

'Both of you. Stop. Mrs Jennings, continue.'

But Harper had forgotten what she'd been talking about. Why was her mind so scrambled? Why couldn't it thaw out like her poor throbbing toes? Hank sat beside her, his hand on her arm. She stared at it, felt its reassuring weight, and closed her eyes, straining to remember what she wanted to say.

'Take your time,' Rivers urged. 'Hypothermia messes with your thought process. It can fog up the memory. Just tell me what you can.'

Harper nodded, opened her eyes, trying to relax and let the memories surface. And recalled Lou, rushing out the door. Where had he been going?

'Mrs Jennings?' Rivers leaned forward, resting her elbow on her knee. 'What happened after you got into the armoire?'

Oh, the armoire? Harper remembered the stink of the cold corpse, its limp slipperiness as she lay on top of it. But Rivers didn't need to hear about that; Harper skipped ahead to waking up in the loft of the barn, shivering, head pulsing, wrists and ankles taped together. She told how she'd freed her hands with a nail. How Evan had held his knife to her skin, promising to kill her. How she'd head butted him out of the loft and he'd fallen to his death.

'Where is this barn?' Rivers asked. 'Do you have any idea?'

Harper blinked. Where was it? She'd left Evan's body there, could see him splayed on the floor, neck broken. She remembered driving away, and Sty jumping onto the truck, popping out the window, lungeing, choking her. She touched her throat, remembering his arm crushing it, her effort to breathe, and then her wild steering as she'd floored the gas pedal, turning and swerving. She remembered all that. But getting to the main road, had she gone left or right? And how many times had she turned? She had no idea, had been thinking only about surviving. Breathing. And after she'd finally thrown Sty backwards and knocked him out, she'd driven around dazed, unable to feel her frozen feet and hands, turning the feeble heater up, following unplowed single-lane roads for who knew how long until she'd found a wider road that had led to another that had miraculously taken her to Route 13, from which she'd found her way home.

So, no. She didn't know where the barn was. Her pulse was too rapid. She rested for a moment before going on. Before telling Rivers about the second body, the one they'd left in the Jeep.

When she finished, Harper leaned back in the bed, drained. Rivers thanked her. Hank kissed her cheek and presented a box of chocolates. She looked at it, unable to reconcile candy with her memories. But she thanked him, offered some to Rivers and Hank, helped herself to a butter cream. It melted slowly on her tongue, its startling sweetness reminding her that it was almost Christmas. She and the baby had survived. And Hank had come home.

Vivian arrived as they were winding up the interview. Her eyes were bloodshot and puffy, but she'd showered and dressed in a big bright red sweater and dark leggings. Her hair was freshly washed. Harper was relieved; apparently, Vivian wasn't trying to kill herself.

'You look nice, Ma.'

'I look like shit.'

'Feeling okay?'

'Why wouldn't I be? Lou will be back in a day or two. I told you.' She picked up the box of chocolates, examined the selection. 'No caramels?'

Rivers' phone rang. She excused herself to take the call.

'Toffee?' Hank suggested.

'No toffee. I like them chewy.' She put the box down.

'So where'd Lou go? Really.' Harper asked while Rivers was out of the room.

'I told you.' Vivian bristled. 'He had to go somewhere but he saw you were involved with the detective and the ambulance, and he didn't want to interrupt. He said to say merry Christmas.'

'Where'd he go?' Harper repeated.

Vivian shifted in her seat, crossed her legs. Eyed the box of chocolates again. Picked it up, selected a nut cluster. Bit into it.

'Ma.'

'Harper, my God. Where Lou goes is Lou's business, isn't it? He went to visit some people, that's all I know.' She popped the rest of the candy into her mouth. 'Now can we please talk about something else? Like when you're coming home? It's Christmas tomorrow and we have presents to open.'

Rivers came back into the room, her head down. She didn't sit. She crossed her arms, took a firm stance and a deep breath. Everyone stared at her.

'What?' Hank asked.

'The call I just got.' She paused, directed her gaze at Vivian. 'I'm afraid it's bad news.'

Harper's unbandaged hand went to her belly. Hank clasped her shoulder.

'Ma'am? Your car is a Toyota Camry?'

Vivian's blood drained from her face. Her hand covered her mouth.

'There's been an accident.'

Harper tried to concentrate but heard only phrases – her mother's car. A crash, a fire. The driver trapped, burned, a gold chain around his neck. Lou's suitcase in the trunk. Dead at the scene.


Vivian didn't move. The light slowly went out of her eyes, and her skin turned gray. 'No,' she said. 'You're mistaken.'

Rivers paused. 'I'm sorry, Ma'am.'

'Oh, Ma. I'm so sorry.'

Hank went to Vivian, leaned his crutches against the wall, sat beside her, held her hands.

Vivian seemed startled at the attention. 'No,' she repeated. 'It's a mistake.'

'The tags are registered to you, Ma'am.'

Vivian's gaze fell to the floor, then rose to Rivers again. 'But it can't be.'

'Ma. He was driving your car. They said he was wearing your Christmas present—'

'Lou was in the car?'

'Yes, Ma'am.'

'Lou?'

'Well, he was pretty badly burned.'

'I want to see him.'

'No, Ma – you don't.' Harper had seen burned bodies, didn't want Vivian to be haunted by the memory as she was.

'It's not true,' Vivian insisted. 'It can't be. We were supposed to go away.' Tears streamed down her cheeks, but she didn't move. She stayed in the chair, repeating that the body wasn't Lou's, that he wasn't dead, that it was a mistake, until Harper asked Hank to call a doctor, and Vivian refused, insisting, despite everyone's concerns about her driving, on going home.

*     *     *

Christmas was funereal. Harper came home from the hospital to find Vivian sloshed beside the tree, which mocked them with its happy decorations, its piles of brightly wrapped presents. The house was quiet. Ominous. Uneasy. Harper tried to nap, couldn't. Sat and watched as Hank replaced the dining-room window, not even asking where he'd gotten the new glass. They ordered Chinese for dinner, but hardly ate. Barely spoke. Vivian didn't even come to the table, kept asking how she could go on, what she would do without Lou.

By nightfall, Vivian was almost comatose with drink. Hank helped her to the guest room, deposited her on the bed. Then he lay beside Harper, his hand draping her belly, and fell instantly asleep. Harper ached to join him, but she couldn't relax. She kept thinking about Lou's sudden death. And Vivian's fragile state. And something else: Sty. How had he gotten away? Where was he?

She watched for his silhouette at the door, listened for his footsteps deep into the night. When she finally drifted off, she found herself back in the loft, then wandering in endless snow. At one point, she woke Hank with a sharp kick, meant for an assailant in her dream. After that, she didn't sleep.

The next day, Hank hobbled on his crutches between Harper and Vivian, not certain who needed attention more. Finally, he called Leslie. Under the circumstances, she agreed to meet with Vivian, even though it wasn't her policy to see a patient's mother.

Vivian went first. When it was Harper's turn, she felt surprisingly uncomfortable. She went into Hank's study, sat on the sofa, poured tea, didn't speak.

'Harper,' Leslie watched her. 'How are you doing?'

'What did she say?' Harper hadn't planned to ask that. The words just popped out. 'My mother – what did she say?'

'You know I can't answer that.'

Of course she couldn't. 'But she's not suicidal?'

'What makes you ask that?'

'Because. In the past, when guys left her, she's tried to kill herself. Once with pills. Once with the exhaust from the car – and that guy wasn't even good to her. So, I'm worried.'

'I don't think you need to worry.'

'She hasn't stopped crying in two days.'

'She's in mourning.'

'Trust me, the only life Vivian is mourning is the one she thought

Lou would give her. She feels sorry for herself, as if his death is just one more awful thing that's happened to her. It's not about Lou. Trust me, she hasn't given a moment's thought to what he went through.'

Leslie paused. 'In the past you've told me that your mother has trouble empathizing. That thinking about others isn't her strong suit.'

'But they were in love. Inseparable. And Lou *burned* to death.' Harper had seen death by fire in the war. Even now, could smell searing flesh, hear silent screams. 'Why isn't that driving her crazy?'

'People do crazy in different ways. Besides, he might have been unconscious from the crash,' Leslie offered. 'Maybe he didn't suffer.'

Harper nodded. 'But maybe he did.'

Leslie didn't argue. 'You've been through a lot this week.'

Harper shrugged.

'Any flashbacks?'

'Not flashbacks. Dreams. About Sty. He comes for me, ambushes me. He tries to take the baby – with a knife.'

Leslie nodded. 'And in the dreams, do you fight back?'

'This isn't about how I handle nightmares. Leslie, Sty is real. He's out there, and he knows I know what he's done. That I'm a threat. Those boys weren't just standard-issue delinquents – they talked about murder as if it were a hobby. Something to do for fun. And Sty's free. He got away because I was careless—'

'You were suffering from shock and hypothermia. You had a concussion—'

'I left him unguarded.'

Leslie sipped tea, waiting a beat. 'You were the victim, Harper. You were kidnapped. Wounded. Half frozen to death. But even so, even in this situation, you refuse to concede that you weren't in control. So let me ask: Why do you feel the need to insist that Sty's escape is your fault?'

'Because it was.' The baby did a somersault; Harper's hand went to her middle.

'No. I think this is about your control issues. We've talked about it before. You can't tolerate having no power. But here you are, powerless. You can't help Lou. You can't help your mother or the kids Sty and Evan killed. And you can't stand that. For you, being powerless is unbearable. I think you'd rather accept blame for Sty's escape – and punish yourself for it with nightmares and worry – than admit you lacked the power to stop him.'

Harper glared, didn't like Leslie's assessment. 'Not everything is because of my personal hang-ups – the issue is that he's still out there. And he might show up . . .' She stopped because there was a knock on the door.

Hank stuck his head in. 'Sorry. Rivers here. Talk now. News.'

Still unopened Christmas presents scattered the floor, and lights still blinked on the tree. Vivian had parked herself in the wingback. Leslie rescheduled, and Harper and Hank sat on the sofa. Rivers was on the easy chair, leaning forward as if ready to sprint.

The news was big. They'd found the abandoned barn several miles south-west of Trumansburg.

'We have Evan's body. It was just as you described.'

Harper nodded, touched the wounds on her jaw and ear. Saw Evan fall, heard the thud of his landing.

'We also found the crashed Jeep with a body in it. And the armoire down the hill, buried under a mound of branches and snow.' Rivers looked at Harper. 'A body was inside. The dead have been identified as two missing students. Sebastian Levering and Steven Mills.' She let those facts sink in for a moment. 'Sebastian had been dead for several days, but the medical examiner could determine from his remains that he'd had a rough time before he died. Beaten. Bones broken. Mutilated.'

A chill ran through Harper's body. She saw the glitter of Evan's knife, felt it gliding along her jaw.

'Motive?' Hank scowled. 'Why?'

He said more, but Harper didn't hear it. A contraction grabbed her, taking away her breath and attention. She held onto Hank's arm, aware of voices but not words. When it eased, she'd lost track of the conversation.

'What's the difference?' Vivian knit her brows. 'Why is that important?'

Rivers eyed Vivian. She paused, cleared her throat. 'Well, Ma'am, since the autopsy showed cause of death to be head injuries and the lungs were clear of smoke, we can conclude he was dead before the fire. That might give you some solace.'

Harper let out a breath of relief, felt a tear well up, hung onto Hank.

Vivian nodded, dabbed at her eyes. 'I suppose.'

'Also, his remains are ready to go. We weren't able to locate any immediate family, so—'

'No, I'll take him. I was his family.'

'Then you can have him picked up—'

'He told me he wanted to be cremated.'

'That's up to you, Ma'am.'

Harper's mind see-sawed between thoughts of Lou crashing and Sebastian being mutilated. Damn. She heard Evan whisper that he would cut her to pieces, and the crack of her forehead slamming his. She closed her eyes, saw the white burst of an explosion, felt her body fly through searing hot air, slamming onto the roof of a burned-out car – no. She had to toughen up, not revisit every bad moment of her past. The cut on her jaw itched; she wasn't aware she was clawing at it until Hank grabbed her hand, whispering, 'Stop.'

'. . . to check him out, we had some surprises.'

Vivian stiffened. 'What surprises?'

Wait, Harper was lost, had again missed part of the conversation.

'Well, for example, Lou wasn't who he said he was. His real name was Ed Strunk. Did any of you know that?' Rivers' eyes bored into Vivian's.

Vivian's were blank, revealing nothing. 'What?' Her voice was low and gruff.

'Actually, at various times, he used various names. Turns out he was a small-time player with the mob—'

'Lou?' Vivian snapped. 'Not possible.'

'Fact is, over time, your boyfriend worked for a long list of mob bosses. Money launderers. Loan sharks—'

'No way. Detective, you're wrong.'

'His last known job was as a bagman for Wally Cobretti. Ever heard of him?'

'Me?' Vivian looked shocked, insulted. 'Of course not!'

'I'm asking because this Cobretti guy's got a bad temper; he's been known to go after people who cross him by going after people close to the people who cross him, if you follow. And Cobretti is not happy with Ed – or should I say, Lou. Which might put people in this room in harm's way. Because, according to our information, your boyfriend was skimming Wally's pot for quite a while. To the tune of over a quarter million.'

'Dollars?' Vivian gasped. Her eyes got wide, and she covered her face with her hands. 'Impossible.' She began to weep, reached for a box of tissues.

Harper watched, speechless, recognizing her mother's technique. She'd seen it often, could almost predict each expression on Vivian's face: shock, indignation, horror and hurt. The sequence was familiar, well practiced. And completely fake. It was her mother's way of dodging confrontation or blame. So what was her mother trying to dodge?

'He ever mention large sums of money? Or bank accounts?'

'No. Lou wasn't rich. I didn't love him for his money.'

'So you have no idea what he did with it?'

'How could I? I didn't know he had it – I still don't believe it.'

Rivers went on. 'Well. I wanted to give you a heads-up. Tomorrow's news will have a story about Lou's mob involvement and the missing money.' She looked at Vivian, then Harper. 'Speculation is that if the crash hadn't killed your boyfriend, Cobretti would have.' She paused. 'Assuming, of course, that the crash wasn't Cobretti's doing.'

Vivian sucked air, appalled.

Hank's arm slid around Harper's shoulder, pulled her close. She leaned against him and studied her mother, convinced that nothing Rivers said had surprised her. That Vivian had known about the mob, the money and Lou's past all along.

And she was right.

As soon as Detective Rivers left, Harper cornered her mother.

'The truth, Ma. Out with it. You knew about Lou, didn't you?'

Vivian opened her mouth, tried to look horrified and appalled. She failed.

'Oh, please stop pretending, Ma.'

Vivian reached for her gin and lime. Lifted the glass, gulped.

Hank looked at Harper. 'What?'

'She'll tell you. Come on, Ma—'

'All right!' Vivian sighed. 'You want to hear it? Fine. It doesn't matter. He's dead. So there's no point keeping it secret any more.' She took another drink. 'The deal was that Lou wasn't supposed to be in the car. The crash was supposed to be staged. And the car supposed to be so mangled that Cobretti would figure Lou couldn't have survived the crash and that the money burned in the fire.' She went on, describing how Lou had a new identity – Oliver Hayes. No – Hines. And, how he'd promised to send for her as soon as he could, so she could join him. And she didn't understand what had happened. How it could have gone so wrong.

Harper listened. Remembering Lou leaving in a hurry, not even saying goodbye, rushing out to the Camry.

Which had been parked in the driveway. Alongside the pickup truck holding Sty.

Harper didn't say anything, but Sty and Lou were about the same height. Lou had a belly and was older, but the body was badly burned – had been identified by the necklace and the car. But all that was circumstantial. So, Lou's body might not be Lou.

She thought it through. Pictured Sty waking up in the back of the truck. Seeing the Camry nearby, thinking he might use it to get away, climbing inside to steal it. Or to just get out of the wind and hide there for a while – He knew they'd look for him at the fraternity, so he couldn't go there. And he couldn't go into Harper's house because he'd be caught. So, yes, he'd hidden in the car – might have been trying to hot-wire it. But then Lou had surprised him, discovered Sty in the Camry, and . . .

And what?

Had Sty killed Lou and crashed the car, setting it on fire?

No. Sty wouldn't have crashed the car. He'd have used it to escape. And he'd have found Lou's money and kept it. Besides, he wouldn't have followed Lou's plan so closely. It was too big a coincidence that the car would crash and burn.

So Lou had must have killed Sty.

And Lou was still alive somewhere.

Harper thought of sharing her thoughts with Hank and Vivian, but didn't. After all, Lou hadn't contacted Vivian, hadn't called to tell her he was alive and where to join him. Probably he'd dumped her, so it was just as well that Vivian thought he was dead.

Her mother was still talking, telling Hank about how Lou had changed. How he'd made mistakes but had been completely honest with her.

Harper said nothing. She was absorbing the fact that, if Sty was the body they'd found in the car, he couldn't come after her any more. Which meant she would be safe. It would be over. Finally, she could relax.

The ashes sat on an urn on the mantelpiece. Vivian had had the cremation done that morning, three days after Christmas. The weather was bleak and the party of mourners small, just Rivers, Leslie, Hank,

Harper and Vivian. Hank had ordered luncheon from a deli and set it out in the dining room. Cold cuts, fresh bread, fruit, pastries.

'I have to decide where to scatter the ashes.' Vivian poured gin into her orange juice.

Hank offered their back yard. Rivers suggested Lake Cayuga. Leslie advised that Vivian hold onto them for a while, that she not rush to a decision.

From her seat on the easy chair, Harper eyed her corned beef sandwich, then looked out the window at the melting snow, the perpetually gray sky. Wondering whose ashes were really in the urn. Sty's? Or Lou's? Surprisingly, she missed Lou; even if he'd been a thief and a gangster, she'd become used to having him around. He'd made great coffee. And he'd taken good care of her mother, acted as a buffer between them. Now, without him, what would Vivian do? Probably Vivian would have to move in with her and Hank, stay at least until the baby was born. And Harper would be back in the life she thought she'd escaped: looking after her mother.

But maybe not. For the last few hours, since the cremation, Vivian had seemed stronger. She'd dealt with the mortician, arranged for transportation of the body from the morgue. She'd seemed, for Vivian, solidly in control. Harper hadn't seen her ducking outside to smoke, or downing as much gin or Scotch. In fact, Vivian seemed uncharacteristically stable. Harper bit into her sandwich, watchful, trying to hear what Vivian was saying to Leslie.

'You're really all right?' Leslie bit into a chunk of honeydew.

'I am.' Vivian's eyes gleamed. 'Lou's death was awful. But I swear, it woke me up. It showed me how short life can be. How important it is to make every minute count.'

Harper shook her head, doubting her ears. Was her mother on some medication? Suffering some delayed form of shock?

'Lou was good to me. I won't find another man like him. Being with him made me – I don't know – stronger. So, even without Lou, I'm going to go ahead and live my life to the fullest.'

'What will you do?'

Vivian grinned. 'I want to see the world. Now that Harper doesn't need me any more, I'm taking a trip.'

'You going?' Hank looked up from his lunch.

'You can't expect me to stay forever.' She winked.

Harper glanced at Leslie, then at Hank. Met their eyes. Shared their confusion.

Rivers asked where she planned to go. Vivian took a drink, listed possibilities. Switzerland. England. France. Ireland. But probably, she'd start someplace warm. Like Mexico.

'Lots of drug cartels down there. Be careful,' Rivers warned, scooping potato salad onto her plate.

'Do you speak Spanish?' Leslie asked.

Harper kept watching her mother. Something was definitely off. How had she recovered so quickly from Lou's death? How come she'd had him cremated so quickly? Unless . . . Had she heard from him? Did she know the body was Sty's? She replayed Lou's last minutes with them, her mother hanging his Christmas gift around his neck. Pictured Lou putting it on Sty's body.

But maybe he hadn't. Maybe Lou was really dead.

Either way, something was up with Vivian. Her whole demeanor was wrong.

'How are you feeling?' Rivers pulled over a dining-room chair. Took a seat beside her.

Harper's cuts and bruises were almost healed, her contractions holding steady. 'Okay.'

Rivers looked across the room at the others. 'Your mom's doing well.'

Harper nodded, didn't share her thoughts. What would be the point? She chewed corned beef, took a sip of iced tea.

'So many funerals coming up. Evan's is Tuesday. Sebastian's and Steven's families will arrange theirs soon, now that the coroner's released them.' She paused.

Harper took another bite, made no comment. The war had given her lots of experience with funerals, with young people dying.

'But I'm disturbed that we still haven't found Sty.' Rivers met Harper's eyes. 'Where could he be?'

Harper chewed, said nothing.

'When you left him in the back of the pickup, how badly hurt was he?'

'He fell and banged his head.' She didn't mention punching him. 'I think he was unconscious the whole ride home. But, truthfully, I was in no condition to—'

'Of course not, Mrs Jennings. But he must have hit his head pretty hard.' She paused. 'Here's what's bothering me: Sty had a bad head injury. He had no car in the area. Temperatures were below freezing, and it was the middle of the night. So let me ask you: In those conditions, how far could he have gotten?'

Harper swallowed. 'You think he went to the fraternity house?'

'We looked that night. He wasn't there. And he wasn't here.'

Harper looked at the urn. Pictured Sty crouching in the Camry. His body burning there.

'When we searched the fraternity, though, we found some other items you'd be interested in. Sty took notes. Meticulous notes.'

Notes? Harper put her plate on the end table, no longer hungry.

'He was trying to be scientific. He wrote out a formal hypothesis – honestly, I couldn't make sense of it. It was long and rambling, and pretty incoherent. But in it, he detailed emotional, psychological and physical changes that he predicted would occur among healthy young men in the face of mounting pain and certain death.' She paused, crossed her ankles. 'He also described the sample group. The victims had to be young white men of height and weight similar to Sty's. He made up standardized forms to be filled out for each victim, but the only ones filled out were for Victim Number One, whom we assume was Sebastian Levering.'

Rivers stopped, took a forkful of potato salad. Chewed. Harper looked away.

'Anyway, Sty noted exactly what was done to Sebastian – step by step, from the abduction on. He detailed Sebastian's reactions, even made audio tapes of his screams.'

Harper smelled burning rubber, felt sand on her skin. She bit her lip. 'Please, don't tell me—'

'Sorry. The facts are disturbing. I'll spare you. But you should know that, by stopping this duo, you've done a great service. They were just beginning. Sty saw their atrocities as research and himself as a genius, conducting innovative studies on pain and death.' She looked around, lowered her voice. 'Mrs Jennings, Sty wrote that killing was a "scintillating intellectual experience" – I believe those were his exact words – and that his work separated him from the "banality of societal norms".'

Harper felt cold, folded her arms. Shook her head.

Rivers went on. 'But even more interesting was what Sty wrote about his partner. He was concerned that Evan was impulsive, that he got a sexual thrill out of inflicting pain. Sty doubted Evan's commitment to science and worried that his sadistic urges could lead to careless – and potentially disastrous – behavior. He was planning to kill him.'

Harper's mouth was dry. She lifted her glass, sipped tea. 'A couple of sick puppies.'

'Indeed. And you'll be interested in this: Sty wrote about a close call with Victim One. He tried to escape; Evan had to chase him and someone – probably the next-door neighbor – saw them and called the police.'

Harper saw him again, naked and terrified, running into the night. 'So the guy I saw—'

'Was Sebastian.'

They sat for a moment.

'This is a bad case, Mrs Jennings. Sty's still loose, and we still have a guy missing – Sebastian's boyfriend. But thanks to you, Evan won't be hurting anybody else. We owe you.' Rivers stood. 'By the way,' she added. 'That key you found? It didn't fit Sebastian's door. If you want, you can have it back.'

Oh Lord. Harper remembered searching for Sebastian in the woods behind the house. Finding a spatter of blood and, beside it on a string, a key. 'No.' She smiled. 'No thanks.'

Harper watched Rivers walk away. There was still time to stop her and tell her that Sty might be dead. But what was the point? Rivers was already talking to Leslie. Besides, telling the police that the body in the car might be Sty's would let everyone – including Cobretti – know that it might not be Lou's.

Vivian banged a spoon against a glass to make an announcement. 'Everybody, listen up.' She projected her voice as if to a large crowd. 'Because of Lou's demise, we never had Christmas. Lou would be upset if he knew our gifts were just lying there. So, as part of his celebration, we're going to open presents!'

Really? Harper looked at the urn, the pile of packages. The faces of the two dismayed guests. Leslie glanced at her watch, said she'd love to stay but had to see a patient in a few minutes. Grabbing her coat, she hugged Harper and Vivian, waved goodbye to Rivers, called bye-bye to Hank and dashed.

Rivers made her apologies; said she'd already stayed too long.

'No. You can't all leave. This is Lou's party!' Vivian had moved into the living room, was dividing gifts, piling a bunch in front of Harper, as if converting the memorial into a baby shower.

'Not my call, Ma'am. I'm on the clock.' Rivers stepped to the door. 'Goodbye, everyone. Again, sorry for your loss—'

Before Rivers was out the door, Vivian shoved a carton the size of a dishwasher at Harper. 'I picked this out myself. Open it first.' She picked up a bottle and refilled her drink.

Harper stared at the box. 'You really want me to open this?' It didn't seem right, after Lou's death.

Vivian answered by ripping paper off boxes, revealing a multi-colored plastic toy chest, a potty seat, a huge stuffed gorilla. And more. A car seat, not the make Harper had chosen. A stroller, not the model Harper wanted. A high chair, not the kind Harper would have bought. Baby clothes – onesies, T-shirts, sweaters, tiny shoes and socks – all yellow. 'That way, it won't matter if it's a boy or a girl,' Vivian grinned.

There were teething rings. Bibs. A little bathtub with washcloths, towels and a cushion. A portable changing mat. Things Harper hadn't even thought of yet.

Harper presented her mother with the cozy slippers; Hank got busy assembling the high chair.

'Ma.' Harper felt suffocated. 'This is way too much.'

'I'm just making sure my grand-baby gets taken care of.'

Harper bristled. Why should Vivian assume only she could take care of the baby? And that she should decide what to buy? What had she left for them to pick out? She'd even selected diapers.

'You shouldn't have bought all this.' Harper's tone was chilly.

'No worries.' Vivian folded onesies. 'Lou picked up the bill . . .' She stopped, met Harper's eyes, as if realizing Lou might have paid with mob money.

'There.' Hank presented the assembled high chair, a depressingly dark, ornately carved thing with a tan plastic tray.

Harper frowned at it.

'You don't like it.' It wasn't a question. 'I knew you wouldn't.'

Really? 'Then why did you get it?'

'Hoppa—' Hank tried.

'I bet you don't like anything I got, do you?'

'I didn't say that—'

'Well, do you?' She held up a pair of shoes.

'Infants don't need to wear shoes.'

'Okay. And what about the car seat? Or the stroller?'

'Ma, you don't want my opinion. If you did, you'd have asked before you bought everything.' Stop, she told herself. What was the point of arguing?

'Sorry, Harper. I only wanted to be helpful.'

'Ma, did you ever think that maybe Hank and I wanted to pick out some things ourselves . . .?'

'Oh, forgive me. Forgive me for giving you so many presents.' Vivian reached for a tissue.

'Ma, please.'

'After all I've been through, Harper. You have no idea – you just don't understand me. You never did. No matter how hard my life has been, I've always done my best for you—'

'Really?' Harper couldn't stop herself. 'For me? Are you kidding? Don't even start—'

'Enough,' Hank ordered. 'Both of you!'

'That's what you think?' Vivian huffed. 'That I'm all about myself? Well, then it's a good thing I'm leaving.'

Harper didn't disagree.

'I'll go tomorrow.'

'If that's what you want.'

'Now. Stop.' Hank faced Harper, his hands firmly on her shoulders. 'Calm down.' He turned to Vivian. 'Not going.'

'I am—'

'Not yet. Not like that.' He glared at one, then the other of them. 'Wait.' He reached behind the tree and took out two small boxes. A silver and turquoise bracelet for Vivian. A turquoise pendant for Harper. 'From. Texas.'

The gifts brought thanks and kisses, apologies for lost tempers. Harper asked her mother to stay; Vivian insisted that she would leave. With Hank home, there was no need for her to remain. And she was eager to move on, had already made plans to go to Mexico. While she talked, Hank cleaned up wrapping paper, ribbons.

It wasn't until he'd tossed out most of the paper that he noticed the last gift, lost in the mass of gifts surrounding the tree. It was a small box, for Vivian, from Lou. Containing a diamond ring.

Vivian sat, gawking at it. 'It's beautiful, isn't it?' she said.

Hank wiped away a tear, grabbed Harper's hand.

Vivian took it out, slipped it onto the third finger of her left hand. Held it up, showing it off. 'It looks good, doesn't it?' Vivian's eyes sparkled, delighted with the diamond, as if she hadn't just cremated the man who'd wanted to marry her.

Hank couldn't watch, got up and walked away. But Harper stayed, transfixed. More certain than ever that her theory was right, that the ashes on the mantel did not belong to Lou.

Suddenly, Vivian was gone. She left the very next morning. Hank went with her, driving her to the airport in Syracuse. By lunchtime four days after Christmas, ten days after she'd seen Sebastian Levering outside her window, Harper was alone, staring at her computer screen, trying not to be distracted by recent events, by the lingering floral scent of her mother's embrace or by the cloud of disappointed loneliness that Vivian always left behind.

Not that there had been any drama. Vivian seemed to have forgotten their spat. She'd thanked Harper profusely for her support after Lou's death, promised to visit after the baby was born, said she'd keep them updated on her itinerary. She'd seemed optimistic, cheery. So cheery, in fact, that Harper had been tempted to ask Vivian if she'd heard from Lou. But she'd held herself back. Vivian might not have heard from him. Even though Lou was probably alive, he might not have been in touch. Might have simply walked away.

Harper stared at the screen and it stared back at her. The Pre-Columbian symbols she was discussing in her dissertation paraded through her head: Jaguars, owls, deer and snakes. Harper yawned, felt the baby swimming around. Thought about the leftover cold cuts. The pastries. Decided to take a break.

Halfway down the stairs, she heard a smashing sound in the kitchen. Probably a melting icicle, crashing onto the deck. She continued down the steps, through the hall. Maybe there was more corned beef. It was salty, but she almost never ate it. Maybe she'd make a special, with cole slaw. On rye.

She headed straight to the refrigerator, had opened it before her mind registered that the deck door was smashed. Harper froze, sensing someone behind her. She wheeled around, holding a bottle of salad dressing like a club, ready to swing. But the bottle was useless.

Sty stood several feet away, holding a gun. Smiling.

Harper gaped, confused. 'I thought you were dead.'

'Really? No, I was just home for Christmas.'

'So, you're alive.' She sounded addled.

'It appears so. But sadly, you're not going to be for very much longer,' he said. 'In fact, not much longer at all.'

* * *

Harper tried to grasp it. Sty was there, alive; his body couldn't have been burned in the Camry. So whose had? She saw Lou, kissing her mother goodbye. Realized that the body was his. That Lou was really, actually dead. A pang of sorrow jolted through her, but Sty stepped closer, his gun aimed at her chest.

'You got out of the truck.'

He watched her. 'Did you expect me to stay there? I had to hide in the effing woods all night until the cops left. And by the way, because of you, there's blood all over my down jacket.'

He'd been in the woods?

'But I'm not vengeful; really, I harbor no hard feelings.' Sty came closer. 'It's just that you're the only witness.'

Harper was trapped by the refrigerator door. Her exit was blocked in three directions. 'The police know everything.' She eyed the gun. 'They found Evan and the kids you murdered—'

'The police won't be a problem once I explain what happened. You see, I was embarking on a fiction project, but unintentionally became involved with a dangerous psychopath.'

'They've read your journal.'

'Oh, the journal. That was written as background material for a character in my novel. But Evan took the plot seriously, actually killing people – beating me up, threatening to kill me when I tried to stop him. Terrifying me so completely that I ran home to my parents, staying there until I heard Evan was dead and it was safe to return. I'm deeply traumatized.' He smiled, stepped closer. 'Don't worry about me; I'll do fine with the authorities. As long as no one contradicts me.'

'I already have. I told them you and Evan were a team. That you planned your murders together.' She watched his eyes, gripped the salad dressing.

'Well, obviously, you misunderstood. After all, you were highly unstable. Hormonally imbalanced.'

Hormonally imbalanced? Again? Why did everybody accuse her of that?

He took another step closer. Stood an arm's length away. 'You were so delusional and depressed that, poor thing, you actually took your own life.' He took a breath. 'Speaking of which, I suppose you should write a note. Come to the table; I have a pen.'

Harper looked right at him, saw a twinkle of amusement in his eyes. Centered her body and swung.

\*     \*     \*

The bottle came at Sty from the side, smacking his cheekbone, dislodging his nose. He reeled, moaning, and fired the gun, shattering something across the room. Before he could regain his balance, Harper pounced, grabbing the wrist that held the gun, knocking Sty backwards, falling onto him. Feeling a bone snap in his arm. Sty howled, and the gun clattered to the floor. She reached for it, but Sty propelled himself forward, his good arm reaching, fingers clawing.

Sty was bigger, heavier. Harper couldn't hold him, saw his hand inching toward the gun. She rolled off him, scuttling backwards, covering it with her body while her arms fought to push Sty away. But she couldn't; he was on his knees leaning over her, his unbroken arm reaching down toward the gun; then he stopped, suddenly withdrawing the arm. And instead of scrapping with her, he raised his torso, made a fist. And aimed it at her belly.

Harper looked at it, at the cold light in his eyes. As Sty lifted his fist to deliver his blow, she lifted her hips to reach under her back. Before he could land his punch, she pulled the gun out and fired.

The police came. The media. The coroner. A cleaning crew. And finally, it was quiet.

Days passed peacefully. Harper's injuries healed; the ones on her wrists left dark jagged scars. The media stopped talking about the deadly duo of Sty and Evan, the murdered students, even about the one still missing. Ornament by ornament, Harper and Hank dismantled the tree; the living room seemed huge and empty without it.

Even on crutches, Hank managed to return most of Vivian's gifts. The stroller, car seat, playhouse, toy chest, even the high chair went back so that he and Harper could buy what they wanted.

They celebrated New Year's Eve with a steak dinner, making lists of baby names, and they fell asleep before the ball dropped on Times Square. They fixed up the nursery. Placed Vivian's stuffed gorilla in the corner. Put her yellow clothing into a new dresser. Hung a monkey mobile over the crib.

Harper's belly seemed suddenly enormous and the baby became relentlessly active. Because her contractions held at a steady rate, she had to continue resting and rarely went out. Leslie came to the house for appointments, but mostly, she and Hank were alone, the house silent. Harper consoled herself with the knowledge that winter break was almost over, that Vicki and her other friends would soon be home. Students would return to campus; the fraternity next door would hop to life. Maybe then she'd stop watching its sulking mass out her window. Maybe she'd stop dreaming of burning cars, of bloody knives. Of Sty appearing in the kitchen. With a gun.

Most days, Harper spent a few hours working on her dissertation. Four days into the New Year, she was at her computer, struggling to complete a sentence, when the doorbell rang and she heard Hank invite someone in.

A moment later, she heard Detective Rivers' voice and stiffened, saving her work. 'This can't be good,' she told the baby. When Rivers came over, it never was.

Rivers nodded at her middle. 'How you feeling?'

'Huge.'

They smiled. Exchanged New Year greetings. Sat in the now tidy living room.

'So, your mom took off? Was she okay?'

'Fine, amazingly. Eager to see the world.'

Rivers watched her. Hank offered coffee; she thanked him, declined.

'Once again, I'm here to give you a heads up.'

The back of Harper's neck tingled.

'It'll be on the news. The last missing kid turned up.'

'Dead?' The word came out unbidden.

Rivers looked at the floor.

Hank sat beside Harper, took her hand.

'Was it – did Evan and Sty do it?'

'Actually, this one looks like it might have been unintentional. The victim was Sebastian Levering's boyfriend. He was in their new apartment. Furniture wasn't even moved in yet.'

Why was Rivers telling them this?

'The kid who rents the adjoining apartment came back from winter break and complained of a smell. The super smelled it and called us, and we found the source.'

'But. How come telling us?' Hank put an arm around Harper, protective.

'Because of this.' Rivers reached into her parka pocket, pulled out a baggie. In it was the key. Harper's key. 'The body was found locked in a closet.'

'Oh God.' Harper sat up straight, staring at the baggie.

'This key opened it.' She put it back in her pocket. 'The door was heavy, and the lock was, too. The kid clawed and rammed and kicked himself bloody trying to get out, but the lock held.' She shook her head. 'Really tough. Looks like he died of dehydration.'

Dehydration? Lord, that took days. Slow, agonizing days. He must have screamed. Why hadn't anyone heard?

'The building was empty for the holidays.'

Oh God.

Rivers sighed. 'Our theory is that Sebastian locked his boyfriend in. Maybe they had a fight. Or maybe it was a practical joke or who knows what. But for whatever reason, it looks like Sebastian got him into the closet, locked the door and left, taking the key. No doubt he planned to let him out when he came back.'

Harper clenched her jaw, braced for what Rivers would say next.

'Except, as we know, he never did.'

Hank walked Rivers out to her car, came back with the mail.

'Your mom. Wrote.'

Harper was making hoagies, popped a piece of salami in her mouth, spun around.

Hank read a postcard. 'Already. Has new boyfriend.'

No surprise. 'Where is she?' She reached for the card.

Vivian was in Mexico, a small town on the west coast, not far from Puerto Nuevo. She was perfectly safe, learning bits of Spanish. And the happiest she'd ever been. She'd met her soul mate. An expatriate who'd made a fortune and retired young. Named Oliver Hines.

What? Harper stared at the name. It was Lou's alias.

But Lou was dead.

'Oliver?' Hank was also puzzled. 'Remember – wasn't it Lou's name?'

Harper pictured Lou kissing her mother goodbye. The new gold chain around his neck. The duffel bag in his hands – had Lou somehow survived?

But how? And, if he was, then the dead guy hadn't been Lou or Sty. So whose body had been in the Camry? Whose ashes were in the urn?

Harper had no idea. But, somehow, Lou had pulled it off. He'd stolen half a million dollars from the mob, and faked his death so they wouldn't come after him. He'd gotten away with it. Nobody – especially not Wally Cobretti – had a clue.

'You think it's him?' Harper stared at the card.

Hank nodded. 'Don't know how, but yes.'

'Me, too.' Harper picked up slices of provolone, layered them on the rolls. 'It's got to be him.'

'Hard to believe.' Hank munched a pickle.

'What?' Harper looked up from the tomato slices.

'Oliver already,' he smirked. 'Never thought she'd. Get over Lou.'

Hank tossed the Best Baby Names book onto the coffee table. It landed on his plate, crushing the uneaten crust of his hoagie roll. 'How about you name. Girl. I name boy.'

Harper frowned. 'How about not? How about we pick a name together?'

'But you don't like my names.' He crossed his arms, pouting.

'I like some of them.'

'Name one.'

Harper stalled, moved closer to him on the sofa, leaned against his shoulder.

'Go on. Waiting.'

'Well, you don't like my names either. You nixed Gabriel and Gideon and Burke—'

'I like Billy. Normal.'

Someone knocked at the door. Neither moved right away, but their eyes met, sharing a thought. It had to be Rivers again. With yet more bad news. The knocking continued. Finally, Harper pushed herself up.

'No, I'll go.' Hank reached for his crutches.

'It's all right.' Harper was already on her way, but Hank got up, too, and was standing behind her when she opened the door.

The person knocking wasn't Detective Rivers. It was a skinny redhead with smeared mascara. And behind her were two huge men, each of whom dwarfed Hank, standing ready like bodyguards. Or thugs.

'We'd like to talk.' The woman's voice was high and scratchy. Almost childlike. 'Can we come in?'

'Sorry—' Harper had been about to say that they must have the wrong house but she stopped, recognizing the black SUV in the driveway.

'You guys wait on the porch, okay?' The woman left the thugs at the door and headed right past Harper and Hank into the living

room, took a seat on the sofa. Pulled a tissue out of her sleeve.
Blew her nose.

'Let's not bullshit,' she said. 'These guys have been watching
your house, so I know you know Lou. I know he was staying here.
I know he had money that didn't belong to him. And I know—'

'Lou's dead,' Hank said.

'Look, whoever you are, Lou was our guest.' Harper crossed her
arms, remained standing. 'That's it. We know nothing about his
money or his work. So, unless there's something else . . .' She
gestured toward the door.

'No, you don't understand. I'm not here about Lou. I know he's
dead. And I don't care about the money.' Her voice cracked and
tears washed mascara down her cheeks. 'Please, sit down. I can't
talk with you standing. Just – please.' She sniffed, dabbed her eyes.

'Who are you?' Harper sat on the easy chair. Hank stood beside
her.

'My name's Rita. I'm an old friend of Lou's. And I'm trying to
locate a mutual friend – Wally Cobretti.'

Harper felt Hank's eyes on her, but she didn't waver, didn't let
on she'd heard the name before.

'Wally had plans to visit Lou Christmas Eve.'

Which was the day Lou left. The day the Camry crashed and burned.

'They were going to meet at noon, but Wally came down early,
to surprise Lou.'

'I don't see how we can help you,' Harper said. 'We were here
Christmas Eve, but didn't see anyone.' Except that, no, wait. They
hadn't been there – she'd just escaped from Sty and they'd gone to
the hospital.

'You didn't see a black SUV? Like the one out front?'

Had she? From the gurney? Harper wasn't sure.

'No,' Hank said. He sounded definite.

'See, we don't even know if he ever arrived here. All we know is
he left to see Lou. And ten days later, nobody's seen or heard from
Wally. And we can't ask Lou if he ever got here, because Lou's dead.'

Harper let herself look at Hank. His eyes were steady, somber.
'Not in papers,' he said.

'No. We don't want anyone to know he's missing.'

Harper raised her eyebrows, trying to seem baffled. 'Did your
friend have enemies? Would anyone want to hurt him?' Other than,
say, Lou?

Rita's eyes widened. 'That's just the thing. He had a lot of . . . rivals in business. And some people hold grudges. So I've – we've been asking around. Nobody admits to knowing anything. But the strangest thing – his car turned up the other day. All the way in Arizona.'

Arizona? Not Mexico? Harper wondered why Lou had dumped it. 'You think he was carjacked?'

Rita shrugged. 'Maybe.' She let out a loud sigh. 'Well, you were about my last hope. I believe you don't know anything.' She met Harper's eyes. 'Honestly, I'm afraid something terrible happened to him.'

Harper didn't know what to say. Certainly not the fact that Wally Cobretti's body had been mistaken for Lou, that his ashes were sitting right there on her mantelpiece.

'I guess this is another dead end.' Rita stood and sashayed to the door where the thugs waited to escort her to the car.

For a moment, neither of them moved.

Then Hank said, 'Lou killed him?'

Harper shook her head. 'Not possible. Lou's dead.'

Hank didn't smile. 'Lou killed this guy.'

'I know.' And her mother was living with a killer. Not that there was anything to be done about it. Who knew? It might have been self-defense.

'Big guys.' Hank came over to the easy chair. 'You okay?'

She nodded. 'You?'

'Could have. Taken them.' He smiled and kissed her neck. He hadn't shaved; his whiskers tickled, gave her gooseflesh.

Harper stood and met his lips. Wrapped her arms around him. Slowly, almost predictably, a contraction took hold. Without ending the kiss, Harper dug her fingers into Hank's back, closed her eyes and hung on.